**W9-BGR-839**

# ONE FATAL FLAW

A DANIEL PITT NOVEL

# ONE FATAL FLAW

# ANNE PERRY

**THORNDIKE PRESS**
A part of Gale, a Cengage Company

GALE
A Cengage Company

LIBRARY OF CONGRESS CIP DATA ON FILE.
CATALOGUING IN PUBLICATION FOR THIS BOOK
IS AVAILABLE FROM THE LIBRARY OF CONGRESS

ISBN-13: 978-1-4328-7607-4 (hardcover alk. paper)

Published in 2020 by arrangement with Ballantine Books, an imprint of Random House, a division of Penguin Random House LLC

Printed in Mexico
Print Number: 01     Print Year: 2020

*To Clare Foss,*
*for her gentle and constructive editing*

# CHAPTER ONE

She sat on the other side of the desk from Daniel, tears sliding down her unblemished cheeks. "They'll hang him, won't they?" she said huskily. "You're a lawyer. You got Mr. Blackwell off, and he would have hanged, for sure. Everyone along the dockside says that." She sniffed and gulped. "Please. You can make them see Rob didn't do it. Please?"

Daniel felt a sudden shiver, even though the room was warm. It was late September, and there was a nice fire burning in the grate. This was his room in the chambers of fford Croft and Gibson, one of the most prestigious law firms in London. It was situated in Lincoln's Inn, naturally, as were all the best. His room was not much more than a very large cupboard, this being his first placement after graduating from university — Cambridge, to be precise.

She was waiting.

"What are they accusing Mr. Adwell of having done, Miss Beale?" he asked. So far, she had not actually told him, only that it was serious, and it concerned a warehouse in the London docks south of the river.

"Setting fire to the building," she replied softly, her gaze lowered.

"What building? And is he accused of doing it deliberately?"

"Would it help if it wasn't deliberate?" She looked up at him, and hope flickered in her eyes.

"I don't know." He must not raise her expectations without cause. "You haven't told me exactly what building it was. Or how bad the fire was."

She looked small, hunched up into herself, and very afraid.

"Miss Beale . . . ." he said gently. "I can't help if I don't know everything about it. Where was it? What time of the day or night? And how much damage was done?"

She hunched her shoulders even more. "It was a big old warehouse, down on Tooley Street, other side of the river, and just before the Pool of London. And it burned in the night. Two nights ago. I suppose it was pretty bad, 'cause there isn't much of it left."

Daniel began to get the feeling that this

might involve a great financial loss, depending on what had been stored there. "Was Mr. Adwell a night watchman there?"

Miss Beale shook her head, setting the soft curls around her face moving. "No . . ."

"Then what was he doing there at night? He *was* there, wasn't he? If not, why do the police suspect him at all?" He wondered if the man had been caught in a robbery that had gone wrong. "Was anyone else there that you know of?"

"Paddy Jackson were there, of course . . ." she said, almost under her breath.

"Who is he?" Daniel asked patiently. "And why 'of course'?"

"Well, he wouldn't have got burned if he wasn't there, would he?" She, too, sounded as if her patience was wearing thin.

Suddenly the room seemed depressingly close, almost airless. Daniel breathed in deeply, but it did not help. "Was . . . was Paddy Jackson badly burned?"

"Oh, yes," she said, looking at him, her eyes brimming with tears. "I'm afraid he was proper burned."

Suddenly it all became horribly clear. He knew what she was afraid of, and why. "He burned to death in the fire?"

She took a deep breath and nodded slowly, her gaze never shifting from his face. She swallowed hard.

He must get control of this. It was too big a case for him to handle. He would have to get Kitteridge in. Toby Kitteridge was his senior by several years, and had a wealth of experience. The Blackwell case, which Jessie Beale had referred to, had not been given to him by chambers. He had taken it privately, actually against orders, because Roman Blackwell was a highly disreputable rogue to whom Daniel owed a debt on honor. Blackwell could not pay anyone. Daniel had earned his undying friendship by pulling a rabbit out of a hat, as it were, and succeeded in proving Blackwell's innocence of murder. Marcus fford Croft, the head of chambers, had forgiven Daniel for taking the case without permission, probably because he was an old friend of Daniel's father's. He would not extend such leniency twice.

Jessie was staring at him, waiting for him to go on. Her face was full of hope, but it was fading even as he watched. This was probably the last place she could go.

"So, it is murder they're charging him with?" he said.

She bit her lip and nodded.

"What was Adwell doing in the warehouse at night? And who is, or was, Paddy Jackson?"

"Paddy was one of the other Jackson boys. I suppose he still is. You don't get out of it just by dying. They'll always reckon he is one of them anyway."

Daniel was beginning to understand. "So, Paddy is dead, and Rob Adwell is blamed for it?"

"Yeah." She gulped.

"And was the fire accidental, or did Paddy cause it? Or someone else altogether?" He tried to keep skepticism out of his voice.

She thought for a moment. "I reckon it could've been an accident, like. But maybe Paddy were setting the fire, and he weren't too good at it. Didn't leave himself a clear way out of it. Or it moved faster than he thought?"

"Seen a few fires, have you?" He tried to sound as if he were asking out of mere innocent interest and not sarcasm.

"No, I haven't," she replied. "I got a decent scare of fires, but I heard people talk. There's a few fires down the docks way, and some of them are accidents, and some of them ain't."

"And this one?"

"I don't know." She spread her hands helplessly and then, looking at his face, quickly took them in again. "Aright! I reckon as Paddy set it, and out-clevered his-

11

self. Rob got away, and Paddy didn't. But that in't Rob's fault, is it?"

"Maybe . . . and maybe not. If two people set out to commit a crime — and burning a warehouse down is a crime — and one of the people gets killed, the other one might be found guilty of his death." He watched the shadows in her face as her emotions changed and she understood the depth of what he said.

"Oh, well . . . it's . . . it's a good thing, in't it, that they weren't together doing something wrong, a crime, like? They wouldn't be doing anything together. Rob hated the Jacksons, and they hated him."

Daniel could not help but wonder if she had made that up on the spot. One thing he was certain of, it was a murky issue, and she was prepared to fight very hard indeed for the man she claimed to love.

"I'll go and see Mr. Adwell," he told her. "And then I'll learn exactly what the police have, and how they are charging him. And what they know about the fire. For instance, how it started. Don't tell me any more . . ."

She gave a slow smile, almost shy. She wasn't really a pretty girl; her mouth was a little large, her cheekbones high, giving her an almost catlike appearance. But she commanded attention, even a certain liking. "I won't tell you nothing more," she promised. "I can pay you . . . but not a lot . . . yet." She smiled properly for the first time, and it lit her face, softening its lines and lighting her eyes. "But I will," she promised.

"That's all right." He cut off whatever else she might say. "I'm going only to see if I can help to begin with." He stood up. Then she rose slowly, clutching her small bag in a gloved hand, almost like a child's. At twenty-five, he felt ridiculously older than her.

She had already given him her address, and he had no need to ask for anything further.

The chambers chief clerk, Impney, was waiting in the hall. He glanced at Daniel, then conducted Jessie Beale toward the main door.

As soon as she was gone, Daniel knocked at Kitteridge's office door. The moment he heard an answer, even though the words were indistinguishable, he opened the door and went in. He shut it behind him.

Kitteridge looked up from the papers he was reading, frowning slightly. "What? If you're bored, there's a whole lot of stuff you could draft replies to over there." He glanced at a table on the other end of his room, considerably larger than Daniel's. But he was ten years older than Daniel and generally considered the most promising barrister in chambers. He was taller also, well over six foot, and gangly, as if his limbs did not get the message from his brain at the same time. Daniel knew that Kitteridge was aware of this, even a trifle self-conscious, his shyness disarming the envy many people might have felt for his extraordinary skills. It did with Daniel; he felt slightly protective of Kitteridge at times, but this was definitely not one of them.

"No, thank you. I've just got a case . . . I think."

"Don't you know?" Kitteridge's eyebrows shot up. His face was not handsome, but it was extremely expressive.

"There's not much money in it, if any at all. And the man might well be guilty . . ."

Kitteridge groaned. "Pitt, you are useless! I keep hoping that one day you'll get the hang of this. We —"

"I want to look into it," Daniel cut across him. "When I find out more, I'll ask your opinion."

"What is it? Petty theft? A brawl in a public house? You can manage that without me. What's the matter? Have you lost your nerve? We all lose cases sometimes —"

Daniel interrupted him again. "No. But Marcus would never allow me to handle this by myself. It's arson and murder."

"What?" Kitteridge jerked upright in his chair, his eyes wide.

"It's arson and murder," Daniel repeated with exaggerated patience.

"Why the devil did they come to you? This is serious. Is it something to do with your father? Is that it?"

Daniel was stunned. "Two ruffians planning to rob a warehouse on the riverbank, not set fire to it, and one of them is killed? Not quite my father's patch." His father was Sir Thomas Pitt, head of Special Branch, the antiterrorism part of the Secret Service concerned with spies, treason, anarchy, and general threats to the public's safety. Daniel was close to his family and proud of his father, and he knew that he owed his position at fford Croft and Gibson to him. But he had an excellent degree from Cambridge and resented even the most oblique suggestion that his practice here was due to his family's influence. Kitteridge's father was the headmaster of a boys' private school and apparently pretty strict, but without the same influence.

Kitteridge saw Daniel's face and must have realized his error. It was one he had made before. He would not apologize, but it would be a while before he made that

15

mistake again. "How did you hear about it?" he asked.

"His girlfriend came to see me just now. I'm going to look into it. I've nothing else to do, except your chores." He indicated the pile of papers on the table. "I'll let you know."

"Let me know before you take the case, not after!" Kitteridge said firmly. "Please?"

Daniel gave a slight, elegant salute and passed through the doorway.

Out on the street, he walked to the nearest main crossroads and in two or three minutes was able to hail a taxi. He always enjoyed these distinctive black automobiles, purpose-built to give the drivers a separate space. They had become standard and very much accepted three years ago, in 1907. He thought of them as a symbol of a new age. Of course, there were still a lot of horse-drawn vehicles in the streets, but everything was changing: not just transport, but fashion, ideas, medicine, art, inventions of all sorts. Most especially — and that is what interested him now — forensic medicine, ways of detecting crime and then proving it in court. Guns had been around for centuries, and knives for even longer. Fire was older than mankind! But the detailed scientific knowledge of them was new. The understanding of why people do things, and how you can work backward from an act to whatever generated it in someone's mind, that was new, and promised all sorts of possibilities unimagined even a decade ago.

The taxi took him across the river; he had not even noticed which bridge they had used. Now they were pulling up at the police station. Daniel paid the fare and a reasonable tip for the driver, and climbed out onto the pavement. He went up the shallow steps to the entrance. He told the desk sergeant his name, and asked if he might speak to the officer in charge of investigating the Tooley Street warehouse fire.

"Yes, sir. Certainly, sir. I reckon as he'll be back in half an hour or so." The sergeant's eyes were bright and amused, and he smiled as he said it.

"I am Mr. Adwell's lawyer," Daniel told him. "Perhaps I can fill in the time by speaking to him first?"

"Perhaps you can, sir, but I'll have to ask Inspector Quarles about it."

"And you have just said that he isn't here," Daniel pointed out. Should he try exerting a little pressure, and risk making an enemy of the sergeant? Or not push him

17

and appear weak? Kitteridge would have known what to do — probably. Daniel hated being as new to his profession as he was, ignorant of so many things. Sometimes he felt as if he was a beginner at everything.

He judged the sergeant to be about Kitteridge's age, mid-thirties. "I expect you've seen a few fires," he said conversationally. "I admit I haven't."

"I expect you will, sir, in time," the sergeant answered sagely.

"This was a bad one?" Daniel asked with interest. This was the nearest police station to the fire. There was bound to have been conversation.

"It was." The sergeant pursed his lips. "Little ones are mostly smoke, though smoke can kill you faster than you think," he went on. "But this one was a lot of flames. Dry wood, you see. And, of course, they reckon quite a bit of whisky. And that burns like hell."

Daniel nodded. "Yes, of course it does. So, how did they put it out? I'm surprised it didn't spread to the buildings on either side of it . . . or did it?" Daniel did not try to hide his genuine awe. "What courage the firemen must have to go in there and put it out." His mind was racing. "It would light up the night! Did you see it?"

"I got there a bit after," the sergeant admitted reluctantly.

Daniel tried to look impressed. "Did you arrest the man right there, at the scene of the fire?"

The sergeant looked pleased with himself. He straightened his shoulders. "Yes, yes, I did. It was . . . pretty conclusive. You should've been there. It was very dramatic."

"I would say I can imagine," Daniel replied, "but I really can't. I've never seen a big fire, a whole warehouse burning. He was lucky to get out!"

"For all the good it'll do him. Other poor fellow didn't. I reckon that's murder, don't you?"

"Probably," Daniel agreed. "We'll see. Who sent up the alarm?"

"What?"

"Who called the fire brigade?"

"Don't know. Why?"

"Just wondered."

"You think perhaps Adwell called them? Doesn't matter. If he set the fire, then once it was really going, he escaped and called the fire brigade, it's still murder."

Daniel could not argue that. He thanked the sergeant and settled back to wait for Quarles.

■ ■ ■

It proved not to be as long a wait as the sergeant suggested. Quarles came in and glanced at the sergeant, who said Daniel was waiting for him. He was a very ordinary-looking man, wearing a rather shabby raincoat, well cut, but worn for too long and too hard. He looked at Daniel with interest, and a smile that totally changed his face. There was light in it, and interest. He held out his hand. "Good afternoon. Quarles. What can I do for you? Our sergeant says you're a lawyer, is that right?"

Daniel stood up and shook the offered hand. "Yes. Daniel Pitt, from fford Croft and Gibson, Lincoln's Inn Fields."

"I've heard of you, at least of your chambers. What on earth are you doing down here?"

"I've come to represent Robert Adwell regarding the Tooley Street fire."

"Adwell? Really?" Quarles's voice was good, deep, and of a pleasing tone. He did not hide his curiosity.

Daniel found himself wrong-footed. He had come prepared for battle and there was nothing to fight. "I'm just looking into it. I haven't met Adwell yet, and I know very

20

little about the case. You arrested him pretty quickly . . ." He left it in the air as a question.

"Not much doubt," Quarles replied. "Come upstairs. I'm gasping for a cup of tea. It's getting cold, and bloody wet outside." He started up the nearby stairs as he said it, and Daniel was pleased to follow him up.

Settled in the small untidy room that was his office, Quarles faced Daniel over his desk piled with pictures, letters, and notices of one kind or another, hard for Daniel to read upside down.

The tea had been brought. It was in enamel mugs and it was hot, too sweet, and very strong.

"Ah!" Quarles said as he had his first sip. "Watch it, it's hot. I suppose the poor devil's got to be defended, but you are going nowhere fast with Rob Adwell. He's not bad, just lazy, and a bit quick to quarrel. Holds a grudge. I would say that's his biggest difficulty."

Daniel put his mug down. It was too hot to hold. "He quarreled with the other fellow, Paddy Jackson?"

Quarles smiled. "Somebody quarreled with the Jackson brothers. Although I'm not sure if they are brothers or cousins. Adwell

21

had his brothers, too, even if they are brothers in interest rather than blood."

"Fighting each other?" Daniel asked. This was beginning to look a lot uglier than Jessie Beale had implied. Did she know all this? Or was she more innocent than he had supposed? He had to think if he had ever been in love enough that it blinded him completely to things that were obvious to everyone else. One or two memories intruded. He forced them away and slammed memory's door closed. "Do you know anything about Adwell's girlfriend, Jessie Beale?" he asked.

Quarles took a deep breath, let it out, and smiled. It was warm, even charming, and rueful. "Is that why you're here? Young Jessie came to find you?" He seemed about to add something else, then changed his mind.

Daniel wondered what it was. He had a strong feeling that something important had just slipped past him, and he had not recognized it. He was not certain how to answer Quarles. He wished to get something from him for an honest reply, learn anything at all.

"Yes. I promised to see Mr. Adwell, that's all. Isn't it as simple as it looks? Two young men plan a robbery, they overturn a lamp, or drop a match, and unintentionally start a fire, which quickly gets out of control. One of them escapes, the other doesn't."

"No," Quarles said simply, a sad smile. "To begin with, they would never undertake anything as allies. They were members of rival gangs, if you'll excuse the word. It's the nearest applicable one I can think of. Members of Adwell's gang might have changed from time to time, but Jackson's gang was family and remained roughly the same. What either of them was doing in the warehouse, we don't know. How the fire began, we don't know yet, but the firemen think it was started in one of the rooms on the ground floor, where highly inflammable goods were stored, and paper, candles, rubbish." He gave a slight shrug. "But he's got to have a defense, so good luck."

Daniel felt his spirits sink. It was far more complicated than Jessie Beale had told him. But then, if she was in love with Adwell, perhaps she saw what she wanted to, or needed to, to keep her beliefs. "Thank you," he said. "I . . ." Then he did not know what he wanted to say.

He followed Quarles down to the prison section of the police station. Quarles stopped outside one of the cells where a young man sat on a bench, his head low, staring at his hands locked in front of him. He did not look up when Quarles's shadow fell across the floor.

"Adwell," Quarles said quietly, "Miss Beale has employed a lawyer to represent you. He's here to see you now."

Adwell lifted his head slowly and stared first at Quarles, then turned to look at Daniel. He seemed totally bewildered. He stood awkwardly, as if his muscles were stiff. He frowned and then shook his head. "I got no money to pay you. Jessie's . . . trying to help, but she can't."

Daniel was aware that Quarles had left and he was alone with Adwell. "Does she want to help because you did not set the fire?" he said quietly.

There was no anger in Adwell that Daniel could see or hear. Was that because he felt nothing, or because he was stunned, frightened, and very understandably did not trust Daniel? "Do you know how the fire started?" he tried again.

"We were fighting," Adwell replied. "I suppose one of us knocked over the lantern."

"Why were you there at all?" Daniel asked. "I understand you weren't friends."

"No." Adwell looked away. "We were planning a way to rob it, so all of us could get something out of it. We knew someone else was going to, and we wanted to be there first."

Daniel was not sure whether he believed that. But at this point, it did not matter a great deal. It made no difference to the fact that they had started the fire when they had no right to be there, so they were committing a crime, and apparently planning another. "But you escaped, unhurt, and Paddy Jackson died," he said. He was trying to form an opinion of Adwell, but so far all he sensed was fear and bewilderment rapidly sliding into despair. "I'll look into it," he promised. "I'll get back to you when I know more. In the meantime, don't say anything."

"I got no money, at least not enough for a lawyer." There was hurt sharp in his voice, and in his face.

Daniel felt a wave of guilt, because he really had no idea of how he could help this young man. Even by his own admittance, he was guilty of planning a crime with the man who had died in the fire, which was either accidental or intentional. Perhaps it being accidental was the only chance he had.

"Don't worry about it now," he said with more assurance than he felt. "Let's see what we can do."

He turned and followed where Quarles had gone out of the room, past the policeman guarding outside, and back up the stairs. He found the inspector in the room at the top.

"Bitten off more than you can chew, young man?" Quarles said. He shook his head. "I suppose you'd better go and see the police surgeon. It's Appleby. You'll probably find him at the morgue. His office is right by there."

"Thank you, yes, I'll do that," Daniel replied.

Daniel found Appleby just about ready to leave for the day. He was a comfortable, untidy man with thick brown hair and a red waistcoat that failed to meet at the front and was missing several buttons.

"Ah," he said when Daniel explained why he had come. "Not nice, my boy. Not nice at all. Poor fellow. Only decent thing is that he might not have known much about it."

"Why do you say that?" Daniel asked. Was it a gleam of light? He looked at Appleby's round face and mild expression, then at his sharp blue eyes, steady, unwavering, staring back at him. There was something else to say, but Appleby was going to wait until Daniel asked. "Did he die of smoke, quickly?

26

That's still a horrid way to go, choking . . ."

"It is, indeed." Appleby shivered involuntarily. "But there was no smoke in his lungs. Shall I show you? Think you're up to it?"

"I believe you," Daniel said quickly. "I'm not sure if we're going to take the case or not. I'll have to go back to chambers and discuss it."

"I can imagine." Appleby did not bother to hide his smile this time.

"So how did he die?" Daniel asked.

"Cracked skull," Appleby said. "Something hit him one hell of a blow. Maybe with a blunt instrument, such as a truncheon." He reached up and touched the back of his own head, just below the crown.

"Any other injury?" Daniel asked, trying to visualize what had happened. "Was there a fight? An ambush? An accident? Where was he found?"

"On the ground floor of the warehouse in Tooley Street." Appleby pulled his mouth into a tight little shape. "At the bottom of the staircase. Been to the warehouse, have you?"

"No . . ." Daniel's mind raced. What was it he had not thought of? There would be no stairs left to show Jackson had fallen down them. And the fire had apparently started at the bottom and gone upward. He gave a deep shrug. "Of course, the police haven't finished looking at it yet. I'll let you know if they find anything else."

Daniel thanked Appleby and left. He could well believe that no one else was likely to take Adwell's case. The only defense was to suggest some kind of accident, and keep any plans for robbery out of it. There was no one else to argue the issue.

The question was, should Daniel take the case? Since the charge was murder, and Adwell was facing the gallows, Daniel would have to sit second chair to Kitteridge. If Kitteridge was willing to take the case. And either of them would need Marcus fford Croft's permission. How likely was that with little or no payment at the end of it? But before he asked Marcus, he must ask Kitteridge. That he would do first thing in the morning.

Daniel thought about it for the rest of the evening. He ate at his lodgings, rather than with any of the friends he often dined with at one of the local public houses. It was pleasant to talk about anything, or nothing, with people who worked in the city, preferably at something other than law, and hear their opinions. But this evening he needed time alone to consider what he was going to do about Adwell.

He hadn't had a case of his own since August. Instead he had spent his time doing paperwork for Kitteridge. The only good thing about it was that he learned several things he had known only intellectually and seen them applied to real cases, which made them all far clearer. To understand the papers was to be able to remember, at least for him.

But a whole evening in silence in his lodgings solved very little, even with Mrs. Portiscale's excellent shepherd's pie, one of his favorites.

When he slept, he dreamed about the blackened ruins of the warehouse and awoke fighting the bedclothes, as they seemed to imprison his arms and legs.

He arrived at the chambers of fford Croft and Gibson a little after half-past eight. As happened rather often, Kitteridge was there before him.

"Well?" he inquired. "How was your arson case?" Unlike many tall men, his height gave him no elegance whatsoever. He looked slightly disjointed, all knees and elbows. Grace was a gift you either had or you didn't. Kitteridge was inclined to be serious, which was a shame, because a sense of the absurd was an asset that made life more tolerable at times. When Kitteridge smiled, it was like a burst of sunshine, but he wasn't smiling now. "Well? Don't stand there! What happened?"

"It's worse than Miss Beale said," Daniel replied, following Kitteridge into his room and sitting in the chair opposite the desk.

Kitteridge rolled his eyes. "When is it ever not? So, what's worse about it?"

"Adwell, the accused, and Jackson, the dead man, went into the warehouse to plan a robbery. Adwell says they quarreled. This was on the ground floor, packed with flammable rubbish. They had a fight, Adwell says, and one of them knocked over a lantern and set fire to the place. Adwell escaped unhurt, except for a few bruises and scars, but he left Jackson there and he was killed. He hit him hard enough to kill him, and left his body to be burned. Probably the blow killed him, and Adwell left the fire to destroy all the evidence."

Kitteridge stared at Daniel. "So what is his defense, for heaven's sake?"

"That he didn't do it, that it was all an accident. But he also says they were robbing the warehouse before someone else did, and I'm wondering if someone else was there and committed the crime of which

Adwell is accused."

Kitteridge put his head in his hands. "You're unbelievable," he said. "Totally —"

"It could be true! Someone might have intended to get Adwell also."

Kitteridge looked at him. "Then they succeeded — rather well!"

"Not yet," Daniel replied stubbornly. "We might win!"

"We?" Kitteridge rolled his eyes.

Daniel waited.

"All right," Kitteridge sighed. "We had better keep your promise."

"Thank you."

Kitteridge gave Daniel a look that defied words.

# CHAPTER TWO

Miriam fford Croft, Marcus's daughter, was alone in the laboratory her father had installed for her in the basement of their house. It was magnificently appointed, with all kinds of modern equipment for a forensic scientist. It was generous of him. She sometimes felt guilty about the amount of money it must have cost. She was an only child, and he would have given her anything within his power to buy, borrow, or pay for with time or labor. But the one thing she wanted was not his to give. Standards would be dangerously lowered, it was said, the whole balance of society upset, if women were allowed to take university courses in such unsuitable subjects as medicine, pertaining to the dissection of bodies, and then practice the skill exactly as a man might. It was more than unsuitable, it was against nature. Women were not made for such things.

Marcus could not change that for her, so she had to be content knowing the medical theory, and turning her professional expertise toward chemistry. Nice and impersonal, not threatening to her delicate sensibilities! Of course, women can bear and give birth, she thought, be a midwife and cope with all that. They can nurse you if you're sick. They can even wash your body when you die, and clean up after you. They've got the nerve and the stomach for that, just not the intellectual stamina.

She put down the beaker in which she had been mixing chemicals. Did the experiment matter? Was anything going to be changed for the better because of it? Was anyone even going to look at it? Probably not.

"Damn!" she said fiercely. It was not ladylike to swear, but it felt satisfying, for a moment or two at least. She had a kettle down here, but it was a good discipline not to mix chemicals with food, or anything you were going to drink out of. Added to which, safety apart, it didn't feel like a break if you didn't leave the laboratory.

Usually the pursuit of knowledge fascinated her, but more recently she had found gaps in her concentration, and they were getting harder and harder to fight her way out of.

Did she use the word *fight*? That made it sound like hard work. Surely, she did not mean that.

She closed and locked the door behind her, and went upstairs to the main house. She had just reached the kitchen when she heard the front doorbell ring. The butler, Membury, would answer it, of course. No friend of her father's would expect him to be at home this hour of the morning. The cook would not come in until the afternoon, and the maid was upstairs.

She filled the kettle with water and set it on the hob.

The kitchen door opened and Membury came in. "I am sorry to intrude, Miss Miriam," he said apologetically. At forty, she was far too old to take pleasure in being called *Miss Miriam,* but he had known her since she was a child, and would always think of her by her given name. He was technically a servant, but in reality he was a friend. He had watched her struggles, her rejections, and her successes.

"Yes?" she said with a smile. "You're not interrupting."

"Mr. Pitt is here to see you. I told him you were busy, but he wanted me to ask you anyway."

"Daniel?" She felt the color rise up her

34

cheeks. She remembered both of the cases they had worked on together. They had been challenging, even desperate, but she had enjoyed them intensely. She had felt more alive than at any other time. It was what forensic science was supposed to be: finding facts that proved the truth of events, of passions, violence, mixed motives, good and bad. It was not just scientific truth, it was the events of people's lives, and they would be either protected or damaged by the decisions made as a result. She had been anything but impractical then. She must answer Membury. "Maybe he has another case. I'm stopping for tea anyway."

"Yes, Miss Miriam." He smiled, but he did not meet her eyes. He turned and went out to tell Daniel he was welcome.

Moments later, Miriam heard Daniel's footsteps in the passage and then stopping at the door. "Come in," she invited. "I'm just going to have a cup of tea. I could do with a break. Would you like tea?"

He stood at the entrance, a slight frown on his face, his hair, with its touch of auburn, flopping forward onto his brow. He looked exactly as she had remembered him, perhaps a little taller. He was naturally graceful, not like his friend Kitteridge.

She turned and invited Membury to join

35

them. She always asked, and he always declined. It would not be suitable for the butler to sit at the kitchen table as an equal to the mistress. But he was always pleased to be invited. It was a small, comfortable ritual they went through.

"No, thank you, Miss Miriam."

Daniel accepted, coming into the kitchen and sitting down at the table, as if he was used to doing so. Perhaps he had momentary flashbacks of them sitting together at the table in the house in Alderney during the case they had fought so hard just a month ago. She had not seen him since then.

There was a moment or two of rather prickly silence. They knew each other in some ways so well, had fought battles side by side. And yet, socially, they did not know each other at all. Her father was Daniel's employer. His father was head of Special Branch, and secretly more powerful than anyone guessed.

She set the water on to boil and put two saucers and cups on the table. "I suppose you have a case," she broke the silence. "I mean, one of forensic interest?" She saw acknowledgment in his eyes and a faint blush in his cheeks.

"Yes, I think so," he replied. "I mean, I've

36

accepted it. I had little choice. Marcus . . . Mr. fford Croft . . . said it will be good for me to learn how to lose gracefully." He smiled and shrugged very slightly.

For a moment, she was taken aback, but she realized how very typical that was of her father. His way of teaching young lawyers in his chambers was definitely unorthodox, but it had been very successful with the best of them, and a little harder on those with less . . . ability? Or just less passion? She knew he had taken Daniel Pitt on mainly as a favor to Sir Thomas Pitt, an old friend. But she also knew that, although Daniel occasionally exasperated him, he liked the young man increasingly as he came to know him.

"Is that what you will be learning to do?" she asked. "Lose gracefully? I don't know that I can help you. I do it often, but not particularly well." She went on quickly, in case that sounded too much like self-pity. She should not allow her frustration to show so nakedly. "What is the forensic aspect to this case?"

"Fire," he said simply, watching her. "Warehouse fire, where two men were inside. One of them died. The other got out with a few bruises and scratches."

She knew he was watching her, waiting

for her answer, although he'd only suggested the problem. "So, he's being charged with the death of the man who did not get out?" she asked.

"Yes. But it's worse than that. The one who died had a pretty badly cracked skull." He stopped abruptly.

"Oh. So intentional murder? Why? Why not an accident? He fell, and your man could see he was dead so there was no point in his risking his own life by carrying him out?"

Daniel shook his head ruefully. "I didn't even think of that."

"It's all right. If that were the case, he would have told you. It wouldn't really be a good thing for you to suggest it to him. Does he admit it?"

"No!" he said quickly. "He just said they were fighting. I don't know whether he doesn't remember very much, or if he's just being very careful what he says to me . . . and he's very frightened."

"They were friends?"

The kettle began to whistle behind her and she turned to take it off the hob and make the tea.

Daniel stood up automatically to help. It would have been a strange thing to do, had they not shared such duties a short while

38

ago, on the island of Alderney. They had been allies in a desperate cause, and such things as who did what in household tasks were of no importance whatever. Now it seemed like an age ago, another world. And that was reasonable. A tiny Channel Island like Alderney *was* another world.

She made the tea and he put the milk and a tin of ginger biscuits on the table. She had no need to ask if he liked them; she already knew he did.

"No, actually they were rivals," he answered the question. "I've a lot yet to learn . . ."

"But you believe he's innocent?" She was puzzled. He was not explaining himself very well, and that was out of character.

"I don't know . . ." He appeared genuinely at a loss. "I felt he could be, but nothing in the evidence so far suggests it." He looked up straight into her eyes. "I didn't intend to take the case. Kitteridge pointed out some of the bad aspects to it, and we went to see your father to ask him what he thought." He was self-conscious at the memory. It was clear in his face. "And somehow I found myself saying I would like to take it. At least, that's what I think I said. Marcus seemed to take it that I did! He said I'd lose, but learn something, so to go ahead." He smiled ruefully. "I think I more or less fell over my own feet."

"You were helped," she observed from experience. Marcus had tripped her up a few times. He looked so perfectly innocuous, until you found yourself going the opposite way from the one you had intended. He used to be brilliant in court, when he was younger. He was now over seventy and he had aged lately. Miriam's mother had died when Miriam was ten, and he had been alone too long. These days he occasionally forgot things, names in particular. She had learned not to fill in for him, at least not to do so too openly. It only made the lapse more obvious.

"What do I even look for?" Daniel asked. "I've got to try, whatever the truth is. The police inspector on the job seems to be competent enough, and the medical examiner, Dr. Appleby, he's always reasonable. They both seem to think that there's no chance he's innocent. The thing that's even worse, I don't think they'll have any problem proving it premeditated." His face seemed suddenly tighter, but at the same time younger, as if the thought had come to him from somewhere unseen, and taken him by surprise. "They'll hang him, won't they?"

She hated admitting it, but to tell him

anything else would be a lie, and that would hurt, without serving any purpose. In the last case, so recently, there had been a high level of trust between them. "Yes, it's a pretty grim thing to do," she agreed.

He swallowed. "Is there any way to prove that it was a spur-of-the-moment thing? A fight that went badly? Adwell got out, but Jackson didn't? Fell over, perhaps, and this caused his cracked skull?"

She shook her head. "They'll be able to tell where the fire started. They can do a lot of things, if they try . . . and they will."

"But can't we do anything?"

"Not if your man really did deliberately kill this Jackson." Again, an honest answer. Difficult, but saying only what he wanted to hear was a waste of time, and an insult to the honesty they had shared.

"We don't know that," he pointed out. "Sometimes the obvious is not the truth."

She knew what he was talking about. The cases they had worked on together, his only two major cases, were complex ones he had gotten involved in more or less by accident. They had developed out of what seemed at first to be minor cases, at least for him, and had turned out to be far more than they had originally appeared. But this was probably exactly what it looked like: a cut-and-dried case of arson and murder. Most cases were mundane, and in the end, sad. Why did she not want to tell him that? To protect his feelings? It was kind, even gentle. It was also unintentionally patronizing, as if she thought he could not take the truth. He would not appreciate it. She smiled deliberately. "But it's usually pretty close. And we've had two complete twisters lately. Rather more than our share, don't you think?"

He smiled back at her, and there was deliberate amusement in his eyes. "I kept all the ordinary ones to myself. Didn't you have ordinary ones you didn't tell me about?"

Since he had not spoken to her since the case that had taken them to Alderney, this had to be true. Most of the work she had been given was pure chemistry, no forensics, and nothing overtly criminal, nothing to stretch her skill or her imagination at all — only her patience! "Yes," she admitted. There was an ocean more to add, but she didn't. This was not the time.

"So, what can we do?" he asked, then flushed slightly. "What can I do? I didn't mean to presume that —"

"We could start by" — she made it inclusive intentionally — "finding the best forensic expert on fire that we can, one whose word will be taken absolutely."

"Is there anyone —" he began. His eyes seemed to judge whether she was being as candid as she suggested, or trying obliquely to comfort him.

Sometimes she could read him so easily, and others, she admitted, not at all.

"Yes," she interrupted him. "With the top ones, their word is pretty well taken as holy writ. For example, Sir Barnabas Saltram. He is so often demonstrably right, and so impressive in being so, that hardly anyone ever argues with him." As she spoke, memories flooded back from twenty years ago. She had been a student, young, desperately keen, and she shuddered at how naïve.

Barnabas Saltram, before his knighthood, had been on the brink of his career, a visiting professor deigning to give some of his already famous expertise to the handpicked best students. He had looked them over and instantly claimed that teaching a young woman was a waste of his time. She would marry and have children, and never practice whatever art or science she was able to learn. He also implied that that would not be much. Any ordinary tutor would suffice.

She felt the blood burn in her face as she recalled it. He had been proven right in her case. Wrong about the marriage and the children, but perfectly right in never having achieved her ambition to practice. Had he said it now, she would have pointed out the example of the brilliant Nobel Prize–winning Marie Curie! And then he would have looked surprised for a moment before reminding her that Marie Curie was as far above Miriam fford Croft as the sky was above the earth. And she would have felt crushed, as he intended.

Daniel was waiting, now looking puzzled.

"We need someone of that caliber to read the evidence for us. Then we'll have a better idea of the truth, and the possibilities." She swallowed, and took a sip of the tea, and then another. "And once you know that, with the certainty his word would carry, you could perhaps make a defense that would fit all the facts."

Daniel looked rueful. "There isn't any money. I'm doing it for . . . for the education. And because it's more interesting than shuffling papers in the office. A man of Saltram's rank would want a fortune, and it's hardly going to be a famous case! Two petty thieves quarrel in a warehouse and set fire to it accidentally. One of them gets out with a few scratches, while the other burns to death. Something like it must happen regularly."

"The crack in the skull needs explaining," she said. "And where each of them was when the fire broke out. If possible, what started it would be helpful to know. If it was accidental, or deliberate, or open to doubt." She was talking, wishing she could make it possible to escape from asking Saltram, because if she could avoid seeing him and asking for anything at all, she would do it.

But a man's life was at stake. That was all Daniel could see, and that was all she wanted him to see. The rest was too ugly, and too painful. It should be forgotten. In fact, she had succeeded in forgetting it for years . . . or almost.

Daniel was studying her face. It was good that he was so perceptive, but there were times she rathered he were not. You should have some privacy, even from friends. In fact, friends were the ones whose opinions mattered the most.

"If you give me his address, I'll go and see if he can offer me any help," Daniel said. "And . . . if you wouldn't mind, a letter of introduction, or recommendation . . ." His voice trailed off.

"It would be better if I just asked him,"

she said, "otherwise you might not get to see him before the trial." She tried to think of how to ask Saltram without emotion getting in the way. She must not taint Daniel's view of him. His client's life might depend on it. Apart from that, if they did not seek and find the truth, it would eat away at them, at their confidence in themselves, in all that they cared about and felt. Lying was like mold: it spread until the whole fabric was rotted with it.

Daniel did not argue with her. His face eased and a warmth filled his smile. "Thank you," he accepted.

She looked away. She did not want him to know how good that made her feel. "Now tell me all you know about the fire, the body as you saw it," she said. "And whatever Adwell told you about what happened. Don't bother to describe the body. You won't have noticed the things that Saltram will want to know. . . ."

When Daniel had gone, Miriam made another pot of tea. The last one had gone cold. She did not really want another, but the simple chore of making it was comforting, and sometimes it was easier to think, or put off thinking about the worst things, if your hands were busy. It was an excuse, and she knew it. What had possessed her to tell Daniel that she would ask Saltram to make a pro bono appearance in his case? She could only imagine what Saltram would say, and how he would say it. She could hear the disbelief in his voice, see the slight sneer twisting his mouth.

As a young man, Barnabas Saltram had been tall and slim, elegant, always immaculately dressed, but his features were ordinary enough. When she had last seen him, a year or two ago, the sides of his dark hair were shot with silver, and it suited him very well. It was still thick with a slight wave, neither receding nor thinning. He was approximately fifteen years older than she, which made him about fifty-five, the professional prime of his life.

She liked to imagine he would have forgotten her. It was twenty years since . . .

She forced him from her mind. It was absurd. No one was injured. There was nothing to remember. For heaven's sake, she must behave like an adult!

But she did remember. All of it! Would he have forgotten? Yes, probably. He was very famous now: the best forensic pathologist, maybe in the world.

No. Be honest. It had been clear in his face, in his eyes, when they were being

47

introduced by some well-meaning person in Madrid, that he had not forgotten.

The kettle was boiling. She made the tea, poured it, sat down again at the familiar kitchen table. There was nothing to do today. Saltram would be busy. He was always busy. If she called his secretary and asked for an appointment, she would be told that he was busy for the foreseeable future. He didn't take cases off the street! If she cared to leave a letter . . . ? She knew all the answers word for word. She had seen him give them to others.

She would go to his offices early. She knew his routine. Between seven and eight-thirty he would be reading new scientific papers, or even writing one. He had written some of the best, but to stay on top one had to publish regularly. His secretary, whoever that was currently, would come in at a quarter to nine and start dealing with the mail, and of course guarding the door from wanderers and would-be trespassers on his time.

What should she wear? Something businesslike, but not too aggressive. Black? No. It suited her very well, with her slender figure, fair skin, and bright hair. With red hair, one expected green eyes, or hazel, but hers were blue, with only a hint of green.

Not black, perhaps dark green. No! Definitely not that. She had been wearing green that day. People expected women with bright auburn hair to wear green. Pink was much cleverer. But for business, that would be absurd. Her cheeks burned when she imagined his remarks. He would be quick, funny — and cruel.

Dark teal, a soft deep color between blue and green. A color you barely noticed at first, subtler, and more glamorous than a peacock, with its unfortunate connections to pride.

Earrings, of course. They were flattering, they gave light to the face, accentuated the cheekbones . . .

What was she thinking?

Would he imagine she had chosen these things to catch his attention, to please him? That was almost enough to make her go in sackcloth. What she chose was to build her own confidence. It was armor. For herself!

She must collect everything she knew of the case, the notes she had made from Daniel's comments, and then it would be a good idea to go out and purchase all of the local newspapers she could find that mentioned the incident. Saltram might not listen to her. Heavens, he might not even let her in the door! But she must be ready.

The next day she was ready, at least as much as she could be. She took a taxi into the city, one of those black, boxy-looking automobiles that were becoming so popular. She had her own car. It was one of the many ways her father had indulged her, and she loved driving in the countryside. But finding a good place to park it in town was difficult, and she could not afford to be driving around in circles looking for a place, when she was, by her own estimate, due at Saltram's office to catch him before the business of the day gave him escape.

She was angry to find herself gulping air, and even shaking a little. She would have liked to say that there was nothing he could do to her, nothing he would even want to do to her! It might even be true.

Or not!

She got out, paid the fare, thanked the driver, and walked across the pavement. She read the carefully lettered gold-embossed plate outside the door, then went inside. A discreet notice told her that his office was on the fourth floor. She called the lift and rode up in the clanking claustrophobic contraption. She was relieved when the door opened and she could step out onto the landing. She read the directions and walked toward his door.

There was still time to change her mind. He would never know she had been here.

But Daniel would. He might forgive her, even though he would never understand. For her, it was the exact opposite: she would understand, but not forgive herself.

Before she could argue with herself any more, she knocked sharply on the door and tried the handle. It opened easily into an empty reception room, furnished simply but expressively, classical etchings on the walls, perfect but impersonal. How like Barnabas. She used to admire that. It was clean and almost antiseptically tidy. A wave of memory washed over her, taking her breath away. That was absurd! She was torturing herself!

She walked across the floor to the door leading into his office and knocked on it firmly.

Silence.

She was about to knock again when it was snatched open from the inside, and she was face-to-face with Barnabas Saltram. More accurately, her face was level with the knot in his perfectly tied cravat.

"Good morning, Sir Barnabas," she said, her voice almost steady.

51

"Who are you, madam, and why have you intruded into my office at this ungodly hour? I do not see clients until half-past nine. If you . . ."

He blinked at her, as if only just realizing that they knew each other. But she had seen the flash of recognition as soon as he saw her hair, even before he met her eyes.

"Because at this hour I will have your attention, at least long enough to tell you why and for whom I am seeking your help." She had rehearsed it several times, but now it sounded practiced, not natural.

He hesitated, as if debating whether to admit knowing her. "Miss . . . uh . . . fford Croft, isn't it?" He sounded less startled now.

"Yes." She must state her case before he had time to refuse her. "It is a forensic matter on which you are an expert — I might say, *the* expert — and I believe the only one anywhere that the court will listen to. You will understand if I say a man's life will depend upon the outcome."

He was surprised. "So why is it you who comes to see me, rather than the lawyer for the defense?" His voice was a little sharp, and he was plainly puzzled, but not unreasonably so.

She stared at him. In the years since she

52

had last seen him regularly, time must have changed him, but so much was still familiar. She knew exactly where the lines had formed in his face from the expressions he wore regularly. His features were neat, nothing too pronounced, everything in control. Almost an aristocratic face. The sudden losses of temper were not yet marked indelibly. Or perhaps he had them in control by now. Fame sat well on him.

She must pull herself together! She was not a girl to be awed by him, as she had been once.

"Miss fford Croft!" He was clearly growing tired of being stared at. "What is this case, and why does it interest you so strongly that you turn up at my doorstep at this hour of the morning to ask a favor of me?" There was a very slight flicker of amusement in his eyes. "Which cannot be easy for you," he added.

She looked at him very directly. His eyes were hazel. Funny, she had thought they were brown. "A little discomfort is hardly of importance, compared to the man's life," she said a little stiffly.

His eyebrows rose. "An innocent man?" He put a weight of doubt into his tone.

"That is what a trial is for, Sir Barnabas. I thought that was one of the things we were agreed upon. You'll get the evidence, all of it, and see what it tells you. What you would like it to be has nothing to do with it. 'Science, gentlemen, science.' " She was quoting him from a class twenty years ago. She had no idea whether he would be flattered at her remembering it, or irritated at being given it back again.

"I see you have finally grasped it, Miss fford Croft," he said with the faintest of smiles. "What can you tell me of this case?" He held up his hand. "Wait! Perhaps I had better see it for myself. I have no idea how diligent you are, and I cannot trust a man's life to your observation of every detail. If I come to swear to it in court, I must ascertain of it myself."

She did not think before she answered. "I would not have come to you if I had thought you had changed so much that you would fight based on someone else's observations." It was a compliment she hated to give, but it was honest. And he would have resented anything else. He could have changed: all this success, the flattery, the almost universal admiration could have dulled his judgment. It did not matter — only that he accepted the case. She waited.

Surprise blinked across his face. Then, as if picking up a gauntlet thrown down, he replied, "Send it to me in writing. You may tell your lawyer that I will testify, but only to what I see in the evidence, only to what I believe."

"Of course." There was nothing to add. She had won, take it and leave! "I shall tell him." She smiled briefly and turned back to go through the waiting room and out the door.

# CHAPTER THREE

Daniel did not find easy the prospect of speaking to Ginger Jackson, the eldest of Paddy Jackson's brothers, but it was something he could not leave undone. He finally ran into him in a public house just off Tooley Street, in the early evening. He disliked doing this alone, but there was no good reason to ask Kitteridge to come with him. Apart from that, Kitteridge was not equipped for a bar brawl, and Daniel did not want to be responsible for his being hurt. He liked Kitteridge. And Daniel had already strained Marcus's tolerance just about as far as it would go.

The meeting had been arranged by Daniel's friend and sometime ally Roman Blackwell, a private inquiry agent and ex-policeman, a man of extraordinary knowledge, inside and outside the law, who had crossed the line rather too often. The last time he was caught had been the most serious. He had been charged with murder, a crime of which he was not guilty. He excelled at forgery, sleight of hand, and letting people's own greed trip them up, but he was not given to violence; in fact, the thought of it offended him. Daniel's skill in finding the true killer had surprised them both and been the beginning of a surprisingly comfortable friendship.

Now Blackwell nursed a pint of Guinness and stared in a friendly fashion across the bench at the very uncomfortable Ginger Jackson, who had had his arm thoroughly twisted to be there.

Daniel had a pint of ale before him, which he had not touched.

"Thank you for agreeing to meet with me, Mr. Jackson," he began.

"Against me principles," Ginger replied. "That bastard Adwell killed me brother. Burned him to death."

"Maybe," Blackwell said before Daniel could answer for himself. "Maybe not. Either way, they can't hang him until there's been a trial, and they can't try him if he hasn't a lawyer."

"So what do you want from me?" Ginger looked at Daniel.

"Did Paddy go to the warehouse to meet Adwell?" Daniel asked.

"Yeah! Ain't that obvious?" Ginger looked at him pityingly. He turned to Blackwell. "I thought you said 'e were clever."

"Just answer him," Blackwell snapped.

"Yeah, 'e did."

"Why?" Daniel asked.

"What d'ya mean, why?"

"Why did he agree to go alone, at night, to a warehouse to meet Adwell? Why not somewhere like here? He must have trusted Adwell . . ."

"More fool him! Murdering swine!"

"Maybe. Perhaps Paddy intended to kill Adwell?" Daniel suggested. "But got beaten to it." Ginger half rose in his seat, and Blackwell pushed him back down again.

"They were to agree on something?" Daniel suggested.

"Unless you want to get lumbered with setting it up, you'd better tell the truth," Blackwell told Ginger.

"All right! All right! We was goin' to go into it together. We needed more men than either of us've got alone," Ginger said grudgingly.

"But they quarreled?" Daniel asked.

"Looks like it, don't it?" Ginger said angrily. "Well, it got them nowhere! Our Paddy's gone, and Adwell's goin' to swing for it. So neither o' them got to lead us.

58

Serve 'em right, stupid sods!"

"A leadership war?" Daniel asked. "At least that's believable, even if it's . . ."

"What?" Ginger glared at him.

"Tragic," Daniel replied. "Looks as if nobody wins."

Ginger drank the last of his Guinness and stood up. "I ain't swearin' to nothin' in court, 'cos I ain't goin'. And you'll be sorry if you make me!"

"I don't think you can add anything," Daniel said. "Thank you, Mr. Jackson."

"You just see to it 'e hangs!" Ginger replied, banged his empty tankard on the table, and left. In seconds he was lost in the crowd around the bar.

"Wonder who's next in line?" Blackwell said curiously.

"For the leadership?" Daniel asked.

"Of course for the leadership." Blackwell smiled widely. "There's a lot of money in that! I mean a real lot."

The morning after meeting with Ginger Jackson, Daniel went with Kitteridge to the club in Regent Street where they were to meet with Sir Barnabas Saltram. It was three days since Miriam had made the appointment for them, and in that time they had collected all the evidence they could

and summarized it on paper, to give to Saltram if he should ask for it. That was as well
as having it in their minds to answer immediately when he asked.

They were both formally dressed, but not
as if they imagined they were members of
such a club. That might be deemed pre-
sumptuous.

Actually, Daniel resented that. He had
grown up with a certain sense of who he
was. He treated everyone with respect, at
least he hoped he did. He had been chided
by his father occasionally for assumptions
not justified. He supposed that was to be
expected. He was an only son, but his sister,
Jemima, who was three years older than he,
never let him assume too much. Like their
mother, she had definite opinions about a
lot of things. Charlotte Pitt had been born
to a high social position but, treating it as a
matter of chance, she never referred to it.

Nevertheless, Daniel did not like having
to show a respect to Saltram that he might
not feel. It irritated him, and he had not yet
even met the man. Kitteridge was completely different. It came as no hardship to
him to defer to Saltram, whether it was on
the subject of pathology or who might win
the next big horse race. Daniel looked at
him now, as they stood on the pavement of

elegant, windy Regent Street. He could read the tension in Kitteridge in a single look. Kitteridge moved his shoulders as if his collar was too tight. He lifted a hand as if to adjust it, and then changed his mind. He was immaculately shaved, and his unruly hair was very recently cut. His suit came as close to fitting him as any garment not tailored for him personally could. His boots were polished to within an inch of their lives.

Daniel smiled at him. "Imagine him in his underwear," he suggested.

Kitteridge's eyebrows shot up. "What?"

"You know what I said! It will make him a lot less daunting. Just don't laugh, or you'll look like an ass."

"I can't take you anywhere!" Kitteridge groaned. "Come on! We've either got to go in or move on. Or they'll have us for loitering!" Without waiting for Daniel, he went up the steps and spoke to the uniformed doorman. "Good morning. Mr. Kitteridge to see Sir Barnabas Saltram. Mr. Pitt is with me." Kitteridge put his card on the doorman's outstretched tray.

The doorman barely glanced at it. "Yes, sir. If you and Mr. Pitt would care to come this way, Sir Barnabas is waiting for you in the dining room."

Daniel let out his breath and followed Kitteridge inside. Saltram had at least made it easy for them this far.

The dining room was very impressive. Daniel had been in several of the better gentlemen's clubs, usually with his father, and he was always amused to see how well Sir Thomas hid the fact that he was a gamekeeper's son, a gamekeeper long ago deported for poaching, at that. Even Daniel, who knew him in many ways so well, would not have known how awkward he felt. Daniel was born to the privilege of financial security. He did not remember the days when his parents lived so very carefully, from week to week, stretching out the money, making do. He had only known the security they gave him, and the excellent education leading finally to Cambridge.

He did not look at Kitteridge to read in his face what he felt. He knew Kitteridge was deeply aware of being provincial, so often the boy who didn't quite fit in. In society, clever, even very clever, was never quite enough. And he was probably more intelligent than three-quarters of the comfortable middle-aged men who sat eating their excellent breakfast in this hushed, deep-carpeted, richly decorated room.

But Kitteridge was not any cleverer than the man sitting by himself at a window table set for three. Saltram's dark gray suit was cut to perfection, shirt and cravat unblemished by even a careless fold.

He saw them coming and greeted them without rising to his feet. He introduced himself and assumed correctly which of them was Pitt and which Kitteridge. Daniel and Kitteridge seated themselves. The usual formalities were observed, the specific tea ordered, and the eggs, bacon, kidneys, tomato, mushrooms, the brand of dark, thick-cut marmalade. Then Saltram turned to Kitteridge.

"Let us not waste time," he said with the slightest of smiles, a mere twitch of the lips. "Your case is arson, that much I know. Tell me the details, the police evidence. I'm not interested in who the young men were, or what the quarrel was between them. That might be relevant to the case from your point of view, but they are not facts as concerns forensics. Mr. Kitteridge?"

Kitteridge sat up straight. He was not going to be hurried. He recited the police evidence as to the origin of the fire, where in the building it had begun, the fact that there was extremely flammable material within a few feet of the point of origin, and what it was said to be.

Daniel watched Saltram's face as he

listened, without interrupting. Saltram made no notes, but Daniel had heard that his memory was prodigious, and he was quite prepared to believe it.

The meal was served and they began to eat. Kitteridge stopped only long enough to take a mouthful now and then. He repeated what Dr. Appleby had said when describing the body.

Saltram interrupted. "You say Appleby described the bones? Did you not see them yourself? Appleby may be efficient. I would rather have your view. His sounds too much like an opinion already formed rather than an observation."

Kitteridge looked slightly discomfited.

Daniel opened his mouth to speak, then decided it would be better to let Kitteridge explain. He would only sound defensive.

"Well?" Saltram said sharply, spiking the last of his grilled mushrooms with his fork, and lifting them to his mouth.

"It was Mr. Pitt who went to see Appleby, and not I," Kitteridge replied. He started to explain why, but Saltram cut him off.

He turned to Daniel, an expression on his face of curiosity, as if he had only just noticed him. "Why?" he demanded. "Why you, and not Kitteridge?"

Daniel had his answer ready. "Because I

was looking into the case before wasting Mr. Kitteridge's time on it. A young woman came urgently to me, and I went to see if there was any case . . ."

Saltram looked as if he had been told a dubious joke. "And what fits you to decide? You have been with fford Croft and Gibson how long?" His eyes were shadowed, clever, and unyielding.

"A year," Daniel replied. "That is why I collect information for Mr. Kitteridge to decide on, rather than to decide on it myself."

"And if you were left to decide for yourself, what would you say?" The question was asked in a level voice, the eyes probing. He could not more plainly have discarded an answer.

"What Mr. fford Croft said to me," Daniel replied without hesitation. " 'You have no chance of winning, unless you can get an expert witness on your side whom no one dare argue with. But every man deserves a defense, innocent or guilty, and you will learn a lot if you pay attention. You're no use around here shuffling papers anyway!' " He held Saltram's gaze. He was surprised to find how much he wished to win, which was ridiculous, because Adwell was almost certainly guilty. What he really wanted was to see Saltram try, as hard as he could, and work a possible miracle.

Did Saltram see any of that in his eyes?

"And what is it you imagine you will learn?" Saltram asked coolly, raising his eyebrows.

Daniel did not waver. "The difference between the best expert testimony and average," he replied.

Saltram nodded slowly. "I'll go and look at this corpse of yours and see what it tells me that you don't already know. Who have you worked with before?" This last was asked almost peremptorily, as if Daniel's reputation depended on the answer.

"Dr. Ottershaw," Daniel answered as he remembered waking up that eccentric man in the middle of the night to help, and finding him perfectly willing, as if it was the most ordinary thing to be asked. They had stayed up all night and shared breakfast, exhausted but victorious, ready for the next step. But that had been a matter of fingerprints, not burned corpses.

Saltram gave a slight shrug. It was a curiously dismissive gesture. "Then fford Croft is right," he said, "you will learn something. I'm not sure how much use it will be to you." He turned away. "Perhaps you will benefit, Mr. . . . uh . . . Kettering, is it?"

Was that a test, to see if Kitteridge was too much in awe to correct him? Daniel longed to do it for him, but that would be no use and might even seem an unintended belittlement. And Kitteridge needed to correct him, not let the error go unremarked.

There was a moment of silence. They heard the clatter of cutlery across the dining room as someone dropped a fork.

"Kitteridge, Sir Barnabas," Kitteridge replied carefully. There was no expression in his face, but Daniel could hear an edge to his voice.

"Oh, yes. More tea, Kitteridge?" Saltram observed.

When they left, neither Daniel nor Kitteridge spoke for quite a long time. They were in the taxi halfway back to Lincoln's Inn when Kitteridge finally commented.

"What the devil have we got ourselves into, Pitt?" he said. "This case is ridiculous! Warehouses don't catch fire spontaneously —"

"They can." Daniel argued the point because there was no reasonable explanation to make, and he knew it. "Flour can explode, you know."

"What? You mean like flour you make bread with?"

"Yes."

"Then why don't we hear of kitchens exploding, or bakeries?"

"It does explode sometimes in warehouses, so perhaps it needs something added to it."

"If you want to suggest to Saltram that the fire was started by exploding flour, I'm not coming with you! I'm going to pretend I never saw you before!"

Daniel groaned loudly. Kitteridge's sense of humor was a unique animal.

"His skull was cracked," Kitteridge said. "That's what you told me. How did that happen if nobody hit him? You've got to strike someone a hell of a blow to do that!"

"That's Saltram's job," Daniel replied. "He won't give up easily!"

"Diligent in the cause of justice . . ." Kitteridge held a slight question in his tone.

"Balderdash!" Daniel said sharply. "He doesn't like being beaten by anyone at all, alive or dead."

That evening, Daniel went to his parents' house for dinner. He liked his rooms in his lodgings well enough, but the house where he had grown up would always be home.

He stepped inside the front door and immediately felt the warmth envelop him. Not that it was so cold outside; it was the familiarity. He realized with surprise that half the fear, the courage, the new knowledge of civilization was good only because there were things that did not change. The past was safe. Nothing could tarnish it, or change the small things that were irrevocably good.

His mother had heard the butler open the door, and she came from the withdrawing room into the hall to greet him. Of course, she had changed a little, day by day, as she grew older, but it was so gradual he barely noticed it. He was the second child, so she had been in her late twenties when he was born. Now she was in her early fifties. Happiness, confidence, passion to fight the battles she believed in, had kept her spirit strong, but softened her temper — most of the time. Daniel supposed most young men thought their mothers beautiful. He knew in his case he was right. She was also warm and funny and knew him far too well for his comfort. Her own faults were mirrored in his, but if her courage was as well, he would be satisfied.

This evening, she was wearing a fashionable dress, the shape of which he did not like. He thought it too exaggerated, too modern. But the color was a deep, soft sort of red, and the vibrancy of it made him smile. He hugged her tightly for a moment and then let her go, to follow her into the withdrawing room that he had known all his life. It was still two rooms in one, the further end with its floor-to-ceiling curtains that this evening were drawn closed, hiding the French doors to the garden. Over the nearer fireplace was a large painting of ships in harbor, all blues and grays, calm water, soft skies, buildings looming in the background. He knew it was Dutch, but nobody worried whether it was an original or a copy. The value was far deeper than money.

There were one or two new cushions on the chairs, or perhaps the old ones had been recovered. Otherwise everything was the same: the books, pictures over the mantelpieces, the ornaments, each one with its own history and associated memory.

His father was standing in front of the nearer fireplace, smiling. He looked Daniel up and down, then came forward and clasped his hand, holding it hard for a few moments longer than necessary. Everything had been said years ago. This was only a momentary reassurance that it was all still the same.

Even the offer of a glass of sherry was the same. And the polite declining, with a smile. They talked of the usual comfortable things

70

until the meal was served. There were the questions about Jemima and her two little girls. One could not think about family and not mention three-year-old Cassie, who wanted to know everything about everybody, and would notice the slightest deviation from the previous time you had answered her. She loved to argue, and was fascinated with the idea that Daniel could argue, and get paid for it! He had unwillingly become "her lawyer," and although he denied it, he loved every moment.

Sophie, the new baby, was also changing all the time. And now that they had met and come to know Patrick, Jemima's husband, any news about him was more interesting.

They were beginning dessert when Pitt finally looked at Daniel and asked what he had been waiting for all evening. It was usual for Pitt to ask after his work, to show just enough interest, yet not seem to be asking for a full account. This evening, Daniel would not have resented it. The Adwell case was heavy on his mind, intruding even on the peace of the evening — especially here. Home was emotional safety, but it had never been a shelter from the darkness of life, the violence or the possibility of violence.

Pitt had been a policeman since before he

married Charlotte. They had met because of a series of murders. One of the victims had been her elder sister, Sarah. Daniel could recall sitting at the top of the stairs, hidden from sight, next to Jemima, listening to the grown-ups talking in hushed voices in the hall, then later around the kitchen table, working at solving murders that reached into the heart of government, even to the edge of the throne.

"I've just taken on a case I'm going to lose," Daniel replied to his father's question. Did Pitt know that he was worried about it?

"Why are you going to lose it?" Pitt asked. Just at this moment, his face was inscrutable.

That was not what Daniel had expected him to ask. "Because I think he's guilty," he replied. "He says he's innocent, but there doesn't seem to be any believable alternative. I did ask Marcus before I accepted it."

Charlotte looked at Daniel, then at Pitt, but she did not interrupt.

"You haven't said why you accepted it," Pitt pointed out. "What was your reason?"

This time, Charlotte cut in. "Was it a favor you owed someone, and now you can't pull out of it?"

Daniel drew in his breath to say no, and

then realized that, most simply, it was because Jessie Beale had looked so helpless. It was a stupid, impulsive thing to do, because now that he examined it a little more, the case looked a lot worse.

He left the answer too long and went for the major effect instead. "I asked Sir Barnabas Saltram to examine the evidence," he said, looking at Pitt, then at Charlotte, then at Pitt again. "You must know of him . . ." He stopped. Just as his father could read him even before he spoke, so sometimes could Daniel in return. "You do know him!"

"Slightly," Pitt admitted, his face curiously inscrutable. "Not enough to give you an opinion, except that I'm impressed you could retain him. There must be something of particular interest to him. The case, or the client." The question was in his eyes.

Charlotte was watching Pitt now, too, a slight frown on her brow.

"Not the client," Daniel said quickly. "He's a young dockworker, when he's working at all. He was in a warehouse on Tooley Street, meeting a member of some rival gang. Possibility of joining forces, I gather. There was a fire, a pretty bad one . . ."

Pitt leaned forward a little, elbows on his knees where he sat in the large armchair. "Bad fire? Was that how your victim died?"

Daniel felt the knot in his stomach tighten. How did Pitt, head of Special Branch, which dealt with terrorists and treason, know about a warehouse fire over on Tooley Street? Was this a whole lot bigger than he imagined? And was that why Saltram agreed to act on it — because the case was about a fire?

"Tell him!" Charlotte demanded.

"It will prejudice his judgment," Pitt replied. "And it may not be —"

"Or it may!" she retorted before he could finish. "Thomas, Daniel's big enough to decide for himself what he thinks of Saltram. Don't try and judge it for him. You're . . . you are too protective."

Pitt looked startled. "I'm what?" he said incredulously. It was almost comical.

"It's very sweet of you," Charlotte said gently, reaching across and putting her hand on his, barely touching him. "But it's not necessary."

"You have no idea!" he began.

Daniel felt himself wanting to laugh, and yet absurdly emotional. His father was determined not to interfere, not to use his personal or political power to help. It would be wrong in his opinion and, just as bad, it would rob Daniel of the value of any achievement. He would always wonder if it

74

was real, or bought for him somehow.

His mother knew and understood that, and yet she protected him as instinctively as a tigress in other things. He could remember as he grew up, it was his father he wanted to please. He wanted Pitt to be proud of him, and yet it was Charlotte he knew would back him and fight to the death. He was far more in awe of her than of anyone else, except Great-aunt Vespasia. But Vespasia was gone now, and there was a hole in his life no one else could ever fill. That was true for all of them. It was one of the hardest parts of growing up. Inevitably, some of the dearest and best would not come all the way with you. Things changed. Some losses eased, but never healed over.

"I asked Marcus's advice," he said, "and he said to get the best expert I could."

Pitt clearly found it hard to believe. His whole expression was skeptical.

"Well, not exactly Marcus," Daniel corrected. "Actually, I asked Miriam."

"And you went to Saltram?" Pitt was unconvinced. "I am surprised he even saw you!"

"Miriam went," Daniel explained. "She offered to, so I accepted. I knew I wouldn't get in. Because of her, Saltram saw Kitteridge and me. At his club . . . for late breakfast."

Pitt was sitting very still, unnaturally so.

"You know him? I mean, by more than repute?" Daniel asked.

"No," Pitt answered. "Really only by repute, but it feels personal. I've seen him testify, and spoken briefly to him in the courtroom."

"A case you cared about?" Daniel insisted. He could see the tension in Pitt. It was discreet, only a combination of tiny things, the way he held his hands, the uncomfortable angle of his head, the smile that was not really humor.

"I knew some of the people involved," said Pitt.

"Tell me."

"It's got nothing to do with this, Daniel. I don't want you to be influenced —"

Charlotte interrupted. "Thomas, he's going to be influenced anyway. Saltram talks about his old cases, if he won." She turned her mouth down at the corners in a rueful smile. "And he always wins."

Daniel's heart should have lifted, but the expression in her eyes made that impossible. "What?" he asked her. "Do you know him, too?"

"Of course not! Sir Barnabas doesn't *know women.* He looked straight through me to

76

your father, who was standing behind me."

"You exaggerate," Pitt interrupted.

"If you sort it out, detail by detail, but you have to get all the pieces together to make a picture," Charlotte agreed. "I exaggerate a little, and do it in one sentence . . . or two . . ."

"A little?" Pitt was smiling now.

She turned to Daniel. "Saltram is very clever, as he will tell you as often as you give him the chance. In fact, he is so clever he is almost as clever as he thinks he is. He dresses very well, but always as if someone else did it for him . . ."

"Charlotte," Pitt cut across her. "You don't know . . ."

"Of course I don't," she agreed. "It doesn't matter. He looks like it. And that's all I said. I suppose, if you prefer, I could have said his clothes are chosen by a valet of exquisite taste, and no character. Is that better?" She managed to make her face in the soft lamplight look totally innocent.

Daniel could not help laughing, but it was nerves as much as humor. He controlled it the moment his mother turned toward him. "I met him," he told her. "And, in a way, I didn't."

"Exactly," she agreed. "But is it about fire?"

77

"Yes."

"Then you should learn the case that made Saltram famous." She looked at Pitt again.

"Not exactly about —" Pitt began.

"For goodness' sake, it's better you tell Daniel the truth, as much as you know, or can remember. If he looks it up, it won't be the same," she insisted.

Pitt gave up gracefully. "Have you heard of Sir Roger Daventry?" he asked Daniel.

Daniel thought for a moment, but nothing came to his mind.

"Twenty years ago," Pitt prompted.

"Oh," Daniel felt very foolish. "I was only —"

"Only five, I know, but it was a famous case. You would have read of it in Cambridge, at least. His was a spectacular defense. Daventry's house was badly burned. Very large place in Herefordshire. Family home for generations. A whole wing burned down before the fire brigade arrived and got it under control. But his wife, Marguerite, was burned to death in her dressing room."

Daniel tried not to imagine it. "If there was a trial, they must have believed that it was deliberately started, but by whom? Her husband?"

"That was the first assumption," Pitt replied. "It usually is."

"But he didn't start it? Who else was in the house? Lots of servants surely? A burglar?"

"They found no trace of a burglary at the time, but stop getting ahead of me."

"Sorry. What about the fire? Was it an accident after all?"

"They questioned Daventry and he claimed total innocence." Pitt picked up the story where Daniel had interrupted him. "He was devastated by the loss of his wife. She was apparently beautiful but, more than that, she had a unique character, imaginative, willful, generous, liked by most people, but not all, and —"

Charlotte interrupted him. She glanced at Pitt, but spoke to Daniel. "He's trying to be impartial, but what he wants to say is that she was the kind of woman toward whom no one is impartial. You liked her or disliked her; agreed with her or disagreed. And really, at the heart of it, you approved or disapproved. Your aunt Emily knew her slightly. Daventry was standing for Parliament, you know."

"And Aunt Emily liked her?" Daniel asked.

Charlotte's younger sister, Emily, was an

excellent figure by whom to measure anyone. She was a complete realist with an outrageous sense of humor, and a very practical eye to anything. She was innately kind and yet had a scathing sense of reality. She had married young and gained a title and wealth and high social position. And yet when her husband had died young, she had grieved deeply. A second marriage had been far less practical, to a handsome man with no money and no prospects, but whom everyone liked, she most of all. He had surprised them all by becoming a respected Member of Parliament. If he had done it for Emily, he was careful not to say so.

She was the opposite of Charlotte, who had married a policeman with no money and no prospects. The early years had been hard, but Charlotte was never bored. She was never ashamed of Thomas, or embarrassed to borrow a decent gown she could not afford, in order to return to "society" on occasion, particularly in pursuit of the solution to a crime.

"So Marguerite Daventry was in society?" Daniel asked Charlotte.

"Oh, yes. She found it fun, and society liked her. A certain type of person always finds it satisfying to be in the company of those who scandalize. It gives them room to

80

pretend they are like someone who doesn't bore them to stupefaction. And they see the occasional price one pays for being interesting."

Daniel wondered if she was speaking of herself, rather than for Emily and the role Marguerite Daventry apparently had chosen. She had died perhaps screaming for help that never came. He had not even heard of her before today, and yet there was a clear picture of her in his mind, and he felt a real stab of pain that she was gone. "What happened?" he demanded.

"They arrested Daventry for it," Pitt replied. "They were never certain what caused the fire, but it looked very like arson. Either that, or a particularly stupid accident by one of the servants. They all covered for one another, and the police believed them. Daventry was tried."

"Don't stop there," Charlotte said urgently. "You haven't got to Saltram yet!"

Daniel saw Pitt's face tighten a little. Was it sadness for a husband's grief, or anger at some kind of injustice? Or just the thought of such a pointless death, whoever it was who had died? He had no idea, except that looking away from his father's face and at his hand on the table, his knuckles were white. "Did Saltram prove he did it?" he

81

asked. He could not let it go now.

"No," Pitt said softly. "He proved there was no murder. She died from the extreme heat of the fire. It burned quickly, the door jammed — probably something fell against it — and she couldn't escape."

"Then why did they accuse Daventry?" Daniel asked, confused. "What did the police say had happened? How did it go to trial if it was unprovable?"

"Mercaston, who led the investigation, was a good detective," Pitt said, staring ahead of him, remembering. "The bones of Marguerite's skull were cracked. It looked as if she had been hit very hard, enough to kill her. Then someone left the room, closed the door, and placed something leaning against it. Chair. Table. Hard to tell from what was left."

Daniel glanced at his mother, then back at Pitt. Now he understood. It was in some ways identical to Rob Adwell's story, at least on the surface. "That's what Mercaston thought?" he asked. "What do you think?"

"I wasn't on the case, I just knew Mercaston a bit. I liked him. I was biased."

Charlotte was growing impatient. "Tell him about Saltram!"

"Barnabas Saltram appeared for the defense," Pitt answered, at last leaning back in his chair and looking at Daniel again. "He proved that the heat of a fire can get so intense in some circumstances, it will actually crack the skull. Of course, he couldn't prove that that was what happened there, but neither could the prosecution prove that it was not. And Saltram was a very impressive man."

"He still is," Daniel said ruefully. "So, if he gives evidence for Rob Adwell, he could get him off."

"He could. And it may very well be what happened," Pitt agreed.

Daniel was puzzled. "Then why is it so bad? Perhaps Daventry didn't kill his wife? Everyone makes mistakes sometimes. Maybe Mercaston was wrong. Daventry might be a bastard, and Saltram, too, but that doesn't make them wrong." He turned to Charlotte. "Do you dislike him because he patronized you?" He said it with a very slight smile. He was familiar with his mother's temper when she was talked down to. She never lost control — that would have been beneath her — but sooner or later she would respond with a verbal icicle.

"Twenty years ago, we were none of us so important," she replied.

She was concealing something, he was certain of it. "But . . ."

She looked at him sharply, then suddenly smiled, and her face was beautiful. "I had to wait," she said simply, and he knew she was not going to add anything more.

Pitt took up the story. "The fire was arson. They caught a young man named James Leigh. He was guilty of burglary, at least it seemed so. He could not explain why he was there, not believably. They blamed the fire on him, too, when they sorted out the evidence."

"And?"

"They hanged him."

"But did he mean to — ?" Daniel could feel his own throat choking. He had never even heard of the young man, but his imagination envisioned the horror of his punishment.

"Doesn't matter," Pitt cut him off. "The fire was set in the commission of a crime. The fire burned the house. A woman died. In the law, that's enough."

"Did he do it alone?"

"Apparently. They didn't find anyone else."

Daniel turned to Charlotte. "Is that why you hate Saltram?"

"I don't hate him!" she answered. "I . . . I loathe him because he took pleasure in his victory, and really, the whole thing was

84

nothing but a tragedy. There were no winners. It shouldn't be about winning and losing, it should be about finding something close to the truth."

Daniel glanced at Pitt and saw the emotion in his face. He was still in love with her as much as he had always been, but he was not going to try again to explain the legal system and how often it gave simplistic answers to complex and painful truths.

"I suppose I should be grateful we've got him," Daniel said without conviction. "We can't pay him!"

"He'll get his money's worth," Pitt answered. "One way or another."

# CHAPTER FOUR

Miriam sat across the dining-room table from her father and ate slowly. Her mind was so full of thoughts about Daniel, the Adwell case, and the intervention she had made with Saltram that she had no idea what was on her plate. Not that she ever gave food the appreciation it deserved. Of course, she thanked the cook; it was merely good manners to acknowledge the care given. She had an idea that the cook was perfectly aware of a great deal about Miriam that she did not express. She had worked for the fford Crofts for most of Miriam's life, and regardless of what she said, there was little that surprised her. She was a comforting figure in the background, like clean smells of the kitchen, drying cotton from sheets on the airing rail winched up to the ceiling, fresh bread, dried herbs, and something baking in the oven.

Miriam could remember her mother only

dimly, a soft voice reading to her from her favorite books, cool hands touching her face when she was feverish, or brushing her hair, rhythmically. She had smelled of something sweet, not as sharp as lavender, more like the scent of narcissus, very pure, very white, if a perfume could be said to possess color.

She glanced across at her father. It had been only the two of them there for thirty years now. They spoke of all sorts of things easily and comfortably, as they always had. But there were other old areas they skirted around. Loneliness was one of them, in its several different guises. Marcus was sufficient for her in intellectual discussions. The law and all its myriad stories, dilemmas, questions of fact or logic were his food for the mind. She always interested him, and occasionally he surprised her. That was exciting. A new thought, a different light on an old one, a truly challenging question.

Was she enough for him? She had no idea. He always had new, young lawyers in chambers, people in whom he took a personal interest because of the promise they offered for the future or for difficulties of the present. Sometimes he would ask her opinion of them.

She could very clearly remember when, about five or six years ago, he had asked her about young Toby Kitteridge. He had been even more awkward then than he was now. Miriam had been in her mid-thirties, just grown beyond the usual marriageable age. She had clearly terrified him at that first awkward dinner, in this same dining room with its faded velvet curtains, rich cherry-wood furniture, and a vulgar, hilarious Hogarth cartoon on the wall. Hardly anyone, except Marcus, even looked at it, which was a shame, because its humanity was the perfect antidote to the dry precision of the law.

She was fascinated that anyone could be so agile of mind and clumsy of body as Toby Kitteridge. She had thought it was her presence, but she later came to realize that he was like that with everyone, until he was speaking of the law. Then he seemed to find words easily, to become centered on thought, and all peripheral pieces came together in a symmetrical whole. He was still a bit like that, but finally he was almost comfortable with her.

Daniel was easier to talk to. She was enough older that the possibility of Marcus viewing him as a suitor for her never arose. Had he given up hope of her ever marrying? That was an idea with too many dark holes in it, too many edges that cut more deeply than she expected.

They never mentioned Wallace, her fiancé, long dead in a house fire.

Fire was a deeply emotional subject for her. She herself had only barely escaped from the fire that killed him. She had a burn scar on one foot she would carry always. It was small, almost invisible, and perhaps no one would recognize it for what it was, but she knew. The skin had healed, but far deeper was the memory of being imprisoned in the heat of consuming destruction and fearing she would never escape. She would be devoured, painfully, dreadfully. There would be nothing recognizable left of her.

Of course, that had not been so. She had been rescued. But the minutes before, even the seconds, were printed on her memory forever. She seldom had nightmares anymore. The residue of grief was for Wallace, for all the things he had never done. That he would die young had never occurred to him. Why should it?

The engagement had been a matter of three or four months. Now it seemed like a different lifetime. Did Marcus imagine his death still hurt? Was that why he never raised it? Actually, she hardly ever thought of Wallace, not because it was painful, but because he had never been the huge part of her life he ought to have been.

Did that say something about her ability to fall in love? Thank heaven Marcus had never asked, whatever he thought or imagined of her!

Would this new case of Daniel's, the one for which she had dug so deeply for the courage to approach Barnabas Saltram again, worry Marcus? It had not seemed to, even though it concerned another fire. She looked at him now, across the polished cherrywood table. His hair was wild, white, as if he had been out walking in a gale — just as it usually looked, in fact. He had on a waistcoat in a strong shade of mauve and a fresh white shirt. He was a highly individual man, but he dressed in the appropriately sober colors of the law. His waistcoats were his only concession to fashion. She had lost count of how many he had. Perhaps he had, too! And he liked velvet jackets, when he was not in chambers, but he kept the colors of those dark, rich, simple.

"Why is he doing it?" he asked, looking up from his plate at her. He expected her to follow his train of thought. Perhaps, she thought, asking him would be to let him down somehow, suggesting either he had not been clever, or she had not been listening. "No money," he added.

"Do you mean Daniel or Saltram?" she asked, as if they were picking up a subject only just dropped.

"Saltram, of course!" he said impatiently. "Young Pitt is never after money. Head in the clouds. But then, he's never been hungry, not literally. Soft touch, that boy. Any stray dog . . ."

"Why is Saltram doing it?" She repeated the question to give herself time to think about it. "For the recognition, I imagine. Why does he do anything?"

"It's a pedestrian case," Marcus argued. "Quarrel between two young men of the borderline criminal class. At odds over a planned theft. It ends badly. What makes that different from a hundred other cases in London in a year?"

"It's someone dying by fire and the question of a possible blow to the head being the immediate, actual cause of death, like the Daventry case. Isn't it obvious?"

"What? Saltram trying to remind us of his first real groundbreaking case? Been out of the news for a few months, and wanted to make a little noise? A sort of cry of *Look at me*?"

"You think he's above such things?" she asked and, hearing the edge of bitterness in her own voice, wished she had worded it

91

differently. Her dislike of Saltram was a private matter and she meant to keep it that way, at least for now.

Marcus looked at her more closely, eyes narrowing a little.

Excuses came to her tongue, but she knew he would see through them.

"I hope so," Marcus said. "But I doubt it. It usually takes a hard fall of some sort to cause an actual crack in the bones. Is Saltram the sort of man to learn humility from failure if he's proved wrong this time? I doubt it. I think he will refuse to accept anything as his own fault, and fight very hard to prove it. And he will not forgive the teacher of that lesson, either way."

Miriam looked at him more seriously, and a chill of fear rippled through her, like the sudden drop in temperature before a storm. "Are you saying I have bought into a tragedy, Father?"

His look softened instantly. "No. No, I'm not. He may well win with this. And I'm not sure, for justice's sake, if that's a good thing or not. This wretched young man is probably guilty and should be put away, where he can't continue his criminal career. But I am relieved that Saltram may well win, and will then not blame you, or young Pitt, for a failure."

"It would hardly be Daniel's fault!" she protested. "He wanted an expert witness! Who could be more expert than Barnabas Saltram?"

"And since when did fault have anything to do with who was actually to blame? Be realistic, my dear." He put his knife and fork down. "Please! Follow all the rational thought you like in science, but please observe reality in dealing with human nature!"

She gave him a long, steady look, uncertain what to say.

"What I don't understand, my dear, is why did you yourself go to Saltram?" he said innocently. He did not pursue any answer, although they both knew he was thinking of the past, of her difficulty with Saltram and his prejudice against women scientists. He worried about her, about her professional life and about her remaining alone since her tragic engagement, but it came out awkwardly, and only in small questions. He very seldom mentioned the past, or anything that she had imagined for her future, as if that, too, might be painful, or evoke answers she could not give.

He took another mouthful of lamb chop and ate it completely before he spoke again. "Do you care so much about this case? Do you think the young man is innocent? Or did Daniel ask you to help him? You do not owe him a favor, you know. Not that he needs one. You like him, don't you." It was a statement, not a question.

"Yes, I like him. And I like Toby Kitteridge, too," she replied. "They have no chance in this particular case, except forensic evidence . . ." She drew a breath to add that she wished she could have helped them herself. But even if she had the knowledge, she had not the qualifications to put on paper to prove it. Saltram was brilliant. She could not deny that, nor did she wish to. But yes, she did resent that she was denied the chance even to compete, to try to be as good, because she was a woman. At every turn her qualifications had to be explained in a way no man's ever were. There was always doubt about her, a lack of immediate acceptance, as if she was an oddity; second best.

What she wished was to achieve exactly what Saltram had. Maybe she had not the skills or the discipline, but she would have liked to put it to the test. No, that was not entirely honest. She would have loved it, given all her mind to it, all her time and dedication. She would have paid what it cost in time, disappointment, to get up and try again until her word was good enough to carry a jury. Better than that, she would have found the truth of whatever it was, and shone a bright light into the darkness, understanding into the confusion.

"Miriam."

She came back to the present with a jolt. "Yes?"

"What are you looking for? Do you want to see Saltram make a mistake and be there, so he knows you've seen it?" His eyes were shadowed with anxiety.

"No, Father, not at all. I saw that Daniel had no idea where to start on the case. There seemed no other possible way forward but for a forensic expert of this caliber to get the truth. That had to be Saltram. I would much rather it did not, but it did. I admit, I am surprised he accepted."

"And disconcerted?" he pressed. His face was carefully devoid of expression, so totally innocent as to be unnatural.

"Yes," she admitted. "But now I have to make the best of it. It is down to me that Daniel is going to have a defense . . . or may have. I must see it through."

"By doing what?" he asked. "Assisting Saltram? Trying to keep peace between them? I cannot imagine Daniel Pitt liking Saltram. Or Saltram liking him. Saltram had a slight brush with Daniel's father, you know? Long time ago, but Saltram is the sort of man who remembers a grudge."

"With Sir Thomas?" She had not even thought of that possibility.

"So, you didn't know? Then possibly Daniel doesn't either. What about you?"

"What about me?"

He screwed up his face. "What about you and old grudges, girl? Don't tell me you've forgotten how he treated you!"

"Of course not, but I didn't know you had noticed that," she tried to brush it off. She had never been sure exactly how he felt about it. Sometimes he understood her with startling clarity. Other times, he seemed to be utterly lost.

"I think I might have made a mistake in asking him." She chose her words carefully. "But he is definitely the best. I sometimes think that if he'd told a young lawyer that someone had spontaneously combusted, he would have believed him."

"Indeed," Marcus nodded. "I've seen some people perilously close to it. But you did ask him."

She told him the truth. "He was the only one who would know that I am fully aware of what I am doing. I could not have explained my interest, or my knowledge, or why I had chosen him to speak in a hopeless case. Dislike him as I may, I would not deny his skills." She was about to add other reasons, then reminded herself that one motive was stronger than several. They tended to look like an attempt at justification. She smiled back at him, agreeing, no more.

There was a sharp gleam in his eyes that suggested he had followed her train of thought exactly.

"Anyway, it's done now," she said briskly. "He's agreed to take the case, and we shall have to go along with it."

"We? Do you mean you and Daniel? Or Daniel and I? Or . . . all three of us?" She knew what he meant. He was afraid for her, and not only for the remembrance of past times when she was Saltram's student. He might have known, or even guessed, what else beyond that . . . or almost.

Or was he worried that it still hurt her that there was no road ahead for her in the profession she loved so deeply? He could see that. He had always seen, and known that any change would be so slow, it would not be in time for her. He had hoped once, even if reason told him otherwise.

Did he wish she had married Wallace? Did he think if she had settled down with him, probably had children, that that would have been enough?

Passionately, with total conviction, she believed it would not. Was that an acceptance of pain, or a refusal to admit that she was exactly like all other women, really, just too proud or too stubborn to admit it?

Except it was not all other women, by any means. She knew of all sorts of women who had followed their dreams and crusaded for justice, studied medicine or archaeology, astronomy, art — or gone up the Congo River in a canoe, for heaven's sake. Not all women sat at home and did as they were told.

"Miriam!" His voice cut across her thoughts.

"Yes?"

"Are you helping young Daniel?"

"I wish you wouldn't call him *young Daniel.* You make him sound like a child we've adopted." The words were out before she could stop them.

"He is young!" Marcus said with surprise.

She wanted to respond, *Not to me,* but that opened up a whole new subject she'd rather leave closed. "He's learning," she said instead.

"Don't help him too much! He'll come to depend on you!" he warned.

"Nonsense. I know nothing about the

law," she said immediately, rising from the table.

"You know a good deal about human nature," he said sternly. "And tenacity."

"So does Daniel. And he didn't get it from me."

"He probably gets it from his mother. You'd like her. But he doesn't need your encouragement. He's stubborn enough by himself. This was a ridiculous case to take up."

He placed his knife and fork on his plate and stood up also. "Well, I've got to go and see . . . ." He frowned. "His name escapes me. But I know where he is. Remember what I said, Miriam: Don't encourage Daniel on hopeless cases."

She started to say that it was he who had encouraged Daniel to take the case, but his forgetting the name he wanted sent a warning that stabbed sharply at her, like a thin needle hitting a nerve. He was forgetting names more often recently, and it frightened her.

"I won't," she said immediately, but he was already out the door.

She spent the rest of the day busy in her father's library, studying past cases of death by fire. She might as well give in to it, and read all she could find. It was a subject about which she already knew more than she wished to, but details slip the memory over time, and she had avoided it long enough to have lost the sharp edges of recall.

She had supper alone. Membury brought it to her on a tray, and she ate by the fireside in the sitting room. And then she looked at the newspaper, but her mind was not in it. She read the same paragraph three times and gave up. She wished to be sure of sleeping. Tomorrow, she would busy herself with other things, small jobs. She was not fooling herself. She was filling time. Wasting it. Wasting precious life.

She went through to the kitchen and made herself some cocoa, a little too hot, and drank it. It would help her sleep.

For a little while, she thought it was not going to work. She lay in bed staring at the ceiling, then turned over and deliberately started counting sheep. Then they became individuals, with faces. She wondered if sheep gave one another names, in whatever language they communicated. Surely, they must. What was life worth, anyone's life, without communicating with someone?

She woke with a jolt, sitting upright in bed, her heart pounding. She had heard the crackling, clearly, loudly, like someone walking on dry sticks — except, of course, it was fire. It was always fire. She could smell it, the sharp, acrid taste of it in the back of her throat. Could she feel the heat already?

Where was Wallace? It was the middle of the night, pitch-dark; of course he was not here. He had been angry when he left. She tried to remember why and it eluded her. Something that did not really matter. That was why you quarreled with people — because you could not say what you really meant. But what had she really meant? That she could not face.

It was getting hotter, louder. But it was all in her imagination, as it always was. There were no flickering lights of the flame, except in her head. No heat. Only the sweat, and it was chilling on her skin, rapidly turning cold. She shivered and closed the blankets around her, lying down again. The details were always the same, the breaking glass, the screaming, the horror when she realized Wallace was here somewhere and she couldn't find him. Why was he here, in the middle of the day? She had been lying on the bed because she was exhausted. What had she been doing? Working all night on some experiment? That was why he was angry. She could see his face in her mind's eye, except that it was fuzzy around the edges, and of course much younger than he would be now, if he were alive.

It had not been her fault. Perhaps it was no one's fault. An old electrical connection, the firemen had said. No, it was her fault that she was alone and Wallace was dead, and she was sorry, very sorry. He should have lived a long, happy, wonderful, useful life — just not with her!

She felt horrified, grieved, lonely, but not desolate. There had been times when she missed him for a moment, when something reminded her of him: things they had done together, music he had enjoyed, the odd turn of phrase only he used. But she also felt relief.

Would it always be that? She had believed then that it was possible for her to have a professional future. He would have made that impossible. She realized only slowly that she was part of his life's plan, when he balanced it just right. But she had been chasing a dream that was impossible, with or without Wallace.

She wrapped the blankets tightly around her, but she was not any warmer for a long time. The dreams were getting better, less frequent, but it had been fifteen years and it still left her with a feeling of incompleteness. Was there something she was afraid of remembering? Fire had always frightened her, the savagery of it, the completeness of its destruction, the sense of a measureless power devouring everything, yet forever hungry. Its submission to the mastery of man was an illusion; it was always waiting its moment — smiling and waiting!

*Don't be absurd,* she said to herself. It's a force of nature, a scientific process that is possible to understand, and to explain. Like all things in nature, men needed it to live, but it had its own entity, too. Only a fool misunderstood that. The strength of water was measureless. The weight of a breaking wave, the power of its suction as it drew back into the ocean. The torrents of a waterfall.

Life itself in forms too many to count, even to imagine: beauty, variety, hunger to live. She was getting warmer. In a little while she would go back to sleep, and perhaps not dream this time.

# CHAPTER FIVE

Three weeks later, Daniel sat beside Kitteridge in the courtroom as the trial began. Robert Adwell was charged with the murder of Patrick Jackson. Adwell stood in the dock, not so much at attention as rigid with fear. Kitteridge had done all he could to assure him that they would do their very best for him, but the fear he himself felt came through his face, his voice, and the white knuckles of his hands.

Daniel understood. Of course he did! Barnabas Saltram's reputation was superb, in fact unimpeachable. But the evidence, to the ordinary man, was unarguable. And Adwell was so paralyzed with terror that he was a poor witness in his own defense. His record did not help. He had been convicted of several petty crimes, none of them actually violent, but they still gained him a bad reputation. And what was he doing in a warehouse late at night, in the company of a thief one step higher on the ladder of crime, if not planning something larger, more ambitious as collaborators? He had not even denied it.

The judge brought the court to order and the trial began. The usual formalities were attended to. Kitteridge entered a plea of not guilty, to the judge's obvious surprise. In fact, it seemed for a moment as if he was going to ask Kitteridge if he was sure of what he had said.

But Kitteridge put on an excellent performance. Daniel knew it was a performance from the clenched fist by Kitteridge's side, hidden from the front by his jacket, but visible from where Daniel sat. He knew he had not much of a defense but he was determined to give his best.

Kitteridge sat down. Daniel looked straight ahead, as if he had not noticed anything other than the great care Kitteridge always took. But he felt guilty. None of them would have this case if he had had enough sense not to listen to Jessie Beale, and then not to ask Miriam for her advice.

The witnesses came one by one and told the sad, destructive story of the fire. Daniel turned and looked at the gallery. It was almost empty. A few scruffy-looking men of varied ages who sat together toward the middle were probably relatives of Paddy Jackson. And, of course, Ginger Jackson was there. There was a certain resemblance among all of them. Or did hungry, frightened men who worked in the docks and timber yards, scrubbed and brought to court, all look much the same to an outsider?

In all the verbal and legal battling, the fight over facts and reputations, they should not be permitted to forget that Paddy Jackson was dead.

The forensic evidence was grim and factual. It took all morning to get the details, which were asked for down to the tiniest thing: smoke stains on other floors, the debris of the fire indicating where it had started, and how far it had reached. What was lost? What was the estimated value? Could that be proved?

Lunchtime came and they adjourned briefly.

"Are you sure Saltram will come?" Kitteridge asked over a roast beef sandwich, which he ate as if it were cardboard.

"Yes," Daniel said with a certainty of which he was trying to convince himself. "He's a perfectionist. He always keeps his word. It is part of how he wishes to be seen."

"How do you know him so well?" Kitteridge said with curiosity, and doubt.

"I don't. Miriam does."

"Oh? How? Well enough to know what he thinks of himself, and why?" Kitteridge's expression was a mixture of anxiety and genuine interest.

Actually, Daniel wondered that himself. How long had she studied under his tutelage? A year? Two years? He tried to think back on his law professors at Cambridge, and how well he knew any of them. Had he ever considered their personal thoughts, rather than their legal opinions, and how they had arrived at them? He could remember certain eccentricities, and good jokes, and even more, the bad ones. But personal feelings? Vulnerabilities? And his studies had been far more recent than Miriam's.

He remembered his friends clearly. He kept up with them, when he had the chance. When the work was light, he went up to Cambridge for the occasional weekend. It was not far on the train. Of course, many of them were in London now anyway.

But would Miriam have made friends so easily? How many of her class were also women? Young women who were supposed to study artistic or literary subjects, or possibly history. And then, of course, to marry. Even in this new century, with all its teeming ideas of social upheaval and new norms, some things remained the same.

What had Miriam done for friendship? He felt a sudden wave of sadness for her, he could imagine her loneliness so vividly. He remembered the first few weeks he had been away from home, knowing no one with whom to share a thought or feeling. He had been nineteen, and suddenly discovering that he did not know nearly as much as he had thought. Or pretended.

It was fine in the mornings when he was full of energy, looking forward to learning something new, trying to make sense of it. But at the end of the day it was different: He was overwhelmed with complex ideas that did not seem to fit together as they were supposed to — as apparently they did for everyone else. He was tired and longed for things familiar, things that came easily.

That had passed, when the weeks turned into months, and friendships developed. He had discovered that most people felt as he did: that loneliness was a feeling, and not a reality.

But what about for Miriam, with her love of knowledge, the pursuit of it, with no degree at the end — because she was a woman?

"Is the answer a secret?" Kitteridge's voice

interrupted his thoughts.

"What?" Daniel could not remember the original question.

"I asked how Miriam fford Croft knew Saltram well enough to understand his judgment of himself," Kitteridge said.

Daniel retreated from the question because he did not want to guess the answer. "She said he prided himself on always being on time, and expected his students to do the same." That was close enough to the truth. What she had said had been more perceptive than that, but he did not want to discuss it with Kitteridge. "Are you going to eat that?" he asked instead, looking at the sandwich.

Kitteridge put the remaining half down. "No, do you want it?"

"No, thanks. Let's go back. We might as well get on with it. I think the next one to testify is the policeman, Quarles."

Kitteridge stood up and straightened his jacket. Somehow, it always seemed to slip sideways on his shoulders, although they appeared perfectly even. Must be the way he stood.

"I can't see any point in questioning him," Daniel went on, leading the way out into the street again.

"It's always cold down here," said Kitteridge. "So near the docks. I don't know how people live in it!"

"Probably no choice," Daniel replied. "You had better say something to Quarles, or else it will look as if you don't intend to fight."

"I know that!" Kitteridge snapped. "So, what do you suggest I ask him? I'm only in this because Marcus told me to be. It's your case."

Daniel bit back a tart reply. Strictly speaking, he had been expecting Marcus to tell them to drop the case. He could understand why Kitteridge was annoyed.

"Make sure he's certain where everything was found, exactly," he replied. "Position of the body, everything anywhere near it, anything Jackson could have tripped on. How far he was from the bottom of the stairs. That sort of thing."

"What the devil for?" Kitteridge's eyebrows shot up. "Are you proposing Quarles should say Jackson set fire to the building and then fell down the stairs?"

"It's not impossible . . ."

"It's bloody unlikely! And what was Adwell doing that he escaped unharmed? Why didn't he at least attempt to help Jackson?" Kitteridge asked.

"I don't know! But there's a big difference between being so scared of fire that you run from it, and hitting someone over the head and leaving them to burn."

"If it wasn't Adwell, then who did hit him?" Kitteridge said reasonably. "You can hardly introduce a third person, unless there was someone else there. Nobody's going to believe that. And if there was, why didn't Adwell mention him before now? Who? One of Jackson's brothers?"

"I'm not suggesting it," Daniel said a little more sharply. "I wish I really thought Adwell was innocent . . ."

"But you don't!" Kitteridge's voice was sharp with the fear he himself felt. They were, as Marcus had said, fighting a hopeless cause. Unless he were a magician, which Miriam seemed to consider possible, God knew why, then even Saltram could not save them.

They walked side by side back to the courtroom. There was nothing useful to say.

The trial resumed with Quarles giving evidence for the police. He was confident, and he spoke simply, without a lot of description. His testimony was the more powerful for being given in a calm and unemotional voice, using the plainest of language.

"Yes, sir, Paddy Jackson died in the fire. We found his body badly burned. No doubt the medical examiner will give you the details."

"But he died in the fire?" the prosecutor insisted.

"He was burned in the fire, sir. I cannot swear to when or how he died."

"But you arrested the accused, Robert Adwell. Why?"

"Because he was in the warehouse before it caught alight, and escaped when the fire was started, and he wasn't much burned."

Kitteridge did not bother to rise to his feet. Challenging Quarles would appear to the gallery as if he was doing his job, but he knew the answer would not help. In fact, it might only end by looking even more futile than it was.

"You know that how?" the prosecutor went on.

Quarles gave the details, including Adwell's own words, and the slight scorching of his clothes.

"So, he admits being there, specifically in order to meet the dead man, and yet obviously he himself is alive and well," the prosecutor said with slight surprise. "He met with the victim, they spoke together, perhaps quarreled . . ."

This time Kitteridge shot to his feet. "Objection, Your Honor!"

"Yes, yes," the judge agreed. He looked at the prosecutor with a frown. "You are over-egging the pudding, Mr. Harris. Do not go off into the realms of fancy. They met. That is sufficient. To go any further is speculation. You weaken your case. Mr. Adwell escaped without harm to anything but his jacket. Hardly a loss. Mr. Jackson suffered a blow to the back of his head, as the good doctor will eventually tell us, and died either as a result of this, or of the fire." He looked surprised. "Have you anything useful to add to that?"

"No, Your Honor." The judge had summed it up for the prosecutor very neatly. He knew to leave it when he was ahead. "Thank you, Your Honor."

"Mr. Kitteridge?"

"No, thank you, Your Honor. The defense does not argue with any of these facts as presented, only the conclusions drawn from them."

Daniel could not relax. The next witness was Appleby, the medical examiner who had looked at the body, and whom Daniel had visited in the beginning. Daniel felt vaguely guilty for calling in Saltram to question his evidence, and possibly destroy it. But slim as it was, it was Adwell's only chance.

Appleby took the stand, looking as untidy as always. His hair was on end, as if he had been out in a high wind, and he wore the same red waistcoat he had been wearing the day Daniel had questioned him a few weeks ago — or one like it, but with all its buttons. He had an air of comfort about him, of humanity. One would have taken him for a family doctor, used to dealing with colds and stomach problems, the odd household accident, rather than one who examined charred corpses to establish the causes of their deaths.

He swore to his name and occupation, and faced the prosecutor expectantly.

The prosecutor would of course have been given the list of witnesses the defense intended to call. Daniel found himself unintentionally stiff, and his hands clenched in his lap. Was their defense going to be demolished here, by this homely and agreeable doctor, before they even got Saltram to the stand?

He looked around him and tried to read Miriam's expression. He had known she would be here, out of curiosity and a feeling that she was responsible for their having called Saltram at all. She also had a sense of loyalty because they had chosen to fight based on her belief that it was possible to win — however unlikely. Would it have been wiser, and more merciful to Adwell, to have pleaded guilty and not strung this out over a matter of days?

It was too late now.

The prosecutor began slowly and carefully. Did the shadow of Saltram already hamper his confidence?

"Dr. Appleby, you examined the remains that the police told you they believed were those of Paddy Jackson, did you not?"

"Yes, that's right."

"Were they burned beyond recognition?"

"Not at all. It was perfectly, clearly a human being," Appleby replied, somewhat surprised. "Surely we have already got that far!"

The prosecutor flushed. "Taking the order of evidence, Dr. . . . Appleby. We first establish that they are human, then, if possible, we establish identity, then the cause of death, if possible, and the manner of death . . ."

"I am aware of the rules of evidence, young man. Since you have seen fit to assemble this court and charge Robert Adwell with murder, we may assume that you got this far, at least!"

The prosecutor was rattled. Appleby was

trying to confuse the jury and imply that these things were still to be proven. "Milord . . ." he began.

The judge's face was a study in careful neutrality. "He's your witness, sir. I suggest you ask him the question he is competent to answer."

The prosecutor stared at the judge in silence, then finally surrendered. "Dr. Appleby, having identified the remains as human, and given the information the police had as to the identity and the circumstances in which the body had been found, did you then ascertain the cause of death?"

"Yes, sir, I did. He died as a result of being struck on the back of the head, extremely hard, by some blunt object." There was a murmur throughout the courtroom, but it subsided as Appleby spoke again. "Something like a length of lead piping, or a cudgel."

"Perhaps a baluster?" the prosecutor suggested.

"You are thinking that someone tore off a baluster from the warehouse steps, and hit him with it?" Appleby was incredulous.

"Unlikely," the prosecutor admitted. "I thought a piece of lead piping possibly lying around, but more likely brought for the purpose. Or a good, old-fashioned hardwood cudgel."

"That would do. Can't say if it was that or not. Apparently, no one has found anything for me to test."

"The building burned down!"

"How inconsiderate. But thoughtful of them to have got the poor man's body out first."

"Indeed. So, you did not see him where he was found? To draw any conclusions from the position of the body, or anything like that?"

"No. And intense heat makes the body change in strange and grotesque ways. Extremely distressing. That was not the case in this man's death."

"You said he did not die from the fire, extreme heat, burning, toxic gases, asphyxiation, or electrocution, but from a blow to the back of the head. What makes you believe this was not caused by falling down the stairs? Did the police tell you that there was a flight of stairs, or the remains of them, a few yards from where they found him?"

"They did. Even drew a diagram for me, from what they could remember, being the building subsequently burned down. And the answer is no, the injury could not have occurred from falling down stairs. There were no other injuries on the part of the body that was whole enough for me to examine, and the injury was on a part of the skull" — he indicated the back of his own head, well below the crown — "that would not be struck in a fall — or not the only part, that is. And there were no other injuries to the skull."

"Thank you, Dr. Appleby, that is all I have to ask you. Please wait there in case Mr. Kitteridge has anything to ask." There was a slight smile on the prosecutor's face, as if he was perfectly satisfied that there could not be.

That was the end of the prosecution's case. It was brief and conclusive. Kitteridge glanced at Daniel only for a moment, then stood up, swallowed as if there was something caught in his throat, and turned to the jury.

"Gentlemen, you have heard a sad and troubling account of a man's death. Whether by fire or by violence, he has still lost his life. We owe it to him, and to the man accused of killing him, to discover the truth. The account you have heard is very believable. To begin with, I believed it myself. But I am not an expert in death by fire. I admit, fire terrifies me. The thought of being caught in it, unable to escape, gives me nightmares. I dare say it does you, too."

Daniel looked at the jury and saw them nodding. They were at least listening. So far, Kitteridge had their attention.

"It is my duty to do everything I can to defend my client, if he tells me he's innocent. And he does. I admit it — I find it hard to believe that. At least I did!" He hesitated a moment.

Not a juror moved. They were so still they might have been painted on the wall as part of the scenery.

Kitteridge moved a little uncomfortably, looking down for a moment, then up again at the twelve men facing him. "But this case attracted the attention of the greatest forensic scientist in England, I dare say even in the world, Sir Barnabas Saltram. You may not have heard of him. How often does the average respectable citizen need the resources of a forensic scientist? His field of expertise concerns the tiniest details, often seen through a microscope, of burned flesh, fabric, even human bones." He gave a long sigh, and then a little shiver. "Because this is Sir Barnabas's expert opinion, we can be certain we know all that human expertise can tell us. There will be few guesses, lots of facts, and a man who has devoted his life, his time, all the power of his mind, to understanding these things." He turned to the judge. "Your Honor, I call Sir Barnabas Saltram to the stand."

The judge offered no criticism, not even any surprise. He, too, clearly wanted to see Sir Barnabas Saltram and hear if, with the mind of a genius, he could possibly interpret the facts differently.

There was a hush in the whole court. No one fidgeted, but several people could not resist turning in their seats to peer at the door.

Daniel refused and sat steadfastly facing forward. He saw Kitteridge's fists clenched, white-knuckled.

The door opened with a slight squeak, and then footsteps sounded very slightly up the aisle. Kitteridge let out his breath and his shoulders lowered a little.

Saltram came level with Daniel and Kitteridge. Then, without glancing at them, he went up to the waiting usher, gave him a nod of acknowledgment, and stepped up onto the witness stand and was very solemnly sworn in.

Daniel looked at the faces of the jurors. They were all impressed, except two, who already had looks of skepticism, and perhaps a certain resentment of privilege, or what they perceived as such. But not even a majority was needed to prevent a verdict of guilty. One was enough.

"Good afternoon, Sir Barnabas," Kitteridge began, and then cleared his throat as if his tie was choking him. It probably was. Daniel knew exactly how he felt.

"Good afternoon, Mr. . . . uh . . . Kitteridge," Saltram replied, bending his neck in the slightest of bows. He said it as if it was a courtesy, not a requirement.

"We very much appreciate your sparing the time to come to this relatively minor case, Sir Barnabas. And, in fairness to certain suspicions I have heard around, namely that some anonymous benefactor, probably with a so-far hidden interest in the case, is paying your fee, I would like to add that you are doing this entirely without remuneration."

Saltram smiled very faintly. "You are mistaken, Mr. Kitteridge, the case is not minor, and it is not uninteresting."

Daniel felt his heart sink. Who was paying? What was the element that he did not know? Every eye in the courtroom was on Saltram, and he had to be aware of it. Apart from his voice, there was not the slightest sound from anyone, not even the rustle of fabric as someone eased position.

"It is a case of life and death," Saltram continued. "A man's innocence or guilt, and

121

therefore his death in one of the most unpleasant of ways, for all that we claim to be a civilized society. But for any such claim to be recognized, we must do everything we can to ascertain the truth. That is one of man's highest callings."

Daniel relaxed, and found himself shivering, in spite of the closeness of the atmosphere in the room, now more crowded than before. Merely the power of Saltram's presence had attracted a much larger audience.

Kitteridge unclenched his hands.

Daniel wondered what was in his mind. Awe? Saltram had earned it already, and he had not even begun the expert evidence yet. He stood in the witness stand, shoulders square, but not by any means stiff. He was perfectly at ease. His fine, strong hands were resting on the rail quite casually, the hands of a surgeon, immaculately clean.

"Many of us know how uniquely qualified you are, Sir Barnabas, but for the court records, would you please tell us your qualifications in this field?"

"Certainly . . ." Saltram listed all his courses of study in medicine and forensic sciences, and the degrees he had obtained, the offices in scientific bodies that he held, and the papers he had published, most specifically concerning death by fire.

"Thank you, sir," Kitteridge acknowledged. "Have you examined the body of the late Patrick Jackson, Sir Barnabas?"

A slight smile touched the corners of Saltram's lips. "I have. Dr. Appleby was gracious enough to permit me to, in my capacity as an expert in the field, and with my interest in the defense of the accused, Robert Adwell."

"And would you please tell the court what you found, sir?" Kitteridge requested.

Daniel glanced across at Miriam's face. She seemed aware of no one other than Saltram, but he could not read her expression. She sat very straight, back stiff, even her shoulders looked as if, were he to touch her, they would be rigid under the dark blue cloth of her costume. Was she worried that Saltram would not be able to help, that there was no forensic evidence that could cause reasonable doubt of Rob Adwell's guilt? Or was she worried about wasting Saltram's time? That he would say she had misrepresented the case?

Why had he come at all? To court publicity? As a favor for an old friend? Daniel did not believe that. For Marcus, perhaps, but not for Miriam. He did not know what had passed between them twenty years ago, but it was not anything as easy as friendship. A

123

debt, perhaps? But what could Saltram possibly owe to Miriam?

Turning from Miriam to Saltram, he tried to imagine what such a debt could be. Saltram was a handsome man, in a serious, chiseled way. His brown hair, touched with gray at the temples, was still thick and sat close to his head, almost sculpting his features. His voice was smooth, every word distinct.

He looked around the room. Saltram had their total attention. The subject was grisly. No one wanted to think of a person reduced to something that could be mistaken for the partial remains of a dog, but he had stirred their emotions.

"This particular body was not badly burned," he said. "It was clearly that of a young, healthy man. There was no difficulty establishing it as that of one Patrick Jackson. Several of his family members have sworn to it." He dropped his voice a little lower. Two jurors leaned farther forward.

Beside Daniel, Kitteridge ground his teeth. The tension in him was like a violin string pulled too tightly. One felt the note would screech like hearing a knife on glass.

"But the cause of death is a different matter," Saltram continued with even more gravity in his voice, and a calm, intense concentration on his face. "That is what this trial is all about. Gentlemen . . ." He said this directly to the jury. "Clear your minds of all preconceptions. This is why we trust you, indeed have chosen you, one by one, with consideration. That is what you have sworn to do . . ."

The prosecutor rose to his feet to interrupt, then saw the jurors' faces and realized he would only earn their dislike. If the mood was shattered, it would be replaced by anger and contempt for whoever would disagree with such a grave tribute.

The ghost of a smile flickered over Saltram's face and dissolved. "A man's life hangs in the balance." His voice rasped a little. "Perhaps justice itself does. One man hanged for a crime he did not commit outweighs all our efforts to be fair. A civilized people who keep the law, not revenge-seekers."

He stopped. Perhaps he realized he had taken that as far as the court would allow him. One glance at the jurors' faces told Daniel there was no breaking Saltram's spell.

"Was the cause of his death the fire that burned at least half the warehouse into a charred ruin? Did it incinerate his body? No. And did its smoke and its poisonous fumes choke his lungs? No. That would be easily provable, were it so. Did he suffocate for lack of oxygen, which the fire itself had consumed? Again, the body would tell us that — and it did not." He inclined the angle of his shoulders toward the jurors, as if they were the only people in the room. And in a sense, they were. They, and they alone, would return the verdict.

But Daniel could see the effect it had on them. They, in return, saw only Saltram.

"The bones of his skull were damaged, cracked badly," he went on. "Such shock to the head often causes unconsciousness, and then death. But had those blows not caused death, then he would still have been breathing, and the smoke, the ash, the poisonous gas, would have been in his lungs. They were not!"

He paused, looking into the faces of each man, and ascertaining that they understood him. "Did he fall, and perhaps injure himself that way? Or did anything heavy fall on him?" He touched the base of his own skull, at the back of his neck, so the jurors would see. "There was nothing near him that could have fallen on him, as a result of the fire. If he had tripped and fallen down the nearby stairs, he would have been bruised in many places. He was not. His body was not actually where he would have landed from such a fall, nor, incidentally, was his neck broken."

Again, that shadow of a smile touched his lips. "What, then, caused his death? Let us consider the body, and the fire. The body was subjected to intense heat, but to the head and shoulders mainly. He was identified by his shoes and pants. There is no doubt it was him. Even the man accused of having killed him admits that. Why the disparity? Is there an explanation?" He smiled a moment, perhaps to make sure everyone in the entire courtroom had his attention. He could hardly doubt it!

"If the fire was not accidental, but intentional, as the fire brigade believes, set with an artificial means of achieving an instant and intense heat, but it moved in the opposite direction from the victim, I do not say he started it, but it is not impossible." He shrugged expansively. "The fire began with an explosive effect, and the heat was immediate and very fierce. It would be enough to crack the bones in his skull, such as I saw, and thus cause his death. That, gentlemen, is an answer that fits all the facts we know, and many we only deduce, or surmise. Yes, Patrick Jackson and Robert Adwell quarreled in that highly flammable warehouse. One of them died — Patrick Jackson. But his injuries do not the fit the story that Adwell attacked Jackson, lit the flammables, and escaped unharmed, while leaving Jackson to burn."

He took a long breath. There was utter silence in the entire room.

"Is it not more likely that Jackson lit the fire? It roared up far more quickly than he had foreseen, and he panicked, got caught in the flames and burned to death, the savage, unbearable heat of the fire he had set cracking his skull almost immediately. Then the draft blew the flames the other way, the way he had originally intended, and left his partially burned body behind?"

At last he turned to the prosecution. "I respectfully suggest, sir, that you cannot be sure that this is not what happened. The intended victim lived, and stands before you today, accused of murder. The real murderer fell in his own fires and perished. I put it to you that justice has served itself."

Saltram remained on the stand, waiting. The hushed air all but crackled.

"Thank you, Sir Barnabas," Kitteridge acknowledged. "I have nothing further to ask you. Possibly the prosecution has?"

The prosecutor rose to his feet looking slightly dazed, as if he had been running easily, and unaccountably found himself lying flat on the ground.

"Sir Barnabas," he began tentatively, "is this suggestion of yours the only possible solution that fits all the facts that you have mentioned?"

"Possibly not," Saltram said reasonably. "It is the one that suggests itself most obviously. The human skull is more easily damaged than one supposes, in some circumstances. And yet, in others, it can survive remarkable assault and remain whole. That is not to say, of course, that the brain inside it is not injured."

"But is . . . ?"

"The skull does not need to be broken in order for the brain to be injured," Saltram explained patiently, his voice falling a note. "A hard jolt, violently from side to side, will shake a brain. But that is not what happened here. The bone itself was cracked, in my opinion, by severe heat."

"Not a blow?"

"It is not impossible. It is far less likely. It is not at an angle where a man of approximately the same height would have struck him. You cannot hang a man for something he could possibly have done, but probably did not. You have failed to make your case, sir. I suggest it is because your

129

man is not guilty. It is the misfortune of the victim to be hoisted with his own petard, as it were, and that there is insufficient evidence to show Mr. Adwell is the guilty party."

The prosecutor gave up. He knew he was not going to shake Saltram.

The judge invited Kitteridge to re-examine. He declined. There was nothing further to say. Saltram was excused with thanks. The jurors watched him leave, their eyes following his tall, erect, square-shouldered figure until the door swung closed behind him.

Final arguments were given and the jury retired.

The judge adjourned the court until the following morning.

"Hell, he was good," Kitteridge said, once they were outside the courtroom and free of the thinning crowd. "Do you suppose he was right?"

Daniel had been thinking about it. "Legally, they can't convict," he said.

"I know that!" Kitteridge snapped. "But is he right? Is that what happened?"

Daniel stood on the courthouse steps in the icy wind. "I have no idea."

"If he says so, then at least it's possible,"

Kitteridge argued.

"Because he says so?" Daniel challenged. He did not like Saltram, and he had no idea why. The man was an expert who earned a fortune for his skills, and perhaps deservedly so. And he had come down to this very minor court to give his expert opinion without charge. Why? For justice's sake? Why was Daniel loath to believe that? Had it been Dr. Ottershaw, the fingerprint expert, he would not have hesitated. Did Saltram remind him of someone he had known and disliked? That would be both childish and unfair.

The jury could not reasonably find Adwell guilty now, even if the judge had to direct them. There would be grounds for appeal, if he did. Daniel should find Miriam and thank her. He had a feeling that it had cost her a great deal to ask a favor of Saltram. He had no idea why, and it would be clumsy, perhaps even intrusive, to ask. Did he even want to know? It lay in the back of his mind like an ache he could not reach to ease.

He saw her ahead of him, a little farther along the pavement, the light from the streetlamp a moment on her bright hair. He excused himself to Kitteridge and hurried to catch up with her. "Miriam!"

131

She turned. "You did well," she offered, but there was no triumph in her face.

"It wasn't us," he replied. "It was Saltram. Up until he took the stand, we were losing hands down."

They were under the lamp now and he could see the almost deliberately blank look in her face, as if she was crowded with emotions and uncertain of them all.

"He is very expert, and has proved it over the years," she said. "People believe him. He has a way . . . a manner that they listen to."

If she had said that before, he would have presumed that to be her admiration for his complete mastery of his profession, which she was competent to judge. Now he was less certain. As they stood together islanded in the lamplight, he saw in her eyes that it was far more complex than that. They had almost certainly won their case, and her intervention was directly responsible for that, and yet he was sure that there was defeat in her, a kind of finality in it.

Could she have been in love with Saltram, in the past, and an echo of that still haunted her? Was he the kind of man who would have awakened longing in her? Tenderness? Even a deep, aching need that still remained?

Why should that hurt? And it did! He could not imagine the cold, clever, self-sufficient Saltram responding to her tenderness, laughing with her, sharing her passion over an experiment, or any of her feelings at all. Or how she could have ever imagined that he would!

But then Daniel had been in love himself, a few times, with women who could never have made him happy. Or he them. Each had been an infatuation. Had Miriam felt this burning inside her all these years? He mildly resented it. Had she an unrequited passion for that icy perfectionist of a man, an image of brains without a heart, without laughter, without the ache of tenderness? Or reality! The whole thing was in Daniel's imagination.

She was still looking at him, waiting for his response. "Daniel?"

"Yes," he said quickly. "I . . . I'm very grateful that you asked him. He never would have done it for us."

She seemed to search for an answer. Was she looking for one that would be polite, and truthful, but not give away too much?

He should never reveal what he guessed; it would be far too intrusive, in fact, unforgivably so! He forced himself to smile. "He probably wouldn't have let us in the door in the first place."

She eased a little bit. Her shoulders relaxed. "Perhaps not, but he took the case for his own reasons."

"Do you think so?"

"I'm certain of it. He always does things for a reason, and it is never just to please someone else. It is always a forensic . . . or a justice . . . reason."

"And you don't admire that?" The moment the words were out of his mouth, he regretted them. He drew in breath to say something that would negate them and could not think of anything.

It was as if his thoughts were written on his face. She smiled, but she was only just in control of herself, and it was too late to avoid, or misread. "He is very clever indeed. I used to imagine I would be as good, but perhaps I was wrong. I could not have the tenacity to pursue excellence or the self-mastery to accept the truth, however ugly or painful it was. He told me that years ago."

Daniel wanted to interrupt, but she hurried on, as if to hesitate at all might prevent her from finishing.

"It's a man's skill, by nature as well as law. Perhaps he is right, and women are not equipped to deal with such horrors. We cannot separate ourselves from our emotions,

134

and pursue pure truths."

He could not remain silent any longer. "Balderdash!" he said fiercely. "Get rid of that old-fashioned thinking. That belongs to the past century! If you have brains, you can get there. And if you want to have the steel, you can have it!" He softened his voice. "Only, if you have it, I hope it doesn't drive out your humanity, as it seems to with him. Pompous ass!"

She gave a little gasp, a choking sound, almost laughter, but he could see the tears in her eyes. Then he knew with certainty, like a cold pool of light showing sharp detail, that she had allowed Saltram to take her dreams, even if she had only just now realized it.

"Miriam . . ." He put his hand on her arm, then knew perhaps he, too, had trespassed where he had no right. Friendship did not give him so much, and he took his hand away. "Saltram is a very good expert, and he is a perfect witness, but don't allow him to dictate what you can do . . . or not do. He's at the pinnacle of his career. Which means it could be downhill from here on."

"Oh, Daniel!" she said in disbelief.

"It could!" But he did not think it true either. "Well, his thinking is last century. About women. Look at Marie Curie!

135

Women can do all sorts of things: Go up the Nile. Collect butterflies in the Middle East. Fight for social change at home. Look at Elizabeth Fry, Annie Besant." He searched his mind for other names. "Mrs. Pankhurst. I'll bet in ten years women will have the vote."

"They're extraordinary women," she said reasonably.

"You can be extraordinary, if you want."

"Do they have crocodiles in the Nile? I don't like crocodiles."

"That's prejudice! I'll bet you've never even met one!"

"Daniel, you're being ridiculous!" It was a genuine smile on her face now.

"No, I'm not, I'm . . . I'm just extending reality a bit."

"A bit!"

"Yes. It's up to you to take it further."

"Maybe . . . but not tonight. I think you won your case."

"I think Saltram won Kitteridge's case, but I know what you mean."

She gave him a real smile, very gentle, and then she turned and walked away down the street.

The following morning, after only half an hour's deliberation, the jury returned with a verdict. "Not guilty." The judge thanked them and they were excused. Journalists rushed to the door to be the first to report the result, which would be the one they had expected.

Kitteridge still looked startled, although he, too, must surely have expected this verdict. He turned slowly to Daniel. "Working with you is like riding on one of those fairground things. They're up and down, as if they're off the rails, and then all over the place. And I never know if we are going to get thrown off, taken to the end, or wind up where we started."

"Do you want to get off?" Daniel asked, hoping that he did not. He liked Kitteridge, and knew that despite all the man's oddities he knew exactly what was right or wrong, cruel or kind, true or twisted out of shape.

"No!" Kitteridge said incredulously. "What a bloody stupid question!"

Daniel had no time to answer. Jessie Beale was coming toward them, her face alight with victory and gratitude.

# CHAPTER SIX

Several weeks later, well past the middle of November, Daniel was sitting in his favorite public house flirting with a very pretty barmaid. He was enjoying it; the weather was vile, rain rapidly turning into sleet, and it was already dark outside. Even the street-lamps offered only pale auras in which to see the brief glint of light reflecting off the increasing ice in the rain. Everything else he could see was a misty darkness in which indistinct shapes came and went.

He was prolonging the conversation because, although he did not really believe it, he imagined there was some chance the weather would ease.

"You look all innocent, like butter wouldn't melt in yer mouth," the barmaid said with a grin. "But I weren't born yesterday neither!"

Daniel had been telling taller and taller stories, and she very nearly believed him, until the last one tipped over into the impossible, and he could not hide his laughter.

A man came in and sat on the next stool, bringing the cold air with him, as if it clung to the rain on his coat and the wet rim of his hat.

"Look what the storm blew in!" the barmaid said cheerfully. "If it ain't Mr. Quarles. You look like a drowned rat! What can I get yer, luv?"

Daniel looked at him. Indeed, it was Quarles, the police inspector who had investigated the Adwell case.

Quarles was shivering and seemed both tired and miserable, only the barmaid's greeting bringing a brief smile to his face.

"Long day?" Daniel asked. When Quarles did not say anything, he reintroduced himself. "Daniel Pitt. The death of Paddy Jackson, in the warehouse on Tooley Street. Remember?"

"Oh, I remember," Quarles replied. "Trying not to, but we're not finished yet!"

"I don't know what else there is to say." Daniel was aware of the anger in Quarles's voice. Did he still think Adwell was guilty?

"You'll find out," Quarles said bleakly. "No doubt she'll send for you. I can already hear her in my head."

Daniel felt he was settling in for a long evening of recrimination. As soon as he responded in a civil way, he would go out into the sleet and make his way back to his lodgings. It would be warm there. Mrs. Portiscale kept all the fires going at this time of year. It was worth the small rise in rent. "Hey, Lillie, please give Mr. Quarles a pint of whatever he wants, on me."

"Coming up!" she replied cheerfully. "Pint of Guinness, eh?"

"Thank you," Quarles accepted. He took it and Daniel paid before Quarles could get his icy hands to his wallet. "Thanks," he said to the barmaid, and then to Daniel. "But you won't thank me when I tell you why I'm in need of a drink. You'll be hearing tomorrow morning, I expect."

Daniel felt a sudden tightness inside himself, a nameless threat. "What will I hear? Stop playing games."

"I've just arrested Jessie Beale for murder. She's bound to send for you, sure as the sun will rise tomorrow. Although, God help us, it doesn't look like it will. Going to be cold, wet, and dark till February."

"Jessie Beale?" Daniel repeated, as if the name was incomprehensible to him. "Why? Whatever happened? She can't have!"

"As no doubt she'll say." Quarles took

another long drink from his foaming glass.

"What are you talking about?" Daniel demanded. If this was a joke, it was not in the least funny. "Who's dead?"

Quarles put his glass down. "Now, I thought you would have guessed, Mr. Pitt. Robert Adwell, poor soul, died in a fire earlier today, when an old storage hut burned down. Big hut, but not quite a warehouse. There was stuff packed in there. Highly flammable stuff. Paint, chemicals, and the like. Got very hot before the firemen could put it out. Hot enough, no doubt, to crack a skull!" He stared very steadily at Daniel, his gaze unwavering.

"Why did you arrest Jessie? Sounds like Jackson's family having a spot of revenge," Daniel answered. He was trying to accommodate his mind to it, playing for time, and Quarles knew it.

"Does, doesn't it?" Quarles admitted. "Do you believe that?" He was almost smiling. It reached his eyes, and then died.

Daniel did not know how to answer. His mind was racing, trying to grasp this completely unforeseen turn of events. Was it possible that this was the way Paddy Jackson's family had taken revenge for his death? It would be understandable if they had killed Adwell in exactly the same man-

141

ner he had been charged with killing Paddy. There was a kind of rough equality to it. No one would argue that. They might actually prove it, if they did not believe Saltram's subtle evidence. Or had not heard it. Many people did not read newspapers. Or read at all! But they heard it by word of mouth. That passed from one to another faster than a bird could fly.

Quarles was watching him, waiting.

"I don't know," Daniel admitted. "It could be either. But yes! Why not Paddy's family, even if not entirely for that reason? They have something of a feud going, so any excuse would do."

"In exactly the same way as Paddy died?" Quarles's disbelief was heavy in his voice.

"Adds to the justice of it," Daniel pointed out. "And why would Jessie do it? She was passionate to get Adwell released. If she wanted him dead, all she had to do was have the law take its course."

"True," Quarles admitted. "But you've got a frozen-in-time judgment of things. I find lawyers often do. Things at the time of the crime, so to speak. Never think as they might move on, on account of the verdict."

"Of course," Daniel responded. "That's the only time you can judge. By the time of the trial, things could've changed. In fact, they probably have."

"Which crime?"

Daniel was about to reply, then realized what Quarles was pointing out. There had been two crimes. First, Paddy Jackson's death, now Adwell's less than two months later. "What's changed?" he asked. "In particular?"

"That's what we need to know." Quarles nodded. He was ignoring his drink. "Did something happen in between that changed things? Me, I think using exactly the same means as Paddy's death, down to the details, is a bit subtle for Ginger Jackson. They'd be far more likely to beat the daylights out of Adwell in a back alley. And another thing, how did they know all the bits and pieces of setting a fire like that, and making sure the injuries were pretty much the same as Adwell's? That was only broadly described in the trial. We're not dealing with clever men here."

"And we think Jessie Beale is clever?" Daniel asked incredulously.

"I damn well intend to find out," Quarles replied.

"But why would she kill Adwell? Not just for the hell of it? If she didn't love him anymore, all she had to do was walk away."

"I don't know," Quarles replied. "But I

will. And I arrested her before she walked away into some other jurisdiction and we lost her. She could just do that nicely!"

"But why did she do it?" Daniel asked. He could think of no reason. "It's a terrible risk, why not simply leave?"

"Because there's more to it," Quarles said grimly. Now all the vestiges of humor were gone from his face. "There's a reason behind it, a payoff of some sort, but I don't know what. There are several robberies unsolved along that stretch of the river where the Jacksons and their rival gangs operate. Big ones. Other people have their ideas as to who is involved, and I've got mine. There is certainly enough money involved to cause a murder, and it's usually money or jealousy that's at the root of it. Vengeance doesn't often need that long."

Daniel felt Quarles's eyes studying him, and it made him uncomfortable. He felt no guilt for defending Adwell. In fact, he had thought him very likely innocent. Was that just because Adwell was so terrified of hanging? If he was indeed guilty, then that was a very fine piece of acting, and Daniel was even more gullible than he had thought. And possibly Kitteridge had known better, but agreed to defend Adwell because the firm, in the person of Daniel, had given its

144

word. Somebody had to be there for him, for it be a fair trial, no matter who was guilty, or what the crime. He felt uncomfortable facing Quarles now.

"What do you think was Jessie's part?" he asked. "Do you think she did it alone? A quarrel over the spoils of some robbery?"

"No, of course I don't think she did it alone!" Quarles said sharply. "She's probably in with the Jackson brothers."

"But she asked me to defend Adwell. Why would she do that if she was in with the Jacksons?" Daniel didn't even pretend to believe that.

"Adwell killed Paddy, just as we charged, and then maybe because Jessie Beale knew about it he threatened her, and so she turned the tables on him."

Daniel looked at him steadily. "You don't believe that!"

"No," Quarles admitted, staring unhappily into his Guinness. "More likely she crossed sides and it was one of the Jackson brothers who killed Adwell. But they're all in it."

"So, you're charging her?"

"If she didn't do it, she knows who did."

"Should I thank you for forewarning me?"

"Probably not, or not much." This time, Quarles really did smile.

■ ■ ■ ■

Daniel was in chambers early in the morning, for once even earlier than Kitteridge. He was on his second cup of tea, watching the minutes pass on the wall clock, when Kitteridge passed by his open door, then turned back and came in. He was wearing a checked coat, so beautifully cut that all the checks matched. And he still managed to look scruffy. Perhaps it was because he wore a knitted muffler against the icy wind, instead of a silk scarf and hat. Or perhaps it wouldn't matter what he wore, he would always look as if he had dressed in a hurry and was color-blind.

Regardless, Daniel was pleased to see him. "Tea?" he offered. "It's fresh. Well, it's still hot."

Kitteridge looked at him suspiciously. "What are you doing here so early? I see you have nothing on the desk."

"It hasn't happened yet," Daniel replied. "But it will." He poured a cup of tea for Kitteridge. He would want it in a moment, if he didn't now.

"What will happen?" Kitteridge hung his coat on the rack and sat down. "You're not making sense, but I suppose you know

146

that." He took the teacup. "You were waiting for me. Why?"

"I met Quarles in the pub last night." Daniel had been rehearsing what he was going to say, but it still did not sound any better.

"And that is worthy of comment?" Kitteridge said suspiciously.

"Yes. Rob Adwell died in a fire yesterday."

"Poetic justice," Kitteridge said flatly. "Or are you saying it was the remaining Jackson brothers' revenge? Mildly interesting, but not our problem. They may well be caught. I mean, factually. We didn't prove him innocent, just not guilty beyond a reasonable doubt."

"Possibly," Daniel put his cup down. "Quarles has arrested Jessie Beale for it, and he believes that this morning she will ask for us."

"Well, I'm not available!" Kitteridge was decisive. "I shall see to it, even if I have to defend some drunk for causing an affray instead."

"Are you going to let me do it alone?" Daniel asked, with an uncertain smile. He did not really want to do it at all, but certainly not without Kitteridge's skill and presence. Even if Marcus would allow him to. But he could see no moral way out of it.

"Not taking the case would almost imply that we thought we were wrong the first time," he said.

Kitteridge stared at him, and the look on his face registered a variety of emotions.

"Even if Marcus asks you to?" Daniel pressed.

"He hasn't!" Kitteridge retorted.

"Of course, he hasn't," Daniel agreed. "Nobody's asked me — yet."

But they had not long to wait. Daniel was in the library looking up references for Marcus when he was asked to go to Kitteridge's office. He went with a sinking heart, certain he already knew what it was about.

He was correct. A young man with an attaché case still in his hands, all eagerness and nerves, was sitting in the chair opposite Kitteridge's desk. His fair hair flopped over his brow, his jacket apparently a hand-me-down since the sleeves were a good inch too short for him. Daniel was annoyed because he felt sorry for the young man immediately. He imagined him blaming himself if his request was refused.

"Mr. Holland, from Hedge and Carter, the other side of the river," Kitteridge introduced him. "He has come with a case his client wishes us to take. The case of Miss

Jessie Beale, to be precise."

"How do you do, Mr. Pitt?" the young man said, rising to his feet before Kitteridge could finish. "I do indeed, because you were so spectacularly successful in an almost identical case, almost a month ago. It seemed impossible, and yet you achieved it. The whole profession is talking about it."

Should Daniel pretend ignorance? It seemed a little disingenuous, and less than honest. "How do you do, Mr. Holland? If you are referring to the Robert Adwell case, it is Sir Barnabas Saltram who really won it —"

"Yes, indeed, of course," Holland cut across him. "But it was you who engaged him. I don't know whether it was your reputation, or some other connections — family perhaps — that obtained his services. The fact remains, you did. And you succeeded in the impossible. The case for which I come on behalf of my client is exactly the same. In fact, almost identical!" He said it as if that was an advantage.

"Perhaps you had better tell me the precise circumstances." Kitteridge gestured to him to take his seat again.

Holland did as directed, and proceeded to tell them more or less the same story as Quarles had told Daniel the evening before.

149

He added a few further details, such as the address of the storage shed in which the fire had taken place, the dimensions, and the features of the fire experts' report. There were no witnesses.

"And, of course, there is the medical examiner's report as well," he added. "We don't have that yet. But it is Appleby again. He is a very good man, but he doesn't have anything like the standing of Sir Barnabas. But then, no one does. No one in England, and I dare say no one in the world. I'm afraid I don't know whether you can call him again, or if referring to his evidence would be sufficient."

"We can hardly quote his previous testimony in another case, and apply it to this one!" Daniel said before Kitteridge could speak. "That was done out of his sense of duty. We can't ask him to do the same again — and so soon. His services are far beyond the reach of most people, and certainly a young woman with no means of her own, such as Miss Beale."

"You mistake me, sir," Holland said a trifle stiffly. "Miss Beale has quite considerable means and would not expect Sir Barnabas to give his time and skills without appropriate compensation."

"Has she?" Kitteridge looked puzzled. He

turned to Daniel. "I thought you did the Adwell case pro bono as well? Did I misunderstand you?" He knew perfectly well that he had not. He was aware of all the circumstances.

"No, you didn't." Daniel turned from Kitteridge to Holland. "I think you had better explain yourself, sir."

"Miss Beale has more than enough means to pay such bills as fford Croft and Gibson would charge. Even with Sir Barnabas added to them."

"This is quite a change in fortune for her, would I be right in thinking?" asked Daniel.

"The fact remains she can foot the bill, whatever it is, and asks that you defend her, since you alone, out of all the lawyers in London, were not only willing to take over the previous case, but won it, when such a thing seemed impossible. We do not think it was a fluke, a sleight of hand, or a mistake of the prosecution. We believe it was your feeling for the underdog, a form of justice, if you like. And we believe — we are sure — that it was extraordinary skill." Suddenly Holland did not look so nervous, so naïve, and the fact that his clothes might have been borrowed was irrelevant.

Kitteridge made three attempts to refuse, casting around for an elegant excuse, and

151

failed to find even one. He had no choice but to accept the case.

"Settle it as quickly as you can," Marcus said drily when he was told. He met Daniel's eyes very directly, so that it should be understood no argument was acceptable.

"Yes, sir," Daniel answered.

It was late. The November darkness was already complete, but the wind was quite moderate. As Daniel went out the door into the street, Kitteridge was on his heels. As one, they turned and walked along the pavement and toward their usual pub. There was a faint cloud overhead, enough to prevent an early frost. The lamps gleamed in a pleasant reminder of order, predictability. They were equally placed along the street, every one lit, nothing broken or uncertain, deeply comforting amid all the chaos that passed beneath them.

They walked in silence. Daniel did not doubt that Kitteridge was turning over the same puzzle he was. And the more he struggled the more inescapable the same truth appeared.

They went into the pub, leaving the silent chill of the street for the very considerable chatter inside, the warmth, and the aroma of beer, cider, and food: mostly steak and kidney pie, steamed suet pudding with treacle over it, slabs of Stilton cheese with butter and crusty bread. There were bursts of laughter, shouts of cheer as someone was recognized. It seemed like a blanket of normality wrapping around them.

They both ordered the steak and kidney with mushrooms. It was almost half eaten when Kitteridge broke the silence. "We have no choice." He stated the obvious. "Do you know the truth? Do you even want to?"

"No," Daniel agreed as soon as he had swallowed his mouthful. "I don't know the truth, and I certainly don't want to, but it matters and we have to pursue it."

"It matters rather a lot to Jessie Beale whether we can convince a jury she didn't kill Rob Adwell. Why did the police accuse her? Do they have evidence worth a damn?"

"What could be not worth a damn?" Daniel asked.

"Anything the Jackson brothers say, unless it's corroborated by someone we can trust. It would probably suit them very well if Jessie was guilty. How did she get the money to pay us — and Saltram — for heaven's sake? She told you she had nothing! At least, that's what you said."

Daniel swallowed another mouthful. "Yes, back in September. Apparently her fortunes have changed dramatically since then."

"Obviously, but how? Theft? Blackmail? Payoff from someone? It might matter a lot."

"All dishonest," Daniel observed. "But yes, it could matter."

"Well, can you think of any honest way a young woman, with no particularly remarkable skill, comes into enough money to pay three kinds of bills in a month?"

Daniel considered it for a moment. "Only inheritance . . . why are you supposing it was dishonest?"

"You have a point, but it is something we should bear in mind. If it's dishonest, we can't take the case. I suppose you have thought of that." Kitteridge picked up his knife and fork and thought for a bit before looking at Daniel for an answer.

"Yes," Daniel replied slowly. Actually, it had occurred to him as they were walking along the street, only a few minutes ago. "Are you supposed to ascertain if every client's money is honest? That would be rather difficult. I can think of a good few of Marcus's clients whose money may not be openly stolen, but still made by profiteering or exploitation of one sort or another."

"Daniel!"

"What?"

"She got it in less than a month, if in fact

154

she has it at all. Don't tell me Adwell's death was another fatal accident the same as Paddy Jackson's almost two months ago. I don't believe it, and neither will anyone else."

"It doesn't matter what you believe," Daniel argued, spearing a piece of kidney with his fork. "It's proof. And if it really is the same, Saltram can't say a different thing this time — he would be contradicting himself. He'd look like a fool, and he will never do that!" He put the kidney into his mouth.

"I know," Kitteridge agreed. "Perhaps he won't agree to come at all. Be busy with something else, frightfully important. But if we handle it right, reverse it without him, that will look like a defeat. He won't allow that.

"If Jessie's innocent, then the perpetrators must be the Jackson brothers, for revenge. That stands up pretty well," Kitteridge continued. "They learned from Paddy's death . . . all the details were spelled out in court. Perhaps they're brighter than we thought?" He looked hopeful.

Daniel considered it for a moment. "But if it comes out in court the same way, then Jessie will get acquitted, too. It's hardly a way for them to get revenge on her."

155

"That is supposing she was in on Paddy's death. Perhaps she wasn't, and it's only Adwell they want to punish." Kitteridge ate the last piece of his pie and put his fork on the empty plate. "And equally possible, they don't care if Jessie hangs for it or not."

"So, what are we going to do?"

"Learn as much of the truth as we can," Kitteridge answered.

"Including where Jessie's money has come from?"

"We can start by seeing if, by any chance, she was married to Adwell," Kitteridge suggested.

"I think she'd have said straight out. She introduced herself to me as 'Miss Beale.' So are you suggesting her money was his and he hid a recent fortune somewhere?" Daniel asked.

"His share of the Jackson brothers' robberies?"

Daniel thought about it as he finished up his meal. "I suppose if it's the proceeds of a robbery, she won't have to wait for probate," he said with a crooked smile. "There have been more than a few robberies lately in that area, so Quarles told me."

"We'll go and see Quarles in the morning, and Appleby," Kitteridge replied. "Make some sense out of this, or at least get to

156

know the facts and assess them, arrange them into some kind of order. And see Jessie," he added miserably. "I'm coming with you. I'm the one who has to stand up and defend her in court, if they stick to the charge. And they will."

"Not if we find . . ." Daniel began, and was unable to go on. There was nothing he could think of.

"Precisely," Kitteridge agreed.

In the morning, it did not look any better. In fact, Daniel found that, without the fuzzy edges of tiredness and the pleasant taste of cider, it actually looked worse. And it showed in his face.

Breakfast today was porridge, scrambled eggs, and toast and marmalade, for which he thanked Mrs. Portiscale sincerely. "Never mind, love, perhaps it will be better today," she said hopefully.

Daniel was her favorite boarder of the five presently living in the house, and she made no attempt to hide it. He appreciated it, but he also felt obliged not to take it for granted, and occasionally to confide in her those details he could, perhaps the day before they were printed in the newspaper.

"Thank you, Mrs. Portiscale," he said, forcing a cheerful smile. "I doubt it, but we'll try."

Outside, it was windy and cold, a day that looked wonderful until you turned an easterly corner and the wind sliced at you with a knife-sharp edge.

He crossed the river and reached the prison early, but still Kitteridge was there before him, leaning up against the wall, facing the sun and looking thoughtful, or perhaps half-asleep. He straightened up as Daniel's footsteps sounded hollowly on the stone.

"Thought of anything useful?" he asked.

"No, have you?"

"No." Kitteridge fell into step beside him. "My father would have had so many things to say," he remarked suddenly.

Daniel was surprised. Kitteridge hardly ever mentioned his family at all, but especially not his father. "Such as what? Helpful?"

"Not in the least. Mostly about how the Lord sees all wickedness, and will expose it at the end. All debts need to be paid."

Daniel could think of nothing good to say.

"My father was a preacher," Kitteridge explained.

"I used to think that having a father who was a policeman was tough, but the more I think of it, the better it gets. At least by comparison."

"It's only a matter of time," Kitteridge continued. "All little boys grow up and become men . . . or at least most do. And the seeds of wickedness are in us when we are born."

"Balderdash!" Daniel said savagely. "And if you were conceived in sin, then it's his sin, not yours. Honestly, you cannot believe such rot! You . . ." Then he looked at Kitteridge's face and saw the laughter in his eyes . . . and the pain. He turned away quickly, his own emotion choking him. How little he really knew. Surface was a coat as thin as paint. Transparent. Compared with Kitteridge, he was as uncomplicated as a child — a very spoiled child at that. Even Marcus, who seemed so fierce and so certain of things, was relatively complicated.

They reached the prison doors, gave their identification papers, and were admitted. They did not speak again until they were in the bare stone interview room, sitting on the opposite side of a wooden table from Jessie Beale. She looked older with her hair tied at the back of her neck, and she was ashen pale.

"I thought you weren't coming," she said the moment the door was closed behind the guard. "Why didn't you come yesterday?"

159

Her voice had a hard edge to it, betraying her fear.

Kitteridge kicked Daniel under the table. "Because we were looking at the evidence," he replied.

Jessie opened her eyes wide. "Isn't it pretty much the same as before?"

"How do you know that?" Kitteridge asked. "I thought you weren't there."

Her expression remained unchanged. "That's what Mr. Quarles told me. Was he wrong?"

Daniel was glad Kitteridge was asking the questions. He wished to sit quietly and study Jessie. Not only her face, but also the tone of her voice, the tensions in her hands lying on the bare wood.

"No, apparently not," Kitteridge admitted. "This fire was hotter. It started with a different, more powerful accelerant."

Jessie took a deep breath and let it out slowly. Was she going to make a suggestion? It might be revealing of exactly how much she knew. But she was innocent, or at least cleverer than that. "What does that mean?" she asked.

"Nothing much," Kitteridge admitted.

"Was there something else stored in the shed?" she suggested.

"Perhaps. Where were you when the fire

160

started?"

She didn't blink. "I don't know, when did it start?"

Daniel let out his breath in a sigh. Kitteridge wasn't going to catch her in a lie; he was wasting his time trying.

She moved her hand gently over the table's scarred surface. "Perhaps it was one of the Jackson brothers, in revenge for Paddy's death . . . and Rob being found not guilty of it. And they learned to copy pretty close to what happened before?"

"Perhaps," Kitteridge had to agree. "But we would be wise not to suggest it."

The faintest of smiles touched her lips. "I'm not going to say anything. I don't have to. The accused doesn't. You can use the same defense you used for Rob. It was brilliant. It worked like a charm."

"And if we refuse to?" Kitteridge asked.

Her body stiffened, but her face remained exactly the same. It was a superb piece of self-control. "You won't," she said quietly. "It would make it look as if you didn't believe it the first time, and Sir Barnabas Saltram never goes back on anything he's said. He thinks he's God . . . didn't you see that?"

Daniel was seized with conviction like a shaft of light. "Jessie, you killed Rob Adwell,

161

didn't you?"

She turned toward him, her smile suddenly bright, her eyes clear and honest, all pretense vanished. "But you'll defend me anyway. You can't not, or you'll be going back on your own word."

Kitteridge jerked around in his chair, staring at Daniel, appalled.

Daniel did not take his eyes from Jessie. "Did you kill Paddy Jackson as well?"

"Wasn't that an accident?" she asked sweetly. "Heat of the fire, as Sir Barnabas Saltram testified?"

"Was it?" Daniel demanded.

"No, of course it weren't," she said with contempt. "But you proved it could've been, and you'll prove this could've been, too. You have no choice!"

She was right, he had none. She had not admitted outright that she was guilty. They both knew it, but she was far too clever to say the words.

# CHAPTER SEVEN

It was drawing toward the end of the afternoon and the coming darkness was already draining the light out of the sky, when Miriam was interrupted in her reading by Membury announcing that Mr. Pitt was at the door and would like to speak with her.

At first, she was flustered. She had taken little care over her appearance, believing the day was almost finished, and she had plenty of time to spare because Marcus was dining out with friends at the club — a place to which she would not be admitted and had no desire to be.

"Ask him to come in," she directed. "Don't leave him standing outside in the wind."

The butler's eyes widened. He had never left anyone standing outside in the wind. Then he saw her smile and realized she was teasing him, something she did at the oddest times, often catching him off guard. It was one of the many unspoken jokes between them.

"Yes, Miss Miriam," he acquiesced. "Would you like tea, Miss Miriam, and perhaps a slice or two of ginger cake? The gentleman looks cold and a bit concerned." Membury was a very moderate man, and any degree of anxiety short of hysteria was warranted no more extreme than that. Nevertheless, there was a gentleness in his voice that she could not miss.

"Yes, please, and thank you."

"Yes, Miss Miriam."

He withdrew and she heard his footsteps outside, in the hall. There was no time to find a comb for her hair, only to straighten the skirt of her dress where it was crumpled.

The door opened and the butler ushered Daniel in. He was shivering and the wind had whipped color into his cheeks.

"Come in," she said, surprised at how pleased she was to see him, even with no warning and at this time in the late afternoon. "Sit by the fire; you look perished. I'll put more coal on it. There will be tea in a minute."

He started to say something, then changed his mind.

"What?" she asked. "Are you in too much of a hurry for tea?" She was disappointed, but she tried to keep it out of her voice.

"No! I have all evening, but I don't want to interrupt whatever you were doing. And I didn't want to run into Marcus . . ." He looked awkward.

"He's not coming back until after dinner. I was only reading." Now she was being too eager. "What did you come to say?" That sounded abrupt, but she was concerned that he wanted to avoid Marcus.

He sat down in the armchair opposite her, the other side of the fire.

"Do you remember how eloquently Saltram turned the case around so the jury had to find Adwell not guilty?"

She felt as if someone had opened the front door again into the dark and the cold. "Of course . . ."

"I'm afraid a lot of us learned from that."

"What do you mean? You're talking about some other jury now, aren't you?"

His mouth tightened. "Yes, someone else has died in exactly the same way: skull cracked by tremendous heat, in a fire in another empty storage building." He stopped. "I'm sorry."

"Don't apologize," she said tartly. "What happened? Don't say it was another accident."

"I don't think so, and neither will anyone

else." His eyes did not move from her face. "This time, the victim is Rob Adwell."

"Oh!" She was startled. She did not know why, but she had expected it to be another of the Jackson brothers. "Why? Do you know? Or, more importantly, who? It looks like revenge — is it?"

"I've no idea. Maybe that's what it's meant to look like."

"They learned from the trial and copied it," she concluded.

"Yes, but it's Jessie Beale who's been arrested."

"But why?" That made no sense! "Why would she . . . ?" Then she understood the shock in his face and sat upright in her chair. "Then Saltram was wrong, wasn't he? Somebody killed Paddy Jackson. Was it Adwell? And the Jacksons killed him in revenge?" She was horrified at the injustice and that she had been so instrumental in it, but there was a tiny corner of her that had a totally different reaction. Saltram had been wrong! Memory flooded back, the time they had known each other so well, very nearly completely. But that was a thorn she pushed away from her savagely, as if tearing it out of her mind, not caring what else it ripped apart. Daniel must never know that.

Daniel was talking to her and she had

missed what he said. He was obviously still cold, but the heat of the fire was beginning to reach him. He was less taut.

Before she could ask him to repeat himself, Membury brought in tea and a large slab of cake, and a knife to cut whatever they wished. He had learned long ago that if you slice it, young men will take one. If you leave them to slice it themselves, they will take one twice the size you would have made it.

When she thanked him and he had gone, she looked at Daniel. "What was that you said?"

"Quarles, the policeman on the case, denied that it was the Jacksons and revenge. He has arrested Jessie, because he believes it was she who killed both of them."

"Both of them? You mean Paddy Jackson as well?"

"Yes."

"Oh, Daniel, no wonder you look so stunned. What are you going to do? Will you defend her? You don't have to, do you?"

"She's asked me to," he replied quietly while she poured the tea.

She searched his face. "Because you got Adwell off? For killing Paddy . . . when she did? Oh, God in heaven, this is dreadful." She put the teapot down before it slipped in her grasp. "What are you . . . what are you going to do?" Her mind raced. Her first thought was that he should walk away, but then she realized he could not so easily do that. He had gained a reputation for saving Adwell, as had Kitteridge and the whole firm of fford Croft and Gibson. They were in the middle of it, exactly as Jessie Beale had no doubt intended. The clever little manipulator! "Daniel! You can't walk away!"

"I know. Believe me, if I could, I would be long gone already. What can I do?" He sat staring at the cake, hopelessly.

"Do you know she did it for sure?" She was grasping at straws.

He looked at her perfectly frankly. "Yes. She admitted obliquely; not outright, so I could escape. She even challenged me to do anything about it. And she says I should ask Saltram again. He'll come, even if it's just to defend his reputation."

"She's right about that. In fact, I have a sinking feeling in the pit of my stomach that she's right about a lot of things." She bit her lip.

"Now I have to try to get it straight in my mind before I go and tell your father about this new twist of events," Daniel said. "I suppose it's up to him, in the end, whether we take the case or not. What do you think he'll say?"

It was a good question. She usually had a pretty close idea of what Marcus would do. He loved the law, he loved a challenge. He was protective of his company's good name. But this was probably a case unlike any other he had faced. He would do what he believed to be right. Whatever that was. The risk in doing otherwise would always be greater in the end.

How could she protect both of them, Marcus and Daniel? And Kitteridge, too, for that matter?

"Is the evidence the same?" she asked, looking at Daniel again. "I mean the material evidence."

"The substance that started the fire was similar. The injuries to the skull are a bit more severe, but in exactly the same place: the back of the skull, just above the neck. Appleby says the variations are insignificant." He looked miserable. "Actually, the same defense would do, almost word for word."

"Yes, it would, but that's irrelevant." She hated saying the words, but the truth was unavoidable. "It's Saltram's name that carries the weight. He'd have to say something really absurd before they'd disbelieve him."

The momentary light vanished from his

face. "I thought so." He sounded defeated.

"But you say she admitted to you, more or less, that she did it?"

"Yes, but no. I can't get out of it by saying I know she's guilty. She didn't tell me how she did any of it, or why. I think that it has to do with the proceeds of a robbery, but I can't prove that either. What can I do, Miriam?"

She ached to have something useful to tell him, but there was nothing. He would have to go through with it, unless Marcus forbade it, and she knew already that he would not.

"We need Saltram," Daniel said, looking up at her. "He might not come." There was a thread of hope in his voice.

"He'll come," she said with certainty. "The Adwell case — I mean, when he was acquitted — got a lot of newspaper coverage, because it seemed like a miracle. He'll come, if only to defend his reputation." The humor of it struck her suddenly. "What am I saying, *if only*? Reputation is everything. I sometimes think he exists only in the minds of other people. Alone in the room, he might actually disappear." Before the words were out of her mouth, she regretted them. Daniel would think she was bitter because Saltram had achieved the pinnacle she had only dreamed about. And even the dreams were fading now. They had never been more than elegant shadows on the wall. She was the only one who could see them, and thought they were cast by some reality.

The ashes settled in the hearth, but neither of them noticed.

Daniel was staring at her. "This case, from the way it looks, will bring him to testify," she said. "And you can wager Jessie's life on it that he will not say he was wrong the first time, no matter what gymnastics of logic he has to perform. And he didn't say Adwell was innocent. Actually, he said there was no proof beyond reasonable doubt. He'll find a way to wriggle out, but he will hate her like hell for using him so effectively to get her lover off from having committed her first murder, and then using the exact plan to kill Adwell and get away with that, too. Using Saltram again!" She was a little ashamed to find herself smiling.

There was an element to this that she enjoyed. Fancy an uneducated girl from the dockside streets using the great Barnabas Saltram to get away with murder — twice!

How long would it take him to see that?

"What's funny?" Daniel asked.

"Just the irony of it," she said. "Jessie Beale wins out over Sir Barnabas Saltram, and not once but twice."

171

Daniel laughed with her. "It's the only amusing thing about this whole sorry business," he said. "The great Sir Barnabas — you admired him once, didn't you?"

"I admired his mind." That was true: She had admired his depth of knowledge and that he was able to see parallels that others had missed, causes and effects that so many had stared at and yet not seen. She had admired his dedication. Perhaps, looking back, she had overlooked the things she had not liked. A lack of humor. A lack of empathy. Of course, they were not the tools of a scientist. Neither humor nor emotion had a place in the search for the truth.

When had she crossed over from looking at him purely as a teacher and started looking at him . . . as a man?

Daniel was waiting for her response.

She could feel the heat burning up her cheeks at the memories: the excitement, the awkwardness, the humiliation. Always the humiliation. And then the ache, and the overwhelming disappointment. She had not been so good at hiding it — then. Long ago. Now she must answer Daniel.

"And his self-discipline," she added, and looked up at him at last. She realized the tremendous truth. "But I don't think I ever liked him. I first met him when I was a student and he made it clear exactly what he thinks of women who presume to want to make a career in science. It's hard to like someone when they have trodden on you because of their own prejudices."

She saw relief in Daniel's face.

"That's how I feel about him," he admitted. "And I've only dealt with him once. But he did save the case, even if we were all completely wrong about it. I don't know why Jessie would kill Paddy Jackson or Adwell."

"Do you need to?" she asked. "I mean, is it necessary for the case?"

"If I'm to . . ." He screwed up his face in distaste. "I don't know how I can honestly defend her, when she hasn't denied doing it. What if I get her off? Then the police will blame the Jackson brothers!"

"They'll have to prove it," she stated. "One step at a time."

"That's what got us into this mess," he said with a note of desperation rising in his voice. "Taking one step when I couldn't see where the path was leading to. I've got to do better than that."

"See what Marcus says. You're not in this alone," she added gently, watching him, to be sure he understood all that she was not saying as well.

"I feel alone. It was my being softheaded, listening to Jessie Beale, believing her, that got me into this mess. Got *us* into it. I wouldn't blame Marcus if he threw me out at the end of this."

She looked at his face. He seemed so young. She could imagine quite clearly the child he had been a dozen years ago. So full of hope, so vulnerable. *Don't be an idiot,* she told herself. *You were a young woman then. Your own face was lineless, no masks of pain or wisdom in it!*

"He won't do that," she said firmly. "He might give you a good dressing down about seeing a bit further ahead, not believing everything a client tells you. On the other hand, he might see that you have learned that already. First thing is to sort out this case."

He stood up. "Thank you, Miriam. And thank you for the tea and cake. I'll go home and think about it. I won't make any decisions until I've talked to your father — and Kitteridge, of course."

"You're welcome, Daniel," she replied.

"I feel like a schoolboy who got all his sums wrong," he admitted. "Why didn't I see through Jessie Beale in the beginning?"

She smiled at him with a dawning relief. "Because you're a man," she replied.

"Women can see through other women far more clearly."

"Oh." He flushed slightly.

"You'll learn," she answered him. "And I dare say, if given enough time, I will learn to read men more efficiently." She meant it. She realized he saw the self-mockery in her as well, but he was wise enough not to say so. Perhaps he guessed to whom she referred.

With a smile, she accompanied him to the front door and the cold night outside.

She thought about many things that night. By morning she accepted a few that she had avoided before. It was time. It was ironic that it was Saltram's skill, his economy of words, as he offered explanations that were accurate and understandable to the jury, that had convinced her at last that the aim of becoming even a shadow of him was impossible to her. She had grown used to the belief that she had the ability, if only she was allowed to exercise it. The law would have to change sometime, just as one day women would have to be allowed to vote. And that would probably happen before women were granted the degrees they earned, let alone trusted by the public to know what they were talking about, in anything other than domestic matters.

It made her angry and hurt, dealing with injustice, the sheer stupidity of it, the waste of talent, of lives, the bigotry, the blindness, the dishonesty. She could go on . . . and had in the past. But what had it achieved for her? Or for anybody?

Nothing. That was the honest answer. Nothing at all, except perhaps the necessity of facing the truth. She needed to acknowledge the defeat that had always been there, that she had just refused to see when everyone else had.

She would go and see Octavius Ottershaw. He was kind, gentle, but oddly guileless. An intelligent scientist, he knew how to tell her the truth in its kindest form, and he never gave up looking for the answers he wanted.

Her taxi pulled up outside his house at half-past ten in the morning, a very civilized hour to make a morning call on an old friend, one who was bound to be working, as she would be herself usually. But she had not the heart to work today. There was not anything that mattered, only a series of tests she had set for herself. Today they looked particularly artificial, an intellectual effort made to convince her of her own relevance.

She found him in. The butler offered her

tea, sandwiches, and cake, if she wished. She accepted, hungry because she had not eaten breakfast. She had not wished to face Marcus, so she had avoided it. She had poured tea in one of the two cups and already eaten one of the sandwiches when Ottershaw came in. He looked pretty much as she had always seen him: his jacket a little crooked, or perhaps it was his shoulders, a cravat rather than a tie, his face neatly shaven.

He sat down opposite her and looked at her plate. "No breakfast this morning?" he observed gravely. "What's wrong? You usually have more sense than to starve yourself, particularly at the beginning of the day." He reached for the teapot. "What is it?" He tested its weight to see if there was enough for another cup inside it. He was apparently satisfied.

"You followed the Adwell case?" she asked.

"What's wrong? You think he did it?"

"I wasn't sure at the time, but he's dead anyway."

Ottershaw's eyebrow shot up. "How?"

She could see that he had not learned the news before. "Exactly the same way as Paddy Jackson," she answered.

"Good heavens! If Oscar Wilde will excuse

177

me: to lose one inconvenient person looks like misfortune; to lose two looks like . . . murder. And don't tell me we have two people running around Tooley Street burning people to death!" He left his teacup full and untouched. "That seems excessive."

"It does, doesn't it?" she agreed. But already she felt better for having shared the news with him. Ottershaw was eccentric, kind. Quietly witty. He reminded her of the White Knight in *Alice Through the Looking-Glass*. Except that unlike that gentleman, he did not keep falling off his horse. "And no, we now think we have one killer, Daniel and I," she added.

"Young Daniel Pitt?"

"Before yesterday he thought that Adwell probably killed Paddy, and he hopes, despite what he's been told, that Paddy's brothers killed Adwell in revenge. But I don't think that hope will last long, never mind through a trial."

"Sounds very plausible. Why would it not last? You seem very sure of it."

"Because the police have arrested and charged Jessie Beale with killing Adwell, and I gather she did not deny it to Daniel. Rather, she said something to the effect of: 'You got Rob off the charge of having killed Paddy, and you can get me off with the identical defense. To refuse would be to suggest you were wrong the first time. And none of you is going to do that.' "

"My, my!" Ottershaw looked shocked. "What a clever girl she is. And she's right. Saltram, at least, would never admit to a mistake. I don't know exactly how he's going to get out of it, but I'll wager my socks that he is."

"No, thank you," Miriam said with a smile, "I don't need your socks. And anyway, I think you're right."

He waited a moment. "And you had no breakfast because your brain was still battling with the problem. I'm sorry, my dear, but you look like a woman defeated, not one entering battle."

He had seen through her. How often before had that happened, but he had been too kind to tell her, because it had not mattered? And perhaps because she was not ready to hear it, and he could see that. He was comfortable with women. He had had a wife to whom he was devoted, but she had died several years before. Still, the gentle memories seemed to surround him. He had a daughter also, who had married the man she loved, and gone to live in Canada. But there were photographs of them around. It pleased her to know that.

"I'm always going to have to ask someone else to make my point," she replied to his comment. "And I'm at last obliged to recognize it." She blinked fiercely, felt her voice slipping out of control. "Maybe they're right and the really brilliant scientists are always going to be men. Women haven't . . . I don't know what . . . courage? Stamina? The ability to look at the facts only and read what they say, and not get tangled in emotion?"

"Barnabas Saltram has never got himself untangled from emotion since he passed his exams to enter university. He was about sixteen, I believe."

"Sixteen?" she said with disbelief. Feelings and memories flooded back unwanted. Barnabas behind her, leaning over her shoulder, correcting her work, praising what was right, she too conscious of his presence to remember anything he said. Barnabas with his head back, laughing at an absurd joke in Latin, which no one else understood. Barnabas touching the side of her face, gently. Barnabas at other moments too intimate to recall without embarrassment and humiliation. Ottershaw must never know that, never even wonder. "He's the coldest man I know," she said, forcing the words out, keeping them level.

"There are cold emotions, too, Miriam. Self-love is one of them, cold . . . and sterile. Remember, Saltram has no room in his heart or his mind for anyone else. They would intrude. They would cast a shadow over the pure light of his brilliance."

She looked at his face, searching it for mockery or impatience that she needed to be told this. Or pity, because she had once thought otherwise. Did he know that? Was she something discussed when no one else was present? What had Barnabas said about her? She looked away from Ottershaw. She could not bear that he should think . . . what? Anything!

She must get control of her thoughts, attend to the very real problem that they faced. What should she suggest to Daniel? What help should she offer to give? And a bigger moral question loomed over them all: What if Jessie Beale was guilty, and Adwell had been guilty, too? "It would be better if I had never asked Saltram to appear for Adwell, wouldn't it?" she asked.

"Possibly," Ottershaw agreed. "Possibly not. The question of Jessie herself being guilty never arose then, did it?"

She was startled. "No!"

"Do you think it was an accident, as Saltram said it could be? And everyone misun-

181

derstood it?" He looked genuinely concerned.

"I did at the time, I suppose, and that's what the law has to go with, lacking any certain proof."

"And now?"

"I'm afraid that Jessie Beale did indeed kill them both, and we'll never prove it . . . or why," she said. "But there's a reason somewhere. Instead, we are going to have to rescue her from her own acts, in order to rescue ourselves. Or at least Barnabas. I don't know what he's going to do, but it's time I did something more than mess around on the edges of cases I haven't the authority or the reputation to testify to in court. It seems I know just enough to be dangerous, but not enough to rescue myself. I thought . . ." She had to stop for a moment. She had fought her battles, believing in ultimate victory, and that defeat had a shockingly bitter taste. If it had been a sudden battle, rather than a long war of attrition, that had forced her to see defeat, it would have been different. But life was slipping away from her, not fully used.

Ottershaw drew in breath to say something, but he saw the look on her face and let it out without speaking.

"Thank you," she said quietly. "Daniel

may call you, because he won't reveal this idiotic position we're in to just anybody. The depth of it lies in the fear that Jessie Beale is guilty, which he also can't reveal. I don't even know what we could look for."

"I'll give it some thought," he replied. "Now eat some of that cake. It's delicious and it will sustain you until lunch."

Miriam looked at the cake and smiled at the absurdity of talking about it in the face of such defeat in all directions, personal and professional, not to mention moral. But starving oneself serves no purpose, so she helped herself to a large slice.

"Young Daniel told me about the ridiculous situation he's in," Marcus said to her over dinner. "That's one of the things I like about him: he's honest. Doesn't try to lay the blame elsewhere, like on his father."

He seemed to be waiting for her to answer.

"Of course he's honest," she said a little tartly. "You would not have taken him into the firm, whatever his marks were in Cambridge, if you didn't believe that. And you didn't take him to please Sir Thomas. You took him because you needed someone and he suited you very well."

Marcus frowned, putting down his fork, looking more closely at her. The room was comfortable. The dull red velvet curtains closed out even the sound of the wind, let alone the occasional spatter of rain. "You are very tense this evening, Miriam. Is it because this latest crime is another fire? I haven't forgotten how Wallace died. No doubt, it still pains you. It is bound to. But it has been many years." His brow was furrowed with concern, and he looked oddly beaten, as if he felt he should have been able to provide her some healing, and it had eluded him.

Her eyes filled with tears. Marcus felt pain for her, and guilt because he could not heal it. He was her father, and in his mind he ought to have been able to protect her.

She put the fork into the food on her plate and realized he was still watching her. She changed her mind and looked up at him. It was more than time for some truth, however painful. And however guilty she felt about it. "Father, I am not grieving for Wallace," she said clearly.

"It's all right, my dear. He was a good man."

She found it difficult to recall Wallace's mild, pleasant face to her mind. "I know he was." She must deal with this properly now, or deliberately perpetuate the lie forever. "And I probably would have liked him even more as I grew to know him better, but he has been dead for fifteen years and I am not still grieving for him. If I ever said it is . . ." She took a deep breath, trying to find the right words, and they slipped out of her grasp.

"You will not find a man like him again," Marcus said gently. "But there could be somebody else, just as good in his own way, if you would."

She kept her temper.

"Give someone a chance, Miriam," Marcus went on. "Another man could make you happy, if —"

"Father," she cut across him. "No one makes someone else happy. Happiness is not anybody else's responsibility. It is up to me if I am happy or not, and one thing I am not happy about is the way I spend my time. I am pretending that one day, in my lifetime, women are going to be recognized for their intelligence and have their professional abilities taken seriously. I am going to accept now that that is not true."

"Miriam, happiness lies in —"

"Don't!" she cut him off, dropping her fork on her plate with a clatter. "Wallace was a nice man, a kind man, gentle, but he wanted to turn me into somebody else. He thought he knew better than I did what I wanted, that all women under the silk or in sackcloth were essentially the same. I suppose I would have gone ahead and married him, if he had lived, and I would have had some happiness, but there would have been an emptiness inside me, muscles of a mind and heart trapped, unused. You think it's wrong to keep birds in cages . . . so it is. Even a gilded cage is still a cage. It's wrong to deny people the choice at least to try to use the skills, the courage, the imagination they have, whatever you judge to be the reason. I missed Wallace at first. I wept for him, not for me. I'm ashamed of that, I am. I should have felt bereft, as if I had lost part of myself. But I didn't. I felt free."

"Miriam! You're overwrought!" He put his knife and fork down as if to stand up.

"Don't patronize me!" She raised her voice to a pitch she had never dared use with him before. "I am not overwrought. I'm accepting with great grief and difficulty that I will almost certainly never be able to use my brains, or my abilities, because I am a woman. Maybe I did have them. Or maybe I am second rate, as Barnabas Saltram told me, but I haven't had the chance to try. In your terms, I have been found guilty without a trial. That's not justice, but it's going to stay like that as long as I can imagine."

He stared at her, puzzled and a little frightened, as if she had changed shape in front of him.

She must explain herself now, she might never have another chance. "You are a brilliant lawyer, Father, you have proved it over and over again in the courtroom. You have found justice for more people than I can remember, and you loved it — good cases hard won, or lost, but you still gave it all you had. You have a great skill, and you magnified it." She shut her eyes for a moment and then opened them and stared straight at him. "How would you feel if you were denied the chance ever to do that? To save the people you did. To make legal history with brilliant arguments. Even to change the minds of everyone who heard you. Because you have blue eyes. Or because you are heir to a title. Or anything else that has nothing to do with your ability."

"Miriam." He shook his head, bewildered.

"I know, I know. You didn't make the law, or the prejudices. Or the ignorance. Or the fear of change. It's not your fault. At least you never said, 'I won't love you if you don't conform to my beliefs of you.' Enough people have faced that."

"That's monstrous!" he protested.

187

"It is, but people don't like change, new ideas, old prejudices proved ignorant and wrong. New ideas are frightening, change is frightening. I wish I wanted to conform; life would be so much easier. I could please everyone, myself included. But I won't pretend, even for you."

"What are you going to do?" he asked very quietly.

"I don't know," she answered, but already she had the beginning of an idea in her mind. At the moment it was vague, hazy, no more, but it was something.

# CHAPTER EIGHT

By morning the idea had crystallized in Miriam's mind, at least the core of it had, and she knew precisely how she needed to act upon it. It was a wet, blustery day and she was obliged to dress in a heavy coat and a hat sufficient to keep most of her hair dry. But she did not leave the house until Marcus had gone.

She took a taxi straight to Octavius Ottershaw's house, lest she lose her nerve and think better of it.

"Has something happened?" Ottershaw asked, as soon as he saw her. He had opened the door himself and relieved her of her wet outer clothes. She stood in the hallway, gently dripping.

"Yes, I've been thinking . . ." She had rehearsed her words over and over again, and they still sounded artificial. There was no help for it, but she must lead up to it slowly. She followed him into the warm sit-

189

ting room. "We know what Saltram is going to say: he has no choice but to repeat essentially what he said before. And as far as it goes, it's the truth. The only part of it we can question is the conclusion that the jury will inevitably accept, and that is that Adwell was not guilty, according to the law. Then logic and every fairness say that with the same crime, and the same evidence, they must find Jessie not guilty either. And we know that she is. She pointedly did not deny it to Daniel. They'll get Saltram, because he won't be able to resist justifying himself. He could never leave it to anyone else."

"That much we know," Dr. Ottershaw agreed. "What is it you are suggesting?" He motioned her to sit down in the large chair next to the fire.

She sat, then took a deep breath and let it out slowly. "Will you help me find some argument to rebut what the defense will say? We know Jessie is guilty, no matter how much the case is like the earlier one. We know the facts from Paddy Jackson's death — at least you and I understand them. If she's repeated the circumstances exactly, there must be something we missed. Something that has more than one interpretation, and we have the wrong one. If we find out what happened, we ought to be able to prove it, oughtn't we?"

"Yes," he said slowly, clearly turning it over in his mind in a new light. "That stands to reason, but I have no idea where to begin." He stood in front of the fire in the shabby, comfortable room where nothing matched, but everything seemed to belong.

"We must look at all the facts that are indisputable, the things that we can test over and over and always come out with the same result. Then look at all the others and see if they can be viewed another way." She smiled, but then the smile fixed on her face, as if frozen. " 'How often have I said to you that when you have eliminated the impossible, whatever remains, *however improbable, must be the truth?*' "

"Sherlock Holmes." Ottershaw nodded. "He makes it sound easy; it's not." He looked at her very gravely. "Of course, it isn't as plain as Holmes says. There are fine distinctions, many things depend on judgment, and even with all the skills we have, mistakes are possible. But yes, of course I will help you all I can. I'm assuming young Pitt will ask for your help."

"Yes," she said with a twisted smile now. "Even if only to ask Sir Barnabas to look at the evidence in the new death and testify again."

Ottershaw's eyes narrowed a little and he moved his head to one side. "You have a big interest in this, don't you? Far more than you have said."

It was a relief to stop concealing it. The words came out in a rush. "Yes, Saltram was my professor at university. He made life difficult for me at times and I feel responsible for the fact that he gained Adwell's acquittal because I was the one who suggested to Daniel that he should ask him . . . and I made it possible. I got his meeting with Saltram and I pleaded his case."

"So, effectively you gained the acquittal?"

"I suppose so, but you have to give Toby Kitteridge credit, too."

"I think if you see Daniel and get justice for . . . or perhaps I should say against . . . Jessie Beale, all within a legal and medical setting, you could leave Toby Kitteridge to rescue himself. I think he is quite clever enough to do that."

"I dare say," Miriam agreed. "But that is not an excuse." He still did not seem to understand what she was asking, or possibly he wanted her to clarify it for both of them. "I think there has to be another answer than letting Jessie get away with it," she went on. "We need to know beyond a reasonable doubt that the law can crawl through, whether it depends on the theory of the heat of fire causing both deaths or not. Do you believe the heat cracked both skulls and not a murder weapon? I mean you, yourself, regardless of proof?"

"No, I do not," he replied, in perfect seriousness now. "I think it is possible that Adwell killed Jackson, and Jessie knew it, but wanted to save him, whatever her reasons. I also think she killed Adwell, or helped the Jackson brothers do it, and I don't know why. But before we can convince the court of it, we must get rid of the mesmerism, if I can use such a term, that Sir Barnabas exerts over the jury. And then show a reason why Jessie would do such a thing. But part of that is for the police. As for the part that lies within medical facts, or possibilities, of course I will help you in any way I can. We work together well. Our skills complement each other."

She felt embarrassed now. She thought that was true, but was she asking far too much? "Just until we have undone the damage I have caused by bringing Saltram into the case . . ." she began.

Now it was he who looked a little crestfallen. "I was thinking of rather longer. Have I taken too much for granted?" There was a world of meaning behind what he was saying. He had never visibly skirted around it, but he knew that she would never carry the weight of evidence regularly as a professional. She had done so by chance for Daniel in two cases. But these occasions were accidents of chance, the right time at the right place, and her observations could be, and were, verified by others.

Miriam knew she should not put Daniel in the position of relying on her. She was taking advantage of his inexperience, and perhaps his sense of injustice.

Ottershaw was waiting for her. Behind the care not to hurt her, what did he mean? She felt shame burn up her cheeks. Was he sorry for her? She wanted to shout at him that she was not pathetic or in need of pity or help, but that was childish. "Let me see if I can be useful in this . . ." she began, and then stopped.

"Of course!" he agreed. "Then if we succeed in convicting Miss Beale, or discovering and proving whatever other truth there is, will you consider putting your abilities to work more often to a purpose? I was thinking of taking on more case work. I find it tests different parts of the mind from purely experimental science. People now are willing to see what has been looming on the horizon for years, perhaps even decades. It is exciting, do you not think?"

She did think. In fact, she agreed suddenly and wholeheartedly. She could stop being selfish and needing to do it alone. Or even to have her name on it at all, never mind being the leader. Ideas didn't belong to people. That was an arrogant notion, ridiculously so. She was being guilty of the very fault she saw so clearly in Saltram. That was a horrible thought! But there was truth in it. "Yes," she said vehemently. "Yes, I would like to explore new ideas, recognize them willingly, and see whatever truths they may show. Yes, I would like to learn to work with you, if you think I can help. But only if you really do."

"My dear Miriam, I have neither the temerity nor the time to patronize you. It would insult us both and definitely not serve either science or society were I to give it to you just because you cannot be another Saltram. If you suggest it again, I shall be as offended by the thought as you are." Then he smiled. "Shall we begin?"

Miriam decided to tell Marcus about her decision immediately. She could not pass it off lightly, because she would be spending very little time at home. He would be unable to help noticing it. It would hurt him quite unnecessarily, and to be honest, she was excited about this opportunity, and she wanted to share it with him, as she had shared so much in the past. It was the beginning of making a step forward, rather than marking time, or hoping without any real grounds.

"I went to see Dr. Ottershaw today," she said almost casually at dinner. Her father did not catch the edge to her voice. For just a moment he seemed to be trying to think who she was talking about, but then his face cleared.

"Good man, Ottershaw," he remarked, cutting into his roast beef. "How is he?"

"Very well. But . . ." She looked at him. His head was down, eyes on his plate. He had not noticed that this was more than polite conversation.

"But what?" Now he looked up. "What's wrong? Miriam?"

"Nothing! We talked about work."

"Was that unexpected?" There was slight amusement in his face now. "It is hardly a subject for surprise from you. Did he say anything of interest about this miserable case we seem to have landed ourselves in? Does he have any suggestions? Should I send Daniel to him? We're floundering! And don't tell me Daniel hasn't mentioned it to you. He talks more frankly to you than he does to me." He had abandoned his meal entirely now and was looking at her intensely.

"Of course! I don't employ him, and I don't know enough to criticize him either."

"Miriam, you're being evasive. Either tell me what Ottershaw said, or speak of something else. You're . . . prevaricating! I don't like it; it's very irritating."

"Yes, Father. We are agreed I'm going to work with Dr. Ottershaw. First, on finding some more sense in the Jessie Beale case. And then after that, in anything else that is interesting, but directing my research toward a specific end, linked to whatever he is working on." She waited for him to reply; surely he would be pleased.

He looked confused. "Why? You don't need to work for anyone else. You can explore anything you want, anything that interests you."

She breathed in and out a couple of times. "Father, I'm playing for my own amusement. I need to apply myself to something that matters, that has a real purpose, not just to fill time. Something that people care about. Otherwise, I'm not part of anything bigger, and I need to be." She stopped because it was so hard to explain without sounding as if she were complaining. Then, as she sat looking at him — wild-haired, eccentric, a cravat around his neck that matched nothing — she felt a belief, even a hope.

He appeared mild; he was hardly ever abrupt, much less rude, but in his own way, he was a crusader and always had been, even if the cause was known only to him.

"You know a great deal about the law," she went on. "You have fought and won many extraordinary cases for justice, where winning seemed impossible."

For a moment, a beautiful smile lit his face, then it vanished. "All very complimentary, my dear, but irrelevant."

"Yes, it is," she agreed, "and yet it's exactly the point. Would it have been as satisfying to you if you had known all that case law and never stood up in court and applied it to a real case? A real man's life?"

"But . . ." he started, then stopped. "You want to take up the sword yourself, not merely sharpen it for someone else. But women —"

"Rubbish! I want to be Boadicea, not Queen Victoria! Know it all? I do nothing but tell somebody else how to . . ."

He kept his face nearly perfectly solemn; only one muscle twitched. "Hardly the same, my dear. Queen Victoria told them what to do and they did it. Believe me, they did!" His eyes reflected laughter now, but there were tears in them also. "She had great power in her pleasure or displeasure, and I realize that you are likening yourself to her in only one way, which robs it of a great deal of meaning. But you have made your point: You do not wish to be protected. I just —"

"I don't want to be protected from making mistakes, failings, being disappointed in myself, and others. The only way never to make a mistake is never to make anything at all, and that is the biggest mistake there can be: never to make anything. But I promise you, I will do everything I can to avoid hurting others. I think Dr. Ottershaw will curb me where necessary, even if only to preserve his own reputation. He seems very mild, but I think underneath he is not."

The following morning, Miriam was at Ottershaw's door, ready for work, by a quarter to nine.

"Hello," he said with a quiet smile, opening the door and welcoming her in. "We have several things to consider, and very little evidence to examine. The more I think of it, the more I believe that any experimenting will be with our own materials to see if the results are consistent. I have been making inquiries as to where we can reproduce the kind of temperature Saltram says is necessary for cracking bones. Come in, come in." He stood back, just realizing they were still in the hallway. "Hang up your coat. It's beastly outside, but it's warm in the sitting room. Can't abide a cold house. We must make a plan. Would you like tea?"

"No, thank you, I've not long had breakfast."

His eyes narrowed. He looked at her very carefully. "Has your father approved this?"

"Are you asking if you have his permission?" she inquired, uncertain if she was angry, or whether he just thought it a matter of consideration for Marcus. That alone would please her.

"I am not," he said briskly. "I simply want to know if I have to be discreet or not. It is so much easier not to be."

She relaxed. "Yes, I explained it to him and he sees that it is the best thing. In fact, perhaps the only thing that would really work."

"Good. Good. Then let us sit by the fire and consider what we know, what needs to be tested to be certain it is correct, what depends upon the testimony of others, who

200

is to be trusted to be accurate, and who is to be trusted to be honest, and who not. Then we may deduce what is left that is discoverable, or not. If it is, we will do so."

"And fit it into a pattern," she added. "It's hard to believe something in which you can see no reason. And I have come to realize that Jessie Beale is very clever. She is at least one step ahead of us, maybe more than that. Perhaps even three or four."

"Then we had better move swiftly." He did not argue. "Are we agreed that we trust the evidence found by the fire brigade, but not necessarily all their conclusions?"

"Yes, if there is anything that doesn't fit, we'll set it aside for the moment," she agreed.

"Medically is another matter. I will trust Appleby to be accurate in his facts and measurements, but the conclusions I would rather draw myself."

She leaned forward a little. "Do you think he would let us see the body? And I expect the fire scene would be interesting, if we understood it better."

"That may be something to learn in the future," he said, nodding. "For now, you will have to take the firemen's word for it. It is testimony of others that we will trust. Although we might ask them to explain how the evidence proves the conclusion, and only that conclusion, don't you think?"

"I believe Daniel will be very glad to propose that," she said with the slightest smile. "And Kitteridge also. Poor soul, he got dragged into this almost entirely against his better judgment."

"I'm sure of it, but who among the witnesses is to be trusted? Either for their judgment or their skills?" He shrugged very slightly. "If any."

"We will have to keep an open mind," she agreed without hesitation. "Even the most honest people can make a mistake. Or be so convinced of something that they never consider an alternative." She gave a sheepish little smile. "I've been known to do that."

He glanced at her, but did not speak. The look was sufficient.

"And we all have vested interests as well," she added. "Beliefs we can't easily give up. The older we get, the bigger the stake we have in it, a more or less certain picture in the world, and can't let go of it."

"Any of it, whatever the truth," he said quietly. "Now, where do we begin?"

With the help of Charlie, the eleven-year-old street urchin Ottershaw had taken in to help them with simple chores, Miriam and

Ottershaw worked all day, and into the evening. Charlie was very good at making tea, and he fetched plates of sandwiches that the butler prepared, then carried back the empty plates, after having finished off any and all scraps. Miriam liked to hear him singing quietly to himself, street songs she could not understand. Occasionally he giggled to himself, and she liked the sound of his happiness.

She and Dr. Ottershaw collected what information they could from the police and the fire brigade, from both officers and men who had attended either of the fires. They were in the same neighborhood, on the long riverside road, Tooley Street, and the fires were in sight of each other. Largely, it was the same men who had attended both.

Miriam found it difficult to listen to the details. Fire fascinated her, but since the fire in which Wallace had died, it also repelled her. Did she need to understand it for some reason now? If she imagined she could master it, she was losing her sense of reality. No one did that. But to see its limits — perhaps that would be a good idea?

She asked questions of the firemen and listened to their answers, making notes nearly all the time. They quite clearly thought she was odd, to say the least, but they seemed to take it well enough. She had always had immense respect for their courage — what sane person could not? — but she gained a new respect for their skill, their knowledge, and their self-discipline. Above all, she learned a new awe for fire itself.

During this time, Daniel and Kitteridge were working also, trying to understand the relationship between the various Jackson brothers and Adwell, and where Jessie had fit into it. Why would she kill Adwell? There had to be a reason, and to learn it would be to understand the core of the whole tragedy.

Daniel asked Miriam that two days later, when they met in the afternoon to compare notes on what they had learned.

"It's in all the newspapers," he said ruefully, as they sat over hot soup in a café near the dockside on the south bank. Tooley Street was less than a hundred yards away. "They're making a big thing of it because of Saltram giving evidence the first time to get Adwell off."

She looked at him. He was obviously tired. It was there in the lines of his face, the pallor of his skin. He was sitting hunched up in his coat. Already the skies were darkening in the east and nightfall would not be long. It was the end of November. Suddenly, she was furious that there was nothing she could do to help. "That could work in our favor," she told him.

He lifted his head a little higher. "How? It just makes it even more certain that the jury will believe him. Sir Barnabas Saltram is validation for almost anything." There was for a moment intense dislike in his eyes.

Miriam answered for what she had been thinking, but not said aloud. "The only person who can undo what he said the first time is himself. But he can't do that unless he takes the stand again."

"I haven't asked him." Daniel looked rueful, a little self-mocking. "I haven't the nerve."

"He'll come," she said.

"Do you believe that?" He was dubious.

What was she thinking? She was walking straight into a trap, one set by her own nature, and not by Saltram. "Yes! If we ask him the right way." She sounded so certain. She was doing this to herself! Where was her scientific detachment? Maybe this was why she would never be as good as Saltram.

"What is the right way?" He might be pretending not to care, not to show hope, but it was there, in his face, his voice, even the way he straightened up a little in his seat.

"I've been thinking about it," she replied, choosing her words. "He must see it as a challenge, not just of the facts, but by those who would damage his reputation. If you drive him to protect that, he'll fight dragons. You are threatening his most precious possession, the thing he has spent a lifetime maintaining, protecting. He'll defend it the way another man would protect his only child."

Was she overstating it? She didn't think so. "Daniel, think!" she urged. "The newspapers are all over it. Find out who is prosecuting."

"A man called Fimber," he answered. "He seems decent enough."

"And Appleby will be the medical examiner?"

"Yes. And Quarles is on the case for the police."

"Good. The trial is going to get a lot of press coverage when it starts. Do you have any idea why? I mean, why did Jessie Beale do it? And then there's the matter of Paddy Jackson. Are you going to raise the suggestion that she's guilty of his murder, too?"

"It'll be Kitteridge, not me. I'm only second chair."

Should she say anything encouraging? No, it was not the time. "Do you know how he's going to play it?" she asked.

"He doesn't himself know yet, but since we're defending Jessie, and defended Adwell, we can't exactly go in saying that, but it may well come out in the evidence. Why?"

"Because if it came out that it was Jessie, you'll have to supply a reason. And if it was an accident and you insist on that, you've painted yourself into a corner. Or, to be more precise, Jessie has. Two identical accidents in the space of two months?"

"But Sir Barnabas will say it was," he pointed out. "He has to! He can't say the first was an accident and the second wasn't."

"No." She gave a small tight smile. "It will be interesting to see what he does say. But I don't think he'll try to wriggle out. He'd never live it down. He has to do some very rapid inventing. When you go to ask him to testify, you might need to point that out. His 'error' will be interpreted by others, if he doesn't get in there himself." There was an element of dangerous pleasure in her thought. Dangerous because she was baiting a tiger, and she knew it, one that had wounded her savagely before. She must never forget, she dare not forget, the rage in his face. She shivered now at the memory, twenty years later.

He would never run away.

But then, neither would she.

Should she warn Daniel . . . somehow? If he were to be hurt, that might be the one thing that would make her back off. "Daniel?"

He was looking at her steadily.

"Daniel, Saltram was a bad enemy. He . . . he hates me. I can't tell you why, because you don't need to know, and it's not a public sort of thing." She could feel the shame burning up her face now. "But he'll never forgive you if you embarrass him, or prove him wrong. If you want to back off, this is the time to do it."

He looked puzzled, and perhaps a little hurt. "Back off? I want to fight him all the way. And Jessie Beale. I just don't know how. I think she murdered Adwell and set the fire that killed Paddy Jackson. But we have to defend her, and she knows it. Do you suppose Saltram knows it, too? Now, I mean? Two accidents like that, in two months? To two men who hated each other. That's preposterous." He closed his eyes and let his breath out very slowly. Then he looked up at her. "I've got to give him something else to believe, haven't I? Or at least Kitteridge has to."

"Yes," she agreed. "One of you has to.

You'd better think of it. If you find the truth, it might help. It could even be proof, or at least corroborating evidence. But be careful what you say to Saltram. Tell him as little as possible. He's usually very, very heavily booked, so you need to go soon. In fact, as soon as you have a trial date."

"Will you come with me? I'm sorry to ask, but despite what you've said, he listens to you . . ."

She was prepared for that. It was foolish, probably putting her head into a noose, but she would be ashamed of herself if she did not go. "Oh, yes. But in the meantime, find a story you can go with that explains it all. Fimber might have one. Or Quarles."

He smiled at her, relief lighting his face. She could not turn back now, whatever Saltram said . . . or did.

Miriam could not force herself to eat breakfast the day she and Daniel were going to ask Saltram to testify. They had to ask. He could not testify unless either the prosecution or defense called him as a witness. Until the night before, she had been perfectly certain he would leap at the chance. In fact, she wondered if he had even considered offering, that he had been tempted to, but refused to give in because he was sure they would have to call him. She realized, of course, that he might have changed since she thought she knew him. She had changed beyond her imagination in those years.

But had she really? She still could feel the same humiliation when he criticized her, the same vulnerability, even the same fear that he could read her as easily as an open book.

Would he make them plead? Was Daniel vulnerable, too?

No, of course he wasn't. He had no emotions in this, except perhaps regret that he allowed himself to believe Jessie when she had first asked him to defend Robert Adwell. But then, unless he knew otherwise, he had to believe his client. And Saltram had proved that he may well have been right to do so.

Miriam dressed very carefully. Black was unimaginative, but it was never wrong at this time of year. And it suited her: her fair skin, the blush in her cheeks, her burning auburn hair. Pearl earrings were always right, too, and flattering, yet unimaginative also. But this was not a social occasion. Above all, it was not personal.

The thought choked her, so that breakfast was impossible.

She had all the information Saltram might

reasonably ask for, written out neatly and ready to leave with him, if he should accept. Why was she thinking "if"? She had been certain of it, right until yesterday evening.

Daniel arrived in a taxi to pick her up. It was one of the new black ones that he liked, very up to date. They rode in silence, and he was looking at her with open admiration. She felt her cheeks grow hot and turned away. It was irrelevant to anything they were doing, but it still pleased her very much.

They arrived at Saltram's office and were ushered into the outer room by the receptionist. Saltram must surely have been expecting them this time; even so, he kept them waiting for a quarter of an hour. Was it to make them uncertain? Nervous? Feeling as if they were petitioners coming to beg a favor? Or just simply because he could?

When he finally came in, he looked immaculate, slim, elegant, not a single smooth hair out of place. "Good morning, Mr. Pitt, Miss fford Croft." He inclined his head courteously. "I apologize if you were waiting."

Daniel drew in breath to say it was of no importance.

Miriam spoke first. "It is unusual for you to be disorganized. I hope we have not disturbed you with this news?" She looked straight at him and met his cold, hazel eyes. She saw the temper flare up, and then instantly fall under control.

"Not at all, Miss fford Croft. I had another urgent case that overran the time I had allowed for it. I was expecting you to come asking my help, sooner or later. In fact, I had expected you to be rather faster than this."

This time Daniel answered before Miriam could. "There was no point in disturbing you with it until we had a trial date, Sir Barnabas. If it is possible for you, that is excellent news. If not, we may plead for a little more time. They will hardly be surprised, if I explain to them that you are necessary to our entire case. They will have foreseen that."

Saltram stared back at him coolly. It was as if the clock had stopped. No one moved.

Then Saltram's eyebrows rose. "Is that your uncouth way of asking for my help in this extraordinary case that you have got yourself into? Or perhaps I should say . . . got yourself back into. I got you out of it once, but you seem to have slid back into it again, God knows why."

Again, there was silence, a breath, two, three.

Miriam spoke. "There are always possibilities that one does not foresee, Sir Barnabas, as I am sure you have experienced at one time or another." She meant him to feel the stab of memory, and of what it felt like to fail.

He had not forgotten. She saw the bitter hatred in his eyes for an instant and knew that he was still an enemy. It was like a cold steel blade inside her. She did not even dare look at Daniel.

"I didn't foresee that she was involved at all, not as directly," Daniel broke the silence. "I thought Adwell might well be guilty, but that it would not be proved beyond a reasonable doubt. I thought it possible you believed so, too."

Saltram looked back at him intensely, as if he could read his mind.

Seconds ticked by.

"I deal in facts, Mr. Pitt. Evidence. I don't presume to judge guilt or innocence. Medical forensic scientific facts. I leave their interpretation to the jury, as you should. You are young and as arrogant as most young men."

Daniel nearly choked, but mercifully did not speak.

"I certainly will not yield to you the charge of finding the truth in this mess you have undertaken," Saltram continued. "I presume you have some details of the case, some facts, or at least evidence to consider? Do you have ideas as to what happened? Or are you expecting me to provide those also?"

"I have facts for you, Sir Barnabas," Daniel answered. "Regarding the fire, the body, the conclusions that Dr. Appleby came to, and the questions that arise from them. There is police evidence that suggests motive for Adwell to have killed Paddy Jackson, and a deduction that makes sense as to why Jessie should have wanted Adwell dead."

Saltram drew breath to answer, but Daniel went straight on.

"But that is to convince the jury to listen to the facts, believe them, and then see who it implicates. A story of motive is only to satisfy them that it makes sense."

"For which you need me," Saltram finished it for him.

"Yes, sir," Daniel conceded a little reluctantly.

"It would take all your skill to make them believe two accidents, with identical results," Miriam interrupted. "And only two months apart." She was shaking with an anger she dared not show. In fact, the whole case had grown in depth and power and complexity.

She did not have any idea what had really happened, but it had an impetus that she had no way to control. She glanced at Daniel and saw that he was as aware of it as she was, even though he had no idea as to why Saltram's hatred was bone-deep and irrevocable.

# CHAPTER NINE

The trial date had been set and time was growing short. Miriam and Ottershaw were working as diligently as they could on the little they had, but they did not know what they were looking for. They knew where the fire had been and obtained permission to search what was left of the building.

Miriam had stared at the charred and broken timbers. There were no photographs of the shed before the fire, but then, why should anyone wish to waste photographic plates on the interior of a storehouse? A large part of the roof was gone, the rain since then having soaked what little the fire hoses had not. They could learn nothing except what the firemen had already told them.

They could estimate the time the fire started, and the investigations of the specialists could tell if there had been an accelerant, and what it probably was. In this case, they said oil such as one might put in the engine of a car. Easy enough to purchase without raising eyebrows, or even being remembered. It would not take much to get it burning. There had been plenty of flammable goods stored on the premises.

Miriam looked at the evidence, at the questions, and hope was sliding away like water between the cracks in pavement, leaving nothing behind. It proved beyond any doubt at all, reasonable or otherwise, that the fire had been arson. But there was not even a suggestion as to who might have set it. It was possibly safe to presume it was not Adwell himself, but even that was not certain.

"It's all there," she said when they were back in Ottershaw's laboratories. "But I can't get any meaning out of it. At least, not any that could be interpreted usefully." She looked across the bench to where Ottershaw was bent over a microscope. "What do we need? Even one thing could shake the jury."

"What do you want this thing to say?" he asked gravely, his face slightly puckered from shifting his concentration to her, instead of remaining focused on the blackened fire ruins in front of him. "They can only say 'Guilty' or 'Not guilty,' or 'We don't know.' Then either the case is dismissed or, more likely, there is a retrial. But the judge would go through several days of 'Go back and try harder.' Then we won't know whether the verdict, if we get one, means that they've really decided, or are so fed up to the back teeth with arguing the damn thing that they just want to go home."

"I think I'm there already." She shook her head.

"Really?" He looked surprised, and hurt.

"No," she said, in a softer voice. "I just don't know what I'm looking for. I'm not even sure about what I want."

"You want the most difficult things possible," he answered with absolute certainty. "So do I. I want to have done a good, honest job, proved Saltram fallible, and Jessie Beale guilty of setting the fire to kill Rob Adwell, and very possibly the fire that killed Paddy Jackson as well."

"We set out to find evidence to help in defending Jessie Beale," she pointed out with a rueful smile, almost exactly like his.

"That's a three-legged dog, isn't it?"

"What?"

"Unlikely to win the race," he elaborated.

"Very," she said ruefully "But it's what we have to work with."

"Anything else?"

"Yes! Prove Saltram a pompous ass! Without morality," she added for good measure.

"And I suppose you don't want to go down with him." Ottershaw looked at her curiously.

"That as well," she added, then smiled to soften the impossibility of it.

"All without his realizing it."

"I don't mind if he realizes it, just so long as he can't get out of it."

"Then we need to do a lot better than we are now, and we have very few days left." The light vanished from his face. "I think we must leave the jury with at least one verifiable fact, once we establish which one will lead inevitably to the others. Which one of the facts . . . those that can't be twisted into another shape?"

She thought for a moment. "Both Adwell and Jackson are dead. Both died in fires that were arson. Both had cracks in their skulls, which might have been caused by the heat of the fires, or might have been caused by an old-fashioned hit on the head, with something hard and round, like a lead pipe or a truncheon."

"And neither of them had smoke or toxic gases in their lungs," Ottershaw added. "So, they stopped breathing before the fire burned for long near them."

"Then how did they die so quickly, if it

took a lot of heat to crack their skulls?" she asked. "We've got a contradiction there."

"Not if they were near enough to the accelerant. It would have burned hot enough to crack both quite quickly. Or burned explosively, in more or less instant heat."

"Supposedly they both had basically the same accelerant: engine oil," she said, widening her eyes in disbelief. "But I think the fire brigade is wrong about that. The only thing I can think of that could be relied on to burn at that heat and to crack bone in so short a time would be phosphorous — the white, not the red. That would do it. We must test for that specifically."

"Where would Jessie Beale get that, or even know about it?" Ottershaw asked. "If we find it, then that is a line of inquiry for the police to work on. And it would be sufficient."

"We must tell Daniel," said Miriam, "and he can tell the police. It's probable that they have looked no further than engine oil, when there were two accelerants used."

"Possibly. They may not be specifically looking for something hot enough to crack bones almost immediately."

"How hot . . . exactly?"

"Five thousand degrees."

"Oh, really?" She was stunned. "Five

thousand degrees. I can't even think of that hot. At least the victim would know very little, just a few moments of unbelievable pain."

"Don't," he commanded. "Don't think of it. We need your brain now, not your emotions." His face was grim, full of pity so deep she could see how it hurt. And she knew he had felt it before, as she had herself, when working on the remains of those who had died in terror or pain. One must deny it, and continue working.

He looked at her face. "Miriam, we are no use to them now, except to find the truth," he said quietly, perhaps as much to himself as to her. "They are beyond pain. Stop it!"

"Yes, I am sorry, we must test for white phosphorous and find out where it is obtainable."

"If we find it, or a residue of it, no matter how small, then that is enough to make a case."

"So what we're looking at are two similar accelerants?" she said skeptically. "With white phosphorous used to create an intense heat, but the other used to spread the fire in the building? Who's going to believe that?"

"Possibly no one, which is what we want. At least, it's the heart of what we want."

"Tell me what to do," she requested. "The

more I think of it, the more of my chemistry comes back. But we could at least know the beginning of something. And we need the police to look into it."

"Right," he agreed. "You may have the pleasure of telling young Pitt, and the police."

She smiled, genuinely this time, with pleasure, not in an attempt to create the illusion of courage.

Fimber, the lawyer prosecuting the case, was actually the next one to turn up at Ottershaw's laboratory. Even the butler showed a small amount of interest when he conducted him into the huge, complex room filled with instruments. Some were as large as a furnace and others as small as tweezers that could lift a single hair less than half an inch long.

Fimber stared in open wonder. "Marvelous," he said softly. "What have you got for me?" He was a slender man, not particularly tall, but his posture made him look larger than he was. His face was interesting, curious and lopsided with humor, even in repose. He regarded Miriam with interest, but it was Ottershaw he spoke to.

"A shred of evidence," Ottershaw replied. "Rather a trace . . . proof that it was there."

Fimber frowned slightly. "Such as what? And where is *there*? The seat of the fire, I hope."

"Yes. In fact, the seat of both fires," Ottershaw replied. "White phosphorous. We went back to the scenes of both Adwell and Jackson's deaths and, knowing what we were looking for, found minute traces."

"And that is important . . . because?"

"It is an extremely quick-burning substance that gets extraordinarily hot, almost immediately."

"How hot?"

"Five thousand degrees Fahrenheit."

"God Almighty!"

"Precisely. Enough to crack a human skull, as it did Rob Adwell's."

Fimber's face had lost some of its color. "And Paddy Jackson's as well? Have you found traces of it there, too? This is important. God, what a case!"

"Yes, there, too," Ottershaw replied. "Very little now, but more than could possibly have occurred in any natural way. It was the accelerant in both cases."

"Why didn't you see that before?"

"Because we weren't looking for it. It doesn't just leap out at you. There are plenty of things easier to find, and less explosive, like the oil or petrol used to start

223

the second fire —"

"But you said white phosphorous," Fimber interrupted.

"Yes, for the heat that cracked the skull, not for the fires that burned down the warehouse and the storage shed. Which is probably why we didn't think of it before. The fire brigade found out what was used to spread the fire and we didn't think any further than that. It was only when Miss fford Croft" — Ottershaw glanced briefly at Miriam — "pointed out the relationship between the heat needed to crack bone and kill the people it did, and the fact that they had very little smoke in their lungs, that we realized there must be two accelerants present. One for the ordinary fire, the other for the heat necessary to kill quickly and violently."

Fimber turned to Miriam with an entirely new expression. "I am amazed, Miss fford Croft, and very impressed. We shall have to think how it can be presented so the jury will understand."

"Dr. Ottershaw will do that," she said quietly, and with a smile. Recognition was enough. She did not need more acknowledgment than that. It blossomed up inside her, wiping out all the old ache of failure. "There will be a lot for the police to do, and of course Professor Saltram will testify as well."

"Professor Saltram?" Fimber said with a slight surprise. "You surely don't —"

"We do," Ottershaw replied. "In fact, everything hangs on it."

"Well, well." Fimber shook his head. "This I must see . . ."

Daniel visited his parents that evening. He had intended to ask his father more about Barnabas Saltram when he could speak to him alone, but his mother was quickly aware of his anxiety, which he thought he had hidden rather well. He should have learned by now that she could read his emotions uncomfortably easily. There had been no nursemaid to care for him, just Charlotte and the young general maid, Gracie. They had been good times, happy and close, and they meant that Charlotte knew her children at times disconcertingly well.

"What is it?" she asked him when they had retired from the dining room to the withdrawing room.

It being early December, the curtains were drawn across all the windows, including the French doors into the garden. The heavy velvet closed out the sounds of the winter weather outside. They could only hear the

225

whickering of the fire, and its warmth filled the room.

Daniel had come specifically because his father had mentioned an earlier case of Saltram's, the one that had originally made him famous, and the case obviously had elements about it that were still heavy in his mind two decades later.

"Only an old case," Daniel said as lightly as possible.

"One of your father's?" Charlotte asked dubiously. She could sense when he was evading a question.

"Not exactly, but one he knows about," Daniel replied. Did she realize that was the reason he had accepted the dinner invitation? He looked at her now, standing in the firelight, its warmth of color reflected on the soft tones of her skin, the touches of auburn in her dark hair, and the gray at her temples. She did not look older to him than any of his memories of her, just a little softer, as if some of the haste to judgment, the anger at injustice, had softened a bit. She was wiser, and just as keen to fight what she thought was wrong. Only now she was more careful, seeing a step further ahead. But she was just as quick to laugh or make a tart reply if it was justified — or if it was not.

"Daniel," she nudged him.

She was always going to take his side, right or wrong; he knew that without even having to think about it. She was also not going to be put off, or to wait for him indefinitely. Years had not tempered her patience.

"Yes," he said, meeting her eyes. He might just as well tell the truth straightaway. She would dig until she got it anyhow, and perhaps she had already guessed. She was not necessarily tactful, but never less than astute. He had heard that his grandfather had been horrified to learn that his middle daughter, in her twenties, read the newspapers' least appropriate articles for a young lady. She should have confined her interests to domestic notes and society pages. Politics and crime coarsened a young woman's mind. That seemed funny now, but the man had been perfectly serious thirty-five years ago.

"The Daventry case, I presume," she interrupted his thoughts.

"You know!"

"Not difficult to guess. You want to ask again about Saltram." She did not give the man the courtesy of his title.

That reminded Daniel immediately what her opinion of him was. He tended to forget how forthright she was. In a way, Miriam was like that sometimes. Perhaps that was why he was perfectly comfortable with her.

He looked at his mother and sighed. "Yes, please. It might help. But don't ask me about the case I'm pursuing, I can't tell you."

"I know you're having trouble with it, my dear, and that is all that concerns me."

"How do you know that?"

She did not even bother to answer, but gave him a withering look, then turned to Pitt as he came into the room and closed the door behind him.

He looked at them inquiringly.

"Daniel wants to go over the Daventry case, particularly Saltram's part in it," Charlotte said in answer to his unasked question.

"I imagine so," Pitt replied, the light catching his face, showing a slight concern as he walked over to his usual chair beside the fire. No one bothered to turn the gas light up. The soft glow from the brackets on the wall, along with the firelight, were enough to see the slightest change in his face, as well as the outlines of the familiar furniture, the gloss on the polished wood, the dimmer forms of chairs and the sofa.

"In some ways it feels as if it were only yesterday," Pitt said.

"Was it your case?" Daniel asked in surprise. "I didn't know that. You didn't mention it before."

"No, it wasn't," Pitt answered, "but it was one we shall all remember, and I feel it is somehow unfinished."

"What do you mean?" Charlotte asked. "What was there left?"

Pitt hesitated.

Daniel seized his chance. "Can you tell me about it again? I've got to face Saltram on the stand in two or three days."

"Isn't he your witness?" Pitt asked, his expression reflecting his certainty that he was right. The whole case confused him, and it was there, in his eyes, the set of his jaw, his mouth.

"Yes," Daniel admitted, "and no."

"That's not an answer," Pitt pointed out.

"Kitteridge will be questioning him. Though actually he's quite unwell, and if he still feels rotten tomorrow, I will do it. I'm prepared. At least, I must be by then."

"And what is going to happen between now and then that will change so much?" Pitt asked. He started to add something else, but changed his mind.

"You're going to tell me about the Daventry case, and the evidence that Saltram gave that launched his rapid rise, and why it was remarkable . . . and why it still matters. Or why not. But I hope it does."

"It's public knowledge," Pitt began.

"What you thought of it isn't."

"It wasn't my case."

"But you know about it and think there was something wrong," Daniel pointed out.

"I still think James Leigh, the young man who appeared to be a burglar, wasn't guilty." Pitt was clearly grieved about it. Now there was pain in his face. "But it seemed like the only conclusion from the evidence."

"Was the evidence wrong, or misinterpreted?" Daniel asked.

"I don't know."

"Tell me, from the beginning."

Charlotte looked at Pitt, then at Daniel, then back again, but she said nothing.

Pitt hesitated, marshaling his thoughts. Then he began, leaning forward a little in the armchair, as if he could not relax. "I'll tell it as the police learned about it. Mercaston, the man on the case, I got to know quite well. He told me about it because it still bothered him. This was a couple of years later."

"Where?" Daniel asked. "It wasn't Special Branch?"

"No, regular police, Herefordshire. Daventry Hall is a big manor house standing by itself. Part of the problem. They had an ornamental pond they could get any amount of water from, but the fire brigade took a while to arrive. Saved the main house, and it's all rebuilt now, but they lost the whole of the old east wing."

"Remind us why the east wing was so important," Charlotte chimed in.

"Sir Roger was out that evening, but Lady Daventry was at home. She went to bed early and was trapped. She was burned to death," Pitt replied very quietly. "For anybody it would have been terrible, but she was young, and a particularly beautiful woman."

"Does that matter?" Daniel demanded. He sounded more critical than he meant to be, but such a facile judgment was unlike his father and it disconcerted him. "She'd be just as choked, burned, terrified, and dead if she had been the ugliest woman in England."

"A great deal of real beauty comes from inside, Daniel," Pitt said grimly. "When you are a little older, with luck you will know that."

Daniel was about to answer when he changed his mind and smiled instead. "I'm old enough to know that now. Go on, what then?"

"There wasn't enough of the wing left to say for certain how the fire started. It was winter and the domestic fires were lit. It looked as if the window was left open, and curtains blew inwards. Something caught fire and it spread from there. There was no one to raise the alarm until it was too late to get Marguerite out. The stairs were old wood, dry and perfect for burning. It all went up very quickly. The fire brigade put it out, but when they got to her, she was dead." He stopped, and his face reflected the sadness he had felt when he had first heard of it.

Charlotte put her hand over his. "Thomas, it's over now, all of it."

"Where did Saltram come into it?" Daniel asked. "Why was he even called? Was there some question as to how she died?"

"Yes, there was," Pitt answered. "The regular medical examiner looked at her body, not as badly burned as you would expect, and injured somehow. Her skull was cracked. He said it was a hard and specific blow to the back of her head. Sir Roger could account for most of his time, but not all. They questioned a lot of people, the servants over and over again. They were all accounted for, and devoted to Marguerite. They ended by charging Roger Daventry with having killed her with blows to the back of the head, and then setting fire to cover his crime."

"He's still alive, isn't he?" Charlotte asked. "He's about sixty now."

"Yes, he was found not guilty," Pitt replied. "On Saltram's sudden and dramatic evidence showing how heat can crack a skull if it's hot enough, and apparently this was."

"Reasonable doubt," Daniel said miserably. "Can't possibly hang anyone if the jury believes he probably didn't do it. Do you really think he did? Why?"

"Why he did it is fairly obvious," Pitt replied. "She had come to loathe him, and most of the local people favored her. His family was well known and well respected, even then. It was growing uncomfortable for him. He wanted to become a Member of Parliament. If she had become even a little more public with her feelings, he would not have had a chance. As it was, he got a great deal of compassion, which he used well. Got his seat in the House. Sympathy vote," he added with sudden bitterness.

"What makes you think he killed her?" Daniel went on. "Do you think he paid Saltram?" He doubted that, but it was possible.

"No, Saltram is far too clever for that,"

Pitt said. His face was tight, jaw shadowed in the firelight. "And even more protective of his reputation. To be paid would mean he needed it; he would never stoop to that. He has delusions of infallibility. He found a reason he could believe as to why the injuries were the result of fire, not violence, and he became one of the most influential and respected forensic experts in Britain, even in Europe."

"And Daventry got off? Walked away an innocent and sympathetic figure?" Daniel asked, feeling his own muscles hurt inside him.

"Yes," Pitt agreed. "Then they found a young man they believed started the fire, a supposed burglar; he could not explain what he was doing there on the night of the fire."

Daniel felt the hurt inside him tighten. "And they hanged him."

"As Marguerite's death was the result of the fire," Pitt said quietly, "yes, they hanged him for it."

Daniel glanced at his mother and saw the tears in her eyes. He looked at his father again. "And you think Saltram was wrong, and the fire didn't kill her. Why?"

"If I had had proof, I would have told anyone who would listen," Pitt replied. "It was doubt, not certainty. Mercaston was sure it was Daventry, and that the young man, Leigh, was innocent, but Leigh was terrified, and they took that for guilt."

"And Saltram?" Daniel said softly.

"Made his name," Pitt answered.

"We're calling him for the defense tomorrow," Daniel replied.

"And your client is innocent? You'll want to use him, Daniel. The fact that he's an arrogant swine is irrelevant."

"No." Daniel mouthed the word almost silently. "My client is guilty. Not only of killing this man like that, but I'm almost certain she's guilty of another murder, too. Trying it out, and if the defense hadn't worked, she probably wouldn't have tried it again."

Pitt swore, something he very rarely did.

"Exactly," Daniel agreed.

## CHAPTER TEN

Daniel lay awake a long time trying to understand why Jessie Beale would have killed Paddy Jackson, and then Rob Adwell. It was carefully and deliberately planned. It was no sudden quarrel, loss of temper, or fear of any kind of attack. Did one follow from the other, or had she planned them both at the same time, before she even began?

Why?

Revenge for something? Such as what?

He pictured her face in his mind, at first glance more or less ordinary, and not especially pretty. Then when emotion moved her, it came to life, vivid, intelligent, strong-willed. Far more intelligent than Adwell. More than Paddy Jackson, too. Or Ginger Jackson, for that matter. Quarles had said that there had been a lot of robberies along the warehouses on Tooley Street, the whole length of the dock on the south side of the river. That required brains, organization, forethought — which were certainly not characteristics of Adwell. Daniel could not see them in Ginger Jackson either. He did not know the other members of the gangs, and he could not easily imagine any of the Jackson brothers with that much discipline of the mind, or of their tempers.

Jessie Beale, on the other hand, was a natural commander. Her only handicap was that she was a woman, a young woman. Or was it such a disadvantage? There were some very powerful women in the criminal world, or on the edges of it: forgers, fences of high-end stolen goods, even smugglers, clever thieves. Jessie was just starting young, creating her own, rather than inheriting a father's or brother's gang.

She had outwitted the civil system, Saltram, Kitteridge, and Daniel himself. So far. But it was not finished yet. He turned over and went to sleep at last.

Daniel saw Kitteridge on the courthouse steps the next morning. Kitteridge was early, walking back and forth with his face to the wind, his hat jammed down and his scarf flying.

He almost bumped into Daniel before he saw him. He squinted in the low winter sunlight. "What is it?" he demanded. "Has something happened?" There was fear in his voice.

Daniel fell in step beside him. "Learned some more that could be useful."

"We know everything about this kind of fire, but it doesn't help. Jessie Beale is guilty, and we've called bloody Saltram to prove she isn't. What have you got that will help that?" Kitteridge started coughing. "Come inside," he ordered, fishing in his coat pocket for a handkerchief.

Daniel obeyed, opening the door for him. "Not sure exactly, although I've been thinking about it all night. I had dinner at home and asked my father about the case that made Saltram famous. I mean not just top rank at university, but the one that made him a household name. It's really pretty awful."

"You can't blacken his name over the past," Kitteridge said, blowing his nose fiercely. "It'll have been tried, and it won't make the jury like you. They practically think he's God."

"I know that, for heaven's sake," Daniel snapped. "Let me tell you what my father told me. It could matter!"

Kitteridge sneezed again, and seemed glad enough to follow Daniel into one of the smaller rooms currently vacant, due to the early hour. As soon as the door was closed, Daniel repeated to Kitteridge, as closely as he could remember, all that Pitt had said that was relevant to the fire and, probably more important, to Saltram's character. Somehow in the cold, rather gray morning light, and with too little sleep, it did not seem as useful, as it had all happened years ago. But it gave them further knowledge of Saltram's mind, his beliefs, and most importantly, his nature.

Kitteridge shook his head. "I don't see a vulnerability," he said frankly. "And even if there are an unlikely number of these verdicts in his past, we haven't got anyone who says otherwise."

Daniel felt his earlier optimism dip. "I know, but we'll spin it out as long as we can. We don't have to call him for a day or two."

"There's not much to spin," Kitteridge said unhappily. "Even if I lose my voice completely, they'll call you to stand in, and you haven't got anything substantial to say, have you?"

"Not yet. Except an idea that makes sense of why Jessie killed both men."

Kitteridge stopped abruptly. "What?" he demanded. "Why didn't you say so?"

"I just did." Daniel had held it back on purpose. He had no proof.

"Well, what?" Kitteridge said sharply. He paused to cough, and then could not stop.

"I think there weren't two gangs, but only one. And the fight was for leadership," Daniel explained.

"And who won?" Kitteridge said between bouts of coughing.

"Jessie."

"She's a girl!" Kitteridge gasped.

"I think she's the brains," Daniel replied. "And if she escapes this, she will be the undisputed leader of the gang."

Kitteridge stared at him. "Are you sure of that?"

"No. But it's possible."

"Makes sense," Kitteridge agreed. "It's about the only thing that does. But none of them is going to admit it." He walked toward the door, clearly making an effort to pull his shoulders back and lift his step a little.

Daniel felt profoundly sorry for him, and also afraid that in a day or two — which they could need to discover anything arguable — they might find nothing at all. By then, Kitteridge might have to excuse himself, and Daniel would take his place. He would not hand the case over to anyone else. He wouldn't tell a soul that Jessie was guilty, and she certainly was not going to.

The trial began with Fimber for the prosecution questioning several different members of the fire brigade. He asked everything he could think of. Where did the fire start? Was there evidence of an accelerant? Were they certain? Could it have been accidental? What was the heat like to begin with? How rapidly did it increase?

"Mr. Fimber," the judge, His Honor Judge Hanover, interrupted him, "is this really necessary? The jurors are ordinary men with average knowledge of the matter of fire. You are raising questions they are not going to ask."

"Not the jury, Your Honor," Fimber agreed deferentially. "But the defense may well ask. Mr. Kitteridge is a highly educated man with some considerable experience."

The judge smiled and shook his head slowly. "Mr. Kitteridge is thirty-five, sir. I happen to have watched his career myself. Very promising, even if he has a most unfortunate cold today. And by the look of him, he may very well have to stand down before he falls down. But he is not persnickety for the sake of it. Mr. Pitt, who may have to take over for him, is cut from a very different cloth, though, so perhaps you are wise to establish your grounds. Proceed. But do not waste our time."

"No, my lord," Fimber agreed. "Thank you for your counsel. I shall bear it in mind. Mr. Pitt is something of an unknown quantity."

"He is twenty-five," the judge observed. "He has to be a newborn babe by comparison with your own experience."

"Just so," Fimber agreed, his face flushing with embarrassment. "And William Pitt the Younger had already been prime minister for a year by the time he was that age. No relation, I think."

Kitteridge sneezed, or perhaps he stifled a laugh.

"The relevance of that, Mr. Fimber?" the judge inquired, keeping his face straight with effort.

"Only that I am getting rid of the objections before they arise, Your Honor," Fimber answered.

"Leave Mr. Kitteridge something to do, and get on with it. We now know more about fire than we will ever remember. And the key to a successful prosecution, Mr. Fimber, is to prove beyond a reasonable doubt that the crime charged actually took place, and that the accused person is guilty of it. If you do that, we shall all be able to follow you."

"Yes, Your Honor." Fimber knew where to stop. He thanked the last witness from the fire brigade and the judge adjourned the court for lunch.

In the afternoon, Fimber called a fire expert who specialized in warehouses and other large unoccupied buildings along the south bank of the river. He specified the man's skills and experience to the last tiny fact. Some of the jurors looked to be impressed, but others were bored. One or two of them showed signs of distaste, as if they feared more ugly details would follow.

Actually, the witness spoke mostly of the chemical aspects of the fire, the terrible damage it caused, and why it was frequently so difficult to tell where a fire had started, how, and when. By the time Fimber felt he was losing the jury, he finally came to the point. "And this particular fire, Mr. Morris, can you say how it started, beyond a reasonable doubt?"

"Yes, sir, it was started with oil, such as you use in motor vehicles. It burns very quickly. Some highly flammable things — paint, turpentine, old cloths, and so on — were stored nearby. The fire would have taken hold very quickly."

"Quickly enough that an unwary person setting such a fire might have got overtaken by it and burned also?" Fimber asked.

Kitteridge rose slowly. "I object, Your Honor. There has been no foundation laid for this supposition. And Mr. Morris is not established as —"

"You are a little ahead of yourself, Mr. Fimber," the judge said, nodding in agreement. "Was there a body found near the seat of the fire? Are you not charging Miss Beale with setting it? She appeared to be unharmed. Am I missing something?" He looked inquiringly at Fimber, then at Kitteridge.

There was an uneasy titter of laughter around the gallery, and two of the jurors shifted in their seats uncomfortably.

"I was intending to prove, my lord, that the accused has some experience in starting fires, and knew exactly what she was doing when she lit this one using oil as an accelerant. However, she misjudged the speed at which it would travel, and then her accomplice got caught by the flames and died horribly."

There was an exhalation of sound in the courtroom. Several people jumped to their feet. One journalist bolted for the door, pen still in his hand. An usher made a lunge for a man who was shouting at the top of his voice, and they both overbalanced and ended on the floor.

The judge shouted for order.

"Where in the hell did that come from?" Kitteridge turned to Daniel, his face aghast.

"No idea," Daniel said honestly, "but it's damn clever. She may not have meant him to die, but if she was part of the crime and he died anyway, then that's murder. Clever beggar."

"I wonder if he just thought of it. He's one to watch."

When order was resumed, the judge looked at Fimber over the top of his eyeglasses. "Are you asking to amend your charge, Mr. Fimber?"

"No, my lord, it stands at murder."

"Premeditated?" The judge raised his eyebrows.

Fimber thought for a few moments. "I think I shall leave that to the jury, my lord. I am more certain of a conviction with *unintended,* but since they were in the process of committing a crime in which both had a part, it is still murder."

"Very well, proceed."

Fimber dragged it out for another hour, but he had by then explored every detail, and had left nothing further for Kitteridge to ask. The cause of the fire had been quite clearly established as arson, and he would have gained nothing by trying to cast doubt on that.

The last witness of the day was Dr. Appleby. Fimber asked him if he could identify the body beyond any reasonable doubt.

"I can," Appleby said immediately.

"How are you so very certain? Is there something unique about him?"

"To me, certainly. I examined him for fitness for trial when he was tried for a murder exactly like this one, less than two months ago. He was found not guilty, obviously, or he would not still have been alive." Appleby's face was almost twisted with emotion, but it was such a mixture of anger, frustration, and grief that it was difficult to read.

It was not exactly the answer Fimber had wanted, but fighting it now would only draw the jurors' attention even more. "How did he die, Dr. Appleby, in your opinion?"

Appleby seemed to consider the question as if it were a difficult one. "Fairly quickly," he replied. "Hardly any smoke in his lungs, which meant he was not breathing for more than a few moments when the smoke was thick. The blow to the back of his neck might well have been the cause. It was hard enough to crack his skull. That seems to be the immediate cause. His heart stopped."

"Someone struck him?" Fimber inquired.

"Something hit him." Appleby was precise. "Whether it was in the hand of somebody else or not, I cannot say. It could as well have been a falling timber, or that he fell against something, such as a stair rail, or even a tread of a step, as it were. It was not the floor; there is no edge to the floor. If you're looking for me to say it was murder, I can't, not for certain. Not beyond a reasonable doubt." Appleby looked very unhappy. It was not the opinion he wished to give. Saltram's evidence in the earlier case hung heavily in the air, as if the silence had just fallen upon it, and Saltram was, in some way, present.

Daniel felt his whole body tense. The last thing he wanted was Saltram justified. He looked across at Jessie Beale in the dock. He almost wished she would smile. It would go against her with the jury if they saw victory in her face. But she was far too clever for that. When he saw her pale skin, slightly disheveled hair, and downcast eyes, he knew she would keep up the act all the way through. She had let it slip for only one moment when he and Kitteridge were interviewing her. She could not resist letting them know, but it was for them only. They could not share it. Now the more he thought of it the more he was certain that this was a bid for leadership, money, the power of the Jackson gang.

Fimber was considering his next question. Perhaps he had only just realized that Appleby was not going to offer any opinion that Saltram could ridicule or tear apart. He would not risk his own reputation, nor would he give Saltram something from which to launch another lecture to inspire the jury with his expertise.

It was Kitteridge's turn. He stood up and faced Appleby. "You say, Dr. Appleby, that the actual cause of Adwell's death was that his heart stopped, which it did as a result of a serious blow to the back of the head, which you know because the skull is cracked visibly. You saw it?"

"Yes," Appleby agreed.

"But you can only say roughly what sort of an object caused this crack, and not whether it was something he fell against, or something that either came loose in the destruction of the fire or was in someone's hand. In other words, you cannot tell us whether it was an accident or murder."

"That is correct." Appleby looked relieved. "It could have been either."

"Or the heat of the fire itself?" Kitteridge added.

"I am not competent to judge that, sir. I have conducted no such tests on a human skull."

"No, neither have I," Kitteridge agreed. "Thank you, Dr. Appleby, that is all."

"Mr. Fimber," the judge asked, "have you any other questions for this witness?"

Fimber stood up, as if to ask something, then noticed the time and sat down. "No, thank you, Your Honor."

The judge adjourned the court for the day. The mood was tense, as if there was a storm to come. The evidence was dragging on, and people were bored with what was actually happening. Still, there was an expectation in the air, almost a foreknowledge that the real violence was coming soon. It was like the oppression before the first drop of rain fell, the lightning flashes on the horizon, then the long seconds before the drumroll of thunder. Then a storm hits with wind and torrential rain, deafening noise, bolts of lightning that strike the ground, kill people and animals, fell trees and start fires.

Rubbish, Daniel told himself. Who did he imagine he was? There was no storm, just a mistaken verdict, a clever and heartless young woman walking free after a murder.

Perhaps two murders. He knew exactly how, and he thought the reason was Jessie's desire for power and control, but he wasn't sure. Did it even matter? Perhaps not, as long as no one else was unjustly hanged for it, as apparently James Leigh had been in the Daventry case.

"What are we going to do?" he asked Kitteridge.

Kitteridge sneezed and blew his nose. He sounded terrible, but Daniel had time only for the briefest sympathy. The cold would get better. The case, he feared, would not.

"Delay," Kitteridge replied. "For as long as possible."

"With what?" Daniel asked.

"Police procedure. Fimber will hold it up as much he can. And we can always add to it, argue."

"It will be obvious what we're doing. Even the judge will see it. I know it's because we haven't . . ." He trailed off.

"Got a leg to stand on?" Kitteridge raised his eyebrows. "We've got too many legs. If we could get our client off, and we don't, we'll be disbarred, and we'll deserve it."

"She's bloody guilty!" Daniel swore. He disliked every part of this, and he couldn't see a way out.

Kitteridge sneezed again, and did not argue.

The next day was the nightmare Daniel expected it to be. If only Miriam and Ottershaw were to make a breakthrough in their experiments, but Miriam had sent word that they were making slow progress. Unfortunately, Fimber was good. In fact, he was very good. He called Quarles to testify in detail as to all his investigations, first those that led him to suspect not just murder, but specifically murder by Jessie Beale. He traced the rise of the Jackson brothers in their criminal enterprises from small beginnings as hired minor players in violence, bullying, and petty extortion, through their current position as major operators in smuggling and stealing works of considerable worth imported from the Middle East. Then he described the rival gang of Adwell, which had frequently threatened them, but never acted.

Kitteridge rose each time he had a point on anything that could be argued. Sometimes Fimber was obscure or made a claim with no substantiation. He came perilously close to being obvious in his carelessness. Every point Kitteridge raised, Fimber was able to clear up, but he did it meticulously, using up time.

Once the judge actually admonished him to be more careful in his presentation. It was impossible to tell whether he knew exactly what Fimber was doing. Intentionally. It was a razor's edge. "You're taking your success for granted, Mr. Fimber," he said critically. "We are dealing with a very serious crime. Mr. Kitteridge is correct to challenge you. He's fighting for his client's life. Address this with a little more persuasion. You are coming perilously close to wasting the court's time. Do not oblige me to chastise you again."

"No, Your Honor," Fimber said contritely.

From where he sat several yards away, Daniel could see the color rise up his cheeks. Fimber had given them all he could and it would be Kitteridge's turn to call his defense witnesses next. He knew that Fimber's time-wasting had been to reinforce his arguments and put off the moment when Sir Barnabas Saltram came to speak in Jessie's defense. Fimber had well proved Jessie Beale's motive for wanting Adwell dead. She was after control of the entire operation.

"We've got to call Saltram," Kitteridge said miserably as they walked up the street in the rain, toward the public house for a hot slice of pie before separating to go to their respective homes.

Daniel knew it. They could not go down without a fight, especially if it was possible to win if they tried hard enough. There were lots of loose ends, other people involved.

"Fimber's left enough loose ends for us to pull," Daniel pointed out as they sat down at a small table and ordered hot food.

"It's a bit early," the waitress said.

Daniel smiled at her. "I know, but we're cold and wet, and we've a long way to go home. And we're losing a case at the court down the road. We need someone to be kind to us. Preferably, someone serving hot food." He smiled again. "Please?"

"You think I'm as soft as butter, don't you?" she asked, putting her hands on her hips and shrugging.

"Hot buttered toast would be good enough." Daniel was not going to give up.

"I'll see if there's anything ready," she compromised.

"Thank you," Daniel said sincerely.

Kitteridge started coughing again.

"Got ter, 'aven't I," she said, looking anxiously at Kitteridge. "Don't want you dying here, and give the place a bad name, do I?"

Daniel brought them ale from the bar, and

253

ten minutes later the waitress brought a steaming hot steak and kidney pie and thick suet crust as light as a feather. "Don't burn yourself," she warned, putting the dishes carefully on the table.

They thanked her profoundly before beginning to eat. As she had said, it was very hot indeed, only just out of the oven.

"Got enough money to tip her well?" Kitteridge asked several minutes later. "She deserves it."

"Not as much as she's worth," Daniel replied. "But about twice the price."

"That'll do."

A quarter of an hour later, they finished the meal and were warm again, but Kitteridge still looked ill.

"You won't make it tomorrow," Daniel stated. "Your passing out in court might cause a lot of attention, even some sympathy, but it won't win the case."

"It won't even delay it," Kitteridge replied grimly. "You've been there all the time. You'd be better than any short-notice substitution chambers would send."

"We could ask for a delay," Daniel said hopefully.

"We could ask for Christmas in July," Kitteridge replied. "But we won't get it."

Daniel did not argue. He knew Kitteridge

was right. The best he would get was that Marcus fford Croft would send a clerk to run errands for him. And possibly look things up.

"Take a taxi home. I'll get you one," Daniel said as they left. "And don't waste the breath you've got arguing. I don't want to have to knock you out and send you home in an ambulance."

"Don't be absurd."

"The state you're in, I could do it!" Daniel replied. He was not one to admit it, but he was as worried about Kitteridge as he was about the case. In fact, rather more. He truly cared about Kitteridge, but it would only embarrass him to say so.

Kitteridge did not argue. Either he understood, or he was too ill to make an issue of it.

# CHAPTER ELEVEN

It was long after dark, and the rain blew in gusts against the windows upstairs, at street level. But down in Ottershaw's laboratory it was almost silent. All the lights were on. Ottershaw was still bent over a microscope. Miriam had finished her last experiment, which had yielded nothing useful. She was tired, her eyes felt gritty and hot, and her back ached from bending over, watching dials, calculating figures that in the end proved nothing. Even Charlie was quiet, seldom singing to himself, and regularly offering to fetch them tea, which he did. It helped.

Ottershaw never complained, but she knew him well enough by now to read his disappointment.

She was not even aware of Daniel just inside the door until he spoke. Startled, the pencil slid out of her fingers and rolled off the tabletop onto the floor.

He looked troubled, soaking wet, dripping all over the floor. Except for where the wind had whipped color into his cheeks, his face was white.

She ignored the pencil. "Oh, Daniel, you look perished! What's happened? Did Saltram let you down?"

He smiled bleakly. "No, I almost wish he had, but he'll be there tomorrow. We telephoned chambers and he's ready. That's not it. Miriam, Jessie's guilty. Fimber all but proved that today. Poor devil strung out the evidence as long as he could, trying to emphasize his point so that it won't be overlooked when Saltram takes the stand; even earned a pretty sharp rebuke from the judge for it."

Miriam was puzzled. "Why did she do it? Was it personal, or something else?"

His face showed his emotions. When he was tired, he was totally transparent, at least to her. "I'm not sure she does anything for personal reasons," he answered. "It's all about the money. It was never Adwell and his crew against the Jackson brothers. It was really all about a fight for leadership. And if she gets away with this, it will be Jessie who wins. So yes, it is about money — and power."

"Are you sure they'd accept Jessie as

leader?"

"Why not? She's clever — and tough . . ."

"Then she didn't kill Paddy Jackson," she said. "That probably was Adwell."

"I doubt it," he said miserably. "He knew she was going to take over and she killed him before he could challenge her. Or maybe he would have killed her to take charge himself?" He winced as if he felt a stab of pain. "Or maybe it was just a trial run for seeing if she could rig a murder by fire and get away with it. If she failed and Adwell was hanged, she was rid of him anyway. And if she succeeded, she still would have demonstrated that rebellion did not pay."

Miriam frowned. "Then why didn't she just let Adwell hang for killing Paddy? You mean you really think she was trying this defense to see if it worked?"

"Yes," he said quietly. "I think she's capable of it."

"Or maybe it was another rebellion? Maybe she actually cared for him, but he had ambitions, too?"

"It will be there somewhere," he answered. "But first of all, we've got to be seen to try our damnedest to get her off, yet see to it that we fail." He smiled grimly, a stark flash of humor there for an instant.

She ached to be able to tell him something useful. "We've got" — she was stretching the truth, and she knew it — "half an idea. But we haven't got the sort of proof anyone will listen to except us. It's a contradiction to Saltram." She sighed and felt tears of frustration and defeat sting her eyes. She so badly wanted to win, this time for Daniel far more than for herself. The case was a double defeat for him.

Ottershaw had at last noticed the intrusion; he left his microscope and came over to Daniel and Miriam. He looked exhausted. His face was deeply lined with weariness and impending defeat that he could not deny much longer.

"Any news?" he asked Daniel.

"A bit," Daniel replied. "At least we have an idea. But even if we're right, there's no way of proving it yet —"

"What is it?" Ottershaw cut across him. "We have very little time left."

Daniel drew in a shaking breath. "The only thing that is really going to make a difference is whether Adwell's death could have been a result of the fire, with no human influence — although that is a barely credible belief. In fact, if Saltram is right, where Adwell is concerned, I don't know if he was guilty or not. But at the core, I really thought he wasn't. I'm inclined toward that. I don't know whether that is reasonable or not, but I had no difficulty in arguing it. This time is different, I know Jessie is guilty."

"Do you?" Ottershaw demanded. It was more than a question, it was an order to answer him completely.

"Yes," Daniel said without hesitation. "She admitted it obliquely once, only for an instant, but I can't forget the challenge in her eyes, and the moment of victory when she knew I understood and couldn't do anything about it. I have to call Saltram to the stand, or I would be derelict in my duty, my legal obligation to do the best I can for her. What can you do to help?"

Ottershaw bit his lower lip and shook his head slowly. "We are on the edge of something that could throw Saltram completely, if we could prove it, but we can't . . . yet. If you call him, he has no choice but to stick to his earlier testimony. His whole career —"

Daniel interrupted him. "I know! I heard all about the Daventry case from my father." He glanced at Miriam. "You'll remember, it was the case that made Saltram's name. He used that same line of argument to defend Adwell, and he has to stick to that if we call him to testify for Jessie. The facts we know are all exactly the same. That the heat of the fire, if it was great enough, would crack a human skull in exactly the way it did Marguerite Daventry's, Paddy Jackson's, and now Robert Adwell's. Jessie probably didn't know about Marguerite Daventry, or she might have read of it. It doesn't matter. She certainly did know about Robert Adwell." He looked utterly miserable, even apologetic. "Saltram will say the same thing again, and we can't prove him in any error."

Ottershaw shook his head. "It's debatable. We're trying to repeat the experiments over again. It does crack the skull, if you get the temperature high enough. At least, we did it five times, but the cracks were in a different place."

"Does that matter?" Daniel asked, a flicker of hope in his face. "I mean, can it prove it was a different cause, rather than just a different fire, in a different building? We have to show the impossibility of it being the fire alone. If the heat is enough —"

"We know white phosphorous gets more than hot enough to crack bones," Ottershaw interrupted. "But across the top of the skull first. Not around the back, just above the neck, where both Adwell's and Paddy Jackson's injuries were. But . . ." he shook his head, "we've tested as much as we can for traces of that. We'll need more to shake Saltram's testimony. In fact, it will help him."

"What?" Daniel pressed. For a moment, he could not see it. "Anyone could have put it there, or stored it there, and it was an accident. It certainly doesn't implicate Jessie."

"Or anyone else in particular," Ottershaw agreed. "And there are no reasons it could not be residue from some legitimate use. It's normally stored in water because it's highly combustible and very easily ignited. And there are plenty of places like that down by the river. It would explain the sudden and extraordinarily intense heat."

"Do we know it was *sudden and extraordinarily intense*?" Daniel repeated with a frown.

"Yes," said Miriam, interrupting for the first time. "We know it was sudden because Adwell didn't escape, and there was hardly any smoke in his lungs. Exactly like Paddy Jackson. And we're still thinking that the heat must then have been intense enough to have killed . . . in both cases. We need to be able to prove it, though."

"You could testify to that," Daniel looked at Ottershaw.

"I would, but no one would believe me against Saltram." His voice was apologetic, as if he felt it was his own fault that he had not the dynamic force, wide reputation, or the certainty of his own opinion that Saltram possessed. He was much too aware of the possibility of error. He listened to others, and valued their knowledge also.

"What do you recommend?" Daniel asked directly. It was more than a question, it was a demand for help.

Miriam took a step toward Ottershaw and stopped abruptly. This was not a time to intervene. Sometimes silence was not only the wiser, but the braver choice.

Ottershaw answered at last. "I think we should find the very best person to stand against Saltram, someone who is equal to him in skill, even if he doesn't accept that anyone could be." He hesitated only a moment, but Miriam noticed the rigidity of his body and knew that he was taking what he believed to be a great risk, more than a step into the unknown, but one into territory that held other dangers also. "Someone who will show no fear of him, and who believes in offending and even outraging people, if they are wrong and in the way of justice."

"Are you making this up?" Daniel asked, his voice loud in the silence. "I'm sorry, are you speaking of a real person? We haven't any time to dream. Kitteridge is sick as a

263

dog. I have very little idea of what I'm doing, but that I have to do it first thing tomorrow morning. And Saltram is fighting for his reputation. He'll eat our client alive if I give him even a quarter of a chance."

"I know," Ottershaw interrupted. "Yes, of course there is such a person. I'm a man of science, not creative imagination. I'm speaking of Dr. Evelyn Hall, just as brilliant as Saltram, although he would never agree to that."

"Is he available?" Daniel asked. "I've never heard of him."

Ottershaw's smile was completely unreadable. "Evelyn is both a man's name and a woman's, I would remind you, and in this case, she is a woman. Although that may not be instantly apparent. She is eccentric, to say the least."

Miriam's heart sank. "A woman has no chance against Saltram."

Ottershaw looked at her, his face unusually stern. It was sufficient to silence her. He turned back to Daniel, ignoring the look of despair that was in his face, too. "She is fully qualified," he asserted, "in Holland, where they have no such prejudices against women. On the contrary, in the unlikely event that they can reach the highest standards, and Dr. Hall does, they are welcomed. Indeed, she exceeds most of them."

Miriam's mind was racing. A woman as good as Saltram! It was possible! In fact, she already existed.

"Holland is no use to us." Daniel could not conceal the sudden hope dashed with disappointment. "I need this witness tomorrow morning."

"She is in London, or I would not have mentioned her," Ottershaw told him. "We need to call upon her tonight, with all the information we have."

"It's nearly eight o'clock now!" Daniel protested. "By the time we make an appointment, if we even can, depending on whether she will see us, it could be ten in the evening before we get there."

"She'll see us," Ottershaw said with certainty. "Unless she's completely changed since the last time I saw her."

"Which was when?" Daniel asked.

"Er, I can't remember exactly."

"Do you even know her?" Daniel's voice was rough-edged with emotion: despair, hope, then despair again.

"Oh, yes," Ottershaw assured him. "She's a bit . . . individual."

Miriam looked at Daniel's expression of incredulity as he stared at Ottershaw, whose hair was standing up on end like a cockatoo's feathers, from running his hands through it in exasperation. He was dressed in a white shirt far too big for him, which he wore as protection for the shirt just the same underneath it. He had carpet slippers on his feet, well-worn and stained from chemicals. His gaunt face was alive with enthusiasm. He spent his money and his life in service to science for its own sake.

"She's a bit eccentric?" Daniel asked more gently, avoiding Miriam's glance.

"Well, quite a bit," Ottershaw conceded. "But she is exactly what we need, I assure you."

Seconds ticked by before Daniel replied. "I suppose we have nothing to lose, except whatever she charges, if she'll come at all."

"If she can, she'll come," Ottershaw said without hesitation. "And she won't charge anything, because to join this battle will be its own reward. But if she does, by any chance, I'll pay."

"Why should you?" Daniel began.

"For goodness' sake, hurry! Go out and find a cab and bring it back here, while Miriam and I pack up the things we need to show her."

"Things?" Daniel looked around at hundreds of chemicals and jars, pots and piles of paper, glass tubes and beakers.

"Copies of testimony," Ottershaw replied sharply. "Lists of chemicals and their qualities. Just do it, please!"

"Yes, sir, I'll do it," Daniel replied, and moved to leave. In the background, he heard Ottershaw making the phone call.

Almost two hours later, they drew up outside a very ordinary-looking house, somewhere south of the river. None of them had spoken much during the journey, both absorbed in their own private thoughts. Probably their thoughts were much the same. It was late, they were tired, and it all seemed rather hopeless. In truth, they were fighting long after the battle was lost.

They got out into the bitter night air. Ottershaw paid the driver and the taxi drove away, a dwindling light disappearing around the corner and leaving them on the footpath.

"Come on." Ottershaw led the way along a very short path to the door. "The answer will not improve with waiting." He succeeded in sounding brave.

Miriam shuddered, holding her coat more closely around her, and followed him. Daniel was carrying the attaché case filled with papers.

Ottershaw rang the doorbell.

It was answered straightaway. Lights

sprang on and the door opened to show not a maid — perhaps the staff had gone to bed — but a middle-aged figure with short gray hair and a face deeply marked by lines of curiosity and good humor. It was impossible to tell at a glance whether this person was male or female. The features were strong but did not seem masculine. The eyes were bright and clever.

"Dr. Hall?" Ottershaw seemed less sure, now that he was here, carrying his conviction into reality.

"Yes?" Deep, but definitely a woman's voice. "You must be Ottershaw. Come in!" She pulled the door wider. "What have you got?" She looked at Miriam first. "Miss fford Croft, I presume. You look perished. And Mr. Pitt, well, well." She stepped back to allow them in. They accepted eagerly and were relieved when she closed the door, excluding the bitter December night. They stood in the hall, embraced already by the warmth. The walls were covered with pictures, most of them photographs of people with deeply lined faces, experience written indelibly on them, each remarkable in its own way.

Dr. Hall noticed Miriam staring. "Good," she said with conviction. "You like faces. Wonderful, aren't they? Hundreds of years

268

of life in this lot. Experience, beauty, tension, isolation, and loss. Come in and have a cup of tea by the fire. Tell me what you've got. No time to waste." She led the way into a drawing room unlike any other Miriam had seen. It was filled with artifacts from at least a dozen different countries, some simple, others amazingly complex.

Dr. Hall pointed out where each of them would sit, in hardbacked wooden chairs around a table some distance from the fire. The chairs were polished and carved, very beautiful, but quite impossible to slouch in. Relaxed, one might well slide off.

"Sit," she ordered. She reached out and took the case from Daniel and set it on the edge of the table, flat, where it could be opened and its contents examined. She looked him up and down. "Young," she observed. "Why are you defending a case like this?"

Daniel was too tired to argue. Miriam wanted to but knew it would be wrong for several reasons. To begin with, Dr. Hall had no time for anything but the truth. She was a soldier preparing for battle. She was concerned only with facts, judgments, if they came at all. And also, Miriam would embarrass Daniel. She was sure he would rather trip over his own feet than be rescued by someone else. So would she!

"My senior partner is ill," he said simply. "He has such a cold he has lost his voice, as well as the ability to —"

"Understood," she interrupted. "And you are facing Saltram tomorrow morning?"

"Yes, he's our only witness."

Miriam winced. It sounded so bare.

Dr. Hall's eyes widened. "And what is he going to say?"

"That the dead man's injuries could as easily have been caused by the heat of the fire as by a blow to the head."

"Are you sure?"

"Yes, he has to, because he gave that opinion in a case almost identical to this about six weeks ago."

"Hoist with his own ropes, hey?" She smiled with deep inner satisfaction. "Poetic?"

"Yes," Daniel said ruefully. "I think by the defendant this time. She was part of the last case, too. This victim was the accused in the first case." He gave a very brief account, a few sentences only.

"So, I shall not be appearing for you," she replied. "But for the prosecution. Does Saltram know that yet?"

"No, ma'am." Daniel smiled, his face full of emotion. "But I do know that my client

270

is guilty. She has very clearly placed me in the position of knowing that, and still having to do the best I can for her."

"I shall be interested to see this young woman," Dr. Hall admitted. "I begin to grasp your predicament. You know this woman's guilt because she has let you know it. Implication rather than words. You cannot betray her, you must prove it to yourself and somehow allow the prosecution to prove it to the jury, without in any way being seen to assist him."

"Yes, and I must do it tomorrow morning," Daniel agreed.

"We shall have tea, then begin," she stated. "Dr. Ottershaw, you will fill in the time until the tea comes by telling me what parts of this you can prove. Feel free to add your own findings, Miss fford Croft."

Ottershaw told her how he and Miriam had gone about discovering what agent had initiated the fire, or accelerated it, and what temperature they believe it had reached. Also, how quickly it reached this temperature, in order to burn the body and cause the skull to crack.

"Set aside the skull for the moment," Dr. Hall interrupted. "The skull is cracked: I will see your pictures. But let me not assume how it got that way. What do you judge from the wood, the other debris? What else was burned? Have you photographs of what was left? Drawings. Architectural plans at least, of what was there before the fire. How large was the fire? How long did it burn before being successfully put out by the fire brigade? What did they destroy? What did they testify to? I want everything."

Daniel unpacked the case and presented her with evidence he had brought, including that obtained by Ottershaw and Miriam. Halfway through, a weary and disheveled maid brought them a large pot of tea and a fruitcake, which she sliced with a meat cleaver. She poured the tea without milk and passed them each a mugful. Miriam tasted hers and all but choked. It was very liberally laced with brandy. In a matter of seconds, she was warmed through very thoroughly, and she helped herself to a piece of cake. She had not realized she was so hungry, yet she knew that she ought to eat something or her breath would catch fire.

Dr. Hall read through all the papers they had brought, as they sat in nervous silence, occasionally glancing at one another. She made no comment, and it cost Miriam all the patience and self-control she had not to demand to know what she thought.

Miriam stared at Dr. Eve, as she told them

she was called by those who knew her well. She could read intense interest and curiosity in her features. She had a remarkable face, reflecting every thought as it entered her mind. Miriam saw anger, pity, puzzlement, some excitement. She never saw boredom or, for that matter, temper. Rage, yes, but not impatience.

The tea was replenished, this time with less brandy. The cake had all disappeared. It had been a large one, almost as big as the plate. The brandy had also disappeared, removed long before it was empty. It was a quarter to five in the morning. They would soon be ready to go to court and present this case. Bright, attentive, eager, exhausted . . . but sober.

"Daniel," Dr. Eve said at last, "present your case based upon the evidence you have. Let Saltram say all he has to say about the bones of the skull and exactly how they crack in the intense heat. The more he wants to say, the better. Every fact he gives is one more we can challenge. I think I know my battlefield. Bring him to it."

Daniel stared at her. "The skull?" He said it as if he would obey her blindly.

Miriam understood exactly how he felt. It was the only tactic they had, and the conflict was just a few hours away. She was so tired her eyes stung, as if they had grit in them, and with every blink they were harder to open.

"Right! Upstairs." Dr. Eve looked at Miriam. "First door on the right. Take your clothes off and get under the eiderdown. I'll call you in a couple of hours." She turned to Daniel. "Second door, same. You can share it with Ottershaw. There are two beds. Sleep. I shall call you in time. Breakfast at quarter-past seven, bacon and eggs, toast and marmalade. And then Mr. Foster will drive you to court."

"But what about you?" Miriam suddenly felt utterly confused and then dismayed.

"I shall take my breakfast with Mr. Fimber." Dr. Eve smiled. "I shall be first witness in rebuttal to Sir Barnabas Saltram. I will inform him of that in the morning. Now go and take care of your welfare. This is your battle, be ready for it. I shall be gone when you get up. Discipline! Discipline! We must fight him together. To lose will be very bad. Now go!"

They all stood up, stiff and dizzy with exhaustion. Miriam looked at Dr. Eve for a moment or two. She had no idea whether to trust this woman or not, but there was nothing else left.

She turned to Ottershaw, then Daniel, and

274

forced herself to smile. "Come on," she said warmly. "We must be awake tomorrow morning."

Daniel smiled, but in bleak amusement and gentleness. "It is tomorrow morning," he replied.

morning."

# CHAPTER TWELVE

A scarce couple hours later, Daniel woke
early with a pounding headache. It was still
dark outside, but he could no longer sleep,
no matter how profoundly he wanted to. He
rolled out of bed, leaving the all-too-brief
warmth. He washed in tepid water, shaved
carefully but not particularly well; he wanted
everyone's concentration to be on Saltram
anyway, not on himself.

He went downstairs, still fuzzy-minded,
and found Dr. Eve in the kitchen. "Good
morning," he said as cheerfully as he could
manage.

"Feel like hell?" she asked perceptively.
"Me, too. Thinking what I'm going to say,
regardless of what you ask me. He's clever,
you know."

Daniel ran his hands through his hair,
leaving it inevitably falling over his brow.
"Yes, I do know. So is Jessie Beale."

"She did it."

"Yes."

"You know?"

"Yes, I know now, but I can't prove it. And I can't ask anyone the questions that would prove it."

"You sure you know what they are?"

"No, I'm not sure," he admitted, looking up at her again. "I have to speak with Saltram this morning, before we start."

"Scared of him?" she said, raising one eyebrow curiously.

He thought for several moments, watching her. She was an extraordinary-looking woman, utterly comfortable with her eccentricity. Her short hair had a heavy natural curl. It was going very gray. He thought prematurely so, but he couldn't be sure. She had probably looked like that for twenty years and would for another twenty. She wore trousers like a man's and a burgundy velvet jacket. She was staring at him, waiting for an answer. His natural instinct was to lie to her, but he really did not want to do that. It would break something that could not easily be mended. An honesty that was only just beginning. "Yes," he admitted. "Not of what he can do, but of what I might try to do to win any way possible."

She smiled quite openly. "He has that effect on people, and then you despise yourself for letting him do that to you. He's wrong, you know, about heat and skulls. The trick is not only to prove the facts, but to make the jury want to believe you, and be glad when you show them that they can, and are still right to."

He looked at her, trying to read her face, what she was saying rather than just the words.

"Come on," she said sharply. "We laugh at who is funny, or embarrassing, and we believe what is most comfortable, even if it is ridiculous. We need to be satisfied with who we are, and that often depends on who everyone else is. We must work out who they are — the jury — and then tell them what they can accept."

He did not reply.

"For heaven's sake, the truth!" she said sharply. "But the part of it that they can accommodate, which is that Saltram is very clever and the time of science has come. But I am cleverer, in this instance. It is not only science that matters. It is all the things man has always believed about truth and religion, and everyday life."

"And how on earth are we going to do that?" he said incredulously.

"Carefully," she replied. "Very carefully, indeed. We will allow them to keep their faith and, above all, their dignity. We must let Mr. Fimber drag it all out, perhaps just a little reluctantly, as if he does not really want to believe it. He is one of them, not a fancy scientist."

"He's not like them," Daniel pointed out. "He's a lawyer, and very clever, and detached from most emotion. At least, in conversation."

"Rubbish!" she said succinctly. "He's an actor, like other lawyers, if he's any good. I must help him, that's all."

Daniel had the beginning of an idea, an understanding, and with it, hope. Jessie Beale had asked for Saltram, the best expert witness, to speak for her, but Fimber may just have found an equal or better in Dr. Hall.

"Leave it to me," she went on. "And don't forget, when I have given you all the testimony Fimber asks of me, you can always cross-question me." She smiled. "Now eat your breakfast. We haven't long. I'm going to see Mr. Fimber and you are going to see Saltram. He's your witness, for heaven's sake, man, play him!"

Daniel ate his bacon and eggs. She was an unexpectedly good cook, as if she had enjoyed doing it.

"What's wrong?" Saltram asked when Daniel arrived at his home and was shown into the dining room by a stiff-faced butler.

"Good morning, Sir Barnabas," Daniel replied. "Nothing yet, as far as I am aware, unless you have something that you have not told me." He sat down, uninvited. The butler withdrew.

Saltram did not offer Daniel tea. "To tell you what you do not know, young man, would take you the rest of your life," he said coldly. "Which I do not have to spare. Either you trust me, or you do not. I presume you do, since I got you out of your earlier case, which was in practical ways identical with this one. Why are you now beginning to panic? I assume Kitteridge has succumbed to his cold and you are taking the lead. A pity. You are not even competent, much less perceptive. But fortunately, you do not need to be. Ask me the questions and I shall answer them. That should not be beyond you."

"No, sir, it is just the same."

"Exactly! If the jurors are literate, they will be able to understand it. I shall explain it carefully. If you understand something yourself, it is usually possible to explain it to others, if they have any sense at all. You have Kitteridge's notes, haven't you?"

"Yes, sir."

"Then go and read them again, and leave me to my breakfast in peace. Stop being such an old woman."

"Yes, sir." Daniel stood up, careful to keep the smile from his face when he considered the *old woman* whom he hoped was going to utterly confound Sir Barnabas Saltram.

A small boy handed Daniel a piece of paper outside the courthouse, a message from Kitteridge which read simply: *Good luck. Your best might just be enough. T.K.*

It made no sense to let such a little thing matter, but it made Daniel feel less alone. He went inside with a lift to his step.

The court was silent, waiting for him, and it was cold, in spite of the number of bodies packed together in every row of the gallery. Perhaps it just seemed like so many because they all had winter coats on, several of them with fur collars.

Daniel knew exactly where Miriam and Ottershaw were sitting. If he turned, he would be able to see them. Surely his mother would be there, too, if he had time to look?

281

In the dock, Jessie Beale was sitting upright, her chin high, looking very pale and very brave and, compared to the guard who stood next to her, very small. Daniel caught her eye for an instant and saw a little smirk on her face. She knew better than to let anyone else even guess at it.

All the usual preliminaries had been dealt with. It was time for him to begin. He had already exercised a dramatic pause. Any more would look as if he was afraid.

"The defense calls Sir Barnabas Saltram," he said in a loud, slightly husky voice, still carrying with him the dregs of last night's all-too-brief sleep.

There was a moment of utter silence. No one sneezed, shuffled, or even cleared their throat. Seconds ticked by. This was not Saltram's revenge, was it? Simply not to show up at all, leave him standing there, looking foolish, intellectually naked?

No, thank the Lord, it was only another dramatic pause for effect, and to make him sweat a little.

Tall, graceful, and amazingly elegant in a perfectly fitting suit clearly made for him, Saltram walked up the aisle, looking neither right nor left. The room might have been empty, for any notice he took of it. He did not even glance at the table for the defense.

He stepped onto the witness stand and was sworn in. Only then did he turn and look inquiringly at Daniel.

Daniel smiled at him very slightly. "We have met before, Sir Barnabas, in very similar circumstances. I know your many accomplishments and your overwhelming qualifications, and much of your unique history." Be careful, he must not praise him too much, or people would become suspicious. "However, for the sake of those in this courtroom who might not have had a previous interest in such things, particularly if they should be one of the jurors, would you please tell us your qualifications in the field of forensic science, which studies what a dead body tells of how a person died . . . and has been a new and most brilliant light on the nature of crime in the last few years? Perhaps it is one of the most important sciences of this new century."

"Indeed, it is," Saltram agreed. "Not only in the study of bones, decaying flesh, and the time and nature of death, but in X-rays, which can see through living flesh to photograph bones, showing injury such as breakage. And in ballistics also, and in the pattern of bloodstains. I predict that within the lifetime of most of us here in this room, most crimes will be solved decisively, and within a week or two of their happening."

Daniel could feel his heart beating, and his mouth was dry. Saltram was staring back at him, as if he sensed battle. They both had something to prove. Daniel knew what it was for both of them. He prayed Saltram did not, and also that Saltram had not seen Evelyn Hall outside anywhere. She was not permitted in, of course, because she was to give testimony.

"You were good enough to testify in the case of the Crown versus Adwell, some six weeks ago, when you proved to the jury's satisfaction that a death very like this one was not demonstrably the crime we assumed."

There was a scuffle in the body of the court and a man with a white beard stood up and shouted. "Liar! Blasphemer! Defender of devils!"

"Sit down, sir," the judge said loudly, "or I will have you removed."

"I tell you, sin is sin, and all your newfangled ideas do not excuse it in the eyes of God. Judgment will be upon you!"

"Remove that man!" the judge ordered, and then sat silently as the usher removed him. He deliberately waited until the room was quiet, and then he proceeded. "Gentlemen of the jury, you must disregard the interruption." He turned to Daniel. "Please proceed."

Daniel picked up where he had been interrupted. "I say you were 'good' because you did it without charging your usual fee."

Saltram was puzzled at the compliment. Although it was true, he was perfectly aware that Daniel did not like him. He could not fail to be, after their last encounter. Good. The less certain he felt of the minor things, the more he might be careless in the things he thought were certain.

"Yes," Saltram agreed. "In the interest of justice, it is even more important to protect the innocent than it is to punish the guilty. Even the most passionate of lawyers have agreed on that. 'It is better that ten guilty men go free, rather than one innocent man be hanged.' The phrase goes something like that."

"Exactly," Daniel agreed, hoping he had not taken it too far.

"Or woman," said Sir Barnabas.

"May I take you through the evidence again, for the benefit of the jury? Forgive me if it seems tedious, but it may well be totally unknown to them. We tried to find a jury not predisposed to any particular decision."

"Of course," Saltram replied, with exaggerated patience, and he began again to describe the manner of death, the cause of death, and then evidence as to the ways it could be interpreted.

"So, you know that Adwell died quite quickly," Daniel interrupted him.

"Yes, that is quite plain from the fact that he did not breathe in more than the slightest amount of smoke. Had he died slowly, he would have breathed in a great deal more, and we would have found it in his lungs," Saltram said with very obvious patience.

"Thank you. I think that is clear to us all." Daniel looked inquiringly at the jury and saw the comprehension in their faces, and a sharpened interest. They did not know where he was going with this line of examining, but he was there to defend Jessie Beale. It had to be with some unforeseen alternative explanation.

The judge leaned forward. "I think you may take it, Mr. Pitt, that the court is with you. You do not need to sort out every detail. We are satisfied that the corpse is that of Robert Adwell, and that he died quickly. If you believe you can prove that it was not from a blow to the back of the head, please get on and do so."

"Yes, Your Honor." Daniel could not afford to move on too quickly. If the jury did not realize the importance of the details, they would not see how Dr. Eve destroyed them. They must see the complete edifice of reason before it would crumble before their eyes. Please, heaven!

"You examined the skull of Robert Adwell, Sir Barnabas?" he asked.

Saltram's expression was faintly supercilious. "Of course. I would not give an opinion on something I had not actually seen."

"Naturally." Daniel frowned. "This is a matter of life and death. Specifically, that of the accused, Jessie Beale. You are used to weighing evidence and giving such decisions. The gentlemen of the jury are not. You must help them to be comfortable that they have arrived at the truth."

The judge frowned and leaned forward again, as if to interrupt.

Saltram must have seen it. He answered Daniel that the discoveries he had made could be interpreted. He faced the jury, as if giving them the importance they deserved, and explained in some detail the structure of the human skull, the parts of the brain protected, and the brain's function in the whole of the body.

The judge may have intended to stop him, but he was as much caught up in the subject as everyone else. It was as if Saltram had woven a spell with his words, delicate as a spider's silk, and as strong. None of it was challengeable.

Daniel clung to his own confidence, his fingers clenched by his sides, as if it were a physical raft he held.

"And the heat can crack it?" he said simply, when Saltram stopped. "This marvelous helmet of bone can be split by heat alone, without any blow at all?"

"Only immense heat," Saltram said. "An enormously hot fire. Normally, an ordinary house fire, even a warehouse fire, does not reach that heat. And the inhalation of smoke and toxic gases would usually cause death sooner than that. There would be smoke in the lungs, even soot."

"And what happened in this case?" Daniel asked, hoping he was not exaggerating his air of innocence.

"An intense heat burned up very quickly indeed," Saltram replied, a little tensely.

"And how did that happen?" Daniel asked.

"An unusual element in the fire," Saltram replied. He was looking exclusively at Daniel now, presumably sensing something wrong. "Either an accelerant was used, as in deliberate arson, or accidentally, because it was already inside the building and close to the seat of the fire."

"Can you suggest such a substance?" Daniel asked innocently.

"You are young, Mr. Pitt, but don't pretend to be so naïve. You will have tested the site for such things. I suggest you have already found it. White phosphorous would be my guess, from this intensity of heat, in the region of five thousand degrees . . . or more."

"Precisely," Daniel agreed. "And this substance fits all you have concluded from the evidence, sir?"

"It does," Saltram replied. "I don't know what they were storing such a thing for, but it would answer every particular of the case, and of the previous case in which you had me testify."

"With no blow to the head, or to anywhere else."

"Exactly."

"Thank you, Sir Barnabas. We are greatly indebted to you for your skill and extraordinary studies. Will you please wait there, in case my learned friend, Mr. Fimber, has any questions to ask you?"

"Of course." Saltram turned very slightly in the witness stand, until he was facing Fimber.

Daniel felt his own muscles clench. Had

he done enough? Was Fimber going to stand up to Saltram? He looked mesmerized, like a man before a snake. Had they chosen the right course? Jessie was guilty, and probably not only of Adwell's death, but of Paddy Jackson's as well. They were going to rack up their ten guilty men going free rather quickly.

"Mr. Fimber," the judge said sharply, "have you any questions for Sir Barnabas?"

Fimber rose to his feet. "Certainly, this witness is very expert indeed, Your Honor. I fear I am not competent to question him in detail . . ."

"For God's sake!" The judge's anger finally ran over. "Then either get someone who is, or allow that the man knows what he's talking about and sit down!"

"Your Honor, with your permission — and Mr. Pitt's, of course — I would prefer to call a rebuttal witness, who I promise will be brief."

"A rebuttal to Sir Barnabas Saltram?" the judge asked incredulously.

"Yes, Your Honor."

"He'd better be good. I will not have any more time wasted."

"She is, Your Honor," Fimber assured him.

The judge looked with extreme disfavor at Miriam sitting in the front row. "I hope you are not going to embarrass Miss fford Croft and oblige me to point out in public that she is not qualified to testify at all, never mind to argue with Sir Barnabas. That would be —"

Fimber interrupted him. "No, Your Honor, not at all. I'm going to call Dr. Evelyn Hall, doctor of medicine and of forensic science, from the University of Amsterdam, professor of chemistry from the University of Paris, and —"

"Does she speak English?" the judge asked with complete bewilderment.

"Very well," he replied. "I believe she was born and raised in London."

"Then why Amsterdam?"

"Because the Dutch are rather ahead of us in realizing that some women have remarkable abilities . . ."

"Well?"

Fimber saw no need to push his luck.

The courtroom was still silent. Daniel could hear someone wheezing for breath two rows behind him. There was tension in the room. The previous outburst had not been entirely forgotten.

"Very well," the judge continued. "I do not wish to be reversed for such a reason. If Mr. Pitt has the nerve to try." He glanced momentarily at Daniel and away again.

"Can you call your doctor?"

Saltram was now sitting only a couple of rows away, to the right of where Daniel sat. The moment Daniel saw his face, he knew Ottershaw had made the right decision.

Dr. Eve came into the room like a roll of distant thunder, just enough to send a chill of warning down the spine, with the knowledge of a storm to come. She looked neither to the right nor left of her and took the oath with a clear, penetrating voice. Not that there was the slightest whisper to challenge her. On Fimber's prompting, she recited her impressive credentials and named some of the major courts in Europe where she had given expert evidence.

Fimber thanked her and took a step forward. Not threateningly, but as if he was going to speak to her privately, more as a friend than an inquisitor. "Dr. Hall, have you made many studies in the course of your practice as to the damage to skulls caused by intense heat from some fires? Particularly as such is involved in this case? I would like to be able to describe it to you, and will do so if His Honor insists, but only in such terms as —"

"I have," she interrupted, with a very slight smile. "I'm afraid the newspapers throughout the city have written it up extensively. You can't go down any street without seeing some headline of the latest revelation. And I am familiar with Sir Barnabas Saltram's cases, deductions, and opinions. You will not find any competent forensic scientist who is not."

From one unsolicited remark, she had dealt with the whole question of prejudgment.

The judge, who had leaned forward to intervene, sat back in his chair, a slight amusement evident in his face.

Saltram, too, looked mildly satisfied.

Daniel hoped profoundly that that was not going to be for long.

"Thank you, Dr. Hall," Fimber continued. "You will have seen many skulls cracked by heat in the course of your examination?"

"I have," she agreed, "and very many cracked by blows of some sort."

"May we dismiss all those, where no fire was involved?" Fimber asked politely.

"From suspicion of burning? Of course," she agreed.

"Thank you. Given only the bones, is there any way you can tell if the damage came from heat or a blow . . . beyond a reasonable doubt?"

"If there wasn't, there would be no point in my being here," she answered. "Sir

Barnabas Saltram does not need my opinion to bolster his own. The answer to your question is that sometimes there is, and sometimes there is not. There are several possibilities. I have brought a few examples in plaster, not actual bone. You may wish the jury to see the difference. And, of course, if you would like Sir Barnabas to examine them, I am perfectly agreeable. I observe that he is still here."

Everyone looked at Saltram.

He made a slight gesture of distaste. "Thank you, but I have no interest in seeing plaster of Paris mock-ups of past cases. I have already seen sufficient human skulls to be acquainted with them. Have your little sideshow, by all means. It will only prove to the jury what I have already said. Let us hope it will not sicken them."

"They are plaster, for heaven's sake," Dr. Eve spoke before Fimber could. "If their stomachs can take the description of what happens to flesh and blood of a human body in a fire of that heat, they can touch a plaster replica."

Fimber took a moment to compose his thoughts. Or perhaps it was to judge the mood of the jury.

Daniel looked at the jury and decided that they liked Dr. Eve, and liked the care she

294

was taking to make sure they understood precisely what she was explaining.

"Get on with it, Mr. Fimber," said the judge. "Show them your plaster skulls, by all means."

"Thank you, Your Honor," Dr. Eve answered, and signaled to the usher, who duly brought in two life-sized plaster skulls and had his assistant follow him with the third.

Dr. Eve thanked him and held up the first skull. "You see, gentlemen, where the skull is quite severely cracked here . . . and here." She pointed to the cracks above the back of the neck. Then she passed it to the usher, who took it to the jury, who all examined it with curiosity.

Daniel glanced at Saltram, whose impatience with the whole performance was evident in his expression.

"That is an exact copy, to the smallest fraction of an inch, of the skull of a thirty-five-year-old man who was struck by a heavy metal bar. As one may imagine, the injury was fatal."

They all looked at it gravely. Several actually touched it with their fingers.

Dr. Eve took the second skull. This one was broken on one side. "Beaten with a bottle in a bar brawl. Struck him on the temple, also fatal. But I suppose you have already deduced that." Her face twisted with a sad expression. "Those two injuries could not have been caused by a fire. This one, however, was. Here, you may examine this also."

She took the third skull, which was cracked across the top. "You will see the injury is in a different place altogether. You will no doubt have broken the glass of a window at some time in your lives, probably in your youth. Or someone else has, and you have seen the results. I am speaking specifically of the star-shaped central crack and the star-shaped web of cracks around it. Instinct, not science, will tell you that it has been struck at the central point. This crack has no point of impact. See?" She held it up for them to observe, then passed it to the usher, who carried it to them.

Daniel looked at Saltram, who moved restlessly, as if the seat was too small for him. His face registered irritation, and something else less easy to read.

"Yes, heat can crack bone, or break it, if it is sufficient," Dr. Eve continued. "But it does not do it in all places. If you think about it, it will make sense to you. A baby's skull takes some time to harden. To begin with, it's very vulnerable. And considering

296

how we come into this world, perhaps that is just as well."

There was a murmur of agreement from the jury and one or two sighs as well, from the body of the court, particularly from women.

"The pressures are not even," Dr. Eve said simply. "Heat will not break a skull at the base, where our victim's skull was broken. This was the result of a heavy blow, such as might be caused by a piece of lead piping or wood, if wielded with some weight behind it."

"Not heat?" Fimber said with wide eyes. "You are certain, Dr. Hall?"

"Yes, I am certain," she replied. "You may examine the skulls, if you wish."

"No, thank you," Fimber replied. "Perhaps when the jury has finished its use for them, the usher could remove them."

"They are a grim reminder of our frail and common humanity, are they not?" Dr. Eve agreed.

They waited while the last jurors looked at the skulls, lifelike, except for the uniform whiteness.

Fimber concluded with a few brief questions, then looked at Daniel. "If you care to cross-examine, Mr. Pitt," he invited.

"Yes, indeed I would." Daniel rose to his

feet. It was all up to him now. He must look as if he was desperately fighting for Jessie's innocence. While at the same time proving her actual guilt — beyond all doubt. And no one must realize he did it intentionally.

Dr. Eve had not told him what he was to ask her. He could swear with absolute honesty that she had given him no hint of what to do, and yet she had left him an opening. What on earth was it? He scrambled to recall everything they had said to each other. Every appeal they had discussed, when he was tired and he could not think anymore. What was the loophole she had left? What was the one weakness he could exploit? The crack in the case he could widen, until it was a gaping hole.

He started very carefully. She must be aware that he did not know what he was looking for. "There is a clear difference, when you point it out, Dr. Hall, between a crack from a blow and that from heat. You have shown us very dramatically. I cannot argue with it. I shall not try to. You must have studied the subject for many years, and with great understanding."

"Of course," she agreed. "As has Sir Barnabas Saltram."

"Indeed. Your qualifications — both yours and his — are, if not unique, at the very

298

least highly unusual."

The judge looked at Fimber, then at Daniel. "Mr. Pitt," he interrupted. "Are you in some way questioning Dr. Hall's abilities?" He said it with evident disfavor.

Dr. Eve smiled at Daniel and nodded imperceptibly. Or perhaps he imagined it. Then she looked at where Saltram was sitting, with a very slight smirk on his face. In the dock, Jessie Beale looked from one to the other, and for the first time seemed uncertain.

Daniel knew now what he was going to do. "Certainly not, Your Honor!" he replied with conviction. "I was going to point out that it takes remarkable intelligence, application, and years of dedicated study to know these things."

"Your point, Mr. Pitt, if indeed you have one?" the judge pressed.

"How could a relatively uneducated young woman, such as the accused, possibly have acquired it? Is she a hidden genius of medicine, pretending to be a very ordinary young woman working in a dockside public house, waiting on tables, living in a single rented room?"

There was a dumbfounded silence so complete that Daniel imagined he could hear people breathing.

Dr. Eve smiled directly at Daniel. He felt a shiver of apprehension.

This was the moment. This was the *thing* she had been leading up to.

"It is complicated. Not an easy subject at all," she replied. "But she is, I believe, a young woman of more than average intelligence and she was taught simply, step by step, by a master . . ." She hesitated.

Was it for effect? He did not think so. She was wanting him to interrupt her.

"A master?" he said softly. "Who taught her? When? How? And above all, for God's sake, why?"

"When?" Dr. Eve gave a very slight shrug. "About as long as six weeks ago. How? Very publicly, in an event very like this one. How? By explaining expertly, slowly and carefully, so that a jury might follow it step by step."

There was a gasp of indrawn breaths.

Daniel saw it all clearly. He did not even glance at Saltram, but he could see the cold, pale, handsome face as clearly as if it was right in front of him. He kept his eyes on Evelyn Hall.

"How a human head supposedly cracks in intense heat," she continued. "Such as that created by white phosphorous, for example. I believe there were traces of it in the fire that killed Paddy Jackson. And in this second one, which killed Rob Adwell, who was accused of having killed Jackson . . . and found not guilty by your brilliant defense of him. If you think back to that trial, you will realize that you yourself learned enough to notice it again. You may not like the comparison, but Miss Beale also noticed it. I can't say that she used it, but it seems by far . . ." She hesitated, then went on. "You did a good job with Rob Adwell. I think he may very well have been as innocent as he claimed, although the crime of which he was accused was no more an accident than this one. This time is an exact copy, down to the presence of white phosphorous accelerant to attain an extreme heat quickly. But it was a blow to the head that caused the death of Mr. Adwell, not the heat from the phosphorous. You ask how such an injury could happen twice and yet not be caused by the intense heat at all, although the phosphorous was also present? Two deaths in exactly the same circumstances? That is not for me to answer. I think the jury can manage it."

"I have no more questions of this witness, Your Honor," Daniel said.

Fimber bowed. "The prosecution rests," he said with a smile he could not conceal.

Thank heaven he did not actually look at Daniel.

The judge gave brief instructions. The jury retired. No one left the room. No one even stood up. Minutes ticked by. Five. Ten. Fifteen.

Daniel had been concentrating on not meeting Evelyn Hall's eyes. They must not seem to anyone to have had an agreement. They had not won yet, but he could not help looking at Miriam, the light shining on her bright auburn hair, making her impossible to ignore. Ottershaw, with his untidy white hair, looked like a small snowstorm beside her.

As if she felt Daniel's gaze on her, she turned and looked at him, almost smiling, as if she could sense victory within her grasp.

Daniel looked away. Not yet. Not yet. And he caught Saltram's eyes on him, with a look of such intense hatred, a sudden understanding of something extremely new to him. It chilled to the bone.

Thirty minutes. The jury returned. They had reached a verdict: Guilty.

They did not say anything else, not that they believed Jessie Beale to have also been guilty of the murder of Paddy Jackson, but it was in the air, dark and unspoken. There was a finality to it. At least Daniel thought so.

Now he looked at Jessie. She was ashen, bewildered, as if she could hardly believe it. Then a strange change came over her as she realized it was true. She had played a great game with fate . . . and had lost. She lifted her chin a little higher. No one would see her weep. If she wept at all, it would be alone.

# CHAPTER THIRTEEN

At first, Daniel was too dazed by the fact that they had won to take in all the other possible implications of the victory. Of course, it looked like a loss to anyone who did not know the truth of it, but it was the right verdict, they all knew that. Daniel and Miriam, Ottershaw and Dr. Hall had done everything they could to bring it about, and that was something they all knew must never be said. It was better that even Marcus not be told in so many words. He was definitely wise enough to know that their silence and his ignorance were best.

It was the look on Saltram's face that Daniel would not forget. He was white with rage. He spoke to no one and strode past the assembled journalists jostling him with questions, as if he did not see them.

Daniel found Miriam. He wanted to hug her with the wave of gratitude and shared victory that overwhelmed him. He had his arms tightly around her before he realized it was possibly inappropriate. "Sorry," he murmured, without letting her go. "But we did it. We did it!"

"I know." She put her cheek to his for a moment, hesitated, then unhooked her arms from around his neck and stepped back. She looked up at him. "We did. I think it was mostly Dr. Eve. I never saw even a flicker of fear in her, but she had to know we just as easily could have lost. I would like to fight like that — without thinking of loss, because I know the cause is right."

He looked at her dark blue eyes. "You must keep your fear hidden from everyone else."

She hesitated. "Perhaps not everyone," she said quietly. "Should they know if I doubt myself? Or not?"

"There's no simple answer to that," he replied. "But what matters is we fixed our mistake. Let's go and celebrate." He looked over Miriam's shoulder, to Dr. Eve, and beyond her, to Ottershaw. "Let's go and have dinner in the best place in the area. Then afterward, I'll go and tell Kitteridge."

It was in the chambers of fford Croft and Gibson early the following morning, where Daniel and Kitteridge were sharing a fresh pot of tea laced with a dash of brandy, ostensibly against the cold, but actually in celebration — when Impney knocked on the door and came in.

"Mr. Pitt, there is a lady to see you, sir. May I take the liberty of bringing an extra cup for her? She looks perished with cold, sir, and her coat is little help against the wind."

"Who is she?"

"Her name is Mrs. Adria Leigh, sir. I said you would at least listen to her."

It was definitely a liberty that he should do this, but the look on Impney's face of polite innocence and determination was unmistakable. Daniel thought of telling the clerk not to do that again but, seeing the expression in his eyes, changed his mind. "By all means, another cup. And I suppose you'd better bring a jug of hot water, too, but no more brandy."

"Yes, sir. Thank you, sir."

"You're going to regret this," Kitteridge said with a sniff. He reached for his handkerchief and blew his nose. "Have you the slightest idea who she is?"

"I have a terrible idea who she is," Daniel replied. And so he did. He would have loved to have turned her away, but it was impossible. He would regret it either way.

"You don't learn, do you?" Kitteridge observed tartly. "Another woman to eat you up and then spit you out?"

"We won, Toby. Jessie Beale was guilty and she was found guilty. She will likely hang, which I don't approve of, but I don't approve of burning people to death either. You can take a piece of cake and go away, if you want."

"It's my damn office, Pitt!" Kitteridge protested.

The door opened and Impney held it for the woman, who came in. She was very thin, but she stood upright. Her dark hair was graying, although still thick. She had a curious face, not beautiful in any traditional sense, but it had a great dignity, almost a grace that was more profound.

Both Daniel and Kitteridge rose to their feet.

"Mrs. Leigh, sir," Impney spoke to Daniel, introducing her. "Mr. Daniel Pitt, ma'am."

"How do you do, Mr. Pitt?" She held out her hand, as a man might have, and her voice was pleasantly low. She had no gloves, and her hands were like ice.

"Have some tea, Mrs. Leigh, and some cake," Daniel offered. "It's really very good. This is my associate, Mr. Kitteridge." Daniel was in fact the associate, but this seemed hardly the time to make such a distinction. The woman was clearly in considerable distress.

Daniel indicated the chair for her, and they all sat.

Impney had brought the jug of hot water, another cup, and an extra plate for the cake.

Daniel served them and then turned to her. "What can I do for you, Mrs. Leigh?"

She was shivering, but whether it was from cold or nervous tension, he could not tell. Rather than prompt her, he decided to wait.

She did not look at him, but somewhere beyond him, as if she dared not see rejection or any kind of judgment in his face. "Mr. Pitt, you won the case against Jessie Beale yesterday, even though Sir Barnabas Saltram spoke for her." She almost choked on the terror rising up inside her.

"No, Mrs. Leigh," he said gently. He had an appalling idea where she might be going with this. "I was defending Miss Beale."

"But she was guilty?" she stammered.

"Yes, I know, but even the guilty have the right to a defense. Somebody has to fight for them. You never know who is innocent until you test it. Someone —" He stopped. He was walking right into the trap. She had not even lured him, he had done it himself.

"Yes," she admitted quietly. "Somebody has to speak up for them. You are too young to remember the Marguerite Daventry case twenty years ago. I dare say you are not much more than that."

"I'm twenty-five," he corrected. Those few years made all the difference.

"The same age as my son," she said, her voice almost choked to silence.

Kitteridge sat in total stillness. One could almost have forgotten he was there.

"You're right," Daniel said. "I don't remember the case, but my father does. He has told me about it, because of Sir Barnabas Saltram's part."

"Exactly," she said, at last meeting his eyes, and with an intensity she had not allowed herself to show before. "Sir Barnabas defended Daventry then, with the same arrogance he used to save Robert Adwell, and with Jessie Beale. Until Dr. Hall showed it could be broken."

"Mrs. Leigh, it won't work as a defense anymore if the evidence is examined better."

"Sir Barnabas isn't God now," she said across him, urgent now.

Was she confident, or desperate? He knew it was the latter. Should he say that he knew who she was? Cut off the hope before it grew too tight? "Mrs. Leigh, was it your husband who was blamed for the fire that killed Marguerite Daventry?"

"Yes." Her voice was barely audible. "He was hanged for it and they are still blaming us, my son and me. He was only five." Her words were swallowed in tears.

He took out his clean handkerchief and gave it to her. Kitteridge passed his over as well.

She fought back tears and finally won, and looked up at Daniel again. "If Saltram was wrong over Jessie Beale — and he was — he could have been wrong over Lady Daventry, too. He can be wrong: you proved it for everyone to see."

He hated saying it, but it was the glaring fact none of them could escape. "But Daventry was tried for the murder of his wife and found not guilty," he said as gently as he could. The words were violent, because the meaning was. "He can't be tried again, regardless if we could prove it beyond any doubt at all. The law says you cannot be tried twice for the same crime."

"I know." She gulped. "But it would prove my husband was innocent and I need that for my son. She was loved, you know, Marguerite Daventry. People remember. They still speak of her. They won't give her murderer's son a chance. Not at school, nor at work, not anywhere. He's an outstanding cricketeer, and they won't let him on the village team." She swallowed, gasping for air, and finally gave in and wept quietly.

"For God's sake, Pitt, you're forever tilting at windmills," Kitteridge said urgently. "If ever a case needed kicking over, it's this. If you don't, you'll regret it the rest of your life."

Daniel stared at him. "I'll probably regret it if I do," he said softly between his teeth.

"So at least do the right thing." Kitteridge sneezed, and sneezed again. "I'll help you."

Mrs. Leigh looked up slowly. Hope made her face beautiful.

Every instinct told Daniel to leave it alone, and every emotion told him to accept it. He might undo at least a small measure of the damage. "Yes, Mrs. Leigh, I'll try."

She nodded, too full of emotion to speak again.

"You . . . what?" Marcus's face was about as white as his hair.

Daniel had expected this. Maybe not quite so fierce, but something like it. "He might not have been guilty . . ." he began.

"Listen to me!" Marcus half rose in his chair. "You . . . imbecile! Leigh was hanged

311

because he set the fire that killed her. They thought it had to be Daventry, but what's-his-name . . . Saltram showed how human skulls, or any other, for all I know, can crack in the heat of a fire, if it's white hot, and this one was. It burned the whole wing of the house, burned it to the ground. Leigh might not have known whether Marguerite was in it or not; it's still a crime within a crime. You know that as well as I do. You know that if in the course of committing a crime someone dies, the death is murder."

"They charged Daventry with it at first," Daniel pointed out, although it was an argument he was bound to lose. Marcus would never let them lodge this appeal. But he had to try his hardest, in order to face Adria Leigh, let alone her son, who was so unfairly blamed for his father's misfortune.

"So they did," Marcus agreed. "And he was found not guilty. Saltram's defense. Of course, it wasn't known as that then. But it damned well is now! It introduced Saltram to top society and he never looked back."

"Well, that's the way he's going to look now." Daniel made it a statement.

"Don't be absurd," Marcus snapped. "Wasn't defending Jessie Beale enough for you? Don't think I don't know it was Evelyn Hall who got you out of that fiasco."

312

"Did Miriam —" Daniel started.

"Miriam didn't tell me anything," Marcus replied. "Neither did Kitteridge, for that matter. But I still have a head on my shoulders and though I may not remember all the cases I ever fought, I know the law and I know lawyers. What do you think is going to happen when you start reversing decisions, eh?" His eyes widened. "You want to relitigate the cases that might be affected? Have you even thought of that? Retry one in ten? Two? Half of them? How about all of them? And if we go back twenty years, to Daventry and Leigh, how much further? When does it stop, eh?"

"No, just this one —" Daniel began.

"So, you do this one and leave every other chambers in London to do the rest?"

Answers came into Daniel's mind, and he knew they were useless even before he bothered to put them into words. Marcus was right. Every other case Saltram had given evidence in, or even affected, would be open to question, and possible retaliation.

"You'll be public enemy number one," Marcus went on. "They'll blame *you,* not Saltram, for disturbing the rats' nest. They were happy with him."

"Even though he was wrong?" Daniel said

indignantly. "What happened to 'It is better that ten guilty men go free than one innocent man is hanged'? Forget that, did we?"

"Oh, Daniel," Marcus said wearily. "You believe every damn thing you hear? If it's too bloody uncomfortable, refuse to believe it!"

"You don't mean that."

"I didn't when I was your age, but I don't even remember that far back now. In fact, I don't remember quite a lot of things. Miriam tries to keep me from realizing it, but I know. And if we undertake this idealistic crusade, what happens to her when we all find there's no work coming our way, eh? Thought of that?"

"No," Daniel admitted quietly. "Are you saying it's not worth the price?"

"No! I'm asking you, do you know what the price is? Have you thought further ahead, to the next step?"

"Not . . . not far," Daniel said. "Do you ever see further than the next step?"

"No, not with cases that are really worth fighting. You dig up a toe bone; you have no idea what sort of a monster it belongs to."

"If I lose," Daniel started, "will that be the end of it? I could do it outside chambers." The rest of what he had been going to say made no sense. He let it go.

"Oh, you'll do that all right," Marcus said. "Was *Don Quixote* part of your education? No one ever won against a windmill, but you might make people think very hard about other cases that weren't ever questioned before. Do you think Saltram will stand by and let that happen? Really?"

"But he was wrong!" Daniel protested. "The jury decided against him. You can appeal for Jessie, if you want, but it won't change anything because she's guilty. Even she didn't deny it."

"Not to you," Marcus pointed out. "I think part of her enjoyed your knowing, and still having to fight for her. But to the court she denied it. She will say whatever she thinks will best serve her interests, either to earn clemency or at least to have revenge. Never assume she doesn't know you, how you meant to get the verdict you did. You asked Dr. Hall the question that gave her the chance to blow the case wide open."

Daniel felt a chill inside him. "Are you saying Saltram will fight any appeal of the Daventry case verdict?"

"I'm saying he's badly wounded, for which he will not forgive you. I'm saying, if you're going hunting for bear, you'd better carry a heavy enough shot to finish him off. You don't want a wounded bear coming after you for revenge. And even more, you don't want two of them."

"Are you telling me to get out of the woods, or to get a bigger gun?"

Marcus smiled very sweetly. It was an oddly benign expression. "My dear boy, I'm not telling you anything, except the facts as I believe them to be. If you can prove them wrong, you have obliged the law to retry a number of cases in which his evidence was crucial. You may have righted many injustices, and you will have upset an unknown number of lawyers and delighted many others. You will have made an enemy for life in Saltram."

"Is that the measure of it?" Daniel asked. Even before he said the words, he knew he would regret them. But the question was valid.

"No," Marcus answered without the slightest hesitation. "But you have to know."

"What is the measure of it?"

"The law," Marcus replied. "If you know the truth at all, you have to pay for it, sooner or later. The price has no end. It can grow like a secret beast inside you, getting hungrier and hungrier, a debt that gathers interest, and you never know when you have to pay back the principal."

"So, I had better not borrow." It was not a question. It was the conclusion.

"Is that what you think I mean?" Marcus sounded puzzled.

"Don't you?"

"No. I don't think I do. You will poke the bear anyway. And if you don't, you will always regret it, because you will think that you could've won and you will blame yourself for not trying. And whether Mrs. Leigh blames you or not, you will believe that she does. I'm not telling you what to do; I'm telling you what it will cost."

"Cost me?"

"Cost everyone, Pitt. You don't stand alone in this. We all have things to gain and to lose. Saltram is quite clever enough to make your family and friends pay, not just you."

"Or the people I defend?" Daniel finished for him.

"Yes, them also," Marcus agreed. "And there will be people you don't expect who will join him, because he has friends. And more powerful than that, he has people who want to keep the same secrets he does."

"You mean other people whose guilt he covered?" Daniel asked, although he knew the answer. He felt a dreadful hollow inside himself and no way to fill it. Who else would suffer? His family? Marcus and the whole of fford Croft and Gibson? Miriam? Kitteridge? Even Ottershaw? Had he the right to make these decisions alone?

Marcus did not move. Daniel looked at him and knew he was not going to help. Should he ask his father? Pitt might have a better idea of what could happen. The risk . . . or the prize. Or perhaps he would tell him gently to grow up and make his own decisions.

What if Aunt Vespasia were still alive? He knew what she would say: *Fight the bastard! If you go down, do it with all flags flying. Never give up without a shot fired. You never know who else will come to your side.*

"No one else is going to fight for Leigh, are they?" he asked. "If I turn away from that, I'll never face forward again. If you need to dismiss me . . ." His voice was shaking. "Then do. I've given Mrs. Leigh my word."

"Are you graciously trying to give me a way of escape?" Marcus inquired. "Or just insulting me?"

"What?" Daniel was momentarily confused.

"Oh, just go and do it, you damn fool!" Marcus replied. "When you've got it all together, bring me the plea and I'll file it.

Just leave Miriam out of it. She can get into enough trouble without your help."

"Yes . . . sir." Daniel was overwhelmed, grateful, relieved, and terrified. "Do you think she'll listen if I tell her she can't be involved?"

Marcus ran his hand through his hair. "Not a chance in hell, boy, but try anyway."

"Yes, sir."

"Then get on with it."

"Yes . . . sir!"

# CHAPTER FOURTEEN

"Don't involve your mother," Thomas Pitt said earnestly. He was in his office in the Lisson Grove headquarters of Special Branch. It was half-past seven in the morning and he had come in specifically to meet Daniel, insisting on talking here and not at home. That would have been easier, and far more comfortable, but Charlotte could not have helped overhearing. He had never lied to her, even by implication, but there were whole worlds of things he had not told her — dark, frightening, and ugly things she did not need to know. She helped him most in her silent understanding of what he could share and what he could not, offering comfort and belief in him without needing to be told the details.

How much would he be able to do the same for his son, who sat opposite him, so tense his body was misshapen in his clothes because of the awkward angle at which he sat? When Daniel was a little boy, Pitt had been able to read his moods with ease. But since leaving for university, an experience Pitt had never had, Daniel had been a separate man with a different background, a different education, a different social class from his father. Pitt only occasionally remembered that he was the son of a gamekeeper unjustly convicted of theft. Daniel was the son of a policeman risen in ranks through determination and remarkable ability, to become head of Special Branch. One of the last men to be knighted by the old Queen before her death.

Daniel had had a youth of high privilege. He himself did not fully realize how high. He might well be reminded, if he followed this crazy crusading path of trying to clear the name of a young laborer executed, almost certainly wrongly, for the murder of Marguerite Daventry. And yet Pitt knew how Daniel would be denying not his social heritage, but his emotional one, his belief in justice, if he turned away from it. It would bring him a lifetime of regret, even guilt, that he would never erase.

Pitt himself had taken on lost causes, battles he could not win, even though he had sworn he would not. He could not save his own father. He had been a child when his father had been unjustly accused of theft. The nightmares inspired by that event still came back to him once in a while, the feelings of helplessness, standing by while those you love are destroyed by injustice. Sometimes in dreams he was standing on the shore when a great wave came out of nowhere and swept him away, as if he had been a mere cork on its surface.

Could a child inherit your dreams, your nightmares, without realizing they were not his own?

And Charlotte? She too had chased uncertain ends. And she had done this before Pitt had ever known her. If the cause awakened her anger or her pity, she had always jumped in without looking first. She still did. It was one of the things in her he loved the most deeply. Courage. Empathy. How could he expect Daniel to be different?

Daniel was looking at him now with disbelief. They were sitting on either side of Pitt's huge carved desk, bookcases lining nearly all the walls, only leaving the windows and a few spaces for old pictures brought from Pitt's home: landscapes, black-and-white drawings of bare trees in the wind.

"I mean, don't discuss it with her," Pitt amended. "She will only feel that she ought to help, and she can't."

"I know that!" Daniel said sharply. "I don't want help either, I just want advice. And I can't get out of this with any decency, so don't tell me how to." There was defiance in his eyes.

Was he afraid his father was going to be defensive of him? Heavy-handed? He was wrong. Pitt must make sure he was wrong. That was another loss this miserable case might bring. Growing up, letting go of childhood trusts and dependencies carried its own dangers, whoever you were.

"You can follow the facts wherever they seem to lead you, or you can decide what the truth is and then look for the facts that seem to prove it. The honest way lies somewhere between the two. In this case, by all means, lean a little toward the evidence that may disprove Leigh was guilty. It will be a lot harder to find. The other will come to you without effort." What he really wanted to do was warn Daniel against the enemies he would make in pursuing this case — and not only Saltram.

"What else?" Daniel saw the hesitation rather than heard it.

Pitt realized, not for the first time, that Daniel had known him for as long as he had known Daniel.

"You were going to warn me of something," Daniel prompted him.

Pitt did not argue. "I don't know if Saltram has many friends, in the sense of people who like him, but he has many people who owe him their success, or even their freedom. He probably has debts he can call in, in places we have no idea."

"Defendants?" Daniel asked.

"No, people who never even came to trial. We don't know everybody who might have been ruined but for Saltram, but you can bet everything you have that he has a list of them. And precisely what they could still lose if certain cases were opened up again." He saw the doubtful look on Daniel's face. "More importantly for us, they will know it," he added. "To stretch the metaphor a bit, you won't be able to find room to set your foot without standing on some sleeping dog's tail."

Daniel smiled crookedly. "I'm beginning to realize that, but it's wrong. Someone has got to disturb it, someday. Can sleeping dogs be said to breed? Like lies? Or do we find the lie easier to live with? I don't want to be part of that."

Sometimes Daniel looked so young that Pitt wondered if he had ever felt like that, and then knew that he had. Special Branch had obliged him to make some very hard decisions, and a few of them had been less good than others. But worse was to abdicate all responsibility and let it lie, hidden from view, until the poison reached everyone.

Daniel looked at him, waiting.

"Warn Mrs. Leigh," Pitt went on. "Don't let her walk into this imaginary victory as if it were certain. It's not. In fact, it's not even likely. And Saltram isn't the only one who fears the truth. There will be a lot of people who don't want old cases retried, either in a court of law or in the court of public opinion. And you won't always know who they are until it's too late."

Daniel looked a little paler, a little more awkward in his chair. "I'll tell her. I won't pretend to her that I'm confident, only that I'll do my best."

"And you won't be insulted if she changes her mind?" Pitt asked.

For a moment Daniel's expression was comical. "Insulted? I'll be intensely relieved! As if I've escaped . . . I don't know . . . something very bad indeed."

"It's your decision."

"No, it's not, it's hers. But I'll be honest," Daniel said earnestly.

"Well, be honest with yourself first," Pitt told him. "And . . ."

"Yes?"

"Call me anytime you need to talk."

Daniel smiled and then climbed to his feet. "Thank you."

Daniel went to visit Adria Leigh at her home in East London, where she had promised she would be. She opened the door immediately, as if she had been standing behind it, and then blushed as she realized how obvious she must appear. He wondered whether to try to seem casual, but the hope and fear in her eyes made pretense absurd.

"Would you like tea," she asked, "or anything else?" She led the way straight into the kitchen.

He barely looked to one side or the other. It was obvious that she lived in this room. It was very bare and cold, and although it contained more than many people had, it was still poverty. There was no covering it. Everything was threadbare, mended several times over.

Should he accept tea? It might be the last she had. But pride was worth more at the moment. "Thank you, that will be very nice," he replied. "I have quite a few questions to ask you."

"Then you might . . ." She bit back the final words. They were not necessary to say; they both knew what they were. Still, she hesitated.

"Things I need you to know, before we begin," he said. "To make certain you understand, and are sure this is what you want to do."

She tried to smile, but instead her eyes filled with tears. "You mean you really will take the case? I don't know how I will pay you, but I will, I promise."

She had nothing, he could see that. What could he say that would not be patronizing? "I have other reasons for wanting to see Dr. Saltram discredited, Mrs. Leigh. We'll put it together and decide who owes what to whom, if we win. If we lose, there will be nothing to share anyway. Is that fair?"

She started to say something and then choked on the words. She turned to the sink to fill the kettle with water and then poked the fire in the stove, and put another piece of wood on it to heat the water.

"What do you want to ask me?" She had been holding back the words as long as she could.

"I can read most of the facts from the trial transcript," he replied. He had already done so. It was bleak and told him little except that it had been a trial without any balance of proof against Leigh, who was convicted in the eyes of the jury from the start. He

327

was a young man of charm who had not yet developed any other skills. He had come from an ordinary background, his father a laborer, his mother a cook. He was an only son with three sisters. His family had stayed loyal to him, at least on the outside, but it had broken them.

At the time of Marguerite's death, he had been married, with a young child. After his hanging, the widow had moved and taken whatever work she could to support herself and her child. People believed him guilty because the alternative would have implicated them all in his death. No one wanted that on their consciences. Any alternative was better than that.

Adria was waiting, watching Daniel's face.

"Tell me about Daventry," he asked. "And tell me the truth, as you saw it then. What kind of a man was he? What was Marguerite like? Honestly — not what the newspapers or the Daventrys' friends say."

She looked a little puzzled.

He was not being clear enough. "Somebody set that fire," he explained. "The firemen and the police are both certain it was not an accident. If it was not your husband, who was it? Someone who hated Daventry? A long-time enemy? Or somebody who needed something in the house destroyed?

Evidence of something? Vengeance for an old wrong? Or a recent one? Did they mean to kill Marguerite, or was it just chance that she was there?"

A light of understanding came into her eyes.

He smiled. "Someone did it. So they were there, with all the makings of arson. What did they intend? And if they meant exactly what happened, was it to punish Marguerite? To punish Daventry? Or just to destroy the house?"

"It would point to them," she said slowly. "So, they would be delighted to find someone else to blame. They might even have designed it that way."

"Yes," he agreed. "But they won't be at all happy to have these things dug up again now, perhaps even less happy than they were then. And not only whoever was guilty, but others who have secrets that this inquiry might open up. Accidental damage on the side, so to speak." He watched her face. It was clear she had not thought of such a thing. All she wanted was what was left of her life back; some hope for her son.

"I'm sorry," he said gently. "I know it's terrible. All sorts of people might suffer. That's what investigations do. Almost always someone suffers who is not guilty of the main crime. But we all have things we are ashamed of, or that embarrass us. Lies told that we don't want exposed now. It's not your fault, and you've paid for it too long already."

"And my son?"

"I'm sure your husband and your son deserve justice. I don't know what the truth will be, or what else it will pull out of the darkness. Or who it will cost. I don't even know if we'll find it. I know it will hurt some people, and probably help others, and I would be prepared to wager my house, if I had one, that a lot of people will do anything they can to keep it hidden. But I am prepared to search for it, if you are willing to take the risk."

"I haven't much to lose," she said, with a tiny, bleak smile. "It is Richard's chance in life. It's all I can give him."

"If at any time you change your mind, it might be too late to stop, but I will do whatever you wish," he promised. "Now tell me about Daventry. And Marguerite."

She thought for several moments, as if weighing every word before she started. "She was beautiful," she began finally. "A mass of dark hair, high cheekbones." She touched her own, as if to emphasize the point. "She was always elegant. She wore beautiful clothes, and she laughed a lot. Sometimes it was because she saw the absurdity in things, but sometimes I thought it was because inside she was sad, and she was determined no one should see it. She liked to go riding alone. She was a very good rider."

"How do you know all of this?" he interrupted. Surely she had not been at Daventry Hall to see Marguerite so often.

"My husband told me," she replied. "But on the occasion I was at Daventry Hall, I could see it for myself."

"Why were you there?"

"I'm a good seamstress. I used to embroider linens and things. I did some work for Lady Marguerite. And I mended the good linen, table linen, when it got damaged."

"I see." He could picture it in his mind. Adria depended for work on people who owned embroidered silks and linens. He could imagine how few that was, and that, when her husband was convicted, the word got round and the work disappeared. He refused to think of it. Such pain was disabling, and pity helped nothing. But perhaps he could help now. "And Daventry?" he urged.

"He was very proud." Again, she seemed to be searching for the right words. "Of himself. Of the house and the grounds, the stables. But particularly of her, of Marguerite. Like a man who loves things, great works of art, and wants his neighbors to come and see them, one by one. I made a lace collar once for a lady whose husband bought a small painting by Rubens from Daventry."

"Did you ever see it?" Daniel asked.

"Once. It was lovely, not really like any ordinary picture. It was almost as if it were lit from the inside. Does that sound silly?"

"Not at all. Some pictures are like that. And some people, too. They carry their own light." His thoughts turned first to his mother, then to Miriam. She was also so intensely alive, as if all her senses were concentrated at the same time. She took some of the light with her when she went away, leaving him suddenly aware of his loneliness. Had Marguerite Daventry been like that? In which case, she might well have stirred all kinds of emotions in others, good and bad, and left room for so many misunderstandings. "Thank you," he said. "I won't go and look at Daventry Hall myself. It would have changed a great deal in twenty years. Has Sir Roger married again?"

"I don't know," she admitted. "I have never wanted to go back either. It's . . ."

"I'm sure it must be terribly painful."

"Yes."

He stayed a little longer, trying to think of anything else to ask her, including whether she was absolutely certain she wanted to go ahead with the plea.

She thought for several seconds, then said "Yes" quite clearly, and looked straight at him. "I am quite sure. If I don't, I will always think I could have tried."

Daniel spent the rest of the day reading yet again all he could find out about the case of Sir Roger Daventry, his family, his career, his wealth, and his reputation.

The next day he set out for Herefordshire on the train from London. His intention was to visit those of Marguerite's family who still lived in the area. He took a small overnight bag with him, in case he could not accomplish it all in one day.

He had made an appointment with Gerard Forrester, Marguerite Daventry's younger brother who was now in his late forties and a very successful dealer in rare books. He was a handsome-looking man, and Daniel could easily believe he had been very dashing in his twenties, when Marguerite had died. Now he had not the energy of youth, but he made up for it with an air of grace, although he was clearly reluctant to speak to Daniel.

Gerard welcomed him into an east-facing office very carefully decorated with an exquisite landscape painting dominating the best-lit wall.

"Yes," he said, noticing Daniel's attention to it. "It's a minor Turner. Lovely, isn't it? I would have one of his major works, but who could afford any of those? Did you know that all those marvelous sunsets he painted were real? The effect of an eruption of Krakatoa, on the other side of the world. Ash in the air all over the globe. Amazing how one thing affects another, isn't it? What can I do for you? Marguerite's death was twenty years ago." He indicated a chair for Daniel to sit down and did so himself in one behind the desk. "All I really remember is the grief."

"I'm sorry to rake it up again," Daniel said. "But certain recent cases connected only by fire and evidence have raised many questions."

Gerard's eyebrows rose. "Such as what? For heaven's sake, man, the whole damn east wing burned to the ground. That was self-evident at the time. Daventry's rebuilt it since then, but it looks new, out of place." He shrugged. "Maybe it's only because my sister died in it, but I hate the place."

"And Daventry himself?" Daniel asked. Seeing the stricken look on Gerard's face, he regretted asking so bluntly.

"Never liked the chap much," Gerard said quickly. "But then, I probably never would have thought anyone was good enough for Marguerite. She was special."

"Didn't Daventry think so, too?" Daniel asked.

Gerard shrugged. "In his own way, I suppose. But . . . no, not really . . . enough." He went on to outline, in his opinion, what Marguerite deserved.

Daniel listened and wondered how much was rose-tinted by loss. Some people sanctify those who die young and remember only what was best in them. He wondered how much Gerard blamed Daventry for her death, obliquely, if not outright. He thought about Jemima, his own sister, and realized that if anything happened to her, if she died young, perhaps he would remember only the good things. It was a natural instinct, even if it would not be very helpful in forming a picture of her.

Finally, he thanked the man for his time and left.

It took him an hour to reach the small town in which Marguerite's sister, Antonia

Llewellyn, lived. He had agreed to meet her in a tea shop. Neutral territory, as it were, and more or less in public.

He had been waiting almost half an hour and was getting impatient when a woman came in with a gust of wind from the open door. She was fairly tall, slender, with a mass of unruly but very beautiful black, heavily curling hair. She gave the air of loveliness, femininity, and total confidence.

"Mr. Pitt?" she asked, coming straight to his table. Perhaps he was the only man sitting alone, obviously waiting for someone.

He rose to his feet. "Yes, Mrs. Llewellyn."

"Of course!" She smiled widely and allowed him to pull out a chair for her. She sat in it, and immediately a waitress came over.

They ordered tea and she spoke straightaway, no pleasantries. "You've already been to see Gerard, and so you have his vision of the perfect woman. Marguerite was better than that."

"Better than perfect?" he asked with a smile of doubt.

"Definitely! Real! Isn't real better than ideal? Formed only by your imagination? Answering your dreams?" She looked at him, as if half expecting disappointment.

"Yes," he said with certainty. He had no

idea why, but he thought of Miriam and the sudden realization that she could so easily be hurt over things that seemed trivial to him. And yet she was brave in others, so decisive where he hesitated. "Of course," he added. "Tell me how she really was."

Antonia smiled. "She could laugh uproariously. Sometimes we laughed so hard we couldn't get our breath, couldn't stop, even if it was inappropriate. I don't have anyone I can laugh with like that." She shook her head, as if angry with herself for acknowledging the loss. "She made some unsuitable friends, even I could see that, and I'm not always wise. She was untidy. She flirted, I'm afraid. I don't think she even knew she was doing it. It infuriated Roger. And it never occurred to him that he bored her to death. I don't think she did it to annoy him. Although, on second thought, it's possible. She was quick-tempered, but she was also quick to forgive. Whereas he never forgave. He stored up injustices as if they were gold or animals that could breed, if he fed them and kept them warm. She said that. It's a disgusting thought, isn't it?"

"Obscene," he agreed with feeling.

The waitress brought them tea and toasted tea cakes with currants baked into them. He could have eaten all of them. He must be careful not to take more than his share.

"Do you think Daventry killed her?" he asked.

She drew in her breath sharply. "What? And the great Sir Thingummy Saltram be wrong?" Then suddenly her face was totally solemn. "I hope not, because if he did, that man we hanged was innocent. And that's hideous. He had a wife, you know, and a young child. That's horrible." Her face was filled with grief at the thought. "Is that why you're here?"

"Yes."

"But Saltram explained it all, about heat cracking bone." She shuddered and looked down at the uneaten piece of tea cake. "How can it be?"

"He's right in some cases, but heat cracks bone in certain patterns," he explained. "I've just won a case on that, and lost one. The first time, I was wrong. I was taken in, in just the same way as the jury in Marguerite's case, and the jury in the one I tried. I lost the second one and . . . it's a long story."

"Tell me anyway," she said. "Please, I really want to know."

He told her about Saltram appearing as an expert witness in Adwell's defense, and then Jessie Beale asking for him in hers. It embarrassed Daniel to admit how easily he

338

had been taken in, but he had in some degree redeemed himself in the end.

"Marguerite would have appreciated that," Antonia said quietly. "It's times like this I really miss her. There was no one else who used to see it the way she did. Please, Mr. Pitt, see that the right person pays for her death. Or, at the very least, that the wrong one doesn't. Damn! That's stupid, isn't it! The wrong one already has. It's a bit late for justice now. Can I do anything to help? Damn! Damn! I should have done it twenty years ago! Is it too late now?"

"I don't know," he said honestly.

"But you won't give up, will you? Who's paying you? I'm sorry, that's rude and it's none of my business. But Mrs. Leigh won't have any money. It's she who asked you, isn't it? Or the boy? What was his name?"

"Richard," Daniel answered. "And yes, he's about twenty-five. I'm not asking for money. You're right, she hasn't any."

"So, Leigh was innocent, then? You're doing this because you believe it, and maybe to expose Saltram. He isn't going to like that. He'll do whatever he can to stop you. Aren't you afraid?"

"Yes," he said with a smile. "The only thing I'm more afraid of is not doing it. I couldn't look at that woman and say I won't." That was the truth. "I'd never sleep again."

"I have money." She made it a cool statement of fact. "If you need a client to justify it, or pick up the odd bill, I will. It's not charity, so don't get all proud. It's a debt to my sister, long overdue. And after it's over, win or lose, tell me where I can find Mrs. Leigh. I'd like to do something for her. For Marguerite, as well as for justice."

"Thank you, Mrs. Llewellyn. I will accept that, if necessary. At the moment, my firm, fford Croft and Gibson, is letting me do what I can. We all feel pretty strongly about it and we have a very good forensic expert, every bit as good as Saltram."

"Good heavens! You blaspheme! Is that possible?" There was black humor in her face.

"If you met Dr. Hall, you wouldn't ask," he replied. "Would you like another tea cake?"

# CHAPTER FIFTEEN

Daniel began with Mercaston, the police officer who had been in charge of the Daventry case twenty years ago. It was a natural place to begin a factual investigation, but it was also the easiest because Thomas Pitt knew him slightly. And so Daniel went in with the door already open.

Mercaston was close to retirement now, just over sixty but still in good health, and regarding the end of his career with mixed feelings. This was a case that had troubled him over the years, as he admitted to Daniel.

"Nasty," he said, sitting at the desk in his very handsome office whose large windows overlooked the High Street of Ledbury. He regarded Daniel with interest. "Your father mentioned it when I saw him the other day. I suppose you have good reason to open it up again? You say you want to."

"Yes, sir," said Daniel, and he told him

about the Jessie Beale case.

Mercaston's face reflected his distaste, but he let Daniel finish before he spoke. "And that's where it is now?" he said. "Fford Croft and Gibson has lodged an appeal on behalf of James Leigh? Not that it will do the poor devil any good."

"It will clear his name, if we win, and that will help his wife and son," Daniel answered.

Mercaston shook his head. "And if you don't, it will just rake the whole thing up again and make it worse, if that's possible. I suppose you've thought of that?"

"Of course," Daniel agreed. "Mrs. Leigh wants to try. She has very little left to lose."

Mercaston pursed his lips. "And you, what have you to lose? Apart from your position at fford Croft and Gibson, and your reputation? And even, perhaps, all the money you will ever earn if Saltram sues you for defamation. Have you thought of that? And then there's your family. He'll go after your father, if he thinks he can injure him, just for the pleasure of it. He's a vindictive swine. And of course, Daventry himself is still alive. The law cannot touch him, but it won't help his reputation."

Daniel was tired, and he had thought of all these things, including Daventry's displeasure. In fact, he had lain awake a good deal of the night thinking of this. "You're right," he said. "We should all just back down and apologize, not challenge anyone, especially Saltram. What's the odd innocent man hanged? And the guilty going free doesn't matter at all. It's the price of justice."

Mercaston's face lit up, reading his sarcasm perfectly. "Where do you get that temper from? Not your father; he always thought before he spoke. Well, almost always."

"My mother," Daniel said tartly, not unaware of the irony in the man's voice.

Mercaston nodded. "A woman of exceptional character, so I hear. If you marry as well as your father did, you should go far . . . if Saltram doesn't eat you first. What can I do to help? I'd dearly like to see that man taken down a step or two. I'll even retire with grace if I can see him go at the same time."

"Thank you, sir," Daniel said, with a bleak acknowledgment of the emotion in his words. "I've already read the official account of it, and the evidence given at Daventry's and Leigh's trials."

"And found anything to appeal?" Mercaston asked.

"No, except the evidence that the skull

was cracked because of the fire. It was put forward as evidence to refute the conclusion that it had to be from a blow. It was a beyond-a-reasonable-doubt argument. Along with lack of motive and Daventry's reputation, there was also testimony that it was a happy marriage and he adored her. The jury argued for two days, but in the end, they agreed it had not been proved."

"So, while they hadn't anything against Daventry, they knew the fire was arson. And I believe they got that right," Mercaston agreed. "But you can always look into it, for what it's worth. They decided Leigh set the fire, so therefore he was directly responsible for Marguerite's death, since she burned to death, trapped by the fire. No fire, then she'd definitely be alive."

"Until the killer tried again," Daniel pointed out. Then a sudden thought struck him. "Did anybody look to see if she had had any close shaves before?"

Mercaston froze. "No, never thought of it. My God, how stupid! I do remember some odd episodes. A fall from a horse even though she was a damned good horsewoman. Wheel came off a carriage once. I never connected them with the later event. You are Pitt's son, aren't you!"

Daniel found himself suddenly acutely

344

self-conscious. It was stupid to let such a casual compliment affect him so deeply, but it did. It was so much to live up to. It frightened him at times; at others it was a challenge to be embraced.

"I'll find out more, if I can," Mercaston went on. "I damned well should have seen it at the time. We put it down to her nature. We should look at what had changed just before that. What prompted this attack, and why then? Was it planned for a long time, or quickly, because it was urgent?"

"Can I help?" Daniel felt a sudden surge of excitement, as if a light had been shone on the path ahead. He had something specific to work on! Any doubt at all regarding the death of Marguerite Daventry, anything that looked like a previous attempt on her life, would cast doubt on the verdict that her murderer was James Leigh, who could not possibly have been there unnoticed on every such occasion. It might throw new light on those involved in the truth or untruth of it.

Mercaston thought for several moments, obviously turning it over in his mind. "I don't think so," he said at last. "If there is anything you can help with, can I reach you at your chambers?" He was obliquely asking if Marcus was fully aware of this case, or if there were certain parts of it that Daniel preferred he did not know.

"Yes," Daniel said with a smile. "Mr. fford Croft knows all about it. In fact, I'd rather he did know. Apart from the fact that it is his company, he might see something that we have missed. He's actually the best lawyer we have."

Mercaston answered him with a smile, genuine, but a little rueful. "He certainly was, but he's getting older." He leaned forward over the desk. "Take care of him. He has plenty of friends, but they're also his rivals. Don't trust him to their mercy. They may have vulnerabilities, too, cases they really don't want opened up again. Perhaps victims now a little . . . suspicious?"

Daniel had never thought of Marcus as vulnerable, but even as Mercaston was speaking he recalled tiny lapses of concentration, small things Marcus had forgotten. They must not be as minor as he had assumed, or how had Mercaston heard of them? There was a little bud of coldness inside him opening slowly. "Vulnerabilities, too?" he repeated.

"You know, a couple of the cases that Saltram affected in some way or another. Do you know all the rest? All the cases that may now be looked at again? We don't know which they are, but you could wager your last penny that the people involved do."

The bud of coldness opened a little wider. "Oh," Daniel breathed out slowly. "Yes."

Next, because he was geographically the closest, Daniel went to see Mr. Yates, the chief of the fire brigade who had attended the Daventry Hall fire. He had been a little more difficult to find because he was retired, but he was still close and perfectly willing to see Daniel.

He lived in a cottage on the outskirts of a village, within walking distance of the small railway line that stopped there twice a day. It was a nuisance, time consuming, but Daniel could not afford to overlook any evidence at all, even if it cost a long walk through the rain and the rising wind.

On the way, he thought of all the questions he might ask Yates. He had learned a lot about fire since Jessie first contacted him, and he had gained a greater respect for it, and for the men who fought against it.

The train journey was short, and he enjoyed seeing the countryside slip past the windows. There was snow already on the higher ground, and all the trees were bare, except for the few pines.

When he got off at the small station, he put his head down and walked into the rain. He felt as if he were soaked through. He had jammed his hat hard on his head, but the wind had still whipped it away and sent it sailing over a wide ditch full of water and into a field of cows beyond.

"You're welcome!" he shouted at a curious cow who lumbered over to look at it. To be honest, being without it didn't make much difference; his hair was dripping wet anyway.

He turned what he hoped was the last corner and was rewarded by the sight of a thatched cottage with a December garden full of dark green laurels, holly bright with berries, and bare trees startlingly delicate in their tracery of branches. Thankfully, there was steady smoke from the chimney, streaming away in the wind.

The front door opened before he could reach for the bell. A large, comfortable-looking woman stood just inside, a smile on her face and the hall light glowing on her hair as pale as snow.

"Come in." She drew the door wider. "Come in, and take your coat off. We might get it dry by the time you leave. Goodness, lad, haven't you got a hat? You're sodden wet!"

"Mrs. Yates?" he asked, just to be certain he had the right place, before he stepped in and dripped pools of water onto their floor. He was so relieved to be there that if he actually got inside, he thought he would not be able to bear to leave again.

"I'd better be," she said with a smile. "For goodness' sake, come in and let me shut the door. Himself is in there by the fire. Give me those clothes. I'll fetch a towel for you to dry your hair. Don't you have a hat? We'd better lend you one. You'll catch your death. Go in and sit down. I'll bring tea, and you might like a roast chicken sandwich, yes?"

"I'd love one," he accepted, smiling as widely as he could. "I did have a hat. The wind took it and gave it to a cow."

"I'll keep a lookout for a cow with a hat," she replied, her face totally serious, then she smiled back. "Get on with you, find the fireside!"

Daniel felt as if he were about ten and had just been temporarily adopted. It was very comforting. "Yes, ma'am," he accepted, and opened the sitting-room door as she had indicated.

Yates was sitting beside the fire, relaxed and warm, his face filled with curiosity. He did not stand but indicated the chair opposite him, on the other side of the hearth, for Daniel to sit. "I've seen drowned rats look better than you, boy," he said cheerfully. "Forgive me if I don't stand up, left leg doesn't work." He offered no further explanation.

Daniel did not look at it, except to notice that there was only one slipper on the floor beneath the rug thrown across his knees. "This drowned rat is getting a cup of tea and a roasted chicken sandwich," he said with a smile. "A curious cow has my hat."

Yates nodded. "You here about the Daventry fire, Mr. Pitt? You finally worked out that Saltram is all intellect and no humanity? Taken you long enough. What reached you at last?"

"A couple of bad mistakes of my own," Daniel replied.

"You can see that? Good start! Tell me."

Very briefly, Daniel told him the story of Jessie Beale, interrupted only when Mrs. Yates brought him first a towel for his hair, then a few moments later a pot of tea and a fresh cut and carved chicken sandwich. He thanked her with heartfelt sincerity.

She hesitated for a moment, as if overwhelmed with emotion herself, then hurriedly left and closed the door behind her.

Daniel wondered if he had offended her without realizing how.

Yates noticed his momentary confusion. "Don't mind her," he said quietly. "Our boy was a fireman, too. We lost him when he was about your age. If she wants to do for you, please let her."

"I'm sorry." Daniel tried to imagine the loss and knew he could get nowhere near the reality. He took up the account of the trial of Jessie Beale and the end result.

"So, you're going after Saltram for this Widow Leigh?" Yates concluded. "Good luck, lad, you'll need it. He's a fly bastard, that one. Although, come to think of it, you're pretty fly yourself. You turned the tables on him. He won't forget. He doesn't forget . . . or forgive. So, what do you want me for? Evidence from the Daventry fire?"

"Yes, please. All you can remember. Particulars, if you are certain that it was arson. What that evidence is, and if anyone has a record of it. What accelerant was used, if any. And why Marguerite couldn't escape."

"Because she was already dead, poor lass," Yates interrupted. "Although you'd need the original medical examiner to prove that. He was overridden by Saltram, saying the fire cracked her skull."

"How could he know that, if she was burned?" Daniel asked. "Is he suggesting she was overcome by smoke, or fumes, and then was burned after that?"

"It would fit the evidence."

"Can you give me evidence, or your informed opinion, as to how hot the fire was? It takes great heat to crack a skull."

"I've never attended a domestic fire where that has happened," Yates said grimly. "Industrial fires, maybe, where there were chemicals that would do that. This wasn't one of them. You want to know what I think?"

"Yes, please, sir," Daniel replied instantly.

"I think Saltram was young and looking to make his name. He knew a lot about the human body, but not so much about fire. He tried out that idea and the jury bought it. It was the beginning of his climb to fame. It was fast . . . and brilliant. Mind, he had a lot of help. Daventry was very grateful and praised him all over the place."

"Are you implying that it was more than gratitude?" Daniel asked, choosing his words very carefully. Other ideas were stirring in his head. "Daventry would have paid him very handsomely anyway, wouldn't he? Experts like that don't come cheaply."

"He wasn't all that expert then," Yates pointed out. "He had just one foot on the ladder, but the other foot followed pretty rapidly. Don't know a lot about it."

"Neither do I," Daniel agreed. "But I'll damn well find out. It won't be hard to discover some things. Like if Saltram changed tailors, shirtmakers, boot makers; if he bought different food and drink, and certainly if he moved to a different neighborhood. I'll start with that, and the clubs he joined and who sponsored him. If it was Daventry, that would be telling."

Yates was looking at him with interest. "And how are you going to do that, lad? Got an in with the gentlemen's clubs in London? If not, they're going to very politely decline to tell you, and then a lot less politely tell you to be on your way."

"I think it matters," Daniel answered. "For any kind of justice."

"They won't take that from you. Even I know that much."

Daniel gave him a tight little smile. "I don't like to use my family influence. It makes me look like I can't do it myself. But I can't. My father is head of Special Branch. I'll ask him. Just for the information, if it's relevant."

"Well, now." Yates sat back in his chair, pulling the blanket closer over his missing foot. "Does he know you're after Saltram?"

"Yes. I wouldn't try to pull a fast one on him. Apart from the fact that I wouldn't get away with it, I don't want to. I don't always agree with him, but when I don't, I rather often find I'm wrong."

Yates laughed, and it ended on a note of pain.

Daniel had no doubt that he was thinking of his lost son. "Thank you, sir," he said. "I have just a few more questions about escaping from fire, and then I'll go."

"Take one of my hats," Yates said. "You'll get wet else."

It was on Daniel's tongue to decline, but he looked at Yates harder and accepted.

Daniel arrived back at the hotel he had booked, tired and wet. It was too late to expect anyone else to answer questions, so he had a quiet dinner and went to bed.

The next morning he made an appointment to ask the original M.E. some questions, partly as a courtesy and partly in case there were some fragments of information that might later turn out to be important.

As it happened, there was nothing to add. The fire had been devastating and the matter of identification had been the M.E.'s principal concern. The identification had been made on the evidence of height and the fact that the skeleton was definitely female, and Marguerite was the only person unaccounted for. There had never been any real doubt. The cracked skull, which Dr. Salisbury had said was caused by a heavy blow to the back of the head, low down, near the top of the spine, would have been instantly fatal because it had broken the bones badly.

Saltram had agreed on all of the details except the cause of the cracks. Marguerite had not tried to escape, or her body would have been found nearer one of the windows. Could she have been dead before she succumbed to the flames? Saltram had sworn that she could have, as a result of intense heat. The only safe conclusion from the evidence was that she had died as a direct result of the fire.

And that was what the jury found. Hence, whoever had set the fire was guilty of murder.

That was not Daventry. There was no evidence against him, and no one had suggested it. The verdict was not guilty, unanimously. He walked away a rich, grieving, and much-sympathized-with widower. The tide of his popularity turned and shortly afterward he was elected to Parliament.

So described Dr. Salisbury's words with more than a hint of bitterness. His candor made their meeting last longer than expected, and Daniel had to rush to his next appointment.

Gonville, the prosecuting barrister when Roger Daventry was on trial, was waiting for him in his office, having delayed all other appointments until he had seen Daniel. He was a tall man of slight build, but wiry rather than thin. He had worn well, assuming that he had been in his mid-thirties when he prosecuted Daventry and was therefore in his mid-fifties now. He still had all his hair, and his face had deep lines of character, but none of them bitter.

"Pitt!" He held out his hand and gripped Daniel's firmly. "What the devil are you opening this up for? You have a real hope of sorting it out . . . after all this time?" He indicated a chair on the other side of his desk. "Tea? Coffee?" He raised his hand over the bell to ring for whoever provided such things.

"No, thank you," Daniel replied. "Unless you can tell me far more than I expect."

Gonville's eyes narrowed. "What are you doing this for?"

"To reverse the verdict on Leigh. However slight the chance is, I mean to try. We have new information, some legal judgments," he began.

"The Jessie Beale case," Gonville supplied,

cutting out the need to explain it.

"Yes." Daniel smiled bleakly. "So, everyone knows of it." It would be a long time, if ever, before he lived that one down.

"A neat turn," Gonville observed. "A bit young, aren't you, to go around poking sticks into hornets' nests?"

"I didn't intend to," Daniel began.

"I rather thought not. Too late to go back on it now. What can I do to help?"

"I've read the actual case, as recorded at trial, but I'd like to have your comments. Were you taken by surprise at Saltram's testimony?" It was an honest question to ask. Daniel had no right to an answer, and he knew it.

"Yes," Gonville admitted. "He wasn't known then. He was a young man, on his way up, but nobody expected the meteoric rise that followed after that verdict. It became precedent, as no doubt you know . . ." He smiled. "But I didn't dwell on it. To tell you the truth, I couldn't stand the man, but I believed he knew what he was talking about and had rescued us from hanging an innocent man. The cases you won, and went on to hang, will haunt you all your life, if you're honest. They do me anyway. And this man you say was hanged — Leigh — was he innocent?"

"Well, if Daventry killed her, yes." Daniel looked at him steadily.

"Then we have much to answer for," Gonville agreed. "I think it is something we need to know, by all means. You may have everything I noted, but I'm not sure it will help."

Daniel thanked him, and an hour later he got much the same sort of reply from Waveney, who had defended Daventry. They were sitting in his offices, as unlike Gonville's as the man was personally. The only thing they had in common was a willingness to reconsider the case.

"I honestly thought Daventry was guilty until I heard Saltram. The man was brilliant," he said, shaking his head. His fair hair was receding and he was several inches shorter than Daniel, but there was a sharp intelligence in his face that made him agreeable, even interesting. "He came to see me, you know, offering his services. Seemed he was an expert and had a strong feeling that, if he were allowed to look at the evidence, he could prove that no one had actually killed Lady Daventry. Of course, I leaped at it." He pulled his mouth into a grimace. "I would say it was a good lesson in looking three or even four steps ahead before you commit yourself to a course. But who can see that far ahead, no matter how honest they are, or how hard they look?"

"If you had seen that far ahead, sir, what would you have done?" Daniel asked. He was curious. He could see no honorable way out, any more than there would have been for him, even if he had known Adwell was guilty of Paddy Jackson's death. And nobody at all had even thought of accusing Jessie.

"I would have gotten sick with something severely infectious," Waveney answered his question. "And made damn sure it lasted long enough to disqualify me from the trial!"

Daniel smiled. He knew Waveney did not mean it. "Wouldn't work," he said ruefully. "You thought Daventry was innocent, just as the jury did. You were all thinking so, until Evelyn Hall took Saltram to pieces in the Jessie Beale case."

"Took you to pieces, too, I gather," Waveney said drily.

"Yes," Daniel agreed.

Waveney stared at him with sudden interest. "You know her, this Dr. Hall?"

Daniel smiled. "I do now."

"You knew her before she took the stand. You knew what she was going to say."

"I knew she had something, but not what it was. She is far too astute to have told me beforehand. Left me to flounder, only too obviously not knowing what I was do-

359

ing . . ."

Waveney nodded slowly. "Took a bit of a chance, though, didn't you?" He was smiling very slightly. "What do you want from me? I can't reveal anything Daventry said in confidence, but you know that already."

"Did you like him?" Daniel asked.

"Completely irrelevant," Waveney answered. "As you also know full well."

"Just curious. I was sorry for Jessie Beale at first, that's what got under my skin. When she allowed me to know she'd killed Adwell and Jackson as well, without actually admitting it, there was nothing I could do but defend her to the best of my abilities. Thank heaven I found Dr. Hall, who was cleverer than both of us." He looked directly at Waveney and smiled.

"Ah, indeed," Waveney answered, and smiled back.

Daniel took the late afternoon train to London, feeling reasonably satisfied that he had obtained as much cooperation from the people involved in Roger Daventry's trial as was possible. It was more than he had hoped for. But as far as the whole case of an appeal for Leigh was concerned, this was only the beginning.

He sat in the carriage as it rushed through

the wind and the darkness, the light rain streaming on its windows and being dragged along the glass by the speed they were traveling.

He intended to go through the evidence in his mind, but he drifted off into sleep. It was a quarter to seven by the time the train jolted to a stop and he collected his case. He went out of the door onto the steep steps leading down to the platform. He felt a severe jolt behind him. His foot slipped on the metal and the next moment he was on the asphalt on his hands and knees, one leg slightly twisted under him. A sharp pain ran through him as he tried to get to his feet.

A middle-aged man, well dressed in a pin-striped suit was holding his arm and pulling him up gently. "Easy does it," he said. "Lean on me. That leg all right? Not broken, is it?"

"No." Daniel put his foot gently on the ground. "Thank you," he added.

"Nasty," the man said, still holding on to Daniel's arm, taking some of his weight. "Slight sprain, I dare say. You need to be more careful. Travel can be dangerous these days, if you understand me? Could've been a lot worse. On your way home, are you? I'd get your mother to have a look at that. Good soak in hot water can do a lot. Keppel Street is it, where she lives?"

Daniel froze. He remembered the heavy shove he had felt behind him before he lost his balance. His mouth was dry, and he could not think of any words to say. Not yet.

"Thank you," he said finally. He faced the man, very ordinary-looking, in a city suit, but his cold eyes did not waver. "I'll be fine, I appreciate your help," he added.

"Oh, anytime," the man replied. "Remember that! Any time at all."

# CHAPTER SIXTEEN

Miriam was running an experiment in the laboratory when Ottershaw came in.

"Any luck?" he asked, peering over her shoulder at the work she had been doing. "You should get Charlie to do some of that for you. Where is he?" The boy had exhibited a fierce desire both to learn and to earn the kindness shown him, so Ottershaw was giving him chores to do, and he was actually growing more and more useful.

"He was practically cross-eyed trying to sort those papers," Miriam replied. "He's beginning to get the hang of reading! I told him to go home when he'd finished tidying up the storeroom. Half the time, we're buying new supplies because we haven't time to look for the old things."

"We'd better make sure he's dry and has something to eat," Ottershaw said with a smile. "It wouldn't be the first time he spent the night curled up on the floor. I suppose

it's warmer than his home, poor little beggar."

"That's why I never turn him out," she
replied. "Are you actually sure he's got a
home?"

"No," he admitted. After a pause, his face
softened and he added, "But he has now."

They sat together in silence for a few moments, before Ottershaw spoke again.

"Have you read this?" he asked, holding
up a newspaper.

"You mean the piece Saltram wrote?" She
glanced at it. "I wouldn't have imagined
anyone could write so frighteningly about
the enemies of science, and still make it dry
as sawdust!"

There was no lightness in Ottershaw's
face. "He makes it sound as if they are
enemies of progress, and want to convict all
sorts of people without looking at the facts.
They are only afraid of being misled by
things they don't understand."

Miriam set aside the measurement she
was taking and gave Ottershaw her full attention. His face was tight with distress,
which he was trying unsuccessfully to hide.
His hair was, as always, all over the place.
Two of the buttons on his white coat were
undone, and a third was missing. But they
were only old clothes and he was wearing

them for warmth, not appearance.

"I know," she said more gently. "He's throwing up barricades because he knows Daniel is coming after him. There have been articles questioning all sorts of other verdicts since we won the Beale case."

"Actually, we lost it," Ottershaw reminded her.

"It depends what you'd call a win or a loss. We were on the winning side, so we wanted to lose. The worst loss would have been if we'd won," she reasoned.

A quick amusement flashed in his eyes. "You can make me laugh, even when I really don't want to, but you'd better not say that aloud. You could get us all into a great deal of trouble!"

It would open up a whole new set of rats' nests, and they had already only narrowly climbed out of one.

"I know," she said, "but we'd better be prepared for it. It will occur to somebody one day."

"Right now, Saltram is painting us as intellectual Luddites. As if we want to destroy people's belief in this young century and the new science that will take justice forward in bounds, allowing us to tell the innocent from the guilty, without relying on eyewitnesses who are so often wrong." He

365

kept his expression serious and his eyes grave. "Or upon other testimony of biased people, even those who are really guilty. But science, unbiased, pure and available to all who study it, can prove beyond doubt, reasonable or not, if it is weighed and judged by those who know what they're doing."

"That's rubbish, and we know it!" she said angrily. "Science is sets of facts, measurements, figures, from which we make deductions. It depends upon which facts we use, what deductions we look for, and even what we want to find out. Science is just the latest theory we have, and as soon as another one comes along, a new discovery, a new way of interpreting them, then there's a new answer! It's not like mathematics that always adds up the same way, if you do it right. Science is a method of reaching a conclusion, not a conclusion itself."

"Miriam, I know that," Ottershaw said patiently. "Saltram is putting the emotion into it, not I. He is making an argument for rationality, and using emotion to do it. Fear, mostly. Fear of innocent men being found guilty because lawyers have power, and the victory that brings it to them. Fear of guilty people being let go to wander the streets and prey on the innocent, because we refuse to credit the evidence that might secure them." He slammed the newspaper down on the bench.

"If you look hard enough," he went on, "you will always find a rare incident strong enough to back your point. People don't think rationally, especially when they're afraid. They take what sounds reasonable to them, picking and poking away what they don't really understand. *Bessie has four legs. Dogs have four legs. Therefore, Bessie is a dog.* Right?"

"No!" Miriam said sharply. "She could be a cat. Or a camel. Or a . . . anything. You have to qualify it. *Only* dogs have four legs, or whatever. But it sounds good the other way, if you want it to be true.

"Saltram is using emotion and science dishonestly because he has been caught in a lie. He must again disprove the lie, which he can't. Or else he must blacken the reputation of the people who tell it. He has no alternative. I know, it's disgusting! But it's very human. And yes, it scares me a bit — or a lot."

Ottershaw shook his head, his expression rueful. "It scares me, too, and sometimes it helps to say so, instead of pretending it will all end well."

"It won't," she said with a quick smile.

"You don't know that," he responded sharply. Beneath his certainty and his reason, was he vulnerable after all?

"It won't end," she explained. "There will always be old ideas overturned, and new ones brought in. Sometimes good, sometimes not. Depends upon what we are looking for."

"Or against," he added. "I'm going out to get more supplies. I wish we had something to build on, something useful."

She did not bother to reply. She felt the same. And she was certain he knew it.

It was the middle of the afternoon and Miriam was working on another experiment when there was a knock on the laboratory door. The butler opened it and stood on the threshold.

"Excuse me, ma'am. Sir Barnabas Saltram has called by and wishes to speak to you. Will you see him?"

Miriam drew in her breath to refuse, but she saw Saltram standing so closely behind the butler that he was able to look over the man's shoulder and see her. If she refused, it would be the same as running away.

"Yes, certainly," she replied. "Perhaps you will bring us tea . . . and thank you."

Saltram stepped past the butler and half

turned to speak, his voice relaxed. "Don't bother to bring tea for me. I had a late lunch."

It was a dismissal, and the butler accepted it as such and withdrew, closing the door behind him.

Saltram made sure the door was closed, then walked through the benches and past the experimental equipment, until he stopped about three feet from Miriam.

It was a little too close for her to feel comfortable, but not quite a challenge to good manners. She stood her ground. "Good afternoon, Sir Barnabas," she said quietly. "What can I do for you?"

"Serve the science that you profess to admire so much, for your own sake, as well as everyone else's. You are damaging people's trust in recent fact. You want emotion, which ends in chaos. If you insist on going on this way, you won't achieve a victory, or even a workable order. Look at the future, the real future." He stood almost casually, but there was a tiny muscle ticking in his cheek. Was he aware of it?

Thoughts crossed her mind, arguments that appeared reasonable — but this was not about reason, it was about fear. Fear of progress, the future, proof rather than belief. "We are always on the edge of the future, Barnabas," she replied. His name on her tongue came so easily it took her back twenty years, to the days when they were almost friends, on the verge of becoming lovers. She had said the word in her mind. It was absurd, and yet at the time, she had believed it. She could see the room, even with her eyes open to this familiar laboratory so real around her. He was standing in front of her, twenty years older, smartly dressed, his hair rigidly combed to his head, a few gray threads in it.

She could remember that other time in a quiet room, the lamplight, the bed, and heat burned up her face. The humiliation and the pain as sharp as if it had been yesterday evening. He had been half-dressed then, less than that. She could remember the touch of his hands on her body, the smell of his skin, the warmth of him. She remembered how she could hardly get her breath, for the pounding of her heart.

But nothing happened, nothing at all. The humiliation was his and he had not known what to say, to explain. His solution had been somehow to blame her. She was not beautiful enough, womanly enough. Funny, gentle, graceful enough. It was anything at all but his failure.

Could he remember that now? Please

heaven, no! He had forgotten.

"That's trite, Miriam," he was saying. "Don't try to be profound. You'll only end up looking ridiculous."

She was furious. She remembered the things he had said. She was mannish, boring, humorless. God!

"Looking ridiculous?" she repeated the word incredulously. "Me? Funny you should use that word; it's exactly the one I had in mind."

Scarlet flooded his face. So, he had not forgotten.

For an instant, she was in two times at once. In both of them Saltram was standing a few feet away from her. Only then he had been physically and emotionally nearly naked.

Suddenly he stepped forward. He slapped her so hard she staggered backward, banged her hip violently against the bench, and slid to the floor, hitting her head. For a moment, all she saw was darkness. She felt a hard pain in her upper leg and her shoulder. She crumpled over, protecting her face, her chest.

But he didn't touch her. He turned and strode away. She heard his footsteps retreating farther and farther in the distance.

It took her a few minutes before she could

stop her head spinning, the noise in her ears, and the whirring dizziness. Slowly, she got to her feet, one step at a time. She slipped once, banging her knee on the floor, pain shooting up her leg. She stopped for another few seconds, then tried again.

Then she was standing, hanging on to the bench closest to her. She put her head down, waiting until the room stopped spinning, then looked around. Saltram was nowhere in sight, nor could she hear him, but she could hear something. It was a banging, as if there were people just outside in the street, at the back. No, at the side. She couldn't tell. There was a lot of shouting, angry voices crying out in rage.

Were the doors locked? Would they hold against a mob determined to break in? Where was Charlie? He was still in the storeroom. He might be scared stiff. He was only a child.

The shouting was getting louder. They sounded as if they were right outside the back door. The air was thick with dust here, almost choking. There was a draft, cold air, more dust, clouds of it. It hurt her lungs. This wasn't dust, it was smoke! How had she not known that right away? She knew fire, she knew blinding, suffocating smoke! And she knew the heat inside a ravenous, all-consuming fire.

Wallace . . . he had died in a fire like this, fighting for breath. She had not been close enough to see, or to help, but she remembered the panic, and fighting to get air, any air, into her lungs. She had been nowhere near Wallace. There had never been anything she could have done to help him, and yet she felt guilt more than anything else. Guilt that she had survived, and he had not. Guilt more than grief. That it had not been her fault was just words. They had nothing to do with emotions, or the fact that she felt not only loss, but also relief, an escape from a marriage she knew was wrong.

This was definitely fire, no mistaking it now. Here! In Ottershaw's laboratory. She tore a strip off her petticoat and tied it around her nose and mouth, but it was still difficult to breathe. The acrid smoke burned her throat. Where was Charlie? Had he run away? Could he have fallen asleep and not heard the noise? What about the butler? Was he upstairs in the main house? Or the kitchen? Did he even know what was happening down here, in the converted carriage house?

Had Saltram done this?

She was losing her sense of direction. Which way had she come? Was the storeroom to the left or the right? She stopped, confused, trying to remember. Somewhere to the right there was a shout of terror as the wall collapsed and a great gust of cold air cleared the smoke for an instant. Then, with fresh oxygen, the flames doubled, tripled, and roared up to devour the roof of the carriage house and the stables. She struggled backward; it was the only way she could go. The fire was monstrous ahead of her. It had suddenly become a giant.

She stepped backward, away from it, without any sense of direction at all. It was just like before, except for the fire, eating everything.

Where was Charlie? She had to find him.

The smoke billowed and cleared for a moment. She saw Charlie running toward her, his clothes burning. The fire roared too loudly to hear whether he was screaming.

She caught hold of him and knocked him onto the floor, rolling him over and over to kill the flames. She must be hurting him, driving the burning cloth against his skin, but the alternative was worse.

"Miriam!" She heard someone calling her name. Ottershaw? Had he come back? Saltram? No. He had surely escaped out of the front, as if nothing had happened. But which way was the storeroom? She had thought she knew, but now she was lost. Walls were crashing, breaking down all over the place, cracking, disintegrating in front of her.

"Here!" She tried to shout, but her voice was a croak.

"Miriam!" It was closer than before. A man's voice.

She turned, trying to see through the billows of smoke. It was getting harder to breathe, even through the fabric.

Then she felt her arm caught, held so tightly she could not escape, although she tried as hard as she could to wrench it away. She was going to be trapped and suffocated. She had not even saved Charlie. She felt the dizziness choking her. Would she slip out of consciousness before the flames burned her flesh? Please, God, yes.

"Miriam!"

She was losing her balance, being pulled.

"Miriam, stand up!" The man's voice again.

Had Saltram come back for her? No, it would be intolerable, owing him her life.

"Walk!"

It was a command.

"Charlie . . ." She choked on the word.

"I've got Charlie!"

"Come on, stand up and walk! We've got

to get out quickly!"

She tried to obey, but there was no strength in her legs.

Whoever it was, he was strong, forcing her to walk. Hurting her where he held her arm. Her eyes were stinging so badly she could not keep them open. She was walking. Left foot. Right foot. Left foot. There was a terrible roaring noise, flames consuming the room, taking the air out of everything. And it was getting really hot! Were they even going the right way?

Her legs went from under her and she seemed to be floating. Then . . . nothing.

Miriam opened her eyes and took a deep breath. Her lungs hurt, everything hurt. She was burning, the skin on her arms, her face, her lungs, but the air was cool. Beautiful, cold, drizzling rain.

She breathed in again. It hurt, but it was not unbearable.

"That's right, miss, just take it slow," a man's voice said gently.

She opened her eyes. The tears were streaming down her face from the sting of smoke. But she could see the fire officer's helmet.

"You got me out," she said, but her voice was croaking, distorted. "Where's Charlie?

Have you got him? Is he all right?"

"Yes, miss, if you mean the young gentleman there. A bit of a mess, he is, but he'll be all right. Though I dare say he'll hurt like you will for a few days. Very brave, he was. Or bloody stupid! We got the boy, too, but he's burned a bit nasty, like. Took him to the ambulance."

"Will he be all right?"

"Hard to say, but I reckon so."

She turned to look where the fireman was pointing, and saw Daniel. He looked terrible. His clothes were scorched, burned in several places. Even his hair was singed. There was a red mark on his cheek; beneath the dust and the burns, his skin was ashen. It must have been Daniel who had rescued them, but she had been too terrified to recognize him. It was all tangled in her mind, Wallace, Charlie, Saltram. But Saltram was not there, and yet his presence was: the fear, the heat and burning, and the shame.

But Daniel was all right. She had not even known to be afraid for him. Where was Octavius? He wasn't here. Was he gone, too? She felt as if someone had struck her so hard she could not breathe.

Daniel moved over toward her, awkwardly, shuffling rather than walking. He reached out a hand to touch her but did not know where to place it — what was burned and what was not?

"Ottershaw's all right," he said quietly. "He had been out. The butler smelled the smoke, but didn't know where the fire had taken hold. He's a bit charred, from trying to put it out, but he'll be all right, too. Charlie as well, almost certainly."

"Are you sure?" she asked hoarsely.

"Almost. A crowd had gathered. Some idiot dropped a lantern, the oil spilled and caught fire. Scared the hell out of them, but at least others had the guts to stay and try to fight it, for what that's worth." He found one place where she was not scorched and put his arm around her shoulders. "I'm afraid the laboratory is gone. And part of the back of the house, rather a big part. Poor Ottershaw will have to start again."

She sat silently, letting the tears come.

Minutes slid by.

"And Saltram?" she asked at last.

His face was bleak. "Was he here? Miriam, what for?"

She started to speak, and then choked on her dry, painful throat. "An old quarrel. It doesn't matter anymore. I should put it in the fire, even the memory of it!"

Everything hurt. The bruises, the burns,

her throat raw from smoke, the overwhelming memory of terror from that other fire. The scalding memory of that scene with Saltram. The lost laboratory. And above all, Charlie's face as he ran toward her, the terror and the pain.

Daniel's arm tightened around her, and she leaned against his shoulder and wept.

# CHAPTER SEVENTEEN

Daniel found it impossible to sleep. The doctor had put all kinds of salves on his burns, but none of them seemed to help very much. He'd told Daniel the burns were superficial, and the new skin should grow back without leaving any scars, but that did not stop them from burning and itching.

He lay on his back in the hospital bed. The medical staff would not allow him to go home. They had said something about infection, pain, and that he needed to keep the dressings on the deeper wounds in case the skin left was damaged. They hurt now far more than they had when it first happened. Or perhaps, in the noise and the stark, all-consuming fear of the fire itself, he had been only peripherally aware of them. He wanted to see for himself that Miriam was safe. The residue of that fear was still tight and hard inside him. Lying in this clean hospital bed, he could still see her stricken face in his mind's eye. He would like to forget it, but it was not only her terror. He saw himself in her . . . and understood.

He forced himself to believe that Charlie would be all right. He refused to be treated until he knew that they had done all they could for the boy and Miriam. Which brought him to the question he had been avoiding since the nurse had left him, ostensibly so he could sleep. He had read the pieces in the newspaper about the new inquiry into the Leigh case, which was really the Daventry case. Not all of it, but enough. One journalist in particular, Liam Shand, put into very immediate words the way the new investigation was threatening to rip apart the justice system. If we punish people for murder, he wrote, we run the risk of sending an innocent person to a terrifying and shameful death — a death that is our fault.

Not intentional, of course! Not knowingly. But, he demanded, did that make it all right, since it was the cost of law, peace, for the most part justice? He said we deliberately deceived ourselves that we had made the world safer and that we were more often right than wrong.

Daniel could not help but ask himself, was

he to blame for the unforeseen conse-
quences of opening up the Daventry case
again? It was too late to save Leigh, and no
one could see what the price would be.
Certainly, a great deal of discomfort for
some of the authorities. *Discomfort?* What a
ridiculous word when compared with hanging someone! Shameful!

Some people were saying it would be the
end of the judicial system as it was, if
anyone who made a judgment was subject
to being second-guessed for the rest of their
lives. *Reductio ad absurdum!* Reduction to
absurdity. But if the convicted were always
executed, you could not undo it anyway. So
those in the law would always fear making a
mistake.

That was another argument you could
pursue to the ridiculous. Fear of making a
mistake would paralyze the whole justice
system, until nobody could decide anything.

Daniel moved slightly and felt a sharp
pain. What he was surely saying was, had he
made a mistake in taking Adria Leigh's
case? Had he taken her case because he
could not face her being right and live with
denying it? Did it really have anything to do
with justice? Or was it lack of the strength
to refuse her? Or, even more likely, was it to
get back at Saltram because Jessie Beale had

made a fool of him, using Saltram to attempt to win both cases? Was that really at the core of it? Did he have as great a need to seem to be right as Saltram did?

He drifted off into a pain-disturbed sleep and woke to find a nurse at his side, arranging a bunch of white flowers in a vase on the table near him, where the glass and water jug sat.

"Lady brought these for you," the nurse said. "Wouldn't stay, just wanted to be sure you was all right."

His mother. Why had she not stayed? His mouth was so dry he could not make the words.

The nurse held up the water glass to his lips. "Don't get upset," she said quickly. "You'll feel like that for a little while, but you'll mend."

"The lady?" he tried again.

"Funny name, never heard it before. Atria, or something like that?"

"Adria Leigh?"

"Yes. Looked close to tears, she did. Poor soul. Just stood and looked at you, wouldn't wake you up, but she left these. Pretty, aren't they? Guess the colored ones cost a lot. Actually, I think these are nice. Kind of gentle. I told her you were going to be all right, and so you are. You're young, you'll heal."

Adria Leigh had spent money on flowers and wouldn't stay to be thanked for them. He was being stupid. Tears filled his eyes and his arms hurt when he moved to wipe them away.

The next time he woke up, it was Charlotte sitting beside the bed, watching him, her face filled with concern. What a baby he was, to find her so comforting.

"Don't look like that, Mother," he said croakingly. "Swallowed a lot of smoke, that's all." He stopped to cough and she passed him a glass of water. "I'm a bit scorched around the edges," he added. "Nothing permanent."

"Had to cut a bit of your hair off, at the front," she said, in a voice very nearly steady. "Got a bit burned, but you've still got eyebrows, although one is a little crooked, I think." She turned her head to look at him more closely.

"Miriam," he said, and then stopped.

"She's all right," Charlotte replied. "But she was pretty badly frightened. I think far more than she admitted. I went to see her. She's not as burned as you are. Marcus took her home."

"She was closer to the fire," he started to

argue, then realized he was defending her to his mother, as if Charlotte had criticized her. "She lost her fiancé in a fire a long time ago, and there was a boy badly hurt in this fire. She tried to help him, but she couldn't . . ."

"I know," Charlotte said quietly. "She told me about Charlie. She was worried about him, but he's getting better. I think he's going to have scars, but he'll be all right. She didn't say anything about her fiancé."

Daniel tried to sit up a little higher against the pillows. He felt oddly vulnerable lying down.

Charlotte put one hand on his shoulder and gently pushed him backward. "I'm not criticizing her, Daniel. I don't want to, and I couldn't afford to. I like to think I would have done the same, had I been in her place. She has a quick temper, perhaps acts before she thinks, if she's sure she's right." She smiled a little ruefully. "You didn't really know me when I was her age, but your father will tell you. I acted before I thought . . . sometimes. Your aunt Emily was worse."

"That's not what Father says." He smiled, in spite of himself.

"Well, I suppose he could be right," she admitted. "But Miriam is fine. I've been to see her. It's the scorching inside I'm not so sure about. Be gentle with her, Daniel."

He felt his face heat, but then, he burned a little in several areas where the fire had caught him. "I'm not . . ." he began, but had no idea what he meant to say.

She reached out and touched his brow lightly. Her hand was cool, nice. He felt about ten years old again. He closed his eyes and let the tears seep through his lashes as he thought of Charlie. Who cared about him?

The next time Daniel awoke, it was to see his father sitting in the chair a little way from the bed.

Pitt looked up immediately, his face tired, as if he had been up all night. "Daniel? How are you?"

"It hurts, but it'll pass. Just . . . time. Who set it, do you know that yet?"

Pitt shook his head. "It's not a Special Branch case. I came to see you, not report to you the cause of the fire," Pitt said gently, and with a slight twisted smile.

Daniel sat up a little farther. Perhaps it was his imagination, but he was not quite so sore. "But it was arson."

"A mixture of bad intentions and shared damned stupidity. An old man with a white beard was seen carrying an oil lamp and shouting about hell and damnation. The lamp fell on dry wood. That's all it takes," Pitt replied. "But it still amounts to arson."

"It was very nearly murder," Daniel said. His throat hurt, but speaking was more urgent now than ever. "Was there someone in the crowd who could have done that on purpose? Not just through stupidity?"

"I don't know," Pitt said seriously, "and it's not your concern. You've got a very serious case to prepare." He put out his hand and took Daniel's wrist gently. "It's more than a crowd of stupid people with what they think is a cause. The old man with the beard speaks for many, one way or another. There are a lot of new ideas in the air, more of them every month. Too many things are changing, it's hard to keep up, and you can't rely on what you used to trust. People you think are wicked are proved merely to be different. Tolerance isn't easy to those who think in absolutes. Good and evil. They get confused, frightened, and then angry . . ."

Daniel could suddenly see the man's face in his mind, remembered it from the courtroom. Contorted with self-righteous rage. "I know him. He was in court and had to be removed."

Pitt's face changed. "I'll talk to the commander of the investigation and see that the man is charged. And not just for arson, but attempted murder."

They sat for a moment in silence before Pitt spoke again. "This new science is altering things too quickly."

"Things always change," Daniel argued.

Pitt cut across him. "The old Queen was once young; she ruled for over sixty years. Most of us never knew any other monarch. Now, all of a sudden, everything is different. New sciences, new medical ideas, and the blurring of right and wrong. And social change. New ideas about workers' rights, women's right to vote, the Kaiser throwing his weight around in Germany, and starting to look a bit beyond Germany's borders, even as far as England. It's like a giant who's been stirring in his sleep for a quarter-century. Now he's actually waking up. We don't like the idea of scientists like Saltram — who led us to think he knew the answers — being proved wrong. Nobody wants to think we can be easily fooled. That's at the core of it. Things are slipping out of control."

Daniel stared at him. He understood what he was saying. His own fallibility shook him. But those who had real power, who ruled and guarded the country, made the decisions far beyond his knowledge — that they could be fallible too was a terrifying thought. The idea grew larger, darker, every moment he considered it. He had grown up trusting his father, though he knew intellectually that he was fallible. Pitt had never pretended otherwise. He had never hidden from Daniel that he was as human as anyone else, but he was someone Daniel had always believed was fundamentally right.

It was part of growing up to realize that your parents were subject to error, like everyone else. But if you were lucky — and Daniel was — you never found them seriously wanting. Their mistakes were small errors, never cowardice or betrayal.

The firm edges of things were melting. Foundations upon which things were built were breaking, slipping away, leaving you exposed.

Of course people fought. Not sensibly, but with consuming fear. Fought the people who questioned ideas they trusted, the things they thought to be certainties. The law, the judgments on which civilization was built. You obeyed the universal laws of science, the just, man-made laws of the legal system. If you executed innocent men, then no one was safe. It could be your father next time. Or you! There was nothing to cling to.

No firm ground.

Pitt was watching him, his face gentle and worried. "You've chosen a hard battle, Daniel. Or perhaps it chose you. I'll do whatever I can to help, but I'm not sure what that is."

Daniel stared at him. Pitt was not angry. In fact, there was something quite different from anger in his face. It was the knowledge of danger, what it could cost. But it was also pride. With a wave of buoyancy like the strength of the sea, Daniel realized that his father was proud of him. Not as his child, but as a man.

Daniel reached out and took his father's hand, heedless of the sheet scraping on his burned arm.

# CHAPTER EIGHTEEN

It had taken Marcus weeks of work, calling upon every favor he had ever given in the past or promised for the future, asking everyone to contact the newspapers and demand a retrial to clear the name of James Leigh.

His efforts succeeded. The retrial of James Leigh for the murder of Marguerite Daventry began two weeks into the new year of 1911.

Now he stood in front of the mirror, in the small room where he prepared to go into court and argue the first case he had tried in ten years. His memory from the far past was excellent. He recalled with vivid delight scene after scene from years ago, as if they were yesterday. It was only the memory of recent conversations that eluded him.

Miriam looked at him. He had not worn his wig in a decade. It was made from horsehair, like all others, but disuse had made it seem more prickly than ever. The black gown was a little tight over his shoulders. None of that mattered. What worried her was his ability to recall the words he wanted to use. A slip could be trivial, or it could be disastrous. It might be simple: anyone would know what he meant. Or it might be unintentionally funny, or ribald. Or, worse still, it might be plain wrong. He might lose the case as easily as that.

Should she have tried to prevent him from taking the case? Kitteridge's cold had turned into pneumonia and he was only just back on his feet. Daniel was possibly going to be called as a witness, so Kitteridge was sitting second chair and looking up law references that Marcus might not recall where to find. Every reference must be correct.

The person representing the Crown was Sir John Percival. He was almost Marcus's age. They had known each other for forty years at least, which was an added difficulty because he would see the slowing in Marcus's thoughts, references he lost, points he failed to make.

"Father, you look excellent," Miriam said. "Forget about your appearance now. No one is going to be looking at your gown. Go out and play the best game of your life. You know you're right; you don't have to wonder about it. Kitteridge will be with you and will look up any further reference you need. James Leigh was innocent. Go and make them acknowledge it."

He turned and smiled widely at her, pulling his shoulders back and carrying his head high. But the smile did not reach his eyes.

She followed after him, as far as his own entrance to the court. Then she went to the side used by the public, as close as she could to the front. Partly because she wanted him to know she was there, but mostly because she still had the ridiculous feeling that somehow she could be of help. Whatever the reality, she could not opt out of it, avoid the pain, the embarrassment, the imagining of triumph or disaster, before it came.

She looked at Sir John Percival, who in effect was prosecuting the case, claiming the original verdict as correct. She amended his title in her mind. Sir John Percival, KC. He was a King's Counsel now. He had declined to be elevated to the bench because he loved the battle. She smiled to herself, unaware if it was visible to others. The fact that the government had chosen Percival was a powerful indication of how deeply they wanted this conviction to stand. It was a test case for all the others that were called into question by the verdict against Jessie Beale — in effect, against Saltram.

Was it just the principle of it? The fact that it had been high profile even at the time, and had become higher since, as Saltram had risen in fame? It had all the elements of great drama. A beautiful woman had died what was probably a horrible death. Please, heaven, it had been quick. But what was left of her corpse was very nearly unrecognizable, even as human, never mind as the person she had once been. Would they make drama of that this time? It was not relevant except that it was part of the case, but everything that was emotional would be used.

Had Marguerite taken a lover? Was her possessive and dominating husband guilty of murdering her and setting the fire to hide that fact? That was the original charge. Although now, in light of events that had occurred afterward, it seemed more likely that Daventry had had his eye on a seat in Parliament, and all that could follow from that. The only thing in his way was that he was personally unpopular in his constituency, while on the other hand, his wife was beloved. With her tragic death, and his very public grief, he was elected with ease, and for a few years at least he had prospered, and held high office.

But now, if Marcus could prove his point, perhaps that accusation would be resurrected. Except that legally it could not be. Roger Daventry had been tried and found not guilty by virtue of Saltram's groundbreaking, expert evidence. He could never be tried again, whatever evidence Marcus provided. Would it prove James Leigh's innocence, or only stir up a lot of doubt, misgivings about the law itself, about those who could so disastrously have driven it toward tragedy instead of justice?

Deliberately, Miriam did not glance at her father. Of course, he knew she was nervous, but he must be able to imagine she was confident he would win. He needed all the belief he could find.

Toby Kitteridge was seated beside Marcus, with a full transcript of the original trial beside him.

Along the bench from Miriam sat Daniel's mother. There was tension in the way she held herself. She, too, knew something of how much there was to win or lose in this trial.

The court was almost full. There would be people waiting outside, with no chance of finding a seat. The gallery was filled with journalists. Each would have his own view of the importance of this, and all the questions and turmoil that it could bring.

The court came to order. Silence was instant and complete. The formalities were gone through meticulously; the ritual was age-old. Probably the only difference from the first time this was tried, twenty years ago, was that the Crown was now not Queen Victoria, but George V. And, of course, the man accused had already been found guilty and hanged. This would really be the trial of those who had conducted that trial. Would they lay the ghosts to rest? Or find new, and in a way more terrible, guilt?

"It is the verdict in the case of the Crown against James Leigh that we are re-examining," the judge, Lord Justice Walpole, explained carefully. "New light has been shed upon the evidence that convicted him of the murder of Marguerite Daventry." His expression was sour, his face pinched. "He was hanged. Nothing can alter that now. But that is not your concern . . ."

Several people looked anxious. One man with a fierce red face shifted uncomfortably in his seat.

The judge glanced at him. "But if indeed he was innocent, and that is what we are here to decide" — he dropped his voice a little lower — "then his name, his honor, his family's heritage, must be restored."

There was a moment's silence.

Miriam looked toward Marcus, and saw the expression on Kitteridge's face. *Go on!* he seemed to urge silently.

The judge drew in his breath, then let it out. He did not mention the multitude of other cases that would have to be retried if the original verdict in this one was overturned.

Marcus seemed to Miriam a small figure, like a man alone in a great storm, on the bridge of a sinking ship. There was no path through the towering waves, no harbor light ahead in the darkness.

"My lord, we have what looks like a very complicated case before us," Marcus began, "but we are equal to it. We are practical men with common sense. We must trust our wisdom, not our fears. Most of the evidence we will hear is not in question. We will tell you what is, and why. We'll give you as much of the story as we know. Most of the conclusions are not open to question. You might wonder why we are doing this at all. It is because that small part in question affects not only this case, but many, many others, in the past, in the present, and no doubt in the future. It is our duty to discover the truth, that this need never happen again. We will attempt to tell you what is, and why. We will give you as much of the story as we know, so that you may have all the information. Most of the conclusions are not open to question."

Several of the jurors looked a little more relaxed.

Miriam had forgotten how good Marcus was at this. The decade since the last time seemed to disappear, yet she could not relax. She was listening for the hesitation, the word he could not think of.

He questioned Yates, the fireman. He elicited from him a broad description of the blaze that had destroyed an entire wing of the great house. He had the court's attention. He had set the mood and Percival did not interrupt.

But was it to any purpose?

Miriam waited, not realizing she was clenching her hands, and her nails dug into her palms. She momentarily forgot her still-tender scars from the burns. Reluctantly, she made herself relax. At least until she forgot again, and got swept up in the reactions.

What effect was it having on the judge, beyond drawing him in? How much did it matter?

She glanced along the row to Charlotte

398

Pitt, whose face reflected the same apprehension Miriam herself felt.

"What started the fire, Mr. Yates?" Marcus asked.

"We don't know, sir," Yates answered. "The more I think about it, the less certain I am. It could have been the gas lamp, a candle, a coal fallen out of a fire."

"Unattended?" Marcus asked quickly. "Most of the house would have been unattended, would it not? You could hardly leave a maid in every room."

"No, sir," Yates said patiently.

Was he bored with this, something he must have been through again and again? And did he think Marcus was wasting everyone's time, asking stupid questions?

Marcus spoke quietly. "I was not thinking of unattended rooms, which were possibly not equipped with a fireplace anyway. I was thinking more of passages, corridors, landings, and certainly stairways, which would be kept lit. Wouldn't they?"

"Er . . . yes, sir," Yates responded, relaxing more as he understood. "You would keep them lit all the time. Too easy to have an accident otherwise, and you wouldn't want the staff turning the gas lamps up and down every time they passed. It would make no sense, sir."

"Gets stuffy inside. Open a window. Curtain blows and catches a lamp. Or a candle, maybe? House fires do start that way."

"Yes, sir, a few."

"This one?"

Yates thought for a long time.

An expression of impatience crossed the judge's face, but he did not interrupt. There was no way at all of knowing his thoughts.

"Not this one?" Marcus prompted.

"It doesn't make sense," Yates began.

"Oh, why not?"

"Heat, sir," Yates replied. "That fire had a terrible hold before anyone knew about it, or else why didn't Lady Daventry escape?"

"I don't know." Marcus said. "The rest of the staff did, didn't they?"

"Yes, sir. Took it they were in the servants' quarters, and she was upstairs in the dressing room."

"So, what do you think happened?"

Yates looked confused.

There was utter silence in the court.

Marcus stood still, as if he had forgotten what he had been about to say.

Sir John Percival rose to his feet.

The judge ignored him. "Mr. fford Croft?" There was a certain solicitude in his face.

Miriam felt a sudden coldness. Had he

forgotten what he was going to say?

Kitteridge leaned closer to Marcus and said something.

Marcus cleared his throat. "So, all the servants escaped unhurt, and poor Lady Daventry burned to death, is that right?"

"Yes, sir, I suppose that's the sum of it. Except two of the servants were injured when they tried to get Lady Daventry out, but the fire was between them and her, and they couldn't pass it."

"Thank you, very understandable. Brave of them, and loyal."

"Yes, sir."

"Must have burned up very quickly."

"Yes, sir. Lot of flammable stuff, I'm afraid. Very fine wood paneling. Beautiful . . . rich . . ."

"Yes, dry wood," Marcus agreed. "Burns very hot, does it?"

"Not so much hot as quick."

"I see. Oh, before you go, did you find any accelerant, anything that would make the fire hotter, stronger, harder for Lady Daventry to get out? Hot enough to crack a human skull, for example?"

Miriam relaxed, letting her hands release their grip. She felt tears stinging her eyelids and sliding down her face. Then she was suddenly cold inside. She knew how Marguerite Daventry must have felt. The terror. The choking. The desperation to find a way out. Any way. And then the realization that there was no way. She was going to die here.

Except that Miriam had found the way out. Twice. Once when Wallace had not, and once when Daniel had rescued her — and Charlie. How could you be so hot on the outside, your skin and throat burning, and yet have that tiny spot inside that was so cold?

Marcus was still talking, but he was coming to the end. He was not drawing any conclusion, but leaving the judge thinking, wondering, knowing there was more.

Sir John Percival had nothing to add, but he rose to his feet, tall, imposing, his gown flowing, not bulging like Marcus's. He declined to ask this witness anything more. "I'm sure we are all acquainted with the material facts, such as they are."

Marcus called Mercaston, the policeman in charge, and kept both questions and answers brief. He marshaled the facts and asked for his conclusions.

Percival only reconfirmed them. It added nothing to what everyone knew.

They adjourned for lunch and Miriam ate alone. She knew Marcus would be talking with Kitteridge. She would only be a distraction.

As soon as they were reassembled, Marcus called Gonville, who had conducted the prosecution. He went over Gonville's witnesses and summed up their evidence. He was remarkably brief. Had he forgotten something? She sat rigid with anxiety when he stood with his robe sliding a little farther off his left shoulder. All his coats tended to, always had — and it was more pronounced as he grew older. His own white hair poked out from underneath his wig. She should have had him go to the barber. Too late now.

Marcus was standing there silently. Had he lost his thread of reasoning?

He coughed, then cleared his throat. "You know, Mr. Gonville, as well as I do — and I dare say at least half the other people in this room — that we are only repeating what everyone agrees on already. It doesn't change anything. You were not incompetent. Neither was anyone else at the trial that we are replaying so carefully. The meat of this doesn't lie here, not with you. Not with Mr. Waveney, who defended Sir Roger Daventry so ably. At least, I think not. I have no evidence that he was remiss, or dishonest."

Miriam drew in a shaking breath. Why was Marcus drawing attention to this? She wished she were sitting beside Kitteridge so she could ask him. Was Kitteridge going to have to ask for a recess? Say Marcus was ill? Would he dare?

Sir John Percival half rose to his feet and sat down again. He was neither going to help nor hurt, just let the disaster play itself out. With what intent?

Miriam almost hated him, except that wasn't fair. Help would be patronizing, and he did not have a part in this nightmare.

Gonville, on the stand, looked totally confused.

Marcus let out his breath in a sigh. Everyone was staring at him. "We all know how it played out," he picked up the thread. "A sad story. So, let's get to that as soon as we can." He turned to the judge. "Milord, with your permission, may I set up the case with the testimony that matters? Dr. Salisbury, the medical examiner at the time the body was identified, said that the cause of death was a blow to the back of the head which broke the skull. I can have it reread into evidence, if the court wishes?"

"Do you wish it, Sir John?" the judge asked Percival.

"No, my lord, it is a matter of record and we are all aware of it, thank you."

"Very well, Mr. fford Croft," the judge

conceded. "We will call Dr. Salisbury, if necessary. Proceed."

"Thank you, milord," Marcus said graciously, then turned to the witness stand again. "Now, Mr. Gonville, you gathered all the possible evidence as to how the fire occurred, and who was where at the time, did you not?"

"Of course. With the help of the police, naturally."

"Of course." Marcus smiled. "Without wearing out His Lordship's patience with details, were you satisfied that they were diligent in their duty?"

Percival rose to his feet. "My lord, you cannot be convinced of the correctness of the police search if Mr. fford Croft does not take us through it. If he has . . . forgotten . . . any of the details, I can assist him."

Miriam stiffened. Was that condescension? Or was Percival actually trying to get the case moving? Even trying to rescue an older man quite clearly lost? This was awful. Why didn't Kitteridge step in? Did he not dare?

"Thank you." Marcus came alive again. "But none of this is what is necessary." He shook his head vigorously. "We do not contest the evidence, only that it was incomplete in one or two aspects. And that a great deal of it is not there. I propose to save the court's time and not argue the details with which we all agree, my lord." He did not look at Percival.

The judge appeared nonplussed for a moment, then collected his wits. "Very well, continue. But if at any time I feel that we have lost some necessary element, I shall require you to return to it. If you wish, your junior can handle some of it. I see that Mr. Kitteridge is in the seat behind you."

"Thank you, my lord, most considerate of you." Again, Marcus smiled, and very slightly inclined his head. "I have a few questions for Mr. Waveney, if it pleases the court?"

"You mean Mr. Gonville."

"No, my lord, I want to ask Mr. Waveney, who served as Daventry's defense, a few questions."

"Very well. Sir John, have you any questions for Mr. Gonville, before we excuse him?"

"No, thank you, my lord," Percival replied.

Marcus called Waveney and drew from him details on the case he had put together to defend Roger Daventry. "It was successful?" Marcus asked conversationally, even courteously, as if he did not already know.

"Yes, sir." Waveney half smiled. Everyone obviously knew the answer. "Sir Roger was acquitted."

"Ah, there we have it," Marcus agreed. "He was acquitted. The jury decided he was innocent."

"*Not guilty* is the term, sir," Waveney corrected him.

"I think *not guilty beyond a reasonable doubt,*" Marcus elaborated. "But it was Lady Daventry's body, yes?"

"Yes, I'm afraid so," Waveney agreed.

"And she died as a result of the fire."

"Yes."

"Which was arson. It was caused deliberately. It was not a complete accident?" That was a question.

Waveney was beginning to look a little irritated. "Correct, and they caught the arsonist and tried him for the murder of Lady Daventry. And found him guilty beyond a reasonable doubt. He hanged for it."

Miriam winced. She thought of Adria Leigh.

There was a rustling around the room, a little uncomfortable shifting at the mention of the death penalty. Emotion stirred like electricity in the air before a storm.

Lord Justice Walpole was now intensely interested in where Marcus's line of questioning was going. He sat forward in his great chair, a look of concentration on his lean face.

"Yes," Marcus agreed quietly. "Another death, a young man who had never committed a crime before and I believe was acquainted with Lady Daventry."

Waveney stood a little straighter. "Yes, and before you rake up that tragedy again, he was handsome and had ideas far above his social reach. He paid a very high price for it. I think one can leave this in decent peace now."

"Ah," Marcus let out his breath. "Maybe. We'll see. Thank you, Mr. Waveney. Perhaps Sir John has something to ask you?"

"No, thank you," Percival replied. "I am sure there must be more to your case. You have said nothing yet to reconsider any part of the original verdict. If this is all, then you have wasted our time, Mr. fford Croft."

"Oh, it's not all," Marcus assured him. He turned back to the judge. "It's late in the day to call a new witness, my lord. I will do so if you ask me. However, I prefer to keep Sir Roger Daventry until tomorrow. I have rather a lot of questions to ask him."

"You cannot raise the past verdict again, Mr. fford Croft," the judge reminded him. "Whatever you think of it. It is over."

"Yes, my lord, I'm very aware of that. I

am calling Sir Roger as a witness."

"Very well, call him first thing in the morning."

"Thank you, my lord."

Sir Roger Daventry was now nearly sixty, slender, with dark eyes, dark brows, and a streak of silver at both temples. He wore a plain, elegantly cut suit and a grace of supreme confidence as he walked up to the stand and swore to tell the truth and nothing less.

This morning, Marcus looked stressed. His wig was pushed to the back of his head, as if he had not looked at his reflection before leaving the dressing room, and his gown was already sliding off his left shoulder.

"Good morning, Sir Roger," Marcus began, as soon as Daventry had taken the oath. "I am sorry for the tragedy that happened to your family, and for having to rake it up all over again."

"Good morning, Mr. fford Croft," Daventry replied. "It is most unpleasant to have to relive it, but I'm sure you are doing your duty, as you see it." He sounded polite. He had a good voice, smooth, low, and with perfect diction. It was not quite patronizing, but close to it. "I don't know what I can tell you. What I hear from my lawyers is that you have all the information in the case in which I had part. Although it has been over for twenty years."

"Quite, but its effects live on," Marcus replied. He was more than polite, almost respectful. "That evidence made history, at least in the legal and forensic-science worlds."

"I suppose so," Daventry agreed without expression.

"Oh, yes." Marcus nodded. "It has been accepted law in cases with extremely hot fires. I know personally of people who have used that expert evidence and escaped the rope."

"It has been twenty years," Daventry repeated. "I fail to see how that has any relevance to me."

"But you continue to know Sir Barnabas Saltram socially."

Daventry shrugged very slightly, but it was an awkward gesture. "To some degree. I was enormously grateful to him. He worked very hard indeed to experiment, explore theories on heat, bone, chemicals, to prove my innocence. *Thank you* doesn't seem to suffice. Are you trying to paint a picture of me as an ungrateful man?" There was a flicker of humor in his eyes, just for a moment, then gone again.

"I am sure you are not an ungrateful man, sir," Marcus said, his voice stronger, a smile on his face. "I believe you have done quite a lot to further Sir Barnabas's career, both legal and social."

"Is that a question? Yes, of course I did. I paid his bill for forensic services, although through my lawyer, naturally. And I personally extended my gratitude by proposing him for membership in one of the clubs where I have influence. That is how these things work. You recommend those you trust and find decent and reliable, who excel in their professions. I was certain he was bound for success in many spheres, and I was proved correct. What is your point, Mr. fford Croft?"

Marcus hitched his gown up his left shoulder.

"That both of you have proved successful in these twenty years. He saved your life and you, in gratitude, introduced him to a social life and to a success that he no doubt deserved, but could not have achieved without you."

"True, but you are wasting my time, sir. Yours is your own to do with as you wish, but the court's is not."

Marcus looked a little nonplussed. "You

411

seem unusually irritated, Sir Roger. Why?"

Daventry was wrong-footed. "You seem to be implying something improper."

"Was it improper?" Marcus looked startled.

Miriam sat forward, suddenly paying more attention. Did she imagine a pattern, or was it really there?

"No, it was not!" Daventry snapped. "I suffered an appalling loss, a complete devastation. Half my ancestral home, one of the loveliest in England, was destroyed. For over four hundred years my family have lived in it and cared for it. My beloved wife died horribly. Then, as if that were not enough, I was blamed for it, and actually tried in court. For days I feared they would find me guilty and I would be hanged. You talk about repayment?" Now he was undeniably angry.

Miriam sat forward a little more. Did Marcus realize what feeling he was raising in the gallery? Daventry had suffered. More to the point, he had stood trial and been found not guilty. And did he also realize that Daventry mentioned the loss of his home before the death of his wife?

"Not repayment, Sir Roger," Marcus said gently. "Gratitude."

"I'm sorry," Daventry said more quietly,

regaining his composure with an effort. "In spite of all the years, it still hurts. I don't know what you imagine I can tell you that will help. My poor Marguerite was burned to death by whoever set that fire, and the police were satisfied that it was James Leigh. What are you trying to do here, apart from reawaken old pain?"

"If you are not aware, Sir Roger, of the other cases that have arisen because of certain medical evidence and verdicts, I am afraid I am not in a position to tell you. I suggest you continue to attend this trial. Thank you for your attention. And by the way," he added, "I'm sure you intended to put the loss of your wife before the loss of your property."

There was silence in the courtroom.

"Please remain on the stand, in case Sir John wishes to ask you any further questions. Thank you." Marcus returned to his seat, his face unreadable, at least to Miriam, watching nervously.

Percival rose to his feet. "I'm sorry for this distress, Sir Roger," he said gravely. "Have you any knowledge of that tragic fire that you did not testify to in court, at the time you were tried and found not guilty? If you do, you may tell it now." He waited a second — two, three — then nodded his head slightly. "As I thought. Thank you, Sir Roger, I have nothing more."

The court was duly adjourned, and Miriam walked out into the icy air of the street, glad of its sharp chill to concentrate her attention. She was trying to think what on earth Marcus was planning, and how she could help.

# CHAPTER NINETEEN

The following day, Daniel was waiting outside the courtroom. Marcus was going to call him as a witness to the entire Jessie Beale case, from the murder of Paddy Jackson through to the conviction of Jessie herself. Of course, the real purpose was to expose Saltram's flawed evidence.

Daniel was not required to tell anything but the truth, but he knew that Percival would do his best to discredit him, make him seem inexperienced, which he was — and incompetent, which he was not. He hoped Percival would not try to imply that he had deliberately engineered the trial to find Jessie Beale guilty, which he had, but in the cause of justice. And he had done nothing illegal. He had not lied, given the prosecutor confidential information, or tried to serve anything but justice, if rather obliquely.

It was still possible to be tripped up,

exposed for a foolish or unintentional manipulation of the law and the jury in order to get the verdict he personally believed was right. Percival was very experienced, very clever. He was not a King's Counsel without having earned it.

Did Daniel want to be a King's Counsel one day? "Take silk," as it was called? At this moment, he wanted to be anything but a lawyer.

The usher came and called him to go in.

He walked up the central aisle and into the witness box, deliberately not searching the crowd in the packed gallery to see Miriam's bright hair or Charlotte. She would be there somewhere; she had said she would be.

He took the Bible in his hand and swore to tell the truth. Then he turned to face Marcus. The old man looked tense, his face pinched with anxiety, his shoulders even more lopsided than usual. His robes were crooked, clearly. His hair poked out from under his wig in white tufts, making him look as if he were coming unraveled.

"Good morning, Mr. Pitt," Marcus began soberly. "I want you to take your mind back to late September of last year. A young woman by the name of Jessie Beale approached you and asked you for legal assistance. Precisely what was this regarding?"

"Her boyfriend, Robert Adwell, had been arrested and accused of the murder of a rival of his, Patrick Jackson," Daniel replied.

"Did you accept the task?"

"Yes, sir. I asked —"

"That is not necessary, Mr. Pitt," Marcus cut him off. "If Sir John wishes to know the terms, he will ask you. They are not pertinent to my point. You accepted. Did you then find out all you could regarding the supposed crime?"

"Yes, sir."

"To whom did you speak?"

"The police inspector in charge."

"Mr. Quarles?"

"Yes, sir."

"We will get him to corroborate that, if the court wishes. But in the meantime, what did you learn from him?"

Percival moved a little in his seat, but he did not interrupt. He looked to be taking notes.

Daniel cleared his throat. "That the body of Patrick Jackson had been found at the scene of a fire, very badly burned, but still identifiable. That Rob Adwell had been burned less seriously and was much farther from the seat of the fire. They were known to be rivals in minor criminal enterprises:

417

Paddy and his brothers versus Rob Adwell and various people."

"Adwell admitted to being there?" Marcus interrupted.

"He was found there, sir, he could hardly deny it. And he was not hurt very seriously, but definitely had a few nasty burns."

"Did he tell you that he was innocent of Jackson's death?"

"Yes, he was insistent on that. Jackson did not —"

Marcus held up his hand. "Don't tell me until I ask you, sir! 'Yes' will suffice. He claimed innocence, yes?"

"Yes, sir." Daniel realized he must make allowances for Marcus's very natural tension. This was the first case he had tried in a very long time. His skills were rusty, his memory even more so. And this was a retrial on which a great deal depended. If he lost, the Crown would find it very difficult to retry the other cases based on Saltram's evidence. Just as everyone feared, if he won, then heaven alone knew how many must be tried again. How many convictions would be overturned, innocent men — or guilty men — freed.

Was it really worth it? And would Marcus be blamed for raising the issue at all? Was his legacy to be confusion, where there had been certainty before? But what type of certainty was it, if at the price of injustice?

It was worth it.

"Mr. Pitt, pay attention, if you please!" Marcus snapped.

Was he losing his self-control? Or had he heightened his emotion so the court, and the judge in particular, did not let their attention wander? Looking at Marcus's face, Daniel could not tell. "Yes, sir," he said smartly.

"Why was Robert Adwell charged with murder, precisely, if you please?"

"Because the postmortem examination of Mr. Jackson found that the back of his skull was badly cracked, sir, and there was hardly any smoke in his lungs. Which would indicate —"

Percival rose to his feet. "My lord, Mr. Pitt has no medical qualifications that the court has been made aware of. We have heard that my learned friend's daughter has some medical aspirations, but the court cannot hear the secondhand opinion of a young lady, no matter how charming or intelligent she may be."

There was a hiss of indrawn breath around the room, a rustle of movement as people sat upright. Daniel felt as if a hot, dry wind had passed through.

The judge's face was pinched with annoyance, but at whom one could not tell. He looked at Marcus. "Mr. fford Croft?"

"If my learned friend would leave Mr. Pitt to answer, my lord, he will find out he consulted with the medical examiner, the police surgeon, a Dr. Appleby. I can call Dr. Appleby, by all means. The question I asked this witness was why Adwell was charged with the crime. I can call my daughter to the stand, to assure you that she was not consulted by the police in the matter." He looked innocent, not a shadow of a smile on his face. But Daniel would have bet a month's salary Marcus was laughing inside.

"I take your point," the judge said, his face also suggesting a variety of emotions. He turned to Daniel. "Mr. Pitt, you may proceed. The police surgeon, Dr. Appleby, told you that the skull was cracked?"

"Yes, sir," Daniel replied.

"And did he tell you what he believed to be the cause of this damage?" Marcus continued.

"Yes, sir. He believed it to be a heavy blow, with a blunt instrument, possibly some kind of truncheon."

"Not an accidental by-product of intense heat?"

"No."

"But there was intense heat?"

"Yes, sir."

"Did you ask him why he did not think it was the heat that caused the cracks? It would have been a natural question to ask, especially since you were acting on behalf of the defense."

"Yes, sir, I did ask. He answered it was because Mr. Jackson had died before having time to inhale much smoke, which would seem to be well before the heat became great enough to crack a skull."

"Ah, but could he not have died earlier, and then his skull would have cracked after his death, from the heat?"

"It could have happened that way, as far as I know, sir, but then the crack of the skull would not have been the cause of death. There was apparently not enough smoke in his lungs to have choked him. As Sir John has pointed out, I have no medical qualifications, nor did I ask anyone else's opinion. Dr. Appleby's opinion made sense to me and to the police. I accepted it. Anyway, my job was to defend Adwell against what he was charged with."

"Quite so." Marcus nodded his head. "Quite so. Which I believe you did, yes?"

"Yes, sir."

"And he was found not guilty?"

"Yes, sir."

"How did you do that?" He twisted round to look at the judge. "My lord, please indulge me. This is indeed immediately pertinent to the case presently being retried here. It is recent: within three months. The charge was the same in substance, the defense the same. None but the guilty, if indeed there are any, need fear the outcome."

"I will give you a certain latitude, Mr. fford Croft." The judge held his hand up before Percival was any more than beginning to rise to his feet. "But the court is not going to retry any case but this one, if you are hoping for such a thing."

Marcus did not speak. He knew better than to interrupt a judge whose leniency was sorely needed. But he shook his head fiercely.

"Good," said the judge. "If you appear to be making any other legal conclusions, I will stop you. Otherwise, proceed. Tell us, Mr. Pitt, as briefly as you can, how you defended your client."

"I believed Mr. Adwell, that he was indeed innocent," Daniel continued. "Therefore, there had to be another explanation. I had heard the reputation of Sir Barnabas Saltram, and through certain connections I was able to meet him and tell him of the case. He very graciously agreed to look at the evidence and give his expert opinion in court."

"For a price?" Marcus interrupted. "A professional consultation fee."

"No," Daniel answered. "In the interest of justice. That is what he told me, and I considered that I was acting in the same interest. Mr. Adwell had nothing like enough money to pay either of us. Sir Barnabas said he would act without payment to see a fair verdict on the facts."

"You believed him?" Marcus asked, letting a slight surprise into his voice.

"I did. I still do. I believe he quite often gives of his time to those he believes innocent, but who do not have the money to pay for expert opinion."

Marcus nodded slowly. They had already agreed on this much. "Excellent. And Sir Barnabas examined the body of Patrick Jackson and gave you his opinion, which you then had him testify to in court, yes?"

"Yes, sir."

"And that was . . . briefly, if you please?" Marcus's white eyebrows shot up and his eyes remained wide open.

"That the fire had reached a great heat very swiftly, because there were highly flammable substances in the warehouse. It was on Tooley Street, by the docks, where it happened. These substances explained why the heat grew intense almost immediately. It fit in with the facts I knew, and the jury accepted it and found Robert Adwell not guilty."

"Very succinctly put." Marcus nodded, hitching his gown up again.

Everyone in the room relaxed; Daniel could feel it. There was a whisper of fabric against fabric, a sigh as people sat back a little.

Everyone . . . except Marcus. He was far from finished. Daniel dared not look at Kitteridge, or even turn to look for Miriam, though he would have seen her immediately. No one else had hair quite that shade. He did not dare look at his mother. He chose to believe she was still there.

The judge leaned forward to speak, a slight frown on his face. Daniel had much he wanted to say. Where was the relevance to the Daventry case? If anything, Marcus was making Daniel's case for him. Surely Marcus had not lost his thread of the story.

Marcus spoke before the judge could. "Was that the end of the matter, Mr. Pitt?"

"No," Daniel said quickly. "A very short time later — three weeks, maybe — Miss

424

Beale sent for me. She had been arrested for the death of Robert Adwell, which had occurred in exactly the same manner."

"Did you say 'exactly'?" the judge asked, frowning.

"Yes, sir."

All through the gallery, people were gasping, turning to each other as if they had not heard correctly, shifting in their seats.

The judge banged his gavel sharply.

The buzz died away.

The judge looked toward Daniel, frowning. "I hope you are not exercising what you imagine to be some kind of humor, Mr. Pitt. This is a very serious matter indeed. If you aspire to remain part of this legal system, you will give it the gravity it deserves — not in your opinion, in mine."

"Yes, my lord," Daniel said gravely. "I had thought at first there had been some kind of stupid error, and I went to see Miss Beale, where she was being held in custody. And she was perfectly correct. Mr. Adwell had died in a local fire, and she was charged with his murder. The circumstances were identical to those of Paddy Jackson's death."

"And what evidence was there that she was guilty?" The judge shook his head sharply. "This is preposterous!"

"Yes, my lord, that was precisely what I

thought. I wondered if Paddy Jackson's brothers had taken revenge for his death. That would make sense. At least, I thought it would."

Marcus considered it for a while. "I see."

Daniel watched him, anxiety deepening as the seconds ticked by. Had he lost his train of thought? He had not confided in Daniel the path he intended to follow.

Daniel was about to say something, but Marcus drew in his breath.

"Mr. Pitt, did you believe Rob Adwell to be guilty before you obtained Sir Barnabas Saltram's testimony?"

Marcus knew that Daniel had at least thought it was possible. Was he expecting him to tell that truth? He drew in his breath, too. "I feared he might be, but I was not sure, sir."

"And afterward? After Sir Barnabas's testimony?"

"No, sir, I believed him to be innocent."

"And the case against Jessie Beale was exactly the same." He looked curious, polite.

Sir John Percival rose to his feet, but seemed uncertain exactly what he wanted to say. "My lord, I think it might be a good time to take a brief break. Mr. fford Croft seems to have lost his place."

"Not at all," Marcus said with a shake of

his head, which made his wig slip very slightly farther to the left. "Not at all. I am just getting to the point. I will be a little faster, if Your Lordship wishes."

"Perhaps that will be a good idea," Lord Justice Walpole agreed.

Percival sat down again, not looking any happier.

Marcus looked back at Daniel. "Adwell was acquitted. You think it a just verdict. Did you defend Jessie Beale?"

"Yes, sir."

"Why?"

"She asked me to. I felt —" What answer could he give that was honest?

"Would it be fair to say that she tricked you, and you had no good reason to deny her? For one thing, it might have prejudiced the jury, considering that they were bound to know of Adwell's case," Marcus suggested.

"Yes, sir."

The judge frowned. "You are leading the witness, Mr. fford Croft. Please, let him get there by himself . . . or not."

"I'm sorry, my lord." Marcus turned back to Daniel. "Did you believe she also was innocent, and you might use the same evidence to prove it?"

"Yes, sir." At one point, he had.

427

"And did it prove so again?" Marcus seemed innocently interested.

"No, sir."

"And why was that?" Marcus asked.

There was utter silence in the room, except for a very faint rustle of the judge's sleeves across the bench as he folded his arms.

"Because the prosecution called one expert witness," Daniel replied. "A Dr. Evelyn Hall."

"He was as expert as Sir Barnabas Saltram?" Marcus kept his voice almost devoid of emotion, but not quite.

"She," Daniel corrected. "Evelyn Hall is a woman, sir."

"Oh, yes!" Marcus said, as if just discovering that fact. "Evelyn is one of those names that can be either male or female. Is she anything like as well qualified as Dr. Saltram?"

"Yes, sir. She studied in Britain and France, and in Holland, where I believe work is judged entirely on merit. Gender does not come into it."

"Well, well, admirable practice. And what did this Dr. Evelyn Hall tell you?"

"She showed three skulls, sir. One was cracked by extreme heat, caused by a highly flammable substance. White phosphorous

428

goes very quickly to a heat of five thousand degrees. Explosive, you might say. And also two skulls cracked by blows to the head."

"And how did she know this?" Marcus asked.

"She undertook the experiments herself," Daniel said. "The one thing about all the fire-caused fractures was that they occurred only across and around the dome of the skull, with a star-shaped central crack and a web of smaller cracks. Those cracks caused by blows were anywhere, many in the back of the head, where the skull attaches to the spine. It was very distinct. Enough for the jury to conclude that Adwell had definitely been killed by a blow to the head, not by heat. They found Jessie Beale guilty."

There was a heavy, tense silence in the room. Someone dropped a walking stick on the floor, and it sounded like a gunshot.

A woman let out a little shriek.

Daniel's mouth was as dry as the dust on the law books he had not opened since this began.

"Were you shocked?" Marcus asked, breaking the breathless tension.

"No, sir."

"Why not? What did you know that led you to expect this?"

"The case was a mirror image, sir. I came

429

to see that Jessie Beale was possibly guilty of both deaths. The first was more an experiment to see if it worked. It did . . . superbly. She took advantage of the method to get rid of Rob Adwell, also."

"Did you learn why?"

"Yes, sir, at least evidence that is strongly indicative. We had assumed that Adwell and Paddy Jackson were leaders of rival groups of warehouse thieves. It now looks more as if there was only one gang, and the rivalry was for its leadership. It seems Jessie Beale had the brains and was behind everything."

"Indeed." Marcus continued to look startled. "And why did you take on this case? A little drunk with your success?"

"No, sir. I took it on because Mrs. Leigh, the widow of the man they hanged for murdering Lady Daventry, asked me to. And I don't consider my encounter with Jessie Beale to have been a success. She made a complete fool of me." That was the truth.

Marcus pursed his lips. "Not so much," he said gently. "But to move ahead. You got the right verdict both times. Rob Adwell was not guilty, and Jessie Beale was. And when she was charged, you defended her, and lost. So, you still got the right verdict." He turned to the judge, who was sitting bolt upright at his bench. "Thank you, my lord. That is my case for the reconsideration of the guilt of James Leigh. A particular piece of evidence, the cracks on the skull of the victim, has been proved in court by an extremely competent expert witness to be flawed. The man charged then was found not guilty. I ask that James Leigh be found not guilty also, by the same evidence and for the same reasons. His family deserves that much. It is only a very small part of what they deserve."

"Are you suggesting we rule Lady Daventry's death to be an accident, Mr. fford Croft?" the judge asked.

Marcus hesitated. He glanced once very briefly at Daniel, then looked back at the judge. "If it please the court, Your Lordship, Lady Daventry died from a blow to the back of the head. I do not know who started the fire. I believe it would be the justice she deserves, and Mrs. Leigh deserves, to find out who did set it. The evidence against James Leigh was largely uncontested, and he had no known motive for such an act. Certainly, he stole nothing . . ."

"That will be taken care of," the judge answered him. "But the question of Lady Daventry's death remains one of murder now. Deliberate murder, rather than an unintentional murder as a result of an arsonist's fire. That is an issue we cannot leave open."

Percival rose to his feet. "My lord, if I might remind the court, Sir Roger Daventry has already been tried on this charge and found not guilty by a jury of his peers. He cannot be tried a second time for the same offense."

"I am aware of that, Sir John," Walpole said tartly. "Marguerite Daventry was not the only victim of this affair. James Leigh also died, and was dishonored in death. Many people had a hand in that, intentionally or not. And the question remains open as to who started that fire. If Lady Daventry was struck over the head, then it is still a question of murder, clearly by someone already in the house at that time. The one who is totally guilty is the man who set the fire, his crime of arson intended to cover the main crime. When we prove beyond a reasonable doubt who that was, we will charge him with arson, and also the resultant death of James Leigh, who was as surely murdered as if he had been shot with a gun. Except that this was infinitely more cruel."

Percival was still on his feet. His voice was less certain, even a little hoarse. "The case is not quite finished, my lord. I would like tomorrow to have the opportunity to question Mr. Daniel Pitt. We have heard a great deal of evidence about fire, experiments, and conclusions. We have heard of Evelyn Hall only from the other side. There are a great many questions I would like to ask pertaining to her and her qualifications. I have a whole case to present to Dr. Barnabas Saltram tomorrow, if it please the court, and I must, in justice for him, and for this trial, allow the opportunity to defend his reputation, which otherwise may have received possibly irreparable damage. I need creative research before I can question Mr. Pitt, who I believe has much personal interest in this case and its outcome. I will also call Dr. Hall, and possibly Miss Miriam fford Croft, who also has a bigger part in this than the jury now suspects. If it pleases the court."

Daniel felt the room swing around him. It was like one of those pieces of music where, when you think it is the end, it starts again, even faster than before. And louder.

# CHAPTER TWENTY

Daniel reached his lodgings feeling cold, wet, and exhausted. But he had barely closed his bedroom door and taken off his jacket when there was a knock on the outside.

Mrs. Portiscale's voice came clearly from the landing. "Mr. Pitt, there's a gentleman here to see you. Said it's urgent, sir, and very important."

Daniel swore under his breath. "All right, Mrs. Portiscale, I'll be out in a moment. Have him wait for me downstairs, please."

"Says it's important and private, sir. Seems like a real gentleman. I'll put him in my sitting room so you can speak private, like."

"Thank you, Mrs. Portiscale, I'll be right down."

"Yes, sir."

He heard the anxiety in her voice, even through the wood of the door, but she also

434

sounded impressed. Who was it?

He put on a dry, warmer shirt and a casual jacket, and brushed his wet hair sharply back, although it fell forward again before he reached the door. He had relaxed once he stepped inside Mrs. Portiscale's comfortable, familiar house. Now he felt stiff, muscles tight, ready for some unknown battle.

He walked straight to the sitting room and went in without knocking.

Barnabas Saltram was standing by the mantelpiece, almost in front of the fire, which had been freshly stoked and was burning nicely. He must have given his overcoat to Mrs. Portiscale, but the front of his hair was dark with rainwater, and there was an indentation where his hat had been. He looked cold and angry.

"I trust we will not be interrupted by your housekeeper. I do not wish tea or whisky or anything else that she might offer in some misguided idea of hospitality. This is a business meeting."

"I have no intention of offering any hospitality," Daniel snapped. "This sitting room is hers and she offered it to afford a degree of privacy. Or do you prefer to do this in public?"

"This will serve adequately. And it is in

your interest not to do this in public —"
Saltram returned coldly.

"I have no interest in doing it at all," Daniel interrupted in a tone just as curt as Saltram's. "You have chosen to come here to see me. You had better tell me what for. I presume it is not a legal matter, or you would have taken it either to Mr. fford Croft or to Mr. Kitteridge."

Saltram straightened up a little, but he did not move away from the fireplace. "I came to see you because you are the person most likely to be able to stop this before it ruins too many lives. Miss fford Croft is beside the point. She will have little ability to do anything but plead with all of you. And she will not need prompting for that. Kitteridge has no power to make a decision, and I believe he has not the will either. Fford Croft himself is old, forgetful, and half the time has very little idea what he's doing. I am not sure that you do either, and you are emotional, so you have little self-control anyway. But you have the most chance of concluding this sensibly."

In spite of himself, Daniel was curious, and he knew he could not afford to dismiss Saltram without listening. "What is it you propose?" he asked, making sure the sitting-room door was closed.

"I propose that you reconsider your evidence regarding Dr. Evelyn Hall, who is not as above fault as you seem to regard her. We have different opinions on a lot of things. The results of fire on the human skeleton, for one."

"The jury can hear both opinions and make up their own minds," Daniel replied. "Daventry can't be tried again for Marguerite's death, whatever the jury thinks, but Leigh deserves a pardon. Though much good it will do him. Had the jury in that case heard Dr. Hall's evidence and her experiments, they would have found differently, and I believe you know that."

Saltram showed no sign of having heard him, except a slight raising of the eyebrows.

"No doubt you've also considered all the other cases that will have to be raked up and retried, if the jury believes Daventry guilty. Even if they are helpless to do anything about it."

Daniel smiled very slightly. "You mean it will be troublesome."

A flash of temper crossed Saltram's face. "*Troublesome* is a very mild word for the misery it will cause."

"For whom? You? It would cost you more than trouble. It would cost you your reputation for infallibility," Daniel said acidly.

"It could cost much more than that for some," Saltram retorted. "It may well cost you your job with Marcus fford Croft, too. What will his company be worth after this? He's a fool. He forgets his own name half the time." He moved a step away from the mantel. The fire was burning up. "He may owe your father some favor, or perhaps his silence is all he needs. But you'll be unemployable. There's not a decent chambers in London that will employ you after this! Or that fool, Kitteridge, either."

Daniel felt a coldness, a chill running through him, as if the light had dimmed.

Saltram saw it in his face and half smiled. "Exactly. And I am only just beginning." He caressed the word. "Miriam fford Croft. What do you know of her early years? Her education, for example?" He shrugged. "Don't bother answering. Nothing, nothing at all, except what she may have told you. Did she say she was an excellent student? Even brilliant? As good as any of the men?" There was a sneer in his voice. "That she was a fine mathematician? Chemist? That she knew anatomy and could draw an exact skeleton and name every bone?"

"No."

"Well that, at least, is in her favor," Saltram said with a curl of his lip. "She did not lie, except by implication. She was a poor student. She lacked diligence, and application —"

"I've watched her work," Daniel cut across him. "She has the most intense concentration of anyone I have seen."

"Watched her? And did you understand what she was doing, or why? For heaven's sake, man, you could watch a pretty woman for any amount of time you care to waste, and have no idea of what she's doing, to any purpose, if you even understand the discipline she is following. I can watch a chef work and produce a magnificent dish, but I have no notion what he has done, or how."

"The fact that you did not understand how he did it is completely irrelevant to the worth of the dish," Daniel said sharply. "That is a measure of your ignorance, not of his skill. And you don't need to prove my ignorance of medicine or chemistry to judge Miriam fford Croft. Her peers did, and found her excellent."

Saltram gave a bark of laughter. "Don't be absurd. You are too old to be this naïve. That belongs to a schoolboy still in short trousers, learning his Latin grammar. She has no degrees."

"Because she's a woman. She passed the

exams. That ought to be what matters."

"Of course she passed them," Saltram said bitterly. "She's a pretty woman, and at that time she was also young."

Daniel saw Saltram's leer and felt the heat scorch up his face.

"I see you understand," Saltram observed sardonically. "A little slow, but you get there eventually, when it is the only possibility left to you. If you force me to defend myself in court, then I have no choice but to destroy her. I'm sure you understand that?"

"I understand that you are telling me that if I do not back you in the witness box, then you will slander Miss fford Croft and say that such marks as she gained in university were given her because she slept with the masters awarding those marks." Daniel's voice was as bitter and hard as his rage. "Since you were one of them, you're in a position to know that." The moment he said the words, Daniel knew that he had done something irreversible. He had closed every path of mediation, agreement, or negotiation. He remembered Marcus telling him never to shoot the bear unless you could be certain of killing it.

Had that been inevitable? Had he actually changed anything?

"Your colleagues will not appreciate your

stating that they all slept with her, in exchange for giving her good marks," he went on, his voice wavering a little. Was that fear, or outrage? "You put their careers in jeopardy, too. Open to bribery, and to taking advantage of vulnerable students?"

"Oh, don't be such an ass!" Saltram dismissed him with his tone. "She offered, they took her up on it. She was very pretty. It was twenty years ago, and she was young, ambitious beyond anything she could reach, but she had not realized it yet. And she was not so bitter."

"So, you sold her something useless, at the price of her virtue. Admirable," Daniel said, his tone dripping contempt. "The searcher after scientific truth, the man who time and again placed his hand upon the Bible and swore before the court to tell the truth. So, God help you, you tell what truth suits your explanation, what the actual truth is doesn't matter. Are you still available to bend it, if the woman is young enough? Pretty enough? And desperate enough?"

Saltram strode forward two steps and swung his right fist, backhanded, across Daniel's face, sending him sprawling onto the carpet.

Daniel landed hard, but missed hitting his head on the edge of the small table. He was dizzy for a moment and his ears were ringing. Then his head cleared and he climbed very carefully to his feet and regained his balance, watching Saltram all the time, in case he struck again. "That, presumably, is a yes," he said carefully, enunciating each word. He shook his head; his ears were still ringing. He moved his jaw carefully, testing if any of his teeth were loose. "Definitely a yes," he added. "I shall have some nice bruises in the morning."

"A drunken brawl," Saltram dismissed it with a slight wave of his hand.

"Are you drunk?" Daniel asked. "I'm not. And not much of a brawl. There isn't a mark on you, except . . ." He looked at the way Saltram was holding his fine, strong surgeon's hands in front of him, his right cradled in his left. ". . . for the bruises there will be on your knuckles, of course! Are you going to claim I hit your fist with my face?"

"I shall say you were so drunk that I evaded your blow easily and then struck you to stop the fight, before you really did injure me," Saltram replied without a moment's hesitation.

Daniel stared at him. "And all under oath, presumably. My God, how far you've fallen."

Saltram's face was white. "And do you

imagine that will save Miss fford Croft?" he asked. "Really, how little you know people. They will remember that, and whisper about it, joke aloud long after anyone knows or cares that I hit you. *Fford Croft and Gibson* will become a byword for someone who offers their favors to get the results they wish, but cannot earn."

"And *Saltram* will become the corresponding word for one who sells results to someone whose favors they can only buy, but cannot win," Daniel snapped back.

Saltram's face was bitter. "Men buy women's favors every day. It's the oldest trade in history. We all know that — and the kind of women who sell themselves."

There was no more to lose. "And the kind of men who need to buy them," Daniel spat back. He sensed exactly what would hurt. "The kind of men who are clumsy or inadequate. You should be careful about hitting people," he warned, meeting Saltram's eyes. "You'll damage those fine surgeon's hands of yours." He stared straight at him. "I nearly broke an ankle getting off a train a few weeks ago. That could happen to you, too!" He saw the slightest shadow cross Saltram's face and knew he had understood. That answered the question as to who had sent the man in the pinstriped trousers.

"I warn you, Pitt! I'll not attack you in court," Saltram said. "I'll be so courteous it will make your teeth ache, but I will tear Miriam into such little pieces there will be nothing left to put back together."

Daniel opened his eyes wide. "My God, she really did refuse you, didn't she! That's the unpardonable sin against vanity: to laugh at it."

Saltram strode to the door and flung it open, then slammed it shut behind him. The sound of it must have echoed through the house.

Saltram really intended to destroy Miriam. What had she done to him? Had she laughed at him in a situation where he felt humiliated? Had her awe, her respect bordering on fear, turned instead to mockery?

Not the Miriam he knew. She would have been as humiliated as he was, and perhaps for once disappointed. She would hardly have told anyone! She would ruin her own reputation, not his — if anyone even believed her!

Was she clever enough to have caught him in another mistake? Something other than the skulls? She had not mentioned anything. Perhaps it was that she had not put it together yet, but the pieces could fall into place anytime, since this recent encounter with Saltram brought it to her mind. That was even more likely if she took the matter to Dr. Hall! That would be sufficient for Saltram to have to silence her.

So Saltram was ready to attack first now.

Who could help? He had to make a decision tonight and be ready to carry it out in court tomorrow. He had no such happy delusion as to think Saltram might not fulfill his threat. Even if there were any doubts, Daniel had no right to take the risk.

Who could he ask? Who had he the obligation to tell? Marcus? Of course. But he wanted to have some further idea in his head before that.

He would have trusted Evelyn Hall. She would understand. But he knew that she had gone back to Holland, at least for the time being.

He hated to tell anyone what Saltram had said about Miriam, so that prevented him from telling Ottershaw. Or even Kitteridge. Saltram was right about one thing: whether people believed him or not, every time they thought of Miriam, they would remember the accusations. Miriam was different from most women, and for that she would be judged harshly. It only took one vicious whisper.

Who could help? At least give some decent

advice, without ever repeating the accusation?

It was late and cold, not a suitable evening to go calling, but he would ask his mother what she would do. Or perhaps he was just putting off having to tell Marcus that he would have to withdraw — and what Saltram had threatened to say of Miriam if he did not! That was what was going to hurt. But he did not doubt that Saltram would carry out his threat, and there was no way to fight against a charge like that. Stories were whispered, innuendo spread, and a reputation was ruined. He could not deny a lie without repeating it first. And when you did that, they had already won.

He put on his heavy overcoat and went out into the foggy night to find a taxi.

It was as black as midnight when he arrived at Keppel Street, although actually, it was still before nine in the evening.

Fortunately, his mother was in and his father had not yet returned from a late meeting.

"What is it?" she asked, the moment the front door was closed behind him.

"I'm in over my head," he replied honestly. "I don't want to tell Father. It's you I need to ask, at least to get it straight in my mind." He stood just inside the door and took off his coat, hat, and scarf, and then followed her as she led the way into the kitchen. This was the house in which he had grown up. He sat on one of the hardbacked chairs under the airing racks pulleyed up to the ceiling. He could smell the clean linen. Looking at the blue and white china and the Welsh dresser was like a trip back in time to childhood, when there was a certain kind of safety that never came back exactly the same way.

"The Daventry case?" Charlotte asked, pulling the kettle across onto the hob.

Daniel could remember back to when they had only one maid, and Charlotte did most of the cooking herself. Her mother had never cooked, nor had her grandmother. Funny what life could do. They had been born to wealth and a certain position in society. Charlotte had married a policeman, definitely a long way down socially and financially. And now she was Lady Pitt.

"Tell me," Charlotte invited.

Over tea, which warmed him through, and a piece of cake that he ate for the pleasure of it, he began, "Saltram came to my lodgings, to threaten me."

"Threaten you? With what?" she demanded, her face immediately dark with anger.

447

"With saying on the stand that Miriam offered to sleep with him to get good marks on her exams, which she didn't deserve . . ."

"And all the other professors, too?" There was a sarcastic edge to her voice.

"Yes. He said she was . . . a complete . . . whore . . ."

"If?"

"If I raise the subject at all, or anything else he doesn't like. And I believe him. He will!"

Charlotte did not hesitate. "You have to tell Marcus," she said gravely. "It is his family. And more complicated, it is his law firm that will be backing away . . . backing away from a fact that has been established and upon which I think many other cases will be judged. It is a big step."

"But you agree, I have to back down and let Saltram win? I hate . . ." It hurt him to say it. It was a bitter defeat, not like being beaten, more like surrender, the cowardice of not even fighting. "I hate to do that, but he's got me, hasn't he? It's not me he's going to hurt, it's Miriam and Marcus."

"Yes," she agreed, her face soft with pity. "That's what clever people do. They threaten someone else you care about. And they are both vulnerable. You like Miriam, don't you?" It was more a statement than a question.

That took him by surprise. "Yes, she's . . ." He couldn't find the right word. In fact, he did not know what it was.

Charlotte smiled. "It's one of the hardest things."

"What is?" He decided immediately that he did not want to know. He was not ready for what else it might involve. Not yet.

"Protecting people who are desperately vulnerable," she answered. "When they have the right to make their own choices. I used to let you fall over, when your father would have picked you up. I hated it. I felt brutal, as if you would think I didn't love you."

"I'm not Miriam's father," Daniel said too quickly. "I'm just a . . . a friend."

"And do you think Marcus is able to look after her, to protect her from this? From Saltram?" Charlotte asked. "Or from what people will say about her?"

Daniel thought hard, struggling for a way to say that if Marcus could protect her, then yes, he thought he would. But he remembered painfully and clearly seeing the look of momentary confusion in Marcus's eyes when he forgot that a law had been updated, changed, that it was not quite what he had assumed.

"Nobody can." He was not answering for

himself, but for Marcus.

"The one thing you can do is give her the right and the dignity of telling her the truth, Daniel, and letting her decide for herself. She's a child to Marcus, but she's not to herself, and she's not to you."

"I should let her face this alone?" he said indignantly.

"My darling, she will always have to face it alone . . . in the end. You can't stop that. Everybody is in the witness stand alone. There are lots of things in life where you can help, but the hardest decisions are made by oneself."

"You and Father —"

"Love each other," she finished for him. "And are separate people, with our own guilts and responsibilities. You must go and tell Marcus, honestly, exactly what Saltram will do. There's no time to find another way around it, whoever else you ask. Perhaps you had better take Toby . . . whatever his name is . . . with you, just to make sure Marcus is all right. You don't want him rushing off and shooting Saltram."

"Oh, Mother, don't be —" He shut his eyes. "You mean that, don't you?" It was little more than a whisper.

"Yes," she answered. "I don't blame him. I'd like to shoot Saltram myself! But it wouldn't help, not in the long run. But don't avoid the truth either. Marcus needs to know, and you have no right to keep it from him. Then you must go and see Miriam. Wake her up, if you have to, and tell her everything, good and bad, and let her make her own decision."

"Saltram will do it, do you realize that?"

"Yes, Daniel, I do, and if Miriam gives in to him, she will have to live with the results of that all her life, too. She will either way, so you must give her the right to make her own decisions. And the knowledge that you will be there, whatever happens."

"I will."

"I know. But make sure she knows it also. It's a very big thing in life to have friends."

His mother touched his bruised face very gently, but she said nothing, for which he felt immeasurable gratitude.

Daniel Found Kitteridge in his pajamas and a rather loud dressing gown. He was half asleep, and not very pleased to see Daniel.

"Sorry. I know you are hardly well yet," Daniel said, "but it won't wait. You'd better get dressed while I tell you what happened."

Kitteridge looked at him bleakly. "Do I care what's happened? Can't I care in the morning?" He ran his bony hands through his hair, leaving it looking like a brown haystack.

"Yes, you do care. Please, just get dressed and listen to me."

Kitteridge sighed and turned back toward the bedroom, signaling for Daniel to follow him. He put on his clothes, considered shaving, but he was too busy concentrating on what Daniel was telling him to bother with anything more than a brief wash.

"Oh God," he said wretchedly as Daniel relayed the night's events. "That's dreadful. What can we do? That's what your mother said, tell them? And let them decide? Are you sure?"

"Not exactly. She said let Miriam decide," Daniel corrected.

"But she's . . . how can she . . . ?" Kitteridge stopped. It was clear in his face how thoroughly he realized he was doing exactly what Charlotte had told Daniel not to do, taking the decision for her, as if she was not capable of making the best choice herself.

"Come on," Daniel said, starting for the door. "You look terrible, but so do I, I dare say. And you're right, it is dreadful."

It was eleven o'clock when Daniel and Kitteridge arrived at Marcus's house. He was still up, sitting by himself in the study beside a dying fire and staring into a balloon glass of brandy. He remained seated, stared at Daniel, then at Kitteridge. "What is it?" he asked grimly. His voice did not shake at all, his hands were perfectly steady. He was bitterly sober, even if perhaps he did not want to be.

Daniel and Kitteridge had already agreed that since it was Daniel to whom Saltram had come, and Daniel who would be in the witness stand tomorrow when Percival resumed questioning, it was also Daniel who should take the lead in this conversation now. Kitteridge would only be a support to make sure that Marcus did not do anything rash. And if his heart suddenly gave cause for concern, the doctor would be called.

There was no time for a preamble. Marcus took one look at their faces and Kitteridge's hair and the bruise beginning to come out on Daniel's cheek and eye, and he knew this matter was very serious indeed. It could only have to do with the case they were handling. Marcus came to the point. "Who hit you?" he asked Daniel.

"Saltram," he answered.

Marcus's face paled. "Ye gods, you're not joking, are you?"

"No, sir. We had a profound disagreement."

"You hit him first?"

"No, sir, he hit me. I did not hit him back."

"Well, well, you have more sense than I judged. Good for you," Marcus said with relief.

Daniel gritted his teeth. "If I testify truthfully tomorrow, regarding the white phosphorous, the cracks in the skull, and what causes them, then Saltram will swear that Miriam got her exam results by sleeping with various professors. Worst of all, he will say that she offered herself to him personally, and he refused her."

Marcus flushed scarlet, so deeply that Daniel was afraid he was going to have some kind of an apoplexy. But when he spoke, it was quite calmly. "And then you told him that that was not so?" That was a challenge that demanded an answer.

"Yes, sir, of course! But I cannot prove he's lying, and I cannot force him to be silent. That kind of poison needs only to be said, not proved, in order to do its damage."

"So, what do you advise?"

Daniel felt dizzy. How could he answer? Marcus was waiting, the hope draining out of his eyes as seconds ticked by. "That I ask Miriam what she wants to do. Tell her the truth and let her judge."

"For God's sake, Daniel," Kitteridge interrupted. "You can't ask her to —"

"I won't," Daniel cut him off. "If she tells the truth about Saltram, he will lie about her, and almost certainly ruin her reputation. She may bring him down, but at a cost to her that will be very high. If she doesn't, she becomes part of his lie of James Leigh's hanging, and of any other wrongful verdict past and future that rests on Saltram's testimony."

"Is that all?" Marcus said very quietly. "Nothing else?"

Daniel shook his head. "If there is, I can't see it, and I'm not going to make that decision for her. Just tell her all the truth that I know. I'm sorry, but I can't see anything else I can do."

"Should I tell her?" Marcus asked. "You know she is staying at lodgings near Octavius Ottershaw's house. They're working daily at salvaging what they can from his former laboratory and setting it up on his new premises. I can go there directly."

"No." This was one thing Daniel was sure of. "It must be her decision, without emotional pressure from any of us. You must send the message that you will back her, whatever she chooses."

"Of course. Daniel." Marcus blinked, and then blinked again while he fought tears. "Daniel, look after her. Don't let her sacrifice everything for my sake. All I care about is her."

"Yes, sir, I know that, and I'll tell her. Now, I'll take a taxi."

"You'll have trouble finding one at this hour. Take my car," Marcus interrupted. "Wake Hilton to drive you. He'll be ready in minutes. He'll look after you."

"Thank you."

Daniel had had no chance to see Miriam since the fire, but he knew she had spent all her time helping Ottershaw. It was a long, dirty, and tedious job, but she had never hesitated in undertaking it, because she knew it had to be done if he was to continue his work . . . and hers.

Marcus had given Daniel the address of the lodging house where Miriam was staying. It was now almost midnight, not a suitable hour to be calling on anyone. But the question of propriety was nothing at all compared to the disgrace that threatened them tomorrow, and he had no hesitation in knocking, ringing bells, and, if need be, throwing stones at windows, in order to speak to her.

As it turned out, another guest was awake and pacing the floor for his own reasons, and was willing to let Daniel in, once he said that he had come from Miss Miriam fford Croft's father's home and had to see her immediately.

"Of course," the man said. "Can I be of any assistance? I hope it is not a bereavement." His face expressed concern.

"Thank you," Daniel replied. "No, Mr. fford Croft is well enough for now, but it is a matter that cannot wait until morning."

The man must have seen Daniel's impatience. He took him upstairs to the door of Miriam's room and knocked. After a few moments, she answered, wearing a dressing robe, but with her hair cascading over her shoulders.

"This gentleman has come to see you about an urgent matter," the young man said. "Is that all right with you, Miss fford Croft?"

The color drained out of her face. "Is it Father?"

"No," Daniel assured her.

Daniel was exhausted, and above all afraid of how he would tell Miriam, but he must. He spared the man a smile and then accepted Miriam's invitation to enter her room.

"The trial?" she asked, the moment the door was closed.

"I'm sorry to come at this hour, but it can't wait. The case is going to close tomorrow, or at least to begin the closing." He had thought of dozens of ways to say this, but they all seemed inadequate, now that he was standing opposite her. He had never before seen her with her hair down. It spread out over her shoulders, like a shining cape. She looked much younger, and in her own way, beautiful.

She was staring at him, at the bruises on his face, now that he was in the light.

"Daniel!"

He dismissed the bruises. "Nothing." He swallowed hard, as if there was a lump stuck in his throat.

"Percival will question me tomorrow," he said, meeting her eyes and seeing a sudden new fear in them. "Saltram came to me this evening, to my lodgings, and warned me that if I don't back down on that evidence about the cracked skulls, and say that we all could have been wrong, he will" — he took another deep breath — "that he will tell lies about you, as a student. He will say you were mediocre, not very good, and that you got your good marks by offering to sleep with your professors." He saw the color flush up her face. Was that rage . . . or shame? And then he forced the idea out of his mind, even the question. He hurried on, his tongue falling over the words. "The only way I can stop him is to go back on my evidence and say we were wrong, and he was right. And Saltram will have his reputation back."

"And James Leigh will still have been hanged, and disgraced," she finished in a whisper, as if her mouth was too dry to speak. "Daventry will remain exonerated, and so will God alone knows how many others. The authorities will be delighted because they won't have to retry all the cases that rested on Saltram's evidence. 'No, my lord, I didn't hit her. It was the fire that crushed her skull.' "

The clerks at fford Croft and Gibson had gathered together records of all the cases affected by Saltram's testimony. There were piles of them.

"He'll do it, Miriam," he said to her. "He isn't making threats, he's warning us. For some reason, he hates you. And it doesn't matter how big a lie it is, it will be repeated, and some people will believe it. Maybe because they want to. It's much less painful to hate someone than it is to envy them."

"And you are willing to lie to save my reputation from this?" She was shaking, as if it was cold in the room. Perhaps it was, if one was wearing only a nightgown and a robe.

"I'm sorry." He did not know what he was apologizing for. Somehow he had let her down that it had ever come to this. "I had to tell you, to explain why I'm doing this, and . . ." He had lost the words again.

"To tell me?" she said shakily. "Or to ask me? Daniel, it is not your decision to make, it is mine!" She stopped. Her eyes were wide in the gaslight. "It is my name that is to be ruined for a lie about my intellect and virtue, for whatever that's worth. My virtue as a pure woman, not as a brave one, or an honest one, not even as a very bright one. Do you think that is worth more to me than the truth? I am trying to be a scientist; do you not understand that? I care as much for scientific truth as you do for truth in the law. And perhaps it is just as difficult to find. I will not say the Earth is flat, so that a lie might be perpetuated in forensic science, and guilt and innocence muddied over, so that a lot of people who don't know or care about me think I am virtuous, but stupid. And a coward as well."

460

"No!" He had not said what he meant, not at all. "No! What I mean is that you have to know the worst, and you have tonight to think about it, so that when you make up your mind, you at least know as much as possible to make the least terrible decision."

"What do you expect me to do? Let you lie, so I can run away? Is that what you want?" She was fighting tears now. Miriam, of all people! She rarely cried.

"No, I . . . I hate it, but I don't know what to do, except give you the right to choose."

She turned her back, perhaps to hide the fact that she was weeping. And that she was afraid also. "Thank you," she said, with a touch of desperate humor. "I think the truth will hurt, but lies will hurt more, and for longer. I imagine Saltram will say that I earned my excellent exam marks by offering myself to various professors, because actually they nearly all gave me very high marks. And that is a pretty serious slander on them. It doesn't apparently occur to him that they may find that offensive, those who are still alive."

"Yes," he agreed. "But he will be fighting for survival. You can't win the war tomorrow if you lose the battle badly enough today."

"He won't name them," she said bleakly.

461

"I will," he answered instantly. "Even if you don't tell me. We can find out easily enough who they are. For that matter, so can the newspapers."

She turned back to face him. "Please don't. They're completely innocent. Think how that would ruin their reputations, even if they are retired . . . or dead. Their families will suffer, not to mention any other women to whom they gave good marks — not that there were many of us."

"Miriam."

"Don't answer," she snapped, then seemed to crumple inside. "He will say I offered to sleep with him. He's right . . . in a way." She looked somewhere beyond Daniel, into the past. "Not for marks. I was confident in them. And if unearned, they would mean nothing anyway. I thought I was in love with him. He was different then. I suppose just as arrogant inside, but it showed less. And I was pretty blind. I imagined he loved me. Isn't that ridiculous! No, you wouldn't know that. I think if you loved anyone, it would be real."

Why did he feel horrified? That was absurd, and totally unfair. He had slept with women from passion, the excitement of it, the hunger, and yes, on occasion, he thought that he might be in love.

462

Still, he did not meet her eyes.

"I was willing." Her voice was a little unsteady. "I almost did, but he was . . . unable."

Now he did meet her eyes. "Unable . . ."

Her face was scarlet. "Nothing happened. He . . . couldn't. Do I have to explain it to you? I'm a student of anatomy, for goodness' sake!"

"No." He tried to imagine Saltram's embarrassment, after all his arrogance.

"He won't ever forgive me for that," she went on, her voice stronger now. "It was humiliating for both of us. Of course, afterward he said I revolted him." Her face twisted ruefully, as if it could ever have been true.

"His impotence was your fault?" he said incredulously. "Don't be ridiculous, you're beautiful! I mean, really beautiful! He was probably just scared of you, like a rabbit."

"I think rabbits are actually quite aggressive that way." She was giggling a little hysterically. "They breed them like mad for science." She put her hand up to her mouth to choke off the laughter and there were tears on her face.

He took a step forward, wanting to put his arms around her, assure her she was lovely, honest, brave, and everything else

that mattered. But considering the conversation only a moment ago, he realized how
inappropriate that might be. In fact, definitely would be. "Tell me in the morning
what you want me to say in court," he said
instead. "But be sure, because once I start,
it may well be too late to change. It's going
to be bad every way, but I'll abide by your
decision."

"I don't need until morning," she said,
her voice perfectly level. "We must go with
the truth. Anything else will hurt us for the
rest of our lives. And every other wrong
decision, every injustice, will be partly our
fault."

He nodded. He should have been sure
that that was what she would say, right from
the beginning.

"But thank you for asking me," she added.

He did not answer, but went out of the
door, closing it quietly behind him.

# CHAPTER TWENTY-ONE

Daniel had slept only fitfully. He looked at
the fine breakfast that Mrs. Portiscale had
made for him and ate a bit of it reluctantly,
but only to please her and to avoid the questions she was bound to ask if he did not.
She would be concerned for his health,
insisting on going back into the kitchen to
prepare something else.

Marcus's driver had brought him home
last night, after he'd been to see Miriam.
Now he was going out the door to look for
a taxi — he would rather be early than late,
even as early as this — when he met a mes-
senger boy.

"Mr. Pitt, sir?"

"Yes." Daniel heard the gritty sound of
his voice, as if he were already tired. He
must control himself. This was no use. Saltram might beat him, but he was not about
to surrender. "Yes, I am."

"Message for you, sir." The boy held it

out, a simple white envelope with his name and address on it. It looked like his mother's writing. He took it and gave the boy sixpence. A little overgenerous, but it was a bribe to fortune. He tore it open and pulled out the paper and read.

Dear Daniel,
We are all thinking of you today, and I will be in court, watching and listening. Remember, Saltram also has much to lose! Perhaps he will remember that! We are all supporting you.

Love, Mother

With a brief smile, he folded the letter and placed it in his pocket, hurrying along the pavement as all that this meant began to sink into his mind, the good and the bad. Charlotte had been so sure that Miriam would fight. That was a good feeling . . . and at once a dreadful one. If he was not equal to it, if he fell, it would be into a hole so vast he would never find his way out. Did his mother hopelessly overestimate him? Her faith in him had bolstered his own, all his life. But he was aware that it was definitely rose-tinted at times! All mothers had an unrealistic view of their children. It was wonderful to have anyone trust in you so completely, and also terrifying.

He found a taxi quite quickly and, in just under three-quarters of an hour, he went up the courtroom steps and inside, out of the wind and the sleet.

Kitteridge came in fifteen minutes later, looking anxious and cold. He was followed so soon after by Marcus that there was no time to speak privately, except for Daniel to say that he was ready and would be staying as close as possible to Marcus.

"Are we going for it?" Kitteridge asked, eyeing Daniel's bruises but forbearing from making any remark.

"Yes, she won't do anything else." Daniel had no need to explain that he was referring to Miriam.

"I thought not," Kitteridge said bleakly. "We really have no choice. I wired Evelyn Hall yesterday . . ."

"In Holland?" Marcus said in surprise.

"No, actually she was in Edinburgh. She said she'd get the night train, and be here this morning . . ." He regarded Marcus approvingly.

"Good," Marcus replied. "Good man . . ." He did not add any more.

Daniel felt the knots in his stomach ease a little. "Miriam told me something in confidence about Saltram," he said. "I may need to use it if Saltram persists in trying to ruin her. I should like to be the one to question him if it comes to that."

Marcus could not refuse, considering what was at stake.

When the court sat at nine o'clock on the dot, Daniel took the stand again, and Sir John Percival rose to cross-examine him.

"Good morning, Mr. Pitt. Please remember you are still under oath from yesterday."

"Yes, sir."

"If I may remind the court, this is a retrial of an old matter, and we are discussing two cases that you defended, based on the evidence we are now calling into question. Sir Barnabas Saltram testified that such cracks in the skull can be caused by extreme heat, and need not arise from any striking of the head by a blunt object. Mr. Pitt, this was a very simple case to begin with. A young woman with no means, no education, and no standing in the community came to you and asked if you would defend her lover, a young man of the same lack of standing as herself. A petty thief who practiced the occasional violence. Is that accurate?"

"Yes, it is," Daniel answered. He was clearly stunned. He was sure Percival was using such dismissive language to irritate him. But he still responded. "The people accused of crime often are of that general description."

A very slight smile creased Percival's face, making him look startlingly human for a few moments. Then it vanished. "I recall that, Mr. Pitt. I began my career much as you are doing, but I don't remember having the professional assistance of a great forensic scientist as a defense witness. Partly since I could not afford to pay such a person. How did it come about that you were so fortunate?"

There it was already.

"I'm acquainted with Miss fford Croft, sir, the daughter of my head of chambers. She was once a student of Sir Barnabas's, and she offered to introduce him on the chance that he would take an interest in the case."

Percival looked surprised. "Miss fford Croft was a student of Sir Barnabas? Studying what, if I may ask."

"Forensic sciences," Daniel answered. "Chemistry, anatomy, and I believe some aspects of medicine."

"Good heavens, what for?"

Daniel glanced at Marcus. He seemed to be frozen.

"For the love of science, I believe. If you wish for more than that, you will have to ask her. I cannot answer for her."

"That would be some twenty years ago?" Percival asked.

"I believe so."

"She is not married, Miss fford Croft."

"Neither is Sir Barnabas, I believe," Daniel said tartly. "Neither am I, for that matter."

"You'd be hard put to keep a wife on your salary, as a junior barrister, in your first years of practice," Percival commented.

"Is that a question?" Daniel asked.

Percival smiled. "I stand chastised, Mr. Pitt. It is irrelevant and unimportant. Back to Miss fford Croft. Did she introduce you to Sir Barnabas?"

"Yes. And to save your asking each question separately, he was most agreeable and inquired as to the details of the case, then offered his assistance. He testified and we won. Robert Adwell was found not guilty."

Percival inclined his head graciously. "Thank you. You've summarized excellently for me. How about the next case, when Miss Beale, the young woman in question, was accused of having murdered Mr. Adwell in exactly the same circumstances, and you found yourself morally obliged to defend her? Did Miss fford Croft again ask Sir Barnabas to testify for the defense? That must have been embarrassing for her, considering the very odd circumstances of the case."

"Is that a question?" Daniel asked.

"An observation, perhaps. Nevertheless, he obliged, did he not? And again, also for no charge?"

"Yes."

"And did you win . . . again?"

"No," Daniel replied. "As you are aware, we lost."

"Which is why we all find ourselves here, with the shadow hanging over us of questioning any case in the past for which this testimony was given." Percival adjusted his gown very slightly, just long enough for the jury to grasp the full import of what he was saying about the unknown number of other cases. "You seem to play a very pivotal role in this chain of events, Mr. Pitt," he continued. "But not quite as pivotal as that of Miss fford Croft. Before you ask me if that is a question, let me answer you. You are a young man from a fairly comfortable and sheltered background. You went to a good school and then Cambridge University. Now you are with an old and reputable law firm led by an eccentric but deeply regarded man who has no son of his own — only an unusual daughter . . . forgive me . . . whose ambitions far exceed any possible ability she might have to fulfill them. Women are not accepted in the profession she aspires to, or used to aspire to. I'm not sure if she still does."

Daniel knew he was being baited, and tensed every nerve to avoid allowing this self-assured man to trip him. It was not a direct question, so he offered no answer.

"I'll be brief," Percival said irritably. "You have got us all, the whole law of the nation, into an ungodly mess because your ignorance of women is only exceeded by your arrogance of imagination. First, Jessie Beale made a fool of you . . . twice. Then Miriam fford Croft, and then Evelyn Hall. You have turned Marguerite Daventry from the tragic victim of a fire into a woman whose husband murdered her. Can there be a more wretched end for any woman? You have branded Daventry a murderer, although he has been tried and found not guilty of that crime. You have given Adria Leigh false hope that her husband may be pardoned posthumously. And now you have attempted to ruin the finest forensic scientist in England. I would even say in Europe."

"Objection!" called Marcus, almost jumping to his feet.

"Sir John," said Lord Justice Walpole, "this is a multitude of claims to hurl at Mr. Pitt. Please confine yourself to questions and give the witness the opportunity to answer."

"Yes, my lord," said Percival. "I apologize. I mean these to be questions and I will now give Mr. Pitt the chance to answer every one of them."

Daniel could feel himself shaking, his mouth dry. He had been wrong. It was not Miriam they intended to ruin, it was him! "I will answer them all, as I see them in order," he said, his voice shaking a little. "I defended Robert Adwell and Jessie Beale, because that is what I do: defend people." He gripped the rail of the witness stand with both hands. "There can be no just trial unless both sides to the case are represented. I asked Sir Barnabas Saltram to give evidence in those two cases. At first, I thought that he was right. By the time of the second, I had another opinion. That of Dr. Evelyn Hall. The jury believed her, and so do I. That angers you, because it seems highly possible that you, the establishment, have made several wrong decisions, relying on Barnabas Saltram's evidence, and not looking any further. And, of course, you don't want to have to look at all these cases again."

He turned momentarily to Kitteridge, who passed him a bundle of files, which he held up for the jury to see, before handing them back. He took a deep breath. "That is not my fault, and you do not do yourselves any favors by trying to move the blame onto someone who was five years old when you started out on this course. You won't sweep your mistakes under the carpet. If you take them out and look at them honestly, you'll possibly find a few where you made errors, and at least repair them, even if the victims are dead. And their families ruined."

Percival looked startled. He had not expected Daniel to fight back. He turned to the judge. "My lord, we have not heard from Miss fford Croft. I do not like doing this, but Mr. Pitt has leveled some very serious charges at Sir Barnabas Saltram. They, I think, are what lie at the bottom of this whole tragedy. Sir Barnabas has asked us if he may defend his own testimony and I think it only just that we should do so. After all, it is his reputation that is at stake. May I call Sir Barnabas Saltram to the stand?"

"I suppose you may," the judge replied. There was sharp interest in his face now. "Make it brief . . . and relevant."

"Yes, my lord, thank you."

Daniel went to sit with Kitteridge, and

beside Marcus, who looked very pale. Daniel felt hollow inside. He thought he had won, but now he knew better. He did not look at Marcus.

Saltram swore to all his high honors and then looked inquiringly at Percival.

"I know, Sir Barnabas, that you have wished to avoid this, but the issue of your expert testimony now lies at the heart of this case and many others. We have no alternative but to settle this now. You have heard Mr. Pitt's opinion of how you came to be involved in this charade. Will you please now tell us your recollection of it?" Percival inclined his head toward the judge. "My lord, you may recognize in the gallery two of the most distinguished gentlemen of our medical establishment." He indicated two elderly men near the front. "Sir Reginald Osterman and Sir Osbert North, both of the Royal College of Surgeons. Sir Osbert is also principal of the university at which Sir Barnabas lectures."

"Indeed, I do," the judge acknowledged, his expression impossible to read. "I think it may be that scientific history will be made here today . . . or unmade. Please proceed."

"Thank you, my lord." Percival turned to Saltram. "If you please, Sir Barnabas."

Saltram looked very pale, but he stood

stiffly to attention, facing straight ahead, into the distance. "I used to teach a great deal, earlier in my career," he began. "I can produce the particulars, if you wish, but the point is that there were very many students and occasionally these were young women. Some who wished to learn anatomy to be better nurses, or orderlies, or other appropriate occupations. Nineteen-year-old Miriam fford Croft wished to be a doctor and a forensic pathologist, both of which are not careers open to women. She was pretty enough, as are most women in their youth, but she had an exaggerated opinion, of both her charms and her intellect."

There was no movement in the gallery. Even the jury seemed frozen in place.

He took a deep breath, then continued. "The inevitable happened. I had to give her far lower marks on her examination papers than she thought she deserved. She came and offered herself to me, if I would give her higher marks, enough to pass the exams. She intimated that this had happened with other professors. She said she was well on the way to passing with honors. The thought made me sick. It is a betrayal of all that I love and hold sacred. Truth. Science. Service to the law and medicine. Service to the dead and the bereaved. I rebuffed her rather sharply, even cruelly." He lowered his gaze a little. "Understand, please, that I was deeply revolted. Not only for myself, but for my colleagues, some of whom had possibly betrayed their callings and their profession. I find it hard to forgive them for that. Nevertheless, I agreed to her request to help the defense of the Adwell case and, I regret to say it, a young lawyer who seems to be very easily seduced, morally, if not sexually, by the daughter of his head of chambers."

"Objection, my lord," said Kitteridge, rising to his feet.

"Sir Barnabas," said Lord Justice Walpole severely, "please keep to the facts and not your personal opinions of character."

"Yes, my lord. I seek only to show how, despite knowing the character of Miss fford Croft, I, for the sake of justice, agreed to stand expert witness in the Adwell and Beale trials."

There was a terrible silence over the entire room. No one spoke. No one even moved.

When, with Marcus and Kitteridge's agreement, it was Daniel's turn to question Saltram, he was shaking as he stood up. He had to end this, whatever the cost. He could not allow Saltram to get away with it.

"Sir Barnabas, you have just accused a woman of trying unsuccessfully to seduce

you, although, according to you, she succeeded with several of your fellow professors. All of them, since you do not name
any specifically, can easily enough be looked
up. And now probably will be, by friends
and enemies and, above all, the newspapers.
By your testimony they are shamed, slandered, and all their highest-marked students
thrown under suspicion. You did not need
to say that, sir. You could merely have accused Miss fford Croft of trying to persuade
you to mark her exams favorably, as did all
the other tutors and professors."

"No! It is she who is dishonored. She is a
temptress and a whore who well knows how
to get what she wants —"

"Order!" shouted Lord Justice Walpole.
"It is not Miss fford Croft who is on trial
here. The court is interested in how you
became involved in the Adwell and Beale
cases, and what part Miss fford Croft played
in your involvement. You may continue, Mr.
Pitt."

Daniel steadied himself, breathing deeply.
"Thank you, my lord. Sir Barnabas, are you
really the one professor with such high mor-
als? Or was it that you intended having an
affair with Miss fford Croft? After all, she
was nineteen, vibrant, intelligent, and
beautiful. And, according to her, she be-

lieved herself in love with you."

"Rubbish! I never touched her! I swear on the Holy Bible and the word of God," Saltram said between his teeth, his face ashen.

"Ah, I believe you," Daniel said finally, leaning forward a little. "But not out of honor. When it came to the point, you found yourself suddenly unable to proceed. When faced with a beautiful, clever, articulate woman, you were impotent."

There were murmurs in the gallery, but no one spoke.

Saltram's face was gray, as if all the blood had left it, and his worst nightmare had taken life in front of him. Perhaps embarrassment was his worst fear: humiliation before his peers. To fail, to be laughed at, a butt of public jokes, was worse than to be beaten by fists.

Daniel wanted to be sorry for him. He knew the arrogance was all bravado, and inside the man was fearful. But his fears were mixed with a hatred so deep that it had become a weapon he used in the cruelest way against others.

The silence was waiting for him, before Saltram could spoil it and somehow turn it against Miriam.

"You could not forgive her for that," he said strongly, so the whole room could hear

479

him. "Every time you heard a woman laugh, you thought she had told them and they were laughing at you! You had to blacken her name before she could ridicule yours. Only, she never did. She, too, was ashamed of a grand love affair with a man she admired so much, which turned into a fiasco, an attempt at ruining her. You should have let it go; it happens, it doesn't matter. But you couldn't. When you met her again, you saw a chance to ruin her. Then she did the unforgivable: she set Evelyn Hall against you in court . . . and you lost."

Saltram was shaking with rage. He stared at Daniel with such hatred it seemed almost to consume him. He opened his mouth, but before he could speak, Daniel went on. "Now all your past cases of burned skulls are questioned. James Leigh was innocent, and he was hanged on your evidence. The truth cannot mend that now, but it can give some reparation to James Leigh's family."

The judge was leaning forward over his bench, his face tense, eyes wide, as if fascinated.

He looked at Percival, who appeared a little dazed. He had seen something new, and he was beginning to recognize it.

Daniel took up the argument again, before anyone could interrupt him. "Perhaps your argument about heat cracking skulls, without any help from injury, was groundbreaking twenty years ago. But you used it too quickly, and you have kept at it too long. It can happen, but not in all the circumstances you have used it! I —"

Percival shot to his feet. "My lord! Mr. Pitt is a lawyer, and a very junior one at that. He has no qualifications in medicine and forensics. You cannot possibly put his very partisan opinion above that of Sir Barnabas Saltram, who is the preeminent expert in the field!"

The judge held up his hand to silence Percival. He turned to Daniel. "Sir, on what grounds do you base your assertions?" His tone was mild, interested.

Not a soul in the room moved.

"Upon the opinion of Dr. Evelyn Hall, my lord, who also examined the skulls in this particular case. I can call her again, if you wish. It may take an hour or two. She came down on the night train from Edinburgh, in case she should be needed."

"Did she, indeed?" The judge sat up even more to attention, if it were possible. "A battle of the Titans? I think not. Not that it wouldn't make legal history, and no doubt great entertainment to the press, but I do not think it is necessary."

"My lord, Sir Barnabas has slandered Miss fford Croft, but he has also slandered the good professors of Oxford University by saying that they extorted several favors of certain young women, to give them good marks that they were not entitled to. I am prepared to call those gentlemen if necessary. And unless Sir Barnabas withdraws all his allegations, unreservedly, I think it is necessary . . ."

"I agree. Although they were not pertinent to the James Leigh case, those accusations have been made in public, for the press to repeat. That is unacceptable. Sir Barnabas will withdraw them unreservedly, or will face damages, not only to those gentlemen but to the young women whom he also slandered, beginning with Miss fford Croft. But that is a matter for a separate hearing."

Saltram's face was scarlet. "I —" he began loudly.

"We want that!" Daniel cut across him. "It is fair. And James Leigh's name cleared, publicly. No reparation is enough for his life lost, but we can see that his widow and her son never want again in their lives."

Saltram stared at him with blazing hatred.

Daniel looked back. "All you want is revenge. That is not justice, Sir Barnabas. When you go to dig your enemy's grave, you should dig your own as well, because sooner or later you will find it in front of you."

Daniel sat down suddenly, as if his legs had given away. What had he done?

Kitteridge put his hand on Daniel's shoulder firmly. Daniel could feel the weight of it, even through the cloth.

"You are excused," the judge said to Saltram, who stepped down from the witness stand and stood motionless, holding onto the end of the rail and looking at the crowd, his face like a mask.

Daniel followed Saltram's eyes and saw the two bearded, bespectacled scientists, led by the principal of his university, rise from their seats and leave the court without glancing back, as if, for them, Saltram no longer existed.

Daniel caught sight of his mother. She was sitting toward the front. She gave a very slight smile and nodded. Just a tiny movement, but he saw it. Saltram was finished; they all knew it.

Where was Miriam? He looked around. Had she not come after all? Perhaps she couldn't bear it. Then he saw her hugging Marcus fiercely, while he stood with a smile so wide he could hardly contain himself. She moved past her father and Kitteridge, and came up to Daniel and kissed him lightly, gently, on the cheek.

"Thank you," she whispered. "I'd like to say I always knew you would do it, but I didn't. I was so afraid, until I saw you really angry for those he had hurt, and I knew it would be all right. We are all grateful . . . but especially me."

He looked at her face, her shining eyes, and could not think of anything to say, so he returned the kiss.

There was a slight noise behind him and reluctantly Daniel turned. It was a moment or two before he recognized the woman who was standing a yard away from him. She was striking-looking, smartly dressed and with a mass of dark hair swept up on her head. He knew her but could not think where they had met before.

"Antonia Llewellyn," she said with a smile. "Congratulations. You have won a very big victory indeed. You never knew my sister, Marguerite Daventry, because Roger killed her when you were still a child. But she would have liked you, and she would certainly have approved of your accomplishment today."

"Mrs. Llewellyn, I'm sorry —"

"Don't be!" she cut across him. She shot an appreciative glance at Miriam, then continued to Daniel. "I am here to do what she cannot, what the judge may do but not quickly enough. The law is excessively careful, and therefore slow. James Leigh's name will be formally cleared, but I would like to offer Mrs. Leigh a place to live, if she wishes it, and honorable work. And the same for her son. Perhaps an education in whatever field he is suited for. My estate is large. For Marguerite's sake, and in her memory, I would be pleased to have them. God knows what will happen to Roger. He can be charged with arson, at the very least. Possibly worse. But that lies in the future. In the present, the Leighs can be warm, fed, rested, and able to look forward. Please introduce me to them."

Daniel was overcome for a moment, then he turned round, searching the crowd. For several moments he saw only strangers shaking each other's hands, smiling, applauding. Then he saw his mother and father, then Ottershaw grinning, Marcus shaking hands with everyone, Kitteridge with his tie crooked, and lastly Adria Leigh and a tall, shy young man beside her.

"There," he said to Antonia. He found himself suddenly overcome with emotion. "She's there . . ."

"Thank you," Antonia said, her own eyes

485

suddenly filled with tears as well. She patted him on the arm and turned to walk over to Adria and her son.

Miriam took Daniel's arm and held it tightly. "We were right," she said softly.

"You were right," he said, his voice catching in his throat.

"No, we were right."

# ABOUT THE AUTHOR

**Anne Perry** is the bestselling author of two acclaimed series set in Victorian England: the Charlotte and Thomas Pitt novels, including *Murder on the Serpentine* and *Treachery at Lancaster Gate,* and the William Monk novels, including *Dark Tide Rising* and *An Echo of Murder.* She is also the author of a series featuring Charlotte and Thomas Pitt's son, Daniel, including *Triple Jeopardy* and *Twenty-one Days,* as well as the new Elena Standish series, beginning with *Death in Focus;* a series of five World War I novels; sixteen holiday novels (most recently *A Christmas Gathering*); and a historical novel, *The Sheen on the Silk,* set in the Ottoman Empire. She lives in Los Angeles.

anneperry.co.uk

The employees of Thorndike Press hope you have enjoyed this Large Print book. All our Thorndike, Wheeler, and Kennebec Large Print titles are designed for easy reading, and all our books are made to last. Other Thorndike Press Large Print books are available at your library, through selected bookstores, or directly from us.

For information about titles, please call:
  (800) 223-1244

or visit our website at:
  gale.com/thorndike

To share your comments, please write:
  Publisher
  Thorndike Press
  10 Water St., Suite 310
  Waterville, ME 04901